The Year of the Child

ISBN #978-1-940189-36-9

Cover design by Babski Creative Studios
Cover image courtesy of iStock photos

Printed in United States

Twisted Road Publications

The Year of the Child

a novel by

Elizabeth McCulloch

To Joe

Leanne

Chapter One

I woke up real early. The baby wasn't even awake. As soon as I woke up I couldn't help it, I started thinking about Misty Dawn and what Peter said we was going to do this morning. It was funny, because I was lying there, and I could see by the streetlight that shines in our window that it was foggy out, just like her name.

I wanted to get up then but was scared I'd wake him up. He doesn't wake up when she cries, though, it's always me that gets her. She cried every night this week and I been crying every night too because he said we had to do it.

Last night he said it was him or her. I said I'd take her, being fresh, but meaning it anyway. He grabbed my arm, right where it was bruised from the night before, and yanked me down onto the kitchen chair. It hurt down there. It's only three weeks ago I had the baby. He looked straight in my face and said, "I'll kill you both. Don't think you can hide anyplace I won't find you." He meant it too. With all the times he gets mad, even that time the week before she was born, I never thought he'd kill me, not on purpose anyway. But I could tell by his face this time. It was all white around his mouth and it made his whiskers look ugly. Peter's got a heavy beard but he only shaves in the morning, and never on weekends. I was so scared I said yes, and as soon as I did, he said we'd take her in the morning.

He was real sweet after I said yes, and started playing around, kissing me on the neck, talking to my titties the way he does. He puts his mouth right up against them and talks soft, saying silly things, calling them names, and sometimes his lips are touching them and sometimes it's just warm air blowing on them. It feels real good. But this time it was like I couldn't feel it, like I wasn't there, but in the other room with Misty Dawn.

I wanted to go be with her for this last little bit of time. I rolled over and then waited a little and Peter didn't move, so I took my weight with one hand and foot on the floor and eased off the bed. I crawled out the door, like if I stood up he'd see me even with his eyes closed. Sometimes I get more scared of him in the dark, when he's not even doing anything. I knew as soon as he woke up he'd want to put her in the car and go. He said we have to do it before it gets light. I was thinking, if he sleeps long enough we can't do it today and maybe I can figure out how to get away from him.

But I don't want to get away, I just want things to be different, him loving me and Misty Dawn too, the three of us together like a family. I saw a picture of him and his first wife. He was holding the baby and looked real glad, so I don't see why he can't love Misty Dawn like he loves that other kid. I say first wife, but I guess she's just his wife because they're not divorced even though we're living together. It's just the same as if I was his wife. It doesn't matter if you're married, it's what's in your heart that counts. That's what Peter says, and I think so too, especially after he gave me that wedding ring.

I got into the other room without him hearing anything and stood next to her crib and looked at her lying on her back. Judy says if they lie on their back they can choke if they spit up, but the nurse said if they lie on their stomach they can suffocate. Seems like just being a baby is dangerous, never mind what people do to you. She was breathing okay though. I could hear that little noise and see her chest going up and down. Babies are so perfect, even if they're small. They come out with everything already there. She's got eyelashes and toenails and all the things that you don't never even think about until you see them on a baby.

I wanted to pick her up and cuddle her, but I was afraid she'd wake up Peter. So I was stuck. If I couldn't hold her, it's like I was already giving her up, but it doesn't seem right to pick up a baby when it's asleep and everything's okay. So I just stared at her hard, trying to imagine her when she's one, and then fifteen like me, and then grown up. But I couldn't even get her to one, because I couldn't picture that little bitty thing getting all chunky, staggering around the way babies do, laughing with those little teeth showing. I just didn't see how she could get from here to there, much less turn into all those bigger people.

It's like those pictures I have of Momma and Daddy before we were born. There's one where she's standing behind him with her hands on his shoulders, you can tell she's on tiptoe. He's making a goofy face and they both look like kids. But I never knew them when they looked like that. I guess most people when they start having kids they stop having fun. But I don't think it has to be that way. Peter and me could have all kinds of fun with Misty Dawn if he'd just let us, because she's so cute. When she gets bigger, she'll be lots of fun to play with. It won't always be this crying and diapers and mess.

Maybe Misty Dawn could hear me breathing like I could hear her, because in a couple minutes she started moving around. I never watched her wake up before – she's always the one to wake me up. Her face got all wrinkly, and she hit herself around the mouth with her fist a couple of times, and then relaxed like it was too much trouble and she might as well go on sleeping. She started making little squeaky noises, so I picked her up to keep her quiet but that really woke her up. Her face was getting red and I knew I had to get a bottle in her mouth fast. I went in the kitchen and I'd just got the lid off the formula when I heard Peter roll over and kind of groan and then he was in the door.

"What are you doing?"

"I'm giving her a bottle."

"You don't need to do that. We got to get going before it starts to get light outside."

When I was staring at her in her crib and when I was getting ready to feed her, I think I was pretending I wouldn't have to do this, like there was some way out. Like Peter was just kidding, or he'd forget, so it was almost like I was surprised when he said it. And I thought of something that I think was smart.

"If I don't feed her, she'll be crying when we leave her and we could get caught."

"Okay, feed her fast while I get dressed."

He always sleeps naked, and his cock was standing up like it does in the morning, kind of pointing and nodding at me. Lots of times I'll take hold of it and squeeze it and we do it first thing, but this time it looked ugly, all red and jumpy, and it made me sick to see it.

"What are you staring at? Go ahead and feed the baby."

I was doing like he said but he sounded mad, so I didn't say anything, just got the bottle ready and sat down at the table. Misty Dawn was hollering and soaking wet but I figured I'd change her after I fed her because she always poops when she's getting fed and I don't like to have to change her twice.

Peter came out in jeans and a tee shirt and was putting on his boots. He was in such a big fat hurry. He got his keys out and started jiggling them at me. I wanted to give her a bath for the last time. I love how she is in her bath, when I pour the water over her head and her mouth opens and her eyes get big. But Peter didn't even let me burp her; he said we had to go. So I just changed her quick and put on the booties I made, so she'd have something from her mother. I wanted the pink dress with the rabbits on it that Judy gave me, but Peter didn't give me time to go looking. When I had her diaper and undershirt on he just grabbed her from me and started out the door. I couldn't do nothing but follow. Anyway, she'll have her booties.

I wasn't usually out this early. It was still dark and all foggy. At the truck Peter gave her to me. I got in and he started driving. I hoped she'd take the rest of the bottle in the truck, but she was asleep. All this time he wasn't saying anything and I wasn't saying anything. I had told him that I wanted to leave her at somebody's house, and not at a dumpster like some girls do. He was trying to be nice after he made me say I'd do it. I even told him where I wanted to leave her; that neighborhood with the big old houses and lots of trees. Momma used to drive me there to sell Girl Scout cookies.

We were driving around that neighborhood and Misty Dawn was sleeping. Every time Peter wanted to stop at a house, I'd say not this one. He was getting nervous because it was starting to get light and I knew I'd better choose. One house had flower pots hanging from the roof and a planter by the front door, and a statue of a black and white dog that looked real. I figured nice people probably lived there, so I said that house.

And as soon as I told him it was like I wasn't there anymore. I could see Misty Dawn there on my lap and the way her eyes were moving around in her sleep and I knew I had to do it so I didn't have to think about it at all and when Peter stopped the truck I just opened the door and got out and walked up this little path to the front door and I didn't see nothing around me, all I saw was Misty Dawn and the planter and I moved a stick out of it trying to be quiet and laid her down in it and she didn't wake up and then I walked away from her and back to the truck and I wasn't even thinking anything. I got back in the truck and Peter drove away real fast, spinning the tires so I thought he'd wake up everybody in the neighborhood.

Marybeth

Chapter Two

Marybeth rolled over toward Munro, last remnants of a dream drifting away. Not time yet to open her eyes, though already she could feel her self approaching, ready to take charge and make things orderly. Still, for a few minutes, she could stay unhooked, thoughts drifting by like floaters in her eye. A bird call ended it, a short trill and silence, and then three high notes from across the yard. Morning was here, though still dark, still warm under the covers with the toasty smell of her and Munro together. Careful not to wake him, she folded the sheet off and went into the bathroom, grabbing her clothes off the chair. A faded lavender t shirt and gray shorts, holey sneakers. She never saw anyone on her morning walk.

She took her keys off the hook, stuffed them in her pocket, and opened the front door to the night almost morning, the morning still night, to fog and dampness and cool air, though it was only September and early for these. A world as dark and quiet and private as under the covers, but this shared not even with Munro. No cars passing, neighborhood dogs asleep, no joggers yet. Walking was exercise, but she did it for the silence and solitude, the smells of every season, the better than dream-state of the dark looming trees on the side of the road, the quiet-breathing houses.

She walked up the road and turned into the path that led to acres of tangled woods. In the deep damp she was almost chilly, and she began to truly wake up. She broke a spiderweb with her face, the price of being first in the woods.

When she returned the sky was lighter, Venus almost invisible. The street was still empty, the only sign of life a blue pick-up driving too fast at the far end of the road. She picked up the newspaper and read the headlines as she walked to the front door. Only when she looked up to put her key in the door did she see the bundle.

She knew immediately what it was. The baby lay on its back, the blanket wrapped around it and folded under its head, its face turned to one side, tiny fist crushed under its cheek. It was so implausible that for a moment Marybeth thought she was still in bed. The pre-dawn walk of mist and silence could be a dream before waking. Why not end it with a baby sleeping in the planter? Only a moment though, before knowing that indeed, she was awake, and she had to accept that there was a baby at her front door.

It looked so peaceful, so comfortable. She almost, before rational thought kicked in, left it sleeping. Who picks up a sleeping baby? Of course, reason did kick in, so she tucked the newspaper into her armpit, scooped her hands under the bundle, and carried it into the house, closing the door behind her with her foot. And then just stood there holding the baby out before her like an offering. It was perfect, plain miraculous like any baby. Probably no odder to find a baby lying in the ivy than to have one emerge from the great ungainly shape she had become by the end of each pregnancy. It had always seemed implausible that a whole human being was living inside her.

Now she drew the baby close and thought about what to do. It had come like a gift. It seemed wrong to turn it over to the police as though it were some crime. It was a crime, she supposed, but what could have driven someone to commit it? For the first time, in the slow thinking of her shock, she wondered who had left the baby there. Certainly a woman, and she hadn't meant the child any harm, that was clear, or she'd have left it in a dumpster or thrown it in the woods. Instead, she had left it here at Marybeth's doorstep, magical as a stolen prince in a fairy tale. Or princess.

She couldn't keep calling a baby it. She unwrapped the blanket and tore the tape on the side of the diaper. The baby stirred and opened her eyes, looked without seeing, flailed her arms, and went back to sleep with a couple of tentative sucks on the air. Marybeth shifted her, and two pink clumps fell out of the blanket. Fuchsia yarn clumsily crocheted into booties, twice the size of the baby's feet; they'd never stay on. She laid them on the table by the door and went into the kitchen. She heard Munro coming and turned her back, as if she could hide the sleeping baby.

"Hey honey, good morning." He came up behind her for a hug, looked over her shoulder. "What's that?"

"It's a baby."

"Well I can see that, but where on earth...?"

"Munro, she was there in the ivy when I got back from my walk."

"What will we do with her?" They were both witless in the sudden presence of the child.

"Can we keep her?"

As if Munro were her father and she had brought home a stray kitten, though she didn't want a kitten or a baby either, with their lives so easy now, just the way they'd dreamed when the children were small and they'd stolen a few tired minutes together at the end of a too-long day.

"I think we'll have to call the police," he said.

He went over to the phone and picked it up as if he were calling a plumber for a leak. Of course they'd call the police. They wouldn't keep a tiny baby, washed up on their doorstep out of the fog, but he sounded so matter of fact.

"Munro, you have no feelings at all. Think where this baby must have been. Think about her poor mother."

"Well, I can think about that, I suppose, but I still don't see what you want me to do besides call the police."

"Oh, go ahead and call."

She sat at the kitchen table, glumly gazing down at her bundle. The baby was moving her mouth like a toothless old woman. Marybeth stroked her cheek, and the little red face turned toward her finger and tried to suck on her knuckle.

She couldn't make out anything from Munro's side of the conversation, all yeses and no's until he said, "Can't you come any sooner than that? We have to go to work... I see... Alright." And he hung up.

"He says it will probably be about an hour and a half before they can get here. The social worker on call lives out of town a ways."

"Well, the child's hungry. We have to feed her before the police get here."

"Can't you give her a bottle or something?"

"Of course I could, Munro, if I had one."

"Oh. I thought maybe you'd have one around somewhere."

Over twenty years since they'd had a baby in the house. Did he think she kept a shrine?

"Look, you'll have to go to the store for some formula. I think they sell it in disposable bottles. I'll try to keep her quiet until you get back."

Munro left. She got her coffee and took the baby out to the rocking chair on the deck, to watch day begin in the garden. The child had sunk back into sleep. Maybe she wasn't hungry.

She would have liked to have had a place like this to sit with her own babies. When Ruthie was born, they were living in that little rental house over on Greenway Place. They'd been meaning to buy, but the store kept them so busy.

With the sun almost up the garden was taking shape. The pale western sky barely illuminated the yard, but she could see the driftwood branches of the crepe myrtles, the green mass of the azaleas under the oak, and the bird feeder swinging from the departure of an exuberant cardinal.

She heard the car in the driveway, and then Munro calling her.

"I'm out here." The baby startled and opened her eyes, yawned. Munro came out with a six-pack of formula.

"Goodness, why did you get so much?"

"They came that way. I didn't want to break open a package."

"Well, I guess we can give them to the police when they come. Here, hold her while I go warm one up."

"That's okay, I'll warm it."

He was back in a couple of minutes. The baby was wide awake by now and took the nipple eagerly.

"Come sit by me."

"Let me get some coffee."

"Heat mine up too."

They sat for a while, just rocking, the baby sucking away.

"You look good with that baby. Don't you get too comfortable."

"Don't worry. How long do you think before the police get here?"

"They said an hour and a half. Looks like we got another half hour or so."

"You didn't by any chance pick up some diapers, did you?"

"No. She wet?"

"Worse than that."

"Oh, yeah, I guess I can smell it. Well, they'll be here soon."

Marybeth hated to think of the child lying there filthy, but she didn't know what else she could do. No point sending Munro to the store again, the police would probably be there before he got back. Then she thought of the hideous dish towel that Aunt Winston had brought her from Mexico. She carried the baby inside and found it in the top of the linen closet, covered with printed butterflies, each with its name in a clear script. She rummaged around in her junk drawer and found two safety pins.

She was in the bedroom, just finishing the pinning, when the doorbell rang. She held up the baby and looked at her critically. It was a lot of fabric for such a tiny child, but at least she smelled okay.

Munro let them in. Officer Williams was a tall, balding black man. Behind him was Mrs. Garrity, a large, freckled red head with a leatherette briefcase.

"We need to get some information from you, Mrs. Coggins."

"Why don't you come into the living room and sit down?"

Marybeth sat on the couch, feeling as though she were displaying a prize. She wanted to be sure they properly appreciated the baby.

Officer Williams asked the questions. Time, place, had she seen anyone in the vicinity? She told them about the blue truck. Did she have any idea whose it might be? Did she know of anyone pregnant? Darlene Taylor two blocks over was due any day but she wouldn't give away her child. Nevertheless, the officer carefully wrote down Darlene's name. Why did they think the baby had been left at their door? They hadn't a clue. He was sorry to ask this, but was there any chance the baby might be somehow connected to Mr. Coggins? That question surprised her so that she gave a sudden embarrassing snort of a laugh, while Munro said indignantly, "Of course not." It hadn't occurred to her at all; she had thought of the baby as hers, with Munro having nothing to do with it. When they finished their questions and stood up to leave, she found it surprisingly hard to place the baby in Mrs. Garrity's ample arms. "What will happen to her?"

"We have homes set up for newborns. We'll take her to Opakulla General for a health check, then to the foster home."

"Where is that?"

"Foster homes are confidential. You understand, we don't want the families disturbed."

So the baby had come to her out of nowhere, springing up in the ivy, and would disappear just as suddenly, as though it had never been.

"Will I see her again?"

"No, you won't need to. Our attorney will prepare an affidavit for you to sign. Don't worry about this one; if she's healthy, she'll be adopted in no time. People wait years to get a healthy white baby."

Marybeth was embarrassed, and glanced at Officer Williams, but he was impassive.

"Thank you both for your cooperation – and for the beautiful diaper." Mrs. Garrity smiled, the first crack in her official face. They started out the door.

"Oh, wait, here's some formula for her. I fed her about eight." She stood in the door watching as Mrs. Garrity strapped the baby into a car seat, watching until the car turned right at the end of the block and disappeared.

Munro came up behind her. "I've always said you'd find trouble on those early morning walks."

Leanne

Chapter Three

It was on TV. They didn't show Misty Dawn, just the lady whose house we left her at. She was old; she had gray hair and was sort of fat around the middle. I think she could be a good mom, but the police took Misty Dawn away and the TV didn't say where she is now. They said what she was wearing but nothing about the booties. That's why I'm going to the store. The lady who found her works at Coggins Hardware right downtown. She could of kept the booties or maybe the policeman took them. Sometimes when somebody gets murdered they don't tell you stuff because that helps them catch the killer.

When I woke up this morning I could feel how long I'd been sleeping and I thought something was wrong, why didn't she cry during the night, and then I remembered. Peter was sleeping on his stomach and had his arm over my chest. I looked over at his face that was mashed into the pillow, and I didn't hate him or anything; it was like I never seen him before, and I didn't want his arm on me. It was funny, last night we had such a good time you'd think I'd be loving him now.

I didn't do much after we left Misty Dawn, just watched TV and slept a lot. Then Peter came home from work with weed and a big yellow box of chocolates. We didn't have any weed for almost three months because he said he couldn't find any, but I think he just wasn't sharing. In a way that was okay because I thought maybe it could hurt the baby. But it didn't matter about the baby anymore, and he had this good stuff that was almost all buds.

He said, "Oh honey, look what I got for you," and he gave me the weed and the candy. Then he grabbed himself and squeezed and said, "Just let me take a shower and I got something else for you too." I always liked when he got himself clean before we did it. And when I saw him give that squeeze, and I could see in his jeans that he got big right away, I got hot, and I hadn't been hot in a long time.

The last couple of months before the baby it was like anything I tried to do I couldn't breathe right. So we didn't have sex a lot, and he wasn't home that much. Two times he was gone all night and I think he was over to his old wife's house but I didn't even bother asking him because I was too tired to fight, and scared too. He never hit me till I started showing with Misty Dawn. Once he had me down and kept kicking me in the stomach, so I was just as glad not to have him around at the end.

Something was always getting him mad at me, like the time he came home late and I caught him crying. I was pretty sure he'd been seeing his little boy. Then after Misty Dawn was born we were always fighting, him nagging me to get rid of her. We had sex the day after I came home from the hospital even though I told him the nurse said to wait six weeks, and I didn't feel like it at all. But he pinned me down and just stuck it in. It hurt bad, but luckily he didn't take very long. We didn't do it after that. I think the blood grossed him out.

I didn't think I'd ever feel anything down there anymore after all that hurting when she was born and then when we had sex, but here he just squeezed his cock at me and I got all hot again. He used to tell me I was the hottest little thing he ever knew, but he sure hadn't said that in a long time.

When Peter came out of the shower I had a joint rolled, and he came up behind me and put his arms around me and held onto my titties, and I could feel his cock hard on my bottom and he whispered in my ear, "Go take a shower too so I can love you all over." That meant eat me. That's my favorite thing and I could hardly ever get him to do it even though he made me go down on him all the time.

I took a shower fast and made sure to get myself plenty clean down there. When I came out he had my pink shorty nightgown and told me to put it on. We sat on the bed and smoked the joint and he started touching my face. He just kept stroking my eyes and my cheeks, and once in a while ran his fingers over my mouth. He moved his fingers down my neck, and then he started licking me there and grabbed hold of my nipples and pinched them just a little bit, and I was screaming the way you do when you're hot and stoned. It seemed like he went on forever, just touching me and licking me, and wherever he moved I could feel his cock mashed up against me but he didn't let me touch it. Finally he started licking me down there, but soft and careful like he didn't want to hurt me, and he got me to that place just before coming, and I stayed there and stayed there like you do when you're on weed. When I came it was like everything just melted and collapsed, and I couldn't move. I started crying, and he came up and held me and let me cry, and we fell asleep that way.

Later I woke up and he was turned around so his cock was right by my mouth. It was gross, but like I said he was always making me do that. This time it was different though, it was weird. When I took him in my mouth, I saw Misty Dawn clear as clear, sucking on her bottle, and it was like we were together, and Peter wasn't even there, and I just sucked and sucked. It was like I was her and she was me and I was just loving her and loving her. I think maybe I was going crazy.

So how come when I woke up this morning I didn't even want his skin touching me? I acted just regular, because I didn't want him thinking anything was different. He was all lovey-dovey, but all I wanted in the world was to see him walk out that door and never see him again. But I hadn't figured that part out yet. All I knew for sure was I had to get to that hardware store and find out about the booties. I had to wait to start till Peter went to work. He didn't leave till almost eight. He'd be late again.

It was a real pretty day and I started out feeling good. After you get out of Oak Meadows, there's a long way on the dirt road. I saw some black girls sitting out in a yard with their kids around them. I knew some of my neighbors in Oak Meadow, but I didn't know none of those people out there. They waved anyway when I went by, and I waved too.

It wasn't hot yet. The side of the road was all grown high with weeds and some scrappy-looking pink daisies with yellow middles. Momma knows the names of flowers and she tried to teach me. Some of the names stayed with me, like fleabane and tickseed, just because they sound funny, but only way I can remember what name goes with what flower is if I draw them in the notebook Daddy gave me.

Time I got to the main road my feet were hurting. I looked down the road, all straight and flat and gray, dirt and sand on the side and a little bit of weeds, and it looked hot. I started walking, and it *was* hot too. The sun wasn't all that high but there wasn't any trees between it and me. All the time I was thinking about Misty Dawn, pretending like I still had her, picturing how we could get away from Peter. Maybe he'd die or something, or go back to his wife and leave us alone. That didn't bother me anymore. It was the first time I ever loved someone and then stopped loving them.

I wonder if it was that way for Momma when Daddy left. She said it was a good thing he left; he was never the same man after he started drinking. Maybe it was good for her, but it wasn't for me. We used to do everything together, and he let me do whatever I wanted. Momma was the strict one, and she had all these rules that Daddy said were silly. I think that's the only thing they fought about, or the only thing I ever heard, until the drinking. Daddy always stuck up for me, and sometimes he'd take me for a walk down the road when she got mad.

He left us right after I turned eight. I don't remember much, but Momma says before the accident everything was going good. Daddy was working lots of overtime and she had a job at Greenway Motors. They were saving for a mobile home. They had a piece of land from Daddy's uncle. Then a load of cinder blocks fell on Daddy's foot and crushed it and he couldn't walk for more than a year. They got a lot of money from the company for the accident. They used it for a down payment on a double wide.

Daddy couldn't get another job with his foot still not right, so he stayed home and started building a garage next to the double wide, out of block, like what crushed his foot. Then Momma lost her job because she had a fight with her boss. So they couldn't keep up the payments, and after a while the dealer came and took it away. But lucky by that time Daddy had finished the garage, so we all five moved in there.

That was all right for a little while until Daddy started drinking. Momma said Daddy used to be a big drinker, when they were young, but when Shauna was born he stopped just like that, never touched even a beer. So I never knew before that how he was when he was drinking.

Young as I was, I just wanted us to get out of that garage. But Daddy was the only one who got out. He was watching TV and kept telling us we were making too much noise. Momma argued back at him, and he stood up and punched her in the face. We sure all shut up then, except for some crying. The next morning when we got up he was gone, and we never saw him again. Momma never got a postcard or nothing. It's like he disappeared.

Once I saw a thing on TV about how they'll help you find missing people, and when I saw it I thought maybe we could track down my Daddy. But you have to have money to do it, and anyway Momma said if he wants to come home he knows where to find us. I couldn't tell from the way she said it if she wanted him to come back, or if she even still loved him.

When Misty Dawn gets big maybe she'll want to try and find me. But I don't see how she can, because Peter didn't let me leave any note with her, or anything but the booties. Peter said if they found me, I'd be in big trouble. But I didn't care. I had to find out where her booties were, and maybe find out where she was.

I was glad to reach the edge of town. I got off that main road into the neighborhoods, where there's trees, and right away it was a whole lot cooler. I passed Sullivan Middle School, where I went before I ran away with Peter. Opakulla High is right across the street, and the high school guys would cross over and hide behind the utility building until after first bell so they could all cut together.

Me and Erica used to have the best times with them. It was mostly ninth and tenth graders; they didn't want middle schoolers hanging around, but they said we were different, like more sophisticated.

Ryan was sixteen and had his license. We'd all cram in and go somewhere. If it was hot we'd go to the quarry. We'd all take off our clothes and jump in that cold water. We'd swim around a while, and the boys did cannonballs. Me and Erica would each pick who we wanted to do it with, and they treated us nice because they wanted to go first. We'd go way off behind some bushes. The other guys yelled things at us until they lost interest. Weed makes your mind jump around a lot. And it made the sex nice, with nobody in a hurry. The guy's skin was all cold from the quarry, and his mouth was hot inside when he kissed me. Those were the best times I ever had in my life, I think, except for the very beginning time with Peter.

When we had enough gas money we'd go to the beach, and that's where I met him. It was me and Erica and four of the guys. We had beer that Ryan lifted from his mom's refrigerator and a big bucket of wings. We spread our blankets out on the sand. But the guys were acting extra goofy and I was in a bad mood, so I went walking down the beach to get away from them. Sometimes I just liked to be alone anyway; those guys never shut up.

I was walking along just where the waves came to, playing a game where I couldn't let the water touch my feet. It was the middle of the week and the beach was almost empty. Then somebody whistled at me. I knew it was me because I was the only one around.

I was only thirteen then, but only a couple months till my birthday, and everybody said I could pass for eighteen. I was wearing this pink and green bikini I lifted from Stop and Save. Momma would of killed me if she knew and killed me twice if she saw me in it.

When this guy whistled, I turned around. He was real hot – tall and thin, with nice muscles, a dark tan, and brown hair down to his shoulders. He walked over to me. He had these beautiful gray eyes. His chest was hairy and he looked like he needed a shave. I couldn't believe he was talking to me. You could tell he was way out of high school because he wasn't acting stupid like those high school boys. He asked me my name and where I was from and said what a coincidence we're both from Opakulla. He wanted to know what I was doing, so I told him about my game, kind of embarrassed, but he said it sounded like fun.

We walked along for a while, and he was asking me all kinds of questions. I didn't want him to think I was just a kid, so I said I was working at the Speedyway and saving money for college. He told me he worked at a gas station near the interstate. He wanted to be a mechanic, but he never got to work on the cars because his boss's son got to do all the good stuff. He was thinking about going to OCC, that's Opakulla Community College, to learn to be a mechanic, but he didn't have a lot to learn because he'd been working on cars all his life. But they wouldn't let you do anything if you didn't have a certificate.

By this time we were holding hands. When I looked back, I couldn't even see my friends. He asked if I wanted to go swimming, and when I said yes he picked me up and carried me into the water. I was in love right then. They always say you'll know when it's really love and I sure did. It wasn't anything like fooling around with the guys. So if it was really love, how come it's gone now? It's like all the love I had for Peter, I wrapped it up and gave it to Misty Dawn.

I felt like I'd been walking forever. I was hot and sweaty, my feet were killing me, and I had a bad ache low down in my stomach, like cramps. After I passed the schools, I had about half an hour more to get downtown. On days we didn't cut, we used to walk downtown after school and hang around at the Pizza Party. Coggins Hardware was a block before that.

Marybeth

Chapter Four

Marybeth always opened the store in the morning and Munro closed in the evening. Now she went in and locked the door behind her. Lowry came meowling toward her, ready for breakfast. He twisted around her ankles as she went into the back room where she turned on the coffee pot and filled his bowls.

Marybeth was only nineteen when her father died. She came home from college and convinced her mother to let her take over Coggins Hardware. Two years later, she married Munro, her third cousin who worked in the store. Their courtship was hardware. They hadn't noticed they were courting, they just spent all their days with hardware and each other.

The small back room, little more than a large closet, had been Munro's surprise for her when she returned to the store five months after Ruthie was born. Not that she didn't love the baby, but she was so bored. And she was overwhelmed. The little milk blisters on the baby's lips, the skin so fine that the veins showed through. Those tiny fingers with the nails that seemed to grow overnight, which she bit off because she was scared to use the clippers. All the taking care that a child required. She knew she ought to love it like any natural woman, but she'd only been running the store for five years, and then she had to turn the whole thing over to Munro.

He was the one who urged her to come back. He was puzzled by her discontent but glad to have her working again, and he didn't have any use for her crying all the time and snapping at him. She argued with him, "But I can't leave the baby."

"We'll get Marlene to come all day," he replied. Marlene cleaned their house. She had three children so she knew what she was doing.

But what kind of mother leaves her baby for somebody else to raise? Marlene left her own children every day when she went off to work, but none of Marybeth's friends would have done that.

"What's the difference," Munro argued, "if you leave them to work or play bridge or go shopping? You're gone in any case. And Ruthie loves Marlene."

It was true. Ruthie fussed from morning to night. Marybeth couldn't make her hush, and sometimes she had to struggle to keep from squeezing till the baby shut up. But turn her over to Marlene or Munro and she'd be quiet in just a couple of hiccups.

She never told Munro the wicked thoughts she'd had, but he was the one who convinced her to ignore what people said and come back to work. He'd fixed up this little room for her, and it made her mad all over again, with that Madonna picture of her and the baby up over the rocking chair, like that's what he thought she ought to be. She wouldn't be young again for anything. All the confusion and struggle, hitting out at poor Munro who didn't want anything from her, didn't care what she did as long as it made her happy.

Now, with the babies grown and gone, with time to be best friends again, she loved the little room, though it kept filling up with stuff: the old turntable they were going to take to Geddy's to get fixed, the fishing magazines Munro liked to look through when he was eating his sandwich, the community service award she was planning to have framed, and all the plaques Munro kept bringing home from Kiwanis. Sometimes she'd clean it out, leaving nothing but the coffee pot, the dorm refrigerator they'd bought for Harlan, the little table where they ate their lunch, and the old rocker. The picture of her with Ruthie was still hanging over it, and she had stuck a picture of Ruthie's baby in the corner of the frame.

With Lowry fed, she got some turpentine to clean the gum off the windows, where they had crisscrossed them with tape during the last hurricane warning. The hurricanes roared up the Gulf, chewing away at the shore, and the storms it brought inland were powerful enough that everybody downtown took full precautions. Now they were having a few cool days, a promise that fall was around the corner. The air was drier, the sky a deeper blue. Summer steam was sure to return, but she had cleared away the Labor Day beach display the night before and hoped to get the fall gardening window set up before they opened. She carried trowels, gardening gloves, loppers up to the front of the store, went back for a garden cart, and then stood a minute watching the dusty sunlight stream in the windows. Lowry was already settled again into his corner, his back pressed against the glass, one paw over his nose.

It was almost ten, and she was expecting Munro any minute, when the girl came. She tried the door, and when Marybeth pointed at her watch and shook her head, she just stood there outside the window. She was a scraggly-looking thing, limp hair bleached with roots showing, jeans faded and too tight in the thighs, a loose blouse that made her look pregnant. Marybeth never could understand why these young girls wanted to look like they were pregnant. She wore a lot of mascara but no lipstick. She looked like sixteen trying to be twenty, but dusty and tired-looking, almost as ragged as a homeless person. She stood with her arms hanging at her sides, not moving, and waited.

Marybeth went back for the rakes and leaned them in size order against the side of the display. The girl was still there, her mouth a little open, her face empty, as though she were asleep standing up. She looked too hopeless to be threatening. Marybeth unlocked the door and opened it a little way.

"We're not open till ten, is there something I can do for you?"

"Are you the lady that found the baby?"

"Yes, I am."

"They didn't say anything about her booties."

Marybeth opened the door wider and stood back to let her in. The girl stood just inside the door.

"Did you find the booties?"

"Yes, I did."

"You should have left them with her. I made them for her."

Marybeth could picture them, hideous lumpy things, one much bigger than the other. They were still sitting on the hall table. She'd forgotten to give them to the police.

"Who are you?"

"I'm Leanne Ellsworth."

"You're that baby's mother, aren't you?"

"Yes'm."

Now it was Marybeth's turn to stand and stare. She'd thought of the baby as appearing suddenly in the ivy, like a baby in a cabbage patch. She had wondered about a mother, especially with the police asking questions, but the child had seemed so complete and self-sufficient, lying sound asleep in the blanket. Now here was this other child, showing up out of nowhere too, claiming the baby was hers.

"How did you find me?"

"It said on the TV about you, that you work here. Can you give me back the booties?"

"Well, I don't have them here. They're at the house. How did you get here?"

"Walked."

"Lord, you must be just worn out. Come have some coffee and let's see about you."

Suddenly the girl's face wrinkled up and she started crying, bringing her fists up to her eyes and hunching her shoulders as if she were trying to hide. Marybeth reached out and placed her hand on her shoulder, half pushed her into the back room and into the rocking chair. As she turned to pick up a mug, she heard the back door open and Munro coming through the stock room.

"Hey, honey, I found that …."

He stood in the door. "What's this?"

"This is Leanne Ellsworth, you go on up front, I'll be out in a minute."

He started to protest, and she glared at him. "Go *on*, Munro."

He was halfway to the cash register when he called back, "What about my coffee?" She ignored him.

Leanne had stopped crying. She was slumped in the rocking chair. She was so homely, so lifeless, Marybeth thought. How did she get herself in this situation? Though getting pregnant didn't necessarily require beauty or enthusiasm. Now that she'd brought her back here, what would she do with her? Other than handing her the cup of coffee, of course. But Leanne didn't want it.

"Should I call your parents?"

"My parents?"

"Your mother, your father."

"How come?"

"They're probably wondering about you."

"Naw."

"Where do you live, then?"

"Over to Oak Meadows."

That was way over in the northeast, not even in town. It must have been a good four miles.

"You mean to tell me you walked all that way?"

"Yes'm."

She was pale and miserable-looking, and a thought struck Marybeth. "Did you have any breakfast this morning?"

"No ma'am."

That was something she could do.

"Wait right here just a minute, while I talk to my husband, then we'll get you something to eat."

The Coffee Cup was three doors down from Coggins'. She'd like to go someplace where no one knew her, but she couldn't leave the store for that long. Besides, she couldn't go anyplace in Opakulla without running into somebody. People knew her from her time on the City Commission.

They sat in a booth, and Marybeth handed Leanne one of the menus propped up against the napkin holder. It was in a plastic binder and hadn't changed since Marybeth was a child. Leanne moved her lips as she read.

"And what will you girls have?"

Elise stood by them with her kind smile. She looked like an old bird, with her glasses down her nose, arms like twigs.

"Leanne, what would you like to eat?"

"Scrambled eggs. And can I have bacon?" She was looking at Marybeth, not Elise, as if she needed permission.

"Of course. How about some biscuits and orange juice too?"

"Okay."

"You want that with grits or hashbrowns?"

"Grits."

"And what about you, Marybeth?"

"I'll have wheat toast and a diet Coke." Ever since O.B. was born Marybeth had been on a diet or falling off a diet. While they waited, Leanne kept her eyes averted, studying the pastries in the display case. She seemed so young, hardly any knuckles visible on her small, plump hands – pretty hands, though the nails were bitten down into the flesh. She looked exhausted, but when Elise brought the food she became more animated.

Leanne chewed her eggs with her mouth half open, then stuck in some bacon as an afterthought. She licked the jam off her fingers. Marybeth kept her gaze resolutely on the salt and pepper shakers to avoid the sight. Elise collected them; these were cows with pink mouths and green ceramic grass around their feet.

She wondered where to begin. She had so many questions, but almost didn't want to know the answers. Where were her parents? What about the father? Why wasn't she in school? But most of all, how could she give up her baby? With all the misery of taking care of Ruthie, it would have been as hard to just dump her somewhere as to pick up a knife and cut off her own... well, she hated to think what she might cut off.

Maybe she should just feed the girl and let her go back to wherever she came from. She was so apathetic – the only sign of unhappiness had been when she started crying back in the store – and that seemed to spring more from exhaustion than grief. But she sensed a world behind Leanne that she had never imagined. That baby in the planter connected them somehow, and now she was required to imagine it.

"Leanne...."

She looked up, and then back down at her plate, where nothing was left but a bite of grits. She pushed that onto her fork with a delicate forefinger.

"Tell me about it."

"About what?"

"Why did you leave your baby in my planter?"

"I thought she'd be safe there, if a dog come by or something."

"Come on now, you know that's not what I mean." But Leanne just stared at her, mouth a little open, mercifully empty now. Suddenly Marybeth found herself very angry.

"Why did you throw away your child?" She knew it was harsh, but she was having the same reaction she used to have when her children were stonewalling.

"I didn't throw her away. I left her at your house because I thought you'd be nice, because of the flowers."

"But how could you leave her?"

"I had to."

"What do you mean you had to?"

"He made me."

"Who made you?"

"Peter."

"Is that the baby's father?"

"Yes'm."

"And where is he?"

"At work."

This was unbearable. "How could he make you, did he hold a gun to your head? You don't just put down your baby and walk away like that. Who did you think would take care of her?"

Elise looked over. Marybeth had raised her voice and Leanne's face was crumpling.

"I don't know."

"All right. I'm sorry I got mad. Do you want more coffee?"

And when Leanne just shook her head, rubbing her eyes with her fists again, Marybeth said, "Let's go."

At the cash register, her face froze out Elise's curiosity. Of course she had probably heard about the baby on the news, but had she heard enough this morning to know who Leanne was? By the time she'd paid, Leanne had control of herself again.

"Do you want me to take you home?"

"Yes'm."

She left Leanne in the car while she went in to tell Munro. He was with a customer, and she scribbled a note: 'This is the baby's mother. I'm giving her a ride home. Back ASAP,' and handed it to him. He raised his eyebrows, but stuffed the note in his shirt pocket and went on looking through a box of hose nozzles.

Back in the car she got surprisingly clear directions to Oak Meadows. They drove through town, Leanne sitting silent and miserable at her side, until MaryBeth relented.

"Listen, Leanne, I'm sorry I yelled at you. I know you're having a hard time. I just want to figure out how I can help you."

"Could we go get the booties?"

Of course, that's why she had come to the store in the first place. It was not what Marybeth meant when she offered to help, but her house wasn't far out of their way.

"All right. We'll go to my house and get the booties, and then take you home. We can talk about what you want to do next."

She parked in the garage and took Leanne in through the back. No point in letting the neighbors see her. After the six o'clock news last night the phone kept ringing until Munro got fed up and unplugged it.

Marybeth was surprised to see Leanne wipe her feet carefully on the mat before stepping into the kitchen.

"Your home is pretty."

"Why, thank you." The kitchen was Marybeth's favorite room in the house. After O.B. left home, she began fixing it up. It was filled with maple, blue gingham, shining copper.

"Is it okay if I sit down?"

"Of course. Just wait right there, and I'll go get the booties."

When she came back, Leanne was sitting at the kitchen table with her hands folded in her lap, like a child waiting to see the principal. But she almost snatched the booties out of Marybeth's hands, crushing them tightly in her own.

Marybeth sat down.

"What's your baby's name?"

"Misty Dawn."

White trash, she thought, and then was ashamed of herself.

"That's a very pretty name. Did Peter help you choose it?"

"No, I chose it myself. He said he didn't care."

"Why did he want to give her away?"

"I don't know. He just got real mad with the mess and the crying. Said I wasn't fun anymore. When I was pregnant he said I was ugly."

She was as homely as they come, Marybeth thought, with her close-set eyes and broad face, doughy white skin with a rash on her neck. She was too young to have put her body through all that. Like the women in primitive societies who began childbearing at puberty, she seemed to have worn herself out prematurely. Bruises on her upper arms, and now Marybeth realized it wasn't a rash, but hickeys on her neck. The bruises and the hickeys both from Peter, she supposed. And now Leanne was crying again, snorting and sobbing, her mouth wet and rubbery. Marybeth stood up quickly and grabbed the box of tissues off the shelf, but when Leanne had taken one, she couldn't help bending over to put her arms around her and rock her while she cried. It was over soon.

"Are you crying about leaving your baby? Why did you let him make you? Why didn't you leave him instead?"

"I didn't have no place to go, and besides, he said he'd kill us if I tried to leave. He'd better not find out I come to see you either."

"Didn't you try to get any help?"

"Help for what?" Leanne looked at her blankly.

"There are places, there are organizations. There's a shelter for women whose husbands abuse them." She was embarrassed, as though she were accusing Leanne of something shameful.

"Judy told me about that once, but we didn't know the name of it. Anyway, Judy says they're all a bunch of lizzies."

Marybeth had heard that before, from another Commissioner, when they were considering funding for the shelter. It didn't surprise her too much coming from him, but she was surprised that Leanne was more scared of lesbians than of getting beaten up. All a matter of what you're used to, she supposed. But the remark seemed to close the subject of getting help, while Marybeth didn't have a clue how to enter the subject it opened, or what she could do for the girl other than what she had asked for.

"We'd better be getting you home." She stood up and replaced the tissues on the shelf. Leanne followed her to the car.

Neither said a word until they reached the long traffic light at County Road 118. Leanne sank comfortably into the silence, but for Marybeth it was like waiting for the next drop of water to fall from the tap.

"Leanne, you have to decide what you intend to do."

"Nothing I can do, I guess." It was like pushing string.

"Well, the police said to let them know if I found out anything else, and I have to tell them about you."

The string stiffened up.

"You can't do that. I thought you wanted to help me get my baby back."

"Now look, how can we get your baby back if we don't let them know who you are?" As soon as she'd said it, she realized she'd been tricked. She hadn't had any intention of getting involved.

"You can tell them you want to keep her, and then you can give her back to me."

"It doesn't work that way. They don't just give away a baby to the first person who waltzes in asking for her."

"But you found her. Finders keepers." As if she'd discovered an elementary principle of law. The light changed, and Marybeth turned onto the dirt road to Oak Meadows.

The road was dusty, empty except for a couple of gray shacks with tin roofs, and one new mobile home. Next to a small, freshly plowed field, cows moved through a grove of live oaks.

Underneath the sign at the trailer park entrance, someone had planted red salvia and white periwinkles. The main road was narrow but paved, the trailers lined up in neat rows. A few women sat on rusty metal steps, watching their children. A little boy in a full cowboy outfit was chasing a dog. Two girls played under a clothesline. Marybeth drove slowly, while everybody stopped to watch.

"I'm sorry. I can't take your baby, even if they'd give her to me. I have to tell the police about this."

"You let me out right now." She opened the door, and Marybeth braked quickly. Leanne ran down the row of trailers, clutching the booties, and disappeared behind the third one. Marybeth couldn't follow in the car. And what good would it do? She had nothing left to say. Carefully, she turned the car around and started back out of the park.

Leanne

Chapter Five

I thought I was rid of Peter for good. It had only been two days but it felt like I'd been gone for weeks. When Mrs. Coggins said she was going to call the cops I just panicked. So I was dodging around like I could hide behind some tree, and it came to me clear. I had to get away from the cops and Peter both. If they found me, they'd put me in jail, and if he found me, he'd kill me.

When I seen Mrs. Coggins' car drive away, I went back over to Judy's. I figured I'd ask could I stay with her a while. People were out in the yard talking, probably about me. I didn't have nothing to say to them, just walked right up to Judy's door and knocked, and that damn dog started in to barking. He just tears my nerves.

Judy was still in bed like usual. Her kids dress themselves and get their own cereal. Lots of times they don't go to school, but just hang low till the bus leaves and then play around the rest of the day. If I had kids I'd be up in the morning to see they go to school. But that's Judy's way, and none of my business.

Listening to the dog, waiting for Judy to haul herself out of bed, I wondered how I could stand staying there with the dog and kids, and worse, Creepy Clayton she lives with. He's this little short ugly guy with a great big hairy chest and arms. Even right out of the shower, that man looks dirty. He has hair everywhere – I bet even the bottoms of his feet are hairy. If he ever touched me, I'd get sick. But I didn't know where else to go. None of the other neighbors would help me. They were stuck up and I didn't even speak to them.

Finally Judy let me in. Creepy Clayton was already gone to work. Bruno shut up after she whacked him and he just laid there looking at me. She heated up coffee and got out peanut butter and jelly for lunch, and we sat around a while talking. She said I could stay there, so that was good. I went over to my place and got some stuff, filled three grocery bags. Judy said I could sleep in the kids' room and they could sleep on the couch that makes into a bed, so we moved some of their junk out to the living room. Judy's got a double-wide, so she's got more room than us. The kids' room smelled funny, like some cat had gone to the bathroom in there. But like they say, beggars can't be choosers.

After we got stuff moved, it was fun, like one of those TV shows where girls are living together. Judy made more coffee, and then she said she'd do a makeover on me. She pulled out her baskets of stuff, and it was like she had a whole beauty parlor in there. She went to beauty college for a while, until the owner came on to her and his wife got jealous. But she learned how to do hair and everything before she got fired. She brought a bunch of supplies home from the school. They didn't give her back her money so she figured they owed it to her.

She washed my hair in the kitchen sink, then cut and frosted it. She gave me a cold wave, and it looked pretty good, all loose and dangly. Some of it got a little frizzed, but she said that's just how new perms do and it would loosen up later. When I was pregnant my hair got kind of thin, so I was glad to have the perm because it looked like more hair.

When Judy was done with the perm she made my face up. I liked it. I looked a lot older and my mouth was shiny and red. That's my best feature, big fat lips like I'm Black, Erica used to say, but I thought they looked sexy. Movie stars have operations to get big mouths, like how they make your titties bigger but on your lips instead. It must hurt a lot, and I'm glad I don't need it done to me but just have it natural.

When we were through, we decided to go out and show me off. Judy wanted to go to the Cherry Lounge, but we looked in both our purses and we didn't have more than a dollar and a half between us. It wasn't any problem, she said, cause we could always get a guy to buy us a beer. But that didn't sound fun to me. It's like I had no interest in guys at all. I didn't care if I never saw another one. You'd think I'd be horny but I felt like that was all over with, like I was dead down there. So I told Judy I didn't want to and we decided to go to the mall.

I'd never been shopping with Judy before. It turned out she lifts things. Erica used to do that too. but I only done it that one time at Stop and Save. I was too scared of getting caught. Judy was slipping underpants and lipstick and all kinds of things in her purse. It made me nervous cause I knew the police were probably out looking for me. Mrs. Coggins probably told them what I look like. Good thing I had the makeover.

But I wasn't having any fun, and Judy was getting mad cause I kept telling her somebody was watching. Finally we just left. In the car she told me to go in her purse and look at what she got. It was a lot. She did it in three different stores and never got caught.

When we got home Creepy Clayton was there. He works construction and the job closes down when it rains. Soon as we walked in the door he started.

"It's like a fucking beauty parlor in here. How come you always gotta leave your shit all over the place?"

"Don't make such a big deal out of everything. We just went to the mall and was going to put it away when we got back."

"Well you're back, ain't you?"

I was just standing there the whole time. It was like he didn't even see me. Judy opened the refrigerator.

"Don't bother, there isn't any beer."

"No wonder you're such a grouch."

They both started laughing. I'll say this for Creepy Clayton, he might be all gross and greasy, but he never hits her. And he's pretty good with the kids. Matter of fact, he's probably better with the kids than she is.

"What's she doing here?" he said to Judy. He was asking why I was there, but he was acting like I wasn't.

"She's gonna stay with us a little while till things calm down. She's trying to get away from Peter."

"I don't want any trouble here."

"What kind of trouble? He won't know she's here."

I couldn't stand it anymore, so I went back into the kids' room. I leaned over the dresser and looked at my face in the mirror. Some of the lipstick was gone, but everything else stayed the same. I looked so grown up, like a model in a magazine.

Sometimes I think I done so much in fifteen years I could be thirty. I just feel old, like nothing new can ever happen to me again. But I never had the good stuff I used to think comes when you're grown up. Looking like that, all fixed up, I could have been anybody. Maybe I can get me a job at the mall or somewhere and then I can get my own apartment.

If I had an apartment they'd have to give me back Misty Dawn, I bet, because I'm her mom, and I know they got to put the real mom first. I guess if I want her back, I'll have to let them know who I am, so maybe it doesn't matter if Mrs. Coggins told the police. Only it would be better if I got the job and the apartment first. I'd fix my face and hair up and go right in there to the police station and just tell them I come for my baby. They don't have her I guess, but they know where she is.

With Peter gone I got all kinds of ideas. He was always telling me I didn't know how to do this and I didn't know how to do that, but I knew a lot more than he thought I did. Like after I met him that time at the beach, he said he wanted to see me again, only he lived with his mom who was sick. I guessed right away he was married, but I didn't say anything. I didn't care because I figured if he was out there at the beach looking at me he probably didn't love his wife anymore anyway. And when he carried me into the water, I knew he was the one for me and me for him.

When he said I couldn't come to his place, I was the one figured out how we could meet. Momma was working four days, 11-9, at the

Magnolia Inn. She wanted to get six days of lunch shifts instead so she could be home when I came home from school, but it was okay with me. It meant I could do whatever I wanted.

Six o'clock I was down on the corner across from Peter's gas station, and he was there with his truck almost as soon as I got there. He pulled over and I got in. I remember what he said that first time like it was yesterday. "Move over close to me baby, so I can love you the way I want to." He kissed me soft on my mouth, and run his tongue over my lips. Then he sat back and pulled away from the curb. And he didn't do me any more that night.

He drove to the Marsh and parked down a dirt road a ways. I thought for sure we'd do it, and I wanted to real bad. I never felt that way before, not with any of the guys from school. I mean I liked it and all, but now I had this hot place, and I just wanted him to touch me there. But he put his arm around me and pulled my head down on his shoulder. He turned on the radio and was stroking my hair. He told me all about himself, how he planned to have his own garage, and about this blue Corvette he wanted that wasn't running but he could fix it. He'd done a lot of work for the guy who owned it and the guy said he'd give it to him. He said he never had anybody he could talk to like he could talk to me. Every once in a while he'd kiss me, just on the hair or cheek. Then he said it's time to go and I was thinking he didn't like me, but he drove me back near my house, and he said "Wait for me again tomorrow?" So I knew it was okay.

Every night for a couple of weeks, except for weekends, cause I couldn't get away with it, and I guess neither could he, he took me to the Marsh and we parked, and mostly talked. Sometimes he'd kiss me for a while, always real gentle. One night he opened up my shirt and run his fingers around on my nipples. He said, "You're so beautiful," over and over, looking at my face the whole time till I had to close my eyes. One time he brought some chips and dip and a couple of beers, and he gave me a rose he'd bought at the checkout line. That time we walked in off the road a little and spread a blanket out, and I thought for sure we'd finally do it, but after we drank the beers he just held me close and rubbed around my neck and back and bottom. I could feel he had a big hard on, and other times I could see it in his pants, and he'd get to breathing hard, but he never tried to do a whole lot any one night.

Every time we could only stay about an hour. At first he said he had to get home to fix dinner for his mom, but then one night I told him I knew he was married. Then he told me about his wife, how she was so much fun till they had their little boy, and then she changed, and she never wanted to do anything and was always complaining. He showed me a picture of his little boy holding a play football, and I thought it was so sweet, the way he carried it around in his wallet. The first word he said was Daddy. I told Peter he looked like him, except his hair is black instead of brown, and I could tell he liked me saying that. I wanted to see a picture of his wife, only he said he didn't have one, and it made me feel good. That was pretty dumb of me, cause later when we were living together I found her picture with their little boy Billy, and she wasn't ugly like he said.

Well, we went on like that for a couple weeks. I never been so happy in all my life, not before and not after either. Mostly we'd talk, but every time, he'd touch me just a little, always some different way, and all the touching just stayed on me. I felt him all the time, when I wasn't even with him, kissing me on the mouth, his hands squeezing my bottom, his thumbs rubbing my nipples, his tongue soft in my ear, like he was doing all those things at once. I couldn't think about anything else. Momma got mad, told me to stop mooning around. She should of been glad though, cause I wasn't hanging out with Erica and the guys anymore. I went to school every day, and I'd just sit there and think about him touching me. I never ever knew being in love was like that.

It was a Friday night when he said to me, "I got a place we can use tomorrow for a couple hours, if you meet me." I was sitting with my back leaned against the door, and my feet up on his lap, and he was rubbing them. I was afraid they were smelly but he laughed and said,

"Peeyew" and held his nose, and then started in to rubbing. It was the best feeling in the world, it relaxed me all the way up my legs, and I was lying back almost asleep when he stopped rubbing and started touching them real soft with his fingers, and it woke me right up. Made me feel all the other places he touched me before, and I closed my eyes and just got hot, and then he said it, about having a place where we could go. And when I didn't say anything he said, "Leanne. Do you want that?" I said yes and he pulled me up by the shoulders and gave me a long kiss, almost rough, holding my head so hard and putting his tongue way deep in my mouth.

Where he found for us to go was his friend's apartment who was out of town. That first time, soon as we got in the door he told me to stand still, and he took off all my clothes and just looked at me, and then he took off his clothes too and pulled me into the bedroom and we did it. It wasn't anything like all those other times with the guys. I could still feel all his other touches, and he took a long time before he stuck his thing in, and then he took a long time with that. So I came, and I never did that before, and it was great.

And that was one thing with Peter, I always liked sex with him except when I was real pregnant and right after the baby. Even after he started beating me up, he knew how to turn me on. in fact after the bruises went away, he'd be extra nice to me and that's usually when he'd eat me. I wonder if that's why I didn't run away from him before. But now I got no feelings for him. When I remember all that stuff we did, it doesn't even get me hot. I guess it's good, because I don't want to be with a guy who beats me up.

Momma always said she'd of kicked Daddy out if he didn't go, because he hit her. She taught me you gotta be tough with guys and not let them take advantage. When I get my apartment and my job and get Misty Dawn back, that's all I need. I don't need no guys hanging around bothering me. Unless one of them wants to take me out on a real date, like to a restaurant or a movie or something. I've never been on a date.

After I got sick of looking at myself, I sat on the bed. I started feeling trapped in that room. If I sat in the living room with Judy and Creepy Clayton, I knew I'd be uncomfortable. But that little room was like a box, with only one window that doesn't even open. I was thinking that's what everything is like for me, just trapped in a box. I heard the TV come on and figured I could at least sit out there and watch it, and it wouldn't be like they were ignoring me. I went out, but the door to the other bedroom was closed and I could hear their bed squeaking. I guess they just put the TV on so I wouldn't hear them.

On the TV it was reruns of that old show about the alien family who are made of Jello, only you can't tell. It's pretty funny because they get all confused by humans, so I liked sitting and watching that. Then Judy came out and said she'd make dinner, and she got out these big cans of spaghetti. Soon as she started opening the first can, the door opened and her kids came in. It's like they was cats, that come running when they hear the can opener.

Judy said, "Where you been?" like she was mad, but I could tell she didn't mean it, and the kids could too, cause they didn't say anything. They were going back to their room and she said, "Hey, don't go back there. Leanne's staying here for a while and she's using your room. Don't you see where we hauled your stuff out? You kids can sleep on the couch." They started whining. I didn't blame them; I would too. But pretty soon they sat on the couch and stuck in their thumbs and watched the TV. Trevor and Crystal, both of 'em thumb suckers. I used to watch them for Judy sometimes when she wanted to go out. I tried to play with them but they never wanted to. Mostly they were happy just watching TV or going outside and doing I don't know what. Kids have it easy. They don't got to worry about nothing, except maybe getting a licking.

When the spaghetti was ready Judy called Creepy Clayton to come and get it, and we all sat around and ate. Creepy Clayton wanted to watch some news show, and the kids complained cause they wanted to see The Simpsons. But Creepy Clayton got his way and the kids shut up. It was a show about twenty years ago when the terrorists attacked our country. It showed the airplanes crashing and all these people running down the street, away from a big pile of smoke that was like a monster chasing them. And then they had this part about all the firemen and police who got killed and how brave they were.

Creepy Clayton said they wasn't nothing like the chickenshit cops in Opakulla and then Bam Bam Bam there was pounding on the door. It made me jump. Soon as I stopped feeling surprised, I started feeling scared, cause I knew it had to be Peter. "Shit, who's that?" Creepy Clayton said, and he got up and threw the door open and let Bruno charge out there. It all happened so fast. I saw Peter's face and then he fell backward down the steps. Bruno was on top of him and barking in his face. Peter yelled, "Get this motherfucker offa me." Creepy Clayton stepped out and grabbed Bruno's collar and hauled him back inside, and Peter followed him.

Creepy Clayton said, "What do you want?"

"I come to get her," Peter said, and he jerked his head over at me, didn't even talk to me. But Creepy Clayton turned around and said to me, "You ready to go home?" and I said, "I'm not going back there no more," talking to Creepy Clayton just like Peter did.

Peter looked straight at me and started to shove past Creepy Clayton but he had Bruno ready to go and said, "You ain't making no trouble in front of my kids, get the fuck outa here." Him and Bruno was like a wall between us, so Peter couldn't do nothing but leave. But he said to me, first time he said anything to me, "You won't get away with this. Wait till I get you back over to our place."

I was proud that I didn't go back to him. To tell the truth, after Bruno knocked him down I wanted to make sure he was all right, like I still cared about him. But if I went back that night, I knew he'd beat the shit out of me, could of even killed me. And I figure that was true no matter when I went back, because longer I stayed away the madder he'd be.

I was thinking, good thing I got Creepy Clayton to protect me, when soon as he closed the door behind Peter, he turned around and said to Judy, "I want her out of here."

"Where's she gonna go?"

"I don't give a shit. I don't want her here with that bastard coming around."

"You can't just put her out tonight."

"Okay, well she can stay tonight, but I want her gone first thing in the morning."

Finally he looked at me and said, "You understand that?"

I wouldn't let him see me cry for anything.

"You don't gotta worry; I'm getting out of here tomorrow anyway. I'm getting a place of my own." And I turned around and went back in the kids' bedroom and closed the door. I didn't slam it except in my mind.

I didn't come out the next morning until I heard Creepy Clayton leave. Judy was sitting on the couch smoking a cigarette. Crystal was laying there sucking her thumb with her head on Judy's lap, and Judy was rubbing her hair.

"She's got a fever so she can't go to school," Judy said when she saw me. I got myself a cup of coffee with a bunch of milk, and we didn't say much of anything. But when I finished my coffee, Judy said, "You know you better be going."

"Is it okay if I leave some of my stuff here?"

"Yeah, I guess. You know, Clayton don't want to be mean. He just doesn't want trouble here; he figures it'll end with the cops."

Creepy Clayton's been in trouble so much I guess he figured soon as they saw him the cops would bust him. I went in the kids' room and got my purse, and then came back out.

"Where you gonna go?"

"You don't have to worry about me. I got plenty of places to go."

"Yeah, well, you be careful now, don't let Peter see you." She gave me five dollars from her purse.

And then I was standing in front of her trailer, and she closed the door behind me. It was all gray outside, looked like rain. I couldn't think where to go. I stood there a long time and nothing came to mind. Wasn't nowhere to go but away, so I started walking.

I went down to the main road and stood there trying to figure out whether to go into town or the other way. In town was the hardware store, Mrs. Coggins' house, the police. I didn't want to go to any of them. I guess I went the other way because I didn't know what was out there, so it wasn't any place I didn't want to be.

I walked a long time. It's a funny thing, all the walking I done since Misty Dawn was born. You wouldn't catch me walking before then. And you won't catch me doing it anymore either if I can help it. After about an hour every part of me was hurting.

I'd passed the last gas station a long ways back and I wished I'd gotten me a drink there. It was just stubbly land on both sides of the road, every once and awhile a bunch of trees. Good thing the sun wasn't out. Or that's what I thought until it started to rain. At first I hoped it would cool me off some, maybe I could even get a little drink. But it was that nasty kind of rain, not a whole lot, a drop on my arm and a drop on my face. It wouldn't start and it wouldn't stop, just made me feel sticky.

You get a lot of funny thoughts when you're walking. Like I was thinking, used to be people didn't have cars and I guess they must of walked everywhere they went. They must of spent their whole time walking. How did they ever get stuff done? I guess the rich ones had horses. Or maybe everybody had horses. I never been on a horse but I could of used one then.

How would it be galloping along on a big horse? How do you make it go where you want? I mean, I know you steer them with reins and you kick them to make them go. But what if the horse doesn't want to do what you tell him? I can't believe you can pull on the reins harder than he can pull with his head. It's not like with a car, that just does what you tell it because it's a machine. A horse has a brain and that means it can do like it wants to. I know cars screw up and there's accidents and all, but that's not because the car decides to do something.

Felt like I could walk forever and nothing would change, just stumps and stubble by the side of the road. I mean, every once and a while I saw a house far away in a field, but only one of them looked like anybody lived there. I got scared, not of any one thing that could come hurt me, but just thinking about walking forever and not getting anywhere. And my feet were hurting so bad. I thought about turning around and trying to go back to town, but I didn't think I could walk all that long way. But if I kept going, I didn't know how long it would be before I came to somewhere. So I just stopped and stood there.

It was an awful feeling, worst I ever had. No point in doing anything: forward, backward, nothing. Like I was dead. Felt like a long, long time I stood there. Hardly any cars at all, but a truck went by, and the guy threw a bottle at me. That was so mean, and it would of made me cry, but I didn't have no more crying in me. It did make me feel like I couldn't stand there anymore, so I went and laid down in the ditch. It was awful and prickly, and there was ants, but I didn't care. I just laid there on my stomach with my head on my arms, and after a while I fell asleep.

Marybeth

Chapter Six

Marybeth didn't get back to the store until almost noon, and as luck would have it, they were swamped. As she came in, Munro gave a significant look at the clock, and said, "Lenny called in sick."

"Again?" she mouthed silently, but he just turned back to the register, where three customers waited. Marybeth plucked one out of the line and spent twenty minutes discussing the merits of different gas grills.

Wednesday was their day for reorders. Usually Marybeth did this, but she could see Munro needed a break from customers, so she took over the register and let him go back to the office. Catherine Willers came in. When she was young and beautiful, Mrs. Willers had been helpless as a matter of principle. Now she was condemned to a walker, and never failed to complain about it when she saw Marybeth. Slowly they made their way together to the back to choose the right size nail. Marybeth could hear a string quartet from the office radio. In a good mood, Munro listened to country.

But he never stayed in a bad mood for long, and when it passed, even if it was caused by Marybeth, he seemed to feel he should make amends. As they closed up at 6:30, he said, " "Let's stop at the store and pick up a steak. I'll fix dinner on the grill."

Marybeth wondered what went through his head when he was cross, to make him so sweet afterwards. She had her own guilty thoughts, about two or three alternative lives she liked to imagine, none of which included him. But she cleaned up her conscience every week in church. Munro didn't go to church, so he did penance by taking care of her.

It was close to nine o'clock, well past sunset, when they finished dinner on the deck, but the sky still held some blue. A new moon with the old moon in its arms. Munro sat in the rocker and Marybeth on the lounge chair beside him, pleasantly stuffed and sleepy. She had finished a huge steak and had not neglected the corn on the cob. She reached over to take Munro's hand and told him about Leanne.

"Did you call the police yet?"

"No. You know we were crazy at the store. Besides...."

"What?"

"Well, I wanted to think about it some and talk to you."

Munro just waited.

"I'm afraid she'll get in trouble if I tell them where she is. It probably won't do any good anyway. They won't give her back that baby."

"Good thing, too."

"You think so? What do you suppose will happen to her?"

"The baby? Mrs. Garrity said she'll be snatched up right away."

"No, I meant Leanne."

"She'll go on getting beaten up by that sorry son of a bitch, and probably have another baby to dump on our doorstep in a year."

Munro rarely swore.

"But if I tell the police who she is what do you think they'll do? Do you think they'd put her in jail?"

"Now Maybeth, how should I know? But I don't think you have any choice. You'll be in trouble yourself if you don't. An accessory or something. And didn't you tell her you were calling them?"

"Yes, and she ran away."

In the dark she felt him staring at her.

"Look, honey, this isn't Ruthie. She's nothing to do with us."

"You didn't meet her or talk with her. She's only fifteen, Munro, and in a world of trouble."

"And how many other teenagers out there are in a world of trouble? Do you want to take them all on?"

"No, maybe just the ones who dump their babies on us."

"Great. They'll be beating a path to our door."

"Seriously, honey. I know I'll have to call Officer Williams tomorrow. But can't we do something for her? At least she needs a lawyer."

"We can't afford a lawyer. I'll tell you what, why don't you help her get to Legal Aid? They can probably help her, and then you can get out of this."

As usual, Munro had come up with a good idea. They sat quietly and watched the rest of the stars come out. Such a relief to have cool evenings again.

But all night in bed she tossed, like the hottest nights of summer, kicking off the sheet and pulling it back up, dreaming and waking and dreaming again. Ruthie with her back turned, refusing to speak, and a thin trickle of blood running down one bare arm. A Commission meeting, where she kept voting yes, though she knew she should hold out and vote no. She woke up for good just past 5:30.

As she walked in the dark, the trees dripped around her. She walked automatically, chewing on her lip, sometimes speaking out loud. If she called Officer Williams, it would sever any link with Leanne. She saw her running down the line of trailers, the booties flashing pink. Leanne had assumed Marybeth would help her get the baby back. She hadn't made any promises. Legal Aid was a good idea, but would Leanne trust her if she called the police?

Officer Williams had been replaced by his brother, Detective Williams. He came to the store to take her statement. She took him into the back room and poured him a cup of coffee.

At first she was hesitant, but he was patient and matter of fact. She wasn't going to tell him about taking Leanne to her house. It seemed to make her complicit. But when he looked straight at her and asked, "Is there anything else?" she told him. He simply wrote it down and thanked her.

"What will happen to her?"

"The mother? Well, it's hard to say right now. First, we'll have to find her. That shouldn't be too hard if you'll come out to Oak Meadows with me."

"Oh, I'd rather not. I didn't mean to get involved in this at all, and the store keeps us so busy. I wouldn't want to come looking for her in a police car. I think she sees me as a friend, at least until I said I was calling you. Will you arrest her?"

"We'll pick her up if we find her. Maybe take her down to juvenile court."

"Oh, good. They'll help her there."

He took a breath, opened his mouth, closed it again. He flipped through his pages of notes, asked a couple more questions, drank down the last of his coffee. He stood and took his hat from the table, put it back down.

"Listen, Mrs. Coggins, that baby will be all right. She'll find a family fast. And these young girls getting in trouble, it's not like when you and me were coming up. Used to, a girl got herself in trouble, she'd be ashamed. But they don't think about things the way we did. You can't be worrying about them. They're past saving, at least by any of us."

"But she didn't get herself in trouble. She's married."

"So she says. Married or not, the only one we can maybe put right is that little baby. It's just too late for the other one."

Twenty-two years he'd been a cop, and what had he seen? He knew a lot more than she did about the rough side of life. A good thing too. She'd seen all she cared to.

So what was she doing Sunday afternoon, driving out to Oak Meadows? A beautiful blue day, she could have been digging in the garden. The dead month was over and the heat passing, beds were ready for planting. But they couldn't all just give up on Leanne. Somebody had to be on her side. Marybeth couldn't leave her to deal with the police all alone.

She drove down the dusty road, turned into Oak Meadows, and pulled up next to the row of trailers where she had last seen Leanne. No way to know which was hers, so she walked to the first, climbed the cinder block steps, and knocked.

A dog started barking inside, a chesty, rhythmic bark. With a voice deep as that it must be a big one. She stepped off the stairs, so when the door opened she was looking up at the woman who answered. Thin and bony, knobby-knuckled fingers clutching a cotton robe over her breasts, holding the dog by the scruff of the neck. She was barefoot, and her hair, dark red with darker roots, stood in tufts as if she had just gotten up.

"What do you want?"

"I'm looking for Leanne Ellsworth."

"Not here." She let go of her robe and started to close the door.

"Wait, please."

"What?" She didn't open it again, but didn't close it all the way either, and she was still restraining the dog.

"I don't know where she lives, which trailer. I was hoping you could help me. Do you know her?"

"I know her."

"Can you tell me which one is hers?"

"That one over there. Aren't you the one found the baby?"

"Yes."

"And you had to go call the police. They been out here too, looking for her. She thought you'd help her."

"That's why I'm here. I want to help."

"Too late. She's gone."

"Will you tell me where I can find her?"

"You're kidding."

"Well, maybe I could just leave a message with you. Do you think you'll see her?"

"How should I know?"

"Please, if you do, just tell her I can get her a lawyer. I'll leave you my number." She pulled out a receipt from Food King, wrote her name and phone number on it and handed it to the woman, who let go of the dog to take it. Luckily, the door was open only wide enough for her hand and his snout. She dropped the paper on the floor, hauled him back in, and slammed the door shut. The dog began barking again.

Leanne

Chapter Seven

I probably wasn't asleep very long, but I felt different when I woke up, like I could think again. I thought of every place I could go, and knew the only place for me now was Momma's. I got up, brushed off the dirt and crossed the road. I couldn't walk all the way so I decided to hitch a ride. I never hitchhiked before and when I saw a car it was the hardest thing to stick my thumb out. Felt like I was standing up on a stage or something, everybody watching me. But I didn't see anybody but the woman driving and she didn't even look at me.

Four cars went by before an old guy stopped. I was scared to get in his car but I had to get back to town. He told me I should be ashamed of myself, I could get in trouble hitching rides. He talked like I was lucky he was the one picked me up, like every other car had some rapist driving it.

I couldn't believe how short a time it took before we were back in town. I must of been walking all morning and here it took like five minutes to get back to where I started. He asked me where I wanted to go and I said I wanted to go to my Momma's and told him how to get there. He said he was glad I was going home.

Momma's house is the other side of town from Oak Meadows. There's some mobile homes out there, and a couple of ordinary houses must of been there a hundred years or something, they're so raggedy looking. I got this guy to leave me at the end of our road. Momma had added a deck with a bunch of flowers all around and it looked nice. Mostly though, when I saw it I just felt good inside, like home.

I hadn't seen Momma since the day I moved in with Peter. We'd been doing it in his truck and at his friend's apartment whenever we could, and after about three months he said he found us a house and we could live together. That scared me a little. It was one thing sneaking around, but I never ran away. That's a really big deal.

Peter said he could come get me when Momma was at work. He wanted to marry me when his divorce was done, only I was too young to do it without Momma's okay, but he'd buy me a ring. He said he never loved anybody like he loved me. He had it all figured out. He'd take me to school every morning on his way to work, and I could take the school bus back – he already knew the bus number. When he came home I'd have dinner ready, and he'd hold me in his arms all night long.

I was thinking about my friends. Angela thinks she's so special because she's living with her boyfriend at his parents' house, but her boyfriend is just in eighth grade, and he's not cute - he's got a skinny neck and zits. And they're living with his parents which I can't even believe they let them do that. I bet it's against the law.

It all sounded so cool. All the time he was telling me this he was touching and kissing me, and he got me hot. He pulled off my leggings and panties and took off his clothes and had me pinned under him. He put his dick right up against me and whispered "You want it, Leanne?" When I said yes please yes, he pushed it in just a little bit and then he pulled out and said, "Say you'll move in with me," so of course I said I would.

We moved two days later. He didn't want to come to Momma's place so he said just to meet him across from his job like always, and bring my stuff. I didn't have a lot of stuff, just only my clothes and drawing things, and a radio, and I put them in a laundry bag and met him, and we drove to Oak Meadows.

Peter had called it a house but it turned out it was just a trailer. I was a little disappointed but I didn't say anything. At least the bedroom and living room were separate, not like Momma's. Only I was used to no neighbors, and here there were all these trailers right up close to each other.

Still, it was cool having our own place. Peter bought the furniture from the people who used to live there, and bought new sheets for the bed. He bought food too – a bucket of fried chicken, cereal and milk, canned soup, and three boxes of cookies. He got a six pack of beer but I don't drink beer. It was just like he said it was gonna be. We ate dinner and went right to bed, had sex and watched TV until I fell asleep. I don't know if it was all night long but whenever I woke up his arms were around me.

In the morning I got ready for school. I couldn't wait to tell Angela and Erica about it. But Peter said I'd better skip school for a while, because Momma would be looking for me. He said when I went back to school I couldn't tell anybody, because we'd both be in trouble.

I hadn't even thought about Momma the night before. But when Peter went off to work and I was all alone I started worrying about her, how upset she'd be, and was she missing me, mostly about how she'd have people out looking for me. Every time I heard a car I'd peep out the window thinking it was Momma or the school people. But she never came looking, or anybody else neither, and after a while I figured she just forgot about me.

So now I was standing outside our door, wondering should I knock or should I just go in. It felt weird to knock on my own house door, but maybe I couldn't call it my house anymore. I didn't know if Momma might be mad, so I knocked. It was like more polite that way, and maybe we could start off right, like visitors. I heard some banging around and Momma yell, "Coming" and then she opened the door and we were just standing there looking at each other.

I didn't know what she was feeling. Her mouth was a little open and she was blinking. She looked like a retard if you want to know the truth. I just felt so good when I seen her, and I would of given her the biggest hug if I wasn't scared how she was gonna be. But I didn't need to worry. In a minute she was giving me a hug like she'd never let go, and we both started crying.

After we got calmed down a little, we went inside and sat on the couch and I told Momma almost everything, except for the sex stuff and him beating me up. When I got to the part about Misty Dawn, she said, "I can't believe you just threw away your own baby and never even asked me for help."

I said I was sorry, and she said we'd get that baby back. Then I felt good, cause when Momma sets out to do something, it gets done. So that made me relax a lot, also cause I'd already told her most of the bad stuff.

All of a sudden I was hungry. I asked her what she had to eat, and she got out macaroni and cheese, one of my favorite things. I started in on it but she grabbed it away from me and had to heat it up first. I sat at the table and it was like I never went away, never lived with Peter, never had a baby. That got me confused. If I could've I'd have wiped out everything that happened in the last year, except Misty Dawn. But I couldn't wipe out Peter without wiping out her. It's dumb to think that way cause you can't change what's happened, but I always like playing what if.

Momma said it was time for her stories so we turned on the TV and laid on her bed to watch. She only gets to do it when she's not working. I asked her, and she said she got a job waitressing at John's Homestyle, and she didn't have to be there till five. She said the money there was okay, even if the tips weren't like at the Magnolia Inn, and with only Bailey home anymore things weren't as tight as they used to be.

I was sorry to hear Bailey was still there. I guess I thought he'd be in jail or dead. You'd think he'd get out on his own, he's twenty-one, but Momma said he was staying with her "just till he gets on his feet." I didn't want to say anything to hurt her feelings, so I just shut up. Anyway, you can't argue with Momma about Bailey. Even with him living off her, probably stealing from her purse, I could look around the house and see she was doing okay. The TV and refrigerator were new. And best thing, she's got a car now. It's old, but she says it runs good.

Momma always used to be scrounging ways to get to work, and she did a lot of walking when I was a kid. I never knew what that was like before now. I never knew lots of things about my Momma until I had a baby myself. The way I feel about Misty Dawn, I can even see why she never gives up on Bailey. Even if Misty Dawn turned into a murderer or crack addict or something I don't think I'd ever stop loving her. I guess that sounds dumb because like Momma said I just threw her away. But that doesn't mean I don't love her.

You know, I think I didn't know what it was to feel good the whole time I was gone until I got back there with Momma holding me. When I was a kid and lived there we'd fight a lot, and she had all these dumb rules she'd yell about, but I could do what I wanted cause what could she do about it, her working all the time and never there. I think maybe I forgot about loving her. But now I'm grown, maybe not my age but I'm sort of married, and a mother myself, I feel different. So that's one good thing that came out of all this mess. That and Misty Dawn.

Chapter Eight

When Momma went to work I started thinking about what she said, why I never called her, when she could of helped me. It made me ashamed, and it made me wonder. I never even thought about her, but I don't understand why not. It's like me and Peter and Misty Dawn were the only people in the world. Or like I wasn't allowed to talk to anybody about it. Not that I asked him, I just knew it.

Thing is, it wasn't that long after we moved in together that Peter got bossy. He was still sweet lots of times, but only if I did everything his way.

First fight we had was about school. Every day I was saying can I go to school today. I didn't want to have to do eighth grade all over again, and I was getting bored just sitting in the trailer. But Peter kept saying not today, and finally the second week I got mad, and said I was going to school Monday even if he didn't take me.

Wow. It was like he turned into a whole different person.

"You think you're better than me, Leanne? You can't learn anything in school, all you want to do is hang out with those dumb kids you used to go with."

"But you told me..."

"What about all the stuff you told me, like your job at the Speedyway and saving for college? You been lying to me from the beginning. You're just a dumb slut, can't even cook worth a shit, you ought to watch some TV about cooking instead of that dumb Oprah show you've always got on."

He was right up in my face and I was scared he'd hit me. But he just grabbed a beer and slammed out the door, and then I heard him tearing away in his truck.

I was so surprised I didn't even cry at first. I didn't know what to do. First he loved me, now he didn't. When I was done crying, I got some chips and turned on the TV. I even opened a beer but I just drank a little of it. Beer's nasty.

It was getting dark. I could hear the woman next door calling the kids in, but I didn't know her, I hadn't met any neighbors and I didn't know anyone who could help me. I did think of Momma then. But we didn't have a phone, just his cell, and he took that.

It must of been about nine o'clock I started wondering if he was coming home at all. First I was mad, but then I thought what if he had a accident? I couldn't call anybody to find out. I would just sit there in that trailer by myself and eat all the food and maybe die there. I knew that was dumb, I could knock on somebody's door even if I didn't know them. I ate the rest of the cereal and watched TV until almost midnight to stop thinking about all this stuff.

But when I went to bed I heard noises. Cars and doors and animal noises, someone walking outside. I tried turning on the light but it didn't help. I'd fall asleep a little while and then wake up. I kept going back and forth. Scared about the noises. Mad at him for leaving. Crying because of all the mean things he said. Wondering what I was gonna do. I bet I only slept three hours.

Finally it started getting light outside. I couldn't believe he'd stayed away all night because of a dumb fight. I got up and took a shower and thought about going to school. But what if he came home and caught me leaving? And I was so tired, I didn't know if I could make it all the way to school. So I turned on the TV again and waited.

When I heard kids outside and cars leaving I thought I'd better see if I could use a neighbor's phone. I went next door but nobody answered. I went next door on the other side and this fat old guy just wearing boxers opened the door and said, "What do you want?" When I asked if I could use the phone he just said no, and slammed the door. I didn't dare try anybody else, so I just went back inside.

I ate soup, and watched TV, and slept some. I tried drawing but I was too bummed out.

It was 8:30 when I heard the truck outside. I quick washed my face and turned off the TV. And Peter came in.

"Hey, Leanne, whatcha doin?"

"Nothing."

He was like nothing was wrong, like he hadn't stayed out all night.

"Where were you?"

"None of your business."

"I was scared, like you'd been hurt or something, and I kept hearing noises."

"Yeah, well you can't go making me mad. Hey look, I got you something."

And he handed me a book, "Cooking Basics for Dummies."

"I'm not a dummy."

"Well you don't know shit about cooking, do you? I bought some food. You can look in the book and cook us dinner."

I really was hungry, and I was glad he came home, even if the book hurt my feelings a little. So I made chili. That was the first recipe in the book and it was pretty easy even though I didn't have the kind of knife they said I had to use to cut up an onion. I made cornbread out of the mix he bought too, and he said it was all pretty good except I should of made the chili hotter.

"I did what the book said. You should of bought hot sauce."

"Don't be telling me what to do."

He had beer with his chili, and then he pulled out some weed and we got stoned.

I was lying back on the couch with my eyes closed feeling the high go right through me. Next thing I knew he had all his clothes off and his dick was right by my face.

"Open up."

I didn't want to, I wasn't used to it then, but I didn't want him mad at me again, when he was being nice. I figured I'd stop before he came, that's the gross part, but he held my head so I couldn't get away and then he made me swallow it. I felt like crying. But he cuddled me and called me baby, told me he loved me.

"You're turning into a real little woman Leanne, learning how to please a man. You just do what I say and we'll get along fine."

Now I know I should have gotten away when he was gone, left the whole mess behind me. But I wasn't thinking of that then. I loved him and I wanted things good between us. I just had to be nicer to him, not make him mad.

We went along a couple of months pretty happy. I was sorry not to be in school but by this time I knew I'd just have to do eighth grade over anyway. I got bored sometimes, but TV kept me company, and I was learning to cook. Saturdays he'd choose the dinners he wanted that week – meatloaf was his favorite – and he'd go to the store to get the stuff. I wanted to go with him but he said I should clean up around the house, I'd let things get messy. That made another fight.

"You're the one makes the mess, Peter, throwing your clothes all over. And those beer cans aren't mine."

"Don't get smart with me, Leanne, if you know what's good for you. I want this place clean when I get back. And you'd better learn to keep your mouth shut."

But it was him that kept his mouth shut. He didn't say another thing, just made a shopping list without even asking me, and slammed the door on the way out. He stayed away all day, and when he got home put the bags on the counter and turned on the TV. He didn't talk to me that night. I made dinner extra nice, chicken wings and mashed potatoes. He ate plenty but never said it was good, never said nothing except when we went to bed, he said, "You sleep on the couch, I'm sick of listening to you snore."

It was always little stuff that made him mad. One time he came home and I was cooking like usual, and I was singing. He must of already been in a bad mood.

"Shut up Leanne. What the hell are you singing?"

"Its *Love Me Like You Do*. It's my favorite song."

"You sound like that girl on American Idol last night, the one everybody was laughing at. When's dinner?"

Then he was mad because I said it would be an hour, and when it was ready he didn't want it.

"What is this?"

"It's lasagna, remember, that's what you wanted."

"I can't eat this shit."

And he dumped his plate on the floor, grabbed his jacket, and went storming out the door.

That was the thing, when he got mad he'd either stop talking or just leave. I got used to him leaving, even though I was pretty sure he went to his wife's house. But when he stayed and didn't talk it sometimes lasted two days. And who else could I talk to? I felt like I was going crazy.

Between mean times he could be sweet. One time he brought me flowers. Another time he said I didn't have to cook, and he ordered a pizza and asked me what I wanted on it. And we had sex a lot, and he made it so good, and afterwards lots of times he'd say he loved me. Especially if I went down on him, and if I did that sometimes he wouldn't get mad for a while.

But the worst time, before I got pregnant that is, was when he came home and found me sitting outside, drawing a picture of Judy. Judy and I had got to be friends after one of her kids fell off his bike outside my front door and I went and got her. Most days I'd go over to her house in the afternoon before the kids came home and just watch TV and talk and stuff.

This time it was a nice day, so I told Judy we should take chairs outside and I would draw her. I was doing her face, and I had to keep telling her to stop talking. I pretended it was cause she had to keep still, but really when I'm drawing I like to concentrate. Everything else goes away, nothing but the thing I'm drawing and what's on the page in front of me. I worked pretty fast because I knew she was getting bored, but I was almost done, just some more shading to do, when

Peter got home. He was way early, the kids weren't even out of school yet.

He grabbed my arm hard and pulled me out of the chair.

"What the fuck are you doing Leanne?"

"What do you think she's doing. She's drawing," Judy said.

"No one asked you. You better get out of here before I make you."

"You and who else?" I couldn't believe she talked to him like that, but anyway she left.

He picked up my drawing pad and looked at the picture for a minute – and then he crumpled it up, grabbed the pencil out of my hand and broke it in two pieces.

"Get inside, Leanne. Take the chairs, they'll get ruined sitting outside like that."

I thought he'd come inside too and I was scared, because he'd never touched me rough like that before, never hit me or anything. I was embarrassed to have Judy see it. I was always telling her about the lovey-dovey stuff he did, but never the mean stuff.

He didn't come in, I just heard the truck start up and him drive off. I went outside and got the picture off the ground and smoothed it out. It was pretty good, only the nose looked like a pig's. I always have trouble with noses. The shading on the cheeks was the best part, it showed how skinny and bony Judy is. I brushed off the dirt and got another pencil and wrote the date on it. My art teacher said to always date my drawings so I could see my progress. I stuck it in my folder and put everything under the mattress, where I'd been keeping it. I guess I already knew he wouldn't want me drawing.

I didn't know if he'd be coming back, but I started making dinner just in case. Anyway, I had to eat too, didn't I? It was a beef stew and the book said you should cook it a long time. I'd just started washing the carrots when I heard Peter at the door.

"I don't want you hanging around with that slut. I've told you before – you don't go anywhere unless I'm with you."

He had a bag from Housemart and he took out a doorknob and got his toolbox.

"You won't listen to me, so I'm locking you up." He took off the old doorknob and put in the new one, with the lock on the outside. He kept the key in his pocket and after that he kept me locked in.

I told Momma a lot of this stuff when she got home from work, while we ate. She brought a bunch of fried chicken and half a pie from John's. She didn't say much. When I got done telling about the drawing she asked me, "But he never hit you?"

I said I was sick of talking about it. I was worn out thinking about all that stuff, and it was like talking about it just brought it back, the lousy way I felt most of the time. I knew Momma thought I was chickenshit to do whatever Peter said but I didn't want to tell her about him beating me up because when I think about it I get scared all over again.

Vinnie

Chapter Nine

On her way to work the next day Vinnie was so distracted she stayed at the stop sign, waiting for it to change to green, until a car honked. She couldn't stop thinking about what Leanne had told her. She knew there was more to tell.

When Leanne had been gone two days, and her friends wouldn't tell Vinnie anything, she called the police. They told her to come down to the station and file a missing person's report. There, a bored young man filled out a form. They'd share the information with agencies around the country and put out an Amber Alert. Then it would be on file and on the network.

"But aren't you going to look for her?"

"Where should we look, ma'am? We'll talk to her teachers, her friends. We can't go house to house. Lots of kids run away, usually they come back."

Usually. For him it was routine.

For months, every time the phone rang she held her breath, and when the restaurant door swung open she'd look over, hoping. During the day she told herself Leanne had run away, she was probably okay, she'd come home. At night she thought of kidnappers and murderers. When a year went by without a word, she realized Leanne might be gone for good. When she thought of her, she wrenched her mind away. And now Leanne was home.

The child had been beaten, no doubt about it. Vinnie wanted to forget everything she'd heard. It was so cruel, so humiliating. It didn't take a genius to figure out how to hurt Leanne.

Shauna was 8, Bailey was 6 when Leanne was born. She was an accident, but secretly Vinnie had been missing a baby. She'd forgotten the 24-7 neediness, the exhaustion. But Leanne was an easy baby, like she was born happy. She never fretted or whined, just let out a full-bodied wail until her needs were met, and then was instantly happy again.

They all adored her. Shauna and Bailey fought over whose turn it was to give her a bottle, and Bailey wanted to take her to school for show and tell. But the most besotted was Preston. It had taken him a little while with the other two, but he fell in love with Leanne the moment he saw her head pushing out. Maybe that was the difference – he hadn't watched the other births. Vinnie was shy, Preston was squeamish, but by the time Leanne came along they'd been married almost ten years, and modesty didn't have many secrets.

Preston gave Leanne her first bottle. He wanted her to sleep in bed with them until Vinnie put her foot down, and then she'd catch him when he couldn't sleep, standing and staring down into the crib. Leanne was Preston's baby more than hers.

Like her father, Leanne loved to sing. Preston taught her to sing harmony, and her voice was surprisingly strong for such a little girl. *I know you want to fly from me but I won't let you go.* Vinnie had loved to hear Leanne harmonizing with her favorite singer, Luli Belle, but now the song filled her with horror.

Leanne didn't do very well in school. Shauna was the one invited into the gifted program. But Vinnie always thought Leanne might be the smartest of her children. She liked to wonder why and how, think about what if.

Vinnie had a big portfolio of Leanne's drawings from kindergarten on. No matter what was going on around her, even in the chaos of the garage, Leanne would sit on the floor in the corner with her back to the room and draw. The art teacher said she had a special gift and got her a scholarship at a week-long art camp the summer she turned eight.

That was the summer that Preston left. Vinnie never asked him to go, she never had the chance, he just took off, but Leanne blamed her. For a few months she was extra quiet, you hardly knew she was there.

Vinnie worried and worried about her, but she had her own misery to deal with. She missed Preston, his solid presence, his good advice, even their arguments. She missed his laughter – he had a big ringing laugh, put his whole heart into it – and the comfort of his body. The worst was how he'd just disappeared.

The kids were acting up, and she had to handle it on her own. Shauna was staying out all night, Bailey smoking weed. Leanne didn't give her any trouble, just sat in the corner scowling over her drawing pad. She struggled in fourth grade and had two referrals to the principal.

But it didn't last. In fifth grade Leanne bounced back better than ever. She came home from school, tidied the house without being asked, made herself a snack and settled down to homework. She begged to join the Girl Scouts and threw her heart into it. She won three badges in a year: first aid, gardening, and drawing.

That didn't last either. One day Vinnie woke up to a different child. Leanne's adolescence – budding breasts and vicious tongue – started early, and by the time she was twelve every trace of the bright, helpful girl, the girl who told her mother everything, who asked for and followed her advice, was gone.

Vinnie had always told the girls that once a man hits you, things will never be the same. If Preston hadn't left she would have kicked him out. She wasn't sure she believed it, but she wanted to make sure they understood. Now, for all her efforts to protect them, here was Leanne, running off with the worst kind of son of a bitch. Made her give away that baby – what had he done to her to get her to that point? She hadn't said anything about beatings, but Vinnie knew, and she bet there were scars.

Now Leanne was home again, and she was so sweet now, so happy to be back with her Momma. But Vinnie could see – fat and greasy and dirty, circles under her eyes. She jumped at any noise, locked the door the minute she got inside. And where was her spark, where was her spunk? It was yes ma'am no ma'am, and slumping down again in her chair the minute Vinnie turned away. Before she ran away Vinnie would have been thrilled to hear the yes ma'am and no ma'am, but now she'd welcome a little backtalk.

He'd kept her out of school, away from friends, from home. How had he done it? Sex. That was the other thing Leanne never talked about.

She had never felt anger like this. Locked in that trailer – what was he thinking? If there had been a fire, no, she couldn't think about that. Leanne was home now, safe.

Leanne hadn't told her everything, but there was no hurry. Now she needed rest, she needed care, she needed her Momma.

Marybeth

Chapter Ten

"Is this Mrs. Coggins?"

It was a moment before Mary Beth recognized the voice. She hadn't thought of Leanne but once or twice since she turned away from that trashy woman and drove out of the trailer park. It had always been her gift: if there was nothing she could do, she could let a matter rest. Almost a week had gone by, and she had put Leanne out of her mind, except for the dream.

Her viewpoint shifted in the way of dreams, so that one moment she saw herself and Munro, sitting side by side in the car, their faces blank, content, familiar, and the next moment she saw gray road, pearl sky, dark pines. On the road, a shape lay stretched across the yellow line, resolving into a heap of gut and bone and flesh as they drew nearer, and then as they passed she saw it was a crushed child, and suddenly the road ahead was littered with small broken bodies. "Road kill," Munro said.

A few times those words had come back to her, bringing with them the helpless sorrow of the dream.

Leanne's voice brought back the muddled reality, something she could tackle.

"Judy said to call you. I'm ready to go get the baby."

"I don't think it's that simple. But I think we can get a lawyer to help."

"I can't pay for no lawyer."

Marybeth explained about Legal Aid. She couldn't make an appointment when she didn't know if she'd ever hear from Leanne. Now she didn't want to risk letting her off the phone without some definite arrangement. They agreed she'd pick her up tomorrow at her mother's house. That was a surprise. Like her baby, Leanne had seemed to come out of nowhere.

The next morning Marybeth got briefly lost on the unmarked dirt roads. It was a very odd house, made of unpainted cinder block except for the front, where a big opening had been boarded up and a door installed. A wooden room was stuck on to the side of the building like a wart. In front was a cypress deck, with two levels and a sturdy rail. The whole assemblage was surrounded by flowers, with two big pots of burgundy coleus on the deck. No driveway, so Marybeth drove across the yard to the sandy area under a tree and parked next to a battered Buick.

A chunky, blonde woman in a faded orange romper sat on the ground at the far side of the house, among the impatiens and peacock gingers. Her back was to Marybeth. She dropped weeds and spent blooms into a plastic bowl held between her legs. Twisting and reaching, she looked as if she were doing morning calisthenics. Her bare shoulders were muscular and freckled. She was whistling with impressive rhythm and no discernible tune, oblivious to Marybeth and to the bugs which must be crawling under her bare legs.

Marybeth approached hesitantly. It took two hello's before the woman heard her and looked around. Then she scrambled up, putting considerable strain on the tie that held up the romper.

"You here for Leanne?"

"Yes, I'm Marybeth Coggins."

"I know who you are. Seen you on TV. Course I didn't know then it was my grandbaby you found."

She turned and hollered into the house, "Leanne, that lady's come to get you." Then she eased herself back down onto the ground.

"If you'll excuse me now, I got a lot to do here."

Marybeth stood awkwardly, stuck halfway between Leanne's mother and the door. No sound came from inside the house. She wondered if she should go to the door, but that seemed rude with Leanne's mother sitting right there. She didn't even know her name.

"Your garden is beautiful."

"Thanks. Go on in if you want. She's probably still getting dressed."

She knocked, and when she received no answer, opened the door slowly. With no windows, the room was like a great square cave. In one corner was a double bed, at its foot a television. Yellow stuffing showed through the arm of a couch. Another bed across the room, an old-fashioned wardrobe and chest of drawers beside it. In the center was a Formica kitchen table with three wooden chairs, a blue plastic glass filled with flowers in the middle. Through a door on the right, a small kitchen. It was the wooden room she'd seen stuck on outside. The door next to it, with a full-length mirror, was probably a bathroom.

Leanne stood in front of the mirror, fixing her hair. It looked scorched. She turned toward Marybeth and posed, obviously pleased with herself. She wore a blue and white sleeveless seersucker dress, and blue flats. If it weren't for the hair and makeup she'd look quite nice. Bright red lipstick and black mascara on that pale face.

"Good morning, Leanne. Don't you look nice?"

"Yeah, I had a makeover, and my Momma got me this dress for the lawyer."

"Well, we'd better get going."

They were halfway to her car when Leanne's mother came running after them.

"Wait. Here, take these." She handed Marybeth a glass jar filled with zinnias and firespike. "Thank you for helping Leanne."

Marybeth gave the jar to Leanne to hold. As she pulled out of the yard, she saw her mother standing by the flower bed, looking after them.

"What's your mother's name?"

"Virginia. Only everybody calls her Vinnie."

The Legal Aid office was an old house with a wraparound porch just east of downtown, behind the county hospital. Three women sat rocking and fanning, gazing out over the hospital parking lot, occasionally passing a remark, ignoring the ancient man with a cane who sat in the fourth rocker. The chairs were bright with fresh white paint, but as they walked up the front path Marybeth could see that the roof was missing some shingles, the soffits breaking loose from the eaves, and paint peeling off the supporting columns.

"It's all Black people," said Leanne.

"Shhh."

The door opened into the waiting room, a high-ceilinged room with dark wood paneling, and one stained glass window beside the door. The other had been replaced with clear glass, a single BB hole in the center. Even with fluorescent lights, the room was dark. Gray folding chairs were lined up in rows, almost all occupied. The receptionist, her desk facing the door, was a black woman with a gray Afro, glasses and a big smile for Marybeth when she approached the desk.

"Are you here for a divorce?" she asked before Marybeth could say anything, offering her a clipboard.

Marybeth was startled. "Uh, no. I'm here, we're here... that is, I brought her, I called you yesterday and got an appointment. Her name is Leanne Ellsworth."

"Oh, sure." And she pulled out another clipboard. "See if you can find a seat, and fill out this form."

There were two empty chairs in the second row, and everybody moved down one so Marybeth and Leanne could sit together. It was all women and children, all ages and sizes, black and white. The women sat staring straight ahead or down at their laps, hushing the fidgeting children beside them. A small group of children played with cars in the corner. Occasionally a mother broke silence for a reprimand. One turned to her neighbor. "I can't make that child mind. I tell him he'll turn out like his father if he's not careful," and a ripple of sympathy ran down the row.

Marybeth peeked over at Leanne's clipboard. She had left most of the financial information blank. Her handwriting was round and unslanted, very neat, and she dotted her i's with hearts. Under *names of children* she had written Misty Dawn Sewell, and date of birth August 14, 2021. It startled Marybeth to realize that the child was still less than a month old. Leanne carried the clipboard up to the receptionist.

"Just a few minutes, honey, the lawyer will be out soon."

After the big round wall clock ticked off eight minutes a woman came through the door behind the receptionist. Tall and thin, pale skin and long brown hair, she wore a cotton skirt in dark brown and mustard, and a sleeveless brown cotton shirt. She called Leanne's name. Leanne followed her to the door and then turned around.

"Aren't you coming?" she whispered loudly. She looked so alarmed that Marybeth followed her.

Behind the door was a jumble of small offices created out of wallboard. The woman led them to one, opened the door, and gestured for them to go in. Her office was as colorful as she was drab. On either side of the window were two bright posters: red tulips in a tall yellow vase, and distant sailboats in a blue bay. The view outside was blocked by a lavender crepe myrtle. A low table held a pile of children's books and an electric teapot, with mugs and a box of tea bags. The steel case desk faced the window, empty except for a clean yellow pad, a pen, a phone and a laptop.

"Oh! You've made it so pretty."

"Thank you. I keep looking for a nicer desk, but I haven't found anything I like yet. Please have a seat, both of you."

Marybeth and Leanne sat in the two folding chairs in front of the desk.

"I'm Amy Bradwell."

She read through Leanne's form.

"I guess you must be Leanne. And you're Leanne's mother?"

"No!" they both said at once. Marybeth quickly looked away from Leanne, embarrassed by the mutual fervor of their denial.

"I'm just a friend." Could she really take on Leanne as a friend?

"Well. You say here that you want your baby back. That's Misty Dawn?"

"Yes, Ma'am."

"And where is Misty Dawn?"

"I dunno. They took her."

"Who took her?"

"The police I guess. She had her." Leanne nodded toward Marybeth.

Miss Bradwell turned toward Marybeth, her pen poised over the paper.

"Leanne left the baby at my door. We called the police and they came with DFC and picked her up."

"Oh! I saw you on the news. I knew you looked familiar."

And she began her questions, leaning forward, her head cocked slightly, her gaze absorbed by Leanne as if she didn't even know her hand was scribbling away at the pad. Had Leanne seen the baby since then? How old was she, where was she living, did she have other children, did she have a job? And Leanne answered, "Yes ma'am, no ma'am, I dunno." Miss Bradwell began looking down at her pad more and more, and sat up straight, pulling her chair closer to the desk.

Marybeth wanted to grab Leanne and shake her. But Miss Bradwell seemed to have all the time in the world, and the patience to spend it pulling the thread out from Leanne, inch by inch. It was like putting together a jigsaw puzzle, or questioning a teenager. And of course, she realized again, Leanne was a teenager. She slumped in front of the desk, her answers short and sullen as if she were doing Miss Bradwell a favor to tell her anything.

Miss Bradwell had covered four pages on her pad when she put down her pencil.

"Let's have some tea."

Marybeth declined, but Leanne accepted, and asked for lemon spice.

"How many sugars?"

"Three."

Miss Bradwell put the mug down in front of Leanne.

"There you go."

Then she sat down, leaned her elbows on the desk and rubbed her eyes fiercely. She read through her notes.

"Now, Leanne, you've given me a lot of very helpful information. But if I'm going to be your lawyer, I need to know some more."

"You're a lawyer?"

"Why, yes. What did you think?"

"I don't know, I thought you was a secretary or something. I didn't think you were my lawyer."

"Actually, I'm not your lawyer yet. I need to take all this information, and think about it some, and talk to the other lawyers here, and see if we think there's anything we can do for you."

"I'm not asking you to do nothing but get my baby back for me."

"I know. And I hope we can. But I have to know a little more. You've told me a little bit about Misty's father...."

"Misty Dawn."

"Sorry. Misty Dawn. You said he made you throw, I mean give, her away. Can you tell me a little more about that?"

And Leanne began, speaking very softly, to tell about Peter, how he changed when she began to show. The first time he beat her up. The lighted cigarettes on her neck – she lifted her hair to show them the scars. The night in the hospital when she was afraid he had hurt the baby.

"But didn't the doctor call the police? Send you to the shelter?"

"Naw. She didn't say nothing about it, but she give me pain pills. I got fourteen stitches."

The day Misty was born, when he left her at the hospital and she didn't see him again for three days.

"I think he was with his wife. He came back with lots of flowers."

And the baby crying on and off all one night, till Peter made his decision. Her voice a curious sing-song now, and her face without expression.

Chapter Eleven

"Mrs. Coggins, it's for you."

"Take a message, can't you, Lenny? I'm with a customer."

Lenny managed to be barely adequate in every task they gave him. "I think it's urgent. She says she has to speak with you before five. It's a lawyer."

"Hello, can I help you?"

"Mrs. Coggins, this is Amy Bradwell from Legal Aid. I'm trying to get hold of Leanne Ellsworth."

"Oh, that's right. She doesn't have a phone, does she?"

"No. I didn't realize it until after you left the office. I remembered you work in a hardware store, so I thought Coggins Hardware was a good possibility. I'm sorry to bother you, but all she gave me on the form was a P.O. Box, and I'd rather not wait for the mail if I can help it."

"She lives with her mother. I've only been out to her place once and I honestly can't think how to tell you to get there. I'll go with you if you'd like. I'm sure I can find it again. It's not that complicated, but the dirt roads aren't named and I can't tell you any landmarks."

"That's very nice of you. Could we go this afternoon?"

"No, I have the store."

"Oh, you work full-time?"

"I own it, that is, my husband and I do. I can't go till Sunday."

"I don't work on weekends."

It sounded like a religious principle, with just that smug air of virtue.

"Aren't you lucky. I do, so if you want me to drive you, it will need to be Sunday afternoon."

They arranged to meet at Miss Bradwell's office.

It was another beautiful Sunday, and when Marybeth got out of church, she just wanted to change into her gardening clothes and spend the afternoon outside. She was meeting Miss Bradwell at three, so she had time to weed the side beds if she didn't linger over lunch.

Miss Bradwell was late. Marybeth sat rocking on the front porch of the Legal Aid office and watched the world go by, people visiting at the hospital, carrying flowers, most still in their Sunday clothes. Near the street lounged three young men, watching, passing a joint. The visitors carefully locked their car doors and glanced over at them before going into the hospital.

At quarter after three, a yellow Volkswagen beetle pulled up in front of the office. It was an old one but it was in beautiful condition. "Sorry I'm late," Miss Bradwell called, and swung open the passenger door. She had covered the hard seats with plastic, so though they were admirably clean, they were especially uncomfortable. Marybeth couldn't think how to politely suggest they take her car.

"Which way do I go?"

Marybeth gave directions. They were out of downtown and passing the car dealers when she spoke again.

"Have you been in Opakulla long?"

"Four years. I came here right out of law school."

"Where did you go to law school?"

"Harvard."

"Oh, my. That's a good school."

"They certainly think so."

"Turn left at the end here; we'll be on Jackson Road."

For a few miles they were silent. They passed and smelled Leon's BBQ. Maybe she'd pick up ribs for dinner on the way home.

"Here's 118. You want to go left."

"Are you from around here?" Miss Bradwell asked.

"Here and the next two counties. My family's been here for five generations. They came down from Georgia."

"I didn't realize there was anybody in Florida that far back. I thought it was all jungle till somebody invented air conditioning."

Marybeth needed no further conversation; she did not like this girl. The next turn would be onto a dirt road, but dirt roads kept cropping up every mile or so. Still, that sagging fence looked familiar.

"Turn right here."

The VW had no suspension, and on the rutted road Marybeth felt every bump.

"That's it, there on the left, where the old Buick is parked."

The place looked deserted. She had expected to see Leanne's mother out among the flowers. They knocked on the door. Vinnie opened it and stood with her hand cupped above her eyes. She was wearing sunglasses. The only light in the room behind her was a small lamp by the bed.

"Can I help you?"

"I'm Marybeth Coggins; I'm the one who found the... who took Leanne to see the lawyer. This is the lawyer, Amy Bradwell."

"Of course. I'd of recognized you if it wasn't so dark. Come on in, both of you. Glad to meet you, ma'am, my name's Vinnie Ellsworth. I'm Leanne's mother."

She offered Miss Bradwell her right hand, while her left shot up to shield her eyes.

"It's nice to meet you. Is Leanne around?"

"She's not here right now, but I'm sure she'll be back shortly. Can I get you some tea?"

She poured the tea from a big plastic pitcher with a tangle of mint leaves at the bottom. It was strong and sweet.

"Come sit down here, Miss Bradwell. This chair's good."

Marybeth was already sitting at the table. Miss Bradwell took the seat opposite her, sipped the tea, and put it back down.

"So you're the one that's helping my Leanne."

"Yes, I was hoping to talk with her today, but I guess I'll just ask you to have her call. You don't have a phone, do you?"

"No. We did have one, but Leanne's brother Bailey, he made a bunch of calls, you know how boys will do, and run up the bill so high the phone company wants a five-hundred-dollar deposit to keep service. It's been about seven months now. I been paying on the bill, and I should get it done by next summer. I think about getting a cell phone, but actually, it's kind of peaceful without it."

"Does Bailey still live here?"

"Oh yes ma'am. Well, he's just staying here with me till he can find himself a job. It's funny, I thought my kids was gone for good and now I got two of them back home."

Miss Bradwell was peering around the room.

"I'm sorry it's so dark. I got one of my headaches, and I just can't take the light in my eyes."

"Mrs. Ellsworth, if Leanne got the baby back, would they live here?"

"Well, of course they would. Leanne thinks she's grown, but she's still just a kid. She'll need help with the baby."

"The thing is, it might be a problem. Your place is nice, but it's small for four people. I'm not sure DFC will approve it."

"But a new baby hardly takes up any room, and anyway, Bailey isn't living here, just visiting like. It's really just me and Leanne and the baby. Miss Bradwell, you don't know how I'm aching to see that baby. Have you seen her?"

"No."

"You seen her though, I know, Mrs. Coggins. Is she pretty?"

"She's beautiful."

"Just like Leanne was. Leanne says she's a good baby too, hardly cries at all. I can't wait to get ahold of her."

"It's complicated, you know. It may not be as easy as you'd like."

"Well, that's just ridiculous, now isn't it? I raised three children already. Who do they think can do a better job with my own grandbaby?"

"Mrs. Ellsworth, no need to get upset. They don't know anything about you yet. They don't even know Leanne's name. We just want to think about how to give Leanne the very best chance of getting her baby back. We may need to find her another place to live."

"All on her own with that baby? That won't work. Why, here she's gone out and I don't have any idea where. Been gone since morning, and for all I know may not be back till night. We don't have but the one key, so I guess I'll have to leave the door unlocked for her when I go to work."

"You're not going to work with that headache?" Marybeth couldn't believe it. Aunt Winston had sick headaches just like that, sunglasses and all, and they used to put her out for three days.

"Mrs. Coggins, if I didn't go to work with my headaches, I'd hardly go to work at all. It's the second day, so it's not that bad. I'm just keeping the lights low, try to get it calmed down more before I got to go in. I was off yesterday so that helped. Leanne was a big help to me," she said, turning to Miss Bradwell. "I don't want you to think she's not a good girl, just Bailey gets under her skin. Maybe he'll be gone by the time they come see about us. I got a feeling it could be a couple weeks before things get going."

"It could take quite a while."

"And that baby getting bigger all the time, away from her momma. Who's taking care of her?"

"She's in foster care, with a family."

"Oh Lord, I've known some ladies took in foster kids, they treat 'em like dirt. I never thought I'd see my own grandbaby in one of those places. Could you go see her and check to be sure she's all right?"

"After I talk to Leanne, I'm hoping we can go straight to court, and get a chance for you and Leanne to visit with her."

"Oh, can you do that?"

"Yes, I think so. I'd like to move quickly. With the baby so young, we want to resolve this as soon as possible."

"You haven't drunk hardly none of your tea. Is it too sweet for you? Can I get you something else? I think I got some diet Coke I bought for Leanne."

"No, this is just fine." And Miss Bradwell picked up the glass and drank about half.

"Mrs. Ellsworth, as long as I'm here, I wonder if I could get some information from you. I need to know a lot about Leanne, and if we want the baby to live here, about you and Bailey."

"Sure. I don't have to be at work till five."

"Do you mind talking to me with Mrs. Coggins here?"

"Oh, I can wait outside."

"You don't have to go. You're Leanne's friend. I'm proud to have you here."

Miss Bradwell reached into her big purse and took out a yellow pad. Methodically, she led Vinnie through the history of her marriage, the birth of her three children, Leanne growing up and getting ornery. She found out where Vinnie worked, and how long she'd been there. Then she asked about Bailey. It turned out he'd been back home for almost a year and a half.

"You say he's looking for work?"

"That's what he tells me. You can usually get something at the labor pool, but you got to get there early, like six or something, and Bailey's not used to that."

"Do you see any sign that he's getting ready to get out on his own again?"

"Well, I know he wants to."

"You say he and Leanne don't get along very well."

"No, I'll tell you! When the two of them are home there's no peace around here. She's always been jealous of Bailey, says I love him best, never make him do anything. And you know, maybe in a way she's right. My oldest girl, Shauna, says Bailey will never amount to nothing cause I spoil him. But I'll tell you how it was, Miss Bradwell.

"When Bailey was born I got sick. Nothing physical really, it was all in my head. I could hardly make myself get out of bed. Whatever I was doing, giving Bailey his bottle, or getting Preston's lunch together, tears just rolled out of my eyes. It's the only time I ever hit one of the kids. I never did believe in that and I swear I can still feel it on the palm of my hand. I was standing at the stove warming Bailey's bottle and Shauna's tugging on my leg. She was whining like some damn mosquito, excuse my language, and I turned around and just swatted her in the face. We were both so surprised it took her a minute to start wailing. I just stood there, looking at her, and this time for once I wasn't crying. I propped the bottle on Bailey's blanket and just let him drink it in his crib. I left him in his crib as much as I could. I went straight back to bed and laid there and listened to Shauna cry.

"It only lasted a couple months, but it felt like forever, like I'd always been that way and always would be, with a new baby and a two-year-old pulling on me. Anyway, Bailey didn't get the loving you're supposed to when you're little, and he's been kind of worthless ever since. Yeah, I know he's worthless. Just because I fuss over him doesn't mean I don't see what he is. Or maybe you think because he's no good I don't love him. It's like that prodgigal son in the Bible. Sometimes it feels like I love him most cause I'm the one made him that way."

All the time she was talking she hadn't looked at either of them. She'd been picking apart a zinnia, and now a little heap of orange petals lay on the table. Marybeth stole a look at Miss Bradwell, who was busy writing on her legal pad.

"I don't mean to be rushing you, Miss Bradwell, but it's about time I got ready for work. You got any more questions?"

"Let me see." She flipped the pages over one by one. "Oh, just this here, I didn't get the name of Leanne's school."

She wrote it down, and put her pad back in her purse, took out a business card and handed it to Vinnie.

"Please have Leanne call me tomorrow. I can't decide our next steps without talking to her."

"But you'll fix up that visit for us, right?"

"I'll try for that just as soon as I can get us into court, but I can't file anything until I'm sure Leanne understands about the State's

Attorney. They're not likely to prosecute, but she has to decide if she wants to take that risk."

"Oh Miss Bradwell, she'd go through fire for that baby, I know she would. I'll tell her them to call you first thing tomorrow. I'll drive her to the store myself."

She walked them to the door and swung it open, standing back from the light.

"Mrs. Coggins, I appreciate everything you're doing for my girl. I used to see you on TV, you know, back when you was on the Commission. I never thought I'd be sitting and drinking tea with you like this."

"It was delicious."

"Here, let me get you some of that mint," and she started out onto the deck.

"You don't need to do that. No, really...."

But she was heading around the back of the house, clutching her bathrobe with one hand and shading her eyes with the other. Miss Bradwell was already behind the wheel when Marybeth got in the car carrying a big fistful of mint. As they pulled out onto the road, she waved back at Vinnie.

They drove a little while, Marybeth looking out at the fields, still brown from the summer heat.

"What will you do about the baby?" Marybeth asked.

"How do you mean?"

"Well, I mean, you don't want to try to get the baby back into that house, do you?"

"No, that will be a problem. We'll have to see about getting Leanne some place of her own."

"Do you think she can handle rearing a baby on her own?"

"Well, her mother will help her. She's raised three kids already."

"And look how they turned out. It sounds like Leanne is the best of the lot."

"We don't know about Shauna. You can't expect her to turn out doctors and lawyers. She's dirt poor."

"I'm not looking for doctors and lawyers. Pardon me, but I'm not so sure we need more of them. But worthless is worthless. Plenty of people grow up with nothing and turn out decent. I think Vinnie is one of them. But here you've got a grown man never worked a day in his life, from what I can tell, and a teenage girl acting like a dog in heat and then throwing away her baby. You've got to look at who reared them. And think about that baby – you could get her a wonderful home."

"That's not how it works. You don't just grab away babies and find the best home for them. The mother's got some rights, even if she is poor, and what you call worthless."

"It's not that I'm not sympathetic. It's just... why would you want to raise a baby like that when she could be in a good home?"

"I don't know. Maybe poor people shouldn't be allowed to have kids."

"That's not what I meant."

"Not everybody has to raise their kids the same way you did. Mrs. Ellsworth is like lots of people I've met from around here."

She'd been here four years and this was all she knew. She'd probably write a book someday about southern culture, everybody living in trailers and spitting tobacco.

They were half a block from the Legal Aid office when Miss Bradwell spoke again.

"Don't you think there's something different about Leanne? Something special?"

"How do you mean?"

"She seems so strong, so determined."

"Or you could say stubborn."

It was after six when she got home. Munro was in the living room watching golf. She leaned over him and kissed where the hair was getting thin, squeezed his shoulder.

"I'm going to sit out in the garden a while."

"Okay. This has another half hour to go. You want to get a pizza after?"

"Sure. Or go to Leon's for ribs."

"Whatever. Hey, Ruthie called. Said to give you her love."

And what will I do with it? But she didn't say it. Munro got uncomfortable when she talked about Ruthie like that. It was good that she'd called when Marybeth was out; that way Munro could have a nice long talk with her. Sometimes Marybeth felt jealous, though she was used to it by now. Ruthie always sent her love to her mother when she talked to Munro, but the love she sent was a mingy little thing, not worth the postage.

Funny how Miss Bradwell thought she was so proud of her own mothering. She'd hate to be held to account for Ruthie. Nothing wrong with Ruthie exactly, she was just a little self-righteous, but Marybeth couldn't dig up any kind of feeling for her. Thank the lord for Harlan and O.B.. She didn't have any trouble loving them. Leanne's mom knew her son was worthless and loved him best of all because she blamed herself.

It was harsh to judge Leanne's mom the way she had. She'd probably done the best anybody could, in her circumstances. Maybe you shouldn't hold parents responsible for the way their kids turned out. Raising kids was such a blind and stumbling journey. But to put another baby in that home, with worthless Bailey and trashy Leanne, and only their mother to hold things together? What was she thinking, the baby would be better off with somebody like her? No chance of that, she thought. She didn't want to raise anything anymore but flowers and vegetables. She had plenty of time before sunset to put in the tomatoes.

Leanne

Chapter Twelve

I seen Misty Dawn. Miss Bradwell took me. It had only been three weeks and she was twice as big. She just laid there staring at my face. I could tell she knew me.

The foster care lady didn't know how to hold her right. Her name is Mrs. Paul like the fish sticks. She's Black. I told Miss Bradwell I didn't want her living with Mrs. Paul and she said it's not up to me. I could tell she didn't like when I said that, but

I think people need to stick with their own kind. I don't want Misty Dawn getting mixed up about who she is. The lady from DFC stayed there the whole time I was visiting and so did Mrs. Paul, so I couldn't do my plan. I figured when nobody was around I'd just walk on out of there like she was mine. Which she is mine. But we had to stay in this ugly little room with the DFC lady.

Besides us and Mrs. Paul, a woman was sitting in the corner with two kids, trying to talk to them. They were just standing there saying "yes ma'am" and "no ma'am" and you could tell they wanted to get out of there. They had some junky toys on the floor. It was sad. Thing is, it doesn't matter too much with Misty Dawn just a baby: she doesn't care where she is as long as I'm holding her.

I listened in on Mrs. Paul and the DFC lady. Mrs. Paul said Misty Dawn was sleeping four hours at a time, but there was another baby in the room and they kept waking each other up. She's got four babies and she said it's too much. She asked when they'd move one, and the DFC lady said she was trying but all their baby homes were full.

I never knew all these babies were living away from their mothers. Every minute of every day I'm sorry I left Misty Dawn in that planter. but when I think about it I don't know what I could of done except kill

Peter, and I don't know how I'd of done that. So here I am with Misty Dawn living with Black people, not in that nice house I picked out for her, and me staying with Momma and Bailey.

Mrs. Paul showed me a picture of her house. It's a lot nicer than where we live. It's a real house in a neighborhood, and she says it's bigger than it looks in the picture because they added on when their kids were little, so it's got four bedrooms. One of their kids is still living there; she's in college, and she helps Mrs. Paul with the babies. Mrs. Paul says she loves little babies. They're not aggravation like bigger kids, and all you got to do is love them.

Mrs. Paul was a lot nicer to me than the DFC lady. In court, she was talking to my lawyer and the persecutor and she was mad. I heard her say, "We had a chance to give this child a decent home and Legal Aid is always interfering. They'll represent anybody." Miss Bradwell stayed polite with her. She said that's the main thing when we went to court: no matter what anybody said I had to stay polite and not get mad, especially when I was talking with the judge.

The judge was this old lady with glasses. I was scared when we went into court. When I first called Miss Bradwell, after her and Mrs. Coggins came out to see Momma, she was telling me about if I turn myself in they could persecute me for abandoning my baby. She didn't think they would but she couldn't know for sure till after she told them who I was, and then it was up to them. It didn't make sense to me because it wasn't my fault, and anyway I'm trying to get her back, so I figured they wouldn't do anything to me, and turned out I was right. Miss Bradwell isn't a whole lot older than me but she was acting like my Momma, the way she used to tell me all the trouble I could get into and all the bad things could happen if I do this and do that. I told Miss Bradwell to go ahead and tell. I didn't care if they did persecute me, I just wanted to go to court and get Misty Dawn back.

The persecutor was there in court, and after the judge was done, him and the DFC lady and Miss Bradwell was talking, and they won't do anything to me if I tell him where Peter is, because they might want to persecute him, because he abandoned Misty Dawn just like I did.

Miss Bradwell said I can think about it a couple days. I'm more scared of Peter, I think, than anything that court could do to me. Besides, some funny way I don't want to get him in trouble. I'll talk to Momma about it maybe. But what I think, maybe it's better not to drag Peter into all this. There's no way they can put me in jail, cause then who'd take care of Misty Dawn?

I looked all around for Misty Dawn when we walked in to court, and when Miss Bradwell said she wouldn't be there I almost started crying. Miss Bradwell and this lawyer from DFC went up to the judge's desk and were talking. I was in the front row, but I couldn't hear much of what they were saying. The judge told me to come stand in front of her and Miss Bradwell started asking me all these questions about what I done, and then about where I was living, and could I take care of Misty Dawn.

It wasn't as scary once I got started talking, because the judge acted nice. But when Miss Bradwell was finished, she said I was awful young to take care of a baby, and didn't I think we'd both be better off if I let her be adopted by some nice family. She said DFC could help me while I finished school and maybe find me a job. It made me mad cause I thought we was there to talk about Misty Dawn, not all this other stuff, but I remembered what Miss Bradwell said about being polite.

Then the lawyer from DFC started asking me a bunch of questions and he wasn't trying to be nice at all. You could tell he thought I was making stuff up about Peter, and he asked dumb questions like "How did he make you? Did he hold a gun on you?" Like he couldn't understand what I'd been telling them. It made me feel bad too, like maybe I should of tried harder to get away from him. I mean, far as I know, he didn't have a gun, and there must of been some way I could take Misty Dawn and hide out, only I sure don't know what it was. But maybe cause I didn't, it means I don't love her. No, that's one thing

I know for sure, no matter how confused they try and make me, that baby is mine and I love her and she ought to be raised by her mom.

The judge must of thought so too. When the other lawyer was finished, she sat there looking at all of us and then she said, "Well, I'll tell you, this one is a puzzle to me. Leanne, you know I don't have to let you see that baby. I think maybe everybody would be better off if we just declared her abandoned and let DFC go ahead and find her a family. But Miss Bradwell here has convinced me that maybe this wasn't your doing, any more than if that man did have a gun. So I'm going to let you try and get her back."

And then she was telling us all this stuff about what I got to do and what DFC's got to do. I don't see why they can't just give me Misty Dawn. She's my baby, and like the judge said, it wasn't my fault. But before we got to court Miss Bradwell said even if we win they don't just hand her over. All we could hope for was the judge would give me a chance. So I knew what she was saying was good, and all I could think about was when will I see Misty Dawn.

Three days after we went to court Miss Bradwell picked me up and took me down to DFC to see her. I couldn't believe it was that long, and now they tell me I can't see her again for a month. I was holding her, she was sleeping, and Mrs. Paul and the DFC lady was just talking away. Miss Bradwell came back in the room and the DFC lady said my time was up. They only gave me half an hour, and it wasn't fair, because she was mostly sleeping and they shouldn't count that time. But the DFC lady said she had work to do, she couldn't be sitting there all day, and Miss Bradwell didn't argue with her or anything even though she's, my lawyer. So I said okay, and I asked if I could come back tomorrow, and that's when they said I couldn't see her again for another month. I couldn't believe it, and I started crying, and I guess I yelled some at all of them, and the DFC lady jerked Misty Dawn away from me and gave her to Mrs. Paul and hustled them out of there. The two little kids in the corner was staring at me, and Miss Bradwell was telling me I got to calm down and I got to be patient. I wasn't yelling any more; I only lost it for a minute. When I watched Mrs. Paul walk out of the room with my baby it felt like somebody tore away my skin.

So then Miss Bradwell took me home. I didn't say much because what is there to say? I thought it would be so great to see Misty Dawn and it all went wrong. I wanted to buy her a new dress, but I got in a fight with Momma and she wouldn't take me to the store, and then we made up, but she had to work so she couldn't come on this visit, but she was excited about coming the next time. Now I got to tell her it will be a whole nother month.

I want to show her that baby so bad. I won't tell her I lost my temper, because then she'll think it's my fault we don't get to see Misty Dawn. She won't be home for another two hours. For once I got the house to myself, no Bailey laying around acting stupid. I don't know where he is, maybe he's working, hah hah. He's twenty-one and he never stays in a job more than like a month. It's always the boss was an asshole, or there's no future in roofing. He always makes like he quit but I bet most of them he got fired. Half the time he doesn't even get there on time.

Peter says you can't get anywhere that way. Not like Peter knows everything, but still, he's worked at that garage four years and the boss leaves him in charge when he's gone, and he's getting ready to have his own business someday. That's how I want to do.

Miss Bradwell says I'll have to get a job and probably move into a place of my own. I'd like to stay with Momma. We been getting along pretty good, and she could help with the baby. But Miss Bradwell says the problem is Bailey. She didn't say it like that, just said DFC won't like four people in one room. I guess three in one room is okay if one is just a baby. But four, she's probably right, especially when one of them is Bailey. You'd think Momma would kick him out by now, but no, not her precious Bailey. Maybe when I tell her about Misty Dawn, though. I bet she'd like having a baby here more than him. I'll talk to her when she comes home.

We could have such a good time with Misty Dawn. Maybe I could get a job at her restaurant, just to start, because what I want is to work in an office. But if we was working different shifts at the restaurant, we wouldn't have to get a babysitter. I could save my money to get my own place, and maybe later I could go to business school. I want to stay with Momma for a while, but not years and years like Bailey. Just at first, to help with the baby.

You think about things different when you have a kid. You got to plan for the future. Even Momma, I think about her different now I'm a mom too. It just kills me that she doesn't get to see Misty Dawn for a whole month. It was almost like a present I wanted to give her. She'll be so proud when she sees my beautiful baby.

Chapter Thirteen

Momma says I got to tell them about Peter. She says she can't afford to support all of us without welfare. She didn't say it very nice, either. I think she was feeling bad about Bailey.

Me and Momma and Miss Bradwell had a long talk about what we have to do to get Misty Dawn back. Then Miss Bradwell took me to DFC to meet the lady who'll be in charge when Misty Dawn comes home. It kills me, why I have to have some snoopy lady checking on me. Misty Dawn is my baby, it's not like I'm a foster mom or something. But Miss Bradwell says it's because I left her.

It's a good thing I had a lawyer. We had everything worked out, and then we got into this lady's office and she was talking about how I could visit Misty Dawn once a month, I gotta get a job or go to school, find a place to live and take a class in how to be a good mom, and then maybe after six months my baby might come home.

"No way, Miss Bradwell says I get to see Misty Dawn every two weeks," but Miss Bradwell touched my knee to shut me up, and then she started talking. And it turned out whatever she said the lady said okay. I get to visit every two weeks and as soon as Bailey moves out Misty Dawn can come home if the lady says our house is all right. I got to get my GED, or if I want I can go to New Beginnings at DuBois. I thought that was just where the delinquents go, but it turns out they have lots of different programs. In New Beginnings you have your baby with you and you finish high school. I'll get welfare and food stamps and Medicaid and everything.

Bailey was home when I got back, but Momma was at work. The whole house stunk of weed. I haven't smoked any since I left Peter, and I miss it sometimes. You'd think he'd share, but not Bailey. "You better not let Momma catch you with that," I said, and he goes, What, you think she'll call the cops?" I just ignored him. He turned on the

TV and I went in the kitchen and started washing his dishes. I wasn't gonna have Momma coming home to a mess.

I heated up leftover spaghetti and made a plate for Bailey too, and we sat on the bed watching TV. When a commercial came on, he said, "So, are you gonna get your baby back?" I didn't know if Momma told him about moving out, and I figured it was better if it wasn't me telling him. So I just said we'd have a couple visits with her and then they'd probably give her back to me. "I'll be Uncle Bailey, holy shit."

I'd never thought of that. Being an uncle sounds even older than being a mom, and I started giggling. Then he started, and he got stuck with the giggles because of being stoned, and we were rolling around on the bed, and I got tears in my eyes and a pain in my chest from laughing so much. I didn't think I could laugh that way anymore without being high. When we were little we used to get the giggles, all three of us, and Momma'd be saying, "Now you all settle down and stop acting silly," and then sometimes she'd start in laughing too.

When his giggles was done Bailey went outside to pee. Momma hates that. She says it's trashy, but I think it's okay when there's nobody around. And it's probably good for the trees, like Bailey always said. He used to do it just to bug her, I think, and then it got to be like a habit. I didn't say anything cause we were getting along good.

When he came back inside, he started poking in the refrigerator, but he couldn't find anything he wanted. I seen a box of brownie mix in the cabinet so I said I'd make him some. Soon as they was done we went and sat out on the deck to eat them. I like them hot like that, when they're all melty inside. It was only about five o'clock and the sun was just to the tops of the trees across the road. I loved watching sunset from the deck. The sun goes down and down behind the trees and every time you look things look a little bit different.

I told Bailey how they want me to tell the police about Peter, and he was all on Peter's side. He said I shouldn't do it, said he felt sorry for him, especially when I told him they'd make him pay child support. He asked me how come I left him, and I said I didn't feel the same after we dumped Misty Dawn. He wanted to know how come I did that, and I just kept saying Peter made me. He didn't understand, and kept bugging me, and going on about how rough it was on Peter, so finally I told him about Peter beating me up, but I made him cross his heart not to tell Momma. Soon as I told him he wasn't standing up for Peter anymore. Said he'd get that son of a bitch, he'd be sorry he ever laid a hand on me, wanted to know where he lived. He was walking around the deck with his fists balled up, cussing, saying he'd pound the shit out of that bastard. He'd eaten most of the brownies already because of the weed. I ate the last two and waited for him to cool off.

When he was done he was hungry again, so he said he was going to the store. He asked did I want to go for a ride and of course I did. I love riding on the back of his bike and he hardly ever lets me. He always, "Don't want to get the seat dirty, hah hah," like he's joking.

He put on his helmet and asked me where does Peter live, said we'd ride by there and check him out. You might think I'd be worried about that, but Bailey's chicken. He wouldn't fight Peter in a million years. I told him the address. I memorized it that time I went looking in his wallet.

It was just starting to get cool, perfect for riding. Bailey's only got the one helmet so the wind blew my hair and it felt like we were going a hundred miles an hour. Peter's address was way the other side of town, but Bailey went on the back roads so there was hardly any traffic. I had my arms around him and my cheek on his back. When we went around a corner, we'd lean like one person. Nice to be hugging a guy again, even if it was only my brother. I wouldn't mind a motorcycle gang boyfriend if he was cute, but not one of those fat hairy guys. They go on these long trips and you just get on the back and hang on. I bet it's fun. Only I couldn't do that with Misty Dawn. I never thought about that before, but I guess those motorcycle girls don't have kids.

Peter's address was in a neighborhood called Dogwood. The houses were little but pretty, and a lot of the people had flower gardens. Peter's house was light green with a dark green door. His lawn was a mess, mostly brown spots, with toys all over in the front yard. It didn't look like anybody was home, but after we passed it I asked Bailey to ride around the block and go by it again. It felt funny knowing that's where Peter lived now. If I'd been his real wife, I guess that's where we'd be. Maybe if we'd lived in a nice place like that none of this would of happened.

Just when we was coming around the corner again to the house, the side door opened and Peter's little boy came out. He was cute as his picture, with shiny black hair and big eyes, dark-looking, like an Indian. Looking at him, I all of a sudden realized Misty Dawn's got this whole other family. I'd always thought like it was just her and me. I don't know if it counts though, if Peter doesn't have anything to do with her. I guess I'll tell her about them when she's older. I mean she has to know. What if she grows up and meets her brother and they fall in love and they can't get married?

I wonder if she'll look like him. She's got this greasy black hair, but the nurse said you can't tell what kind of hair she'll have later. But she might end up looking just like Peter's little boy. Or that's what I was thinking until the door opened again and his mother came out, and I could see right away who he takes after. I'd already seen her picture in Peter's wallet, but still it took me by surprise. She was like a hundred times prettier than her picture. She looked like a model or something. She was wearing cut-offs and a t-shirt, and she didn't have on any shoes. Her hair is black and shiny like the little boy's, and her legs are long and tan and muscley and she's got big boobs. Even her mouth is better than mine.

I don't know why it bothered me so much to see how good she looked, when I already knew Peter lied to me about her being ugly. I just wanted to hide somewhere. I said I wanted to leave and Bailey revved the bike and we took off VRROOOM. She looked up when she heard the noise, then we was down the street and I didn't have to look at her anymore.

All I could think about was her and Peter and me and Peter, and what was he doing with me, or more like, what was he thinking when he looked at me? He must of been pretending all the time that I was her. Maybe that's why he closed his eyes when we was kissing. Except he didn't act like it. I mean, he liked looking at me when I was naked and I know I turned him on a lot.

It's not fair. She's got everything. She's beautiful and she's got that nice house and her little boy and Peter, and I don't have nothing. Only who'd want Peter? For a minute I forgot that. I wonder if he beats her up too. I bet not.

Riding back, I was glad I was behind Bailey. I was crying but he couldn't tell. He went to Food King and bought ice-cream bars. They come four to a box, and he only let me have one. He ate the other three without even stopping. He threw the wrappers in the trash and then he came over to the table where I was sitting and looked close in my face.

"You been crying?"

"Yeah. Just a little."

"How come?"

"I'm scared Peter's gonna come after me."

He said not to worry about Peter; he'd take care of him if he tried anything. Then he started talking about Misty Dawn, how he can't wait to see her, and how she'll love her Uncle Bailey, and how much fun it will be with her living there. It made me feel bad, so I was glad when he said he was going out with friends. Then I was sorry when he was gone because we were having fun, and here it wasn't even eight o'clock and I was stuck alone in the house with nothing to do.

I sat out on the deck for a little while but the bugs started getting to me. Then I went all through Bailey's stuff trying to find some weed, but he either hid it good or took it with him. I couldn't find even a roach. I turned on the TV and watched a movie about this woman who's a policeman, and this crazy man holds a gun on her and makes her steal a car. Lots of cop cars chase them and her partner's in love with her but he never told her. It all turns out good in the end. I was tired when it was over. Used to I'd stay up late but it was only about ten-thirty and I was ready to hit the sack. It's like Misty Dawn changed my clock and I'm tired early and I wake up early too.

I was taking a shower when I heard Momma come in. I could tell it was her cause she was whistling the way she always does, whistle or hum, one. When I came out of the shower she was sitting out on the deck with her feet up on the rail. I put on my bathrobe and went out there. She had a glass of tea and was just sitting there looking out at nothing. That time of night, you can't hardly see anything, just the trees like big shadows across the road. I asked Momma should I do her feet. Her feet hurt all the time from waitressing, so she likes for us to rub them.

We didn't say nothing for a while, and then when I put her one foot down and picked up the other one and put it on my lap, she asked me about the meeting with DFC.

She was excited about me going back to high school. Momma never finished high school. I said I wanted to learn computer.

"That's wonderful, honey. That way you won't have to be a waitress, you can work in an office. Your lucky feet."

"Yeah, Misty Dawn won't never have to rub them." Then I was sorry because she might think I was complaining.

"Will I see that child before she gets big enough to rub your feet?"

"Oh Momma yeah, we have a visit next Wednesday! And then soon as Bailey's gone, Misty Dawn can come live with us."

Momma took her foot out of my lap and put both of them back up on the railing.

"Did you talk to Bailey?"

She didn't say nothing, so I asked her again.

"Well, no. He can't move out of here with no place to go, so I thought I'd tell him soon as he gets a job."

"Momma! He's never gonna get a job just living here. You got to tell him. Or I can."

"No, you won't do it right. I'll talk to him tomorrow."

"What will you tell him?"

"Never you mind what I'll tell him."

"Well, you better give him a deadline."

"Thank you, Miss, I don't think you need to be giving me orders."

I knew I should shut up then, but something made me go on and tell her how they want to know about Peter. That's when she said how she doesn't want to be supporting us. I guess I was already planning on telling about Peter, but maybe I wanted to hear Momma say it. I sure hope he doesn't start any trouble. I just worry a lot about all this stuff. If Momma doesn't get Bailey to move out, we won't get Misty Dawn back, and she's getting bigger all the time. She's already seven weeks old.

Chapter Fourteen

Misty Dawn is coming home! Momma and me spent all Saturday getting ready. Momma didn't go to work. She said they could do without her for once, so she got Sue to take her shift. She said, "I'm gonna spend the day with my girl," and we had the best time.

Everything was different with Bailey gone. Momma likes to get up early and we'll be doing that now Misty Dawn is coming home. Babies don't let you just lay around all day. But with Bailey sleeping all morning we pretty much had to stay in the kitchen or outside. Momma was always shushing me, and I couldn't do anything in the morning with Bailey there.

I knew I'd better not ask Momma what she told him, but I didn't see how he'd get a job. Everything I've heard, you can't go looking for jobs at two in the afternoon. Like they say, early bird catches the worm. Actually, that's what Peter used to say when we had sex in the morning. Anyway, Bailey never left the house till after lunch. But then Momma came home from work last Friday and said Mrs. Coggins called and she had a job for Bailey! They needed somebody to help in the store. The best part is he doesn't have to be there till 10. Even Bailey was excited. He said it would be cool selling hardware, and he could move in with these guys who live near the high school. Whatever Momma said to him he sure has been acting different, like he wants to help me out. He left Thursday, the day after DFC brought Misty Dawn over for a visit.

Even though he's usually a big pain in the butt, Bailey was sweet when he saw Misty Dawn. He even got up early because Phyllis from DFC was coming at eleven and Momma said she wanted him dressed. Phyllis was late, but she didn't call even though we finally got a cell phone. She just drove up into the yard, and she didn't park where

Momma's car is. She parked under the big tree and mashed all the ferns.

The three of us came out on the deck to watch. She got out of the car and leaned in the back seat. Her butt was this big green thing, like those crab balls we used to play with in gym. Bailey looked over at me and said real quiet, "Man I'd like to get me some of that." I thought I'd die because I knew I couldn't laugh, and when you can't laugh that's when things are really funny. Momma said "Bailey you hush," quiet but fierce, and went over to where Phyllis was just standing up holding Misty Dawn. I was so excited with that being the first time my baby came to our house. It felt like Christmas only this time I knew what was in the package.

Phyllis handed Misty Dawn over to Momma and Momma just stood there and stared down into her face. I wanted to go over and take her so bad, but it was Momma's first time. She'd only seen that one picture from eight weeks ago when Misty Dawn was born, and she doesn't look anything like that now. I couldn't see Momma's face but I knew just how she felt to be holding that baby. And seeing them together it was like this love balloon was growing bigger and bigger inside me and I was gonna bust from it.

After a little while we all went in the house. It was Misty Dawn's first time to see where she was gonna live. I think she liked it too. Her eyes got big when Momma took her inside, and she was laughing. Not laughing out loud with a sound, I think she's too young to do that, but her mouth opened and she smiled, and you could tell she was thinking a laugh.

It's no wonder she was laughing, the way Bailey was making a fool of himself. He leaned over her, making faces and saying the dumbest stuff in this squeaky voice, "Hey Misty, it's your Uncle Bailey. Hey little girl, how come you don't got teeth," and then he'd laugh. I'm surprised he didn't scare her up close in her face like that. He practically tripped Momma, walking so close, and she said, "Bailey, stop acting the fool. You can hold her if you're careful. Go sit down over there." Which I thought she should have asked me because it's my baby, but I didn't mind, and Momma was so happy. So Bailey sat down at the table and Momma put Misty Dawn in his arms. It was so neat having her home with us instead of over at DFC in that room with those sad little kids.

Momma got Phyllis a cup of coffee and one for herself, and because it was nice outside we went and sat on the deck. Momma kept her talking, so she stayed almost an hour, so naturally Misty Dawn did too. It was the first time I'd been with her that long since we left her at Mrs. Coggins' house. Some ways it feels like just last week, and some ways it feels like forever ago, with all the different stuff that's happened since I done it, and I sure wish I never did. But I still don't know what else I could of done.

When Phyllis got up to go she said to me, "I think Misty will be really happy here with you and your Mom, Leanne. You can come get her next Wednesday. You'll need time to get some things together for her, Vinnie."

I can't help it, maybe she thought she was being nice, but it was like she thought we didn't know nothing about babies. Nobody knows what Misty Dawn needs better than me, because I'm her mother, just like Momma's my mother and she knows what I need. I said all this to Momma after Phyllis left. She said it wasn't any big deal and I shouldn't let people upset me.

Anyway, who cares. Misty Dawn's coming home and like I said, we got everything ready for her. Momma and I got up early Saturday and I made her coffee. We sat down at the table and started a list. Momma won't do anything without a list. We needed a crib and sheets and clothes and diapers and formula; it just went on and on.

I wondered how we could afford it all, but Momma said Phyllis gave her a voucher to shop at a thrift store. I'd like Misty Dawn to have new things instead of stuff some other baby used, but no way we could pay for all those things in a regular store.

As soon as we finished the list I wanted to go, but the store didn't open till ten. We did some cleaning and figuring out where to put

Misty Dawn. Bailey's bed was in the corner with a bedspread up like a curtain for privacy. I'm sleeping there now; I don't have to share with Momma anymore. I wanted to move the bedspread out to make the space bigger and put the crib in there. Momma said Misty Dawn should sleep by herself, so we should put it in the other corner. But then it's like she'd be sleeping in the same room as Momma, so I said we should put up another bedspread to make her own little room. Momma started getting cranky, said it would look like a laundry, but then she said we'd find some screens somewhere, and make it like me and Misty Dawn have our own place. So she put screens on the list.

We got to the store right when it opened. They had so much stuff. We got a crib and crib bumpers covered with yellow ducks, and a string of plastic ducks to hang over it. They didn't have any highchairs, but we got a nice stroller and one of those carrier things. I asked her about car seats and the lady said we could get one at the health department for five dollars.

We carried the stuff out to the car and put the mattress on the roof with all the crib pieces on top and the lady tied it down. I didn't like the mattress on the roof because it would get dirty but Momma said we'd brush it off and it would be okay. We put everything else in the back seat, and then the lady gave us three packages of diapers for a present, and a little book called You and Your Baby.

We got in the car and Momma said, "Well, what's next?" and I said, "Clothes." She said, "We're a good team, Leanne," and started driving. Then she was whistling her favorite song and I sang along, *Telling my sweet baby it'll be all right.*

She was driving like she does when she's feeling good, her hands moving all smooth. I said I want to learn to drive, and she said she'll teach me when I get a learner's permit.

The Goodwill store had lots of baby clothes. They were all so cute that Momma found everything else we needed while I was still trying to choose. I got her lots of red things to go pretty with her black hair. We got some little overalls, and two dresses even though they weren't on the list. One of them is yellow with orange goldfish, and the other is fancy, white with little pink bows.

Momma said we could have lunch at Harrigan's. I hadn't been to a restaurant all the time since I ran away. Sometimes me and Peter did go to the drive-through at McDonald's, but just once in all that time he could of taken me someplace nice. He didn't treat me very good, not just the hitting stuff, but I mean he didn't treat me like a girlfriend, with dates and all, maybe because we were kind of married. If that's what it's like, I never want to get married. I think you should go out together and do fun things, not just stay home and watch TV.

I ordered a turkey club sandwich, fries and a chocolate milk shake. Momma had the meat loaf plate, and it looked so good I wished I'd had that. But I figured a sandwich with turkey and lettuce and tomato is less fattening. I'm still kind of fat from when Misty Dawn was born.

We were talking about how it will be when Misty Dawn comes home. Momma works five to eleven, and I'll be home from school by three, so we don't need a babysitter. Then when I get a job, if it's an office job, most of those go eight to five, so we'll have to find someone to watch her for a little while. Momma says she could drop her off at somebody's house on the way to work and then I could pick her up on my way home. I said I'd learn computer good, and maybe then when I'm working I could start college too.

I don't want a job where you wear a uniform, like a waitress or a nurse or something. I want to wear those suits, like the lady lawyers on TV. Miss Bradwell should dress like that and look more like a lawyer. If I lost ten pounds and got my hair done right, I bet I could look pretty good. I'd have a secretary and my own apartment, and take Misty Dawn to school every day and then she could do her homework while I'm fixing dinner, and after dinner we could watch a video or something or maybe just talk like me and Momma.

I was telling Momma all this and first she was smiling but then she got this funny look. I couldn't tell if she was sad or mad. She said, "Hold on, Leanne, you got Misty in high school when you haven't even started ninth grade yourself." I said I thought I should make plans, and she said that's not plans, that's dreaming. She could see it hurt my feelings, and she apologized. She said her and my dad used to dream a lot but nothing good ever come of it, just disappointment when things didn't work out.

I asked her what kind of dreams. I think she didn't want to talk about it, but I kept bugging her, and then she said how my dad and Uncle Jim were going to start their own construction business. They put a bunch of money down on some land before Jim went into the Army, and then every month my dad paid on it with the money Jim sent and what they could save. They paid for almost two years, and then Jim got killed in Iraq, and they couldn't pay on it anymore and they lost the land.

She said my dad was tore up when his brother died. She used to hear him crying at night and she'd roll over in bed and hold him. They never talked about it in the daytime, but she said even so, the months after Jim was killed brought her and my dad closer. It's funny, we always had a picture of my Uncle Jim in our house, and he was in lots of the pictures of when Dad was little, but they never told us kids anything about him, just said he died in a war. I said me and Peter never had anything like that, and it wasn't like I wanted something awful to happen, but maybe that would of made us more of a marriage. And she said, "You and Peter," sounding snotty, and then she stopped a minute, and I could tell she was deciding not to say whatever she was gonna say.

She stayed quiet a minute, then she said, "If I ever see that man, I don't know what I'll do. I know you haven't told me the worst part."

I said things got worse when I got pregnant. I just wanted to leave it at that, but she got it out of me. She said she wished I'd gotten out of there the first time he hit me. I told her how sweet Peter was afterwards, but she said it's always that way – they beat you up and then they come back all loving. I thought she was talking about my dad, but she said he just hit her that one time, but she'd of left if he didn't, because she'd seen what happened to a friend of hers, and she'd ncver let anyone treat her that way. I said I never would again, and she was glad to hear it.

Then we were quiet for a little while except for me slurping my milk shake. Suddenly Momma said something so quiet I couldn't hear her and I said, "Huh?" And she said, "Nobody made me give away my baby." I thought she was talking about Shauna, and I didn't get it, but then she told me I have another brother! She got pregnant when she was fifteen and Grandma wanted her to have an abortion but she wouldn't. She only got to hold her baby one time before he got adopted. I've got a brother out there somewhere who's twenty-six! I asked if she ever tried to get him back and she said no, he was better off where he was, but she never stopped missing him. It was worse than having your baby die, never knowing what was happening to him. It was like my dad going off that way, she doesn't know if he's dead or alive, maybe he's even got married again and has more kids.

I was just freaking out, thinking I've got a brother somewhere and maybe Daddy had more kids. Then I asked if she thought I should give away Misty Dawn, not that I ever would. She said no, you couldn't ask a girl to do that after she knows her baby. That's why it was so awful what Peter did to me. What about what's good for Misty Dawn, I asked her, you said you feel like your baby was better off. "Oh, Misty will be just fine, you'll see, we'll take good care of her." But I felt like she thought it would be better if I'd gave her away when she was born. I know that's not true. A baby belongs with her mother, and that's me. I'm gonna show Momma that Misty Dawn is lucky to have me for a mom.

Marybeth

Chapter Fifteen

Marybeth stood on Vinnie's deck, knocking on the door. WELCOME HOME, MISTY DAWN! was written on a giant sheet of paper on the door, each big letter carefully colored in. She heard footsteps, and Leanne opened the door, Misty in her arms. The baby wore a white dress with pink rosettes and smocking and a sock with a lace cuff on one foot, and her face was growing rapidly redder. Just as Leanne said, "Hi Mrs. Coggins," the baby began wailing and flailing her fists, arching her back and struggling so that Leanne had to hold on with both arms.

"Come in Mrs. Coggins, I'll be right there," Vinnie called from the kitchen. "Leanne, come get this bottle and feed that child."

"Well I'm coming, Momma. I had to get her dressed, didn't I?"

Leanne looked as if she might begin wailing too. Her red-rimmed eyes had dark circles underneath, and her skin looked splotchy.

"Sit over there and I'll get her bottle."

Marybeth sat at the table and put down her gift. Vinnie and Leanne came out of the kitchen together, Misty already frantically sucking on the bottle.

"I guess I shouldn't of woke her up, but I wanted her ready for the party, and then she pooped so I had to give her a bath before I dressed her, and she got real hungry."

"I told you...." but Vinnie stopped and began again. "Mrs. Coggins, it surely was nice of you to come help us celebrate. I'm looking for Bailey any minute, and we're hoping Miss Bradwell, the lawyer, will be coming too. Leanne said we had to invite her even though I said she'd probably have better things to do. You probably did too."

"Why, I'm happy to be here and see that beautiful baby again."

She was drinking peacefully now, restored to a normal pink. Clear skin, big eyes, and a cap of silky black hair.

"Well Mrs. Coggins, what do you think of my granddaughter?"

"She's growing like a weed, she looks so healthy and alert. You're doing a wonderful job."

"It's not me. Leanne just loves her baby. She gets up whenever she hears a peep out of her. I tell her she'll spoil her. She does all the night feedings, no matter how tired she is. And I swear Misty knows her. When she's fussy I can't do anything with her, only Leanne will do."

"How old is she now?"

"Well, she was born August 14, let's see, that makes her, September, October...."

"She's ten weeks Momma. And she's at the top of the chart in size. She's bigger than any of the other babies at school."

Leanne was sitting in a rocker with two pink balloons tied to the back. They had strung crepe paper on the walls, and more balloons hung from the ceiling. Misty sucked energetically, fist clutching and loosening on Leanne's finger, eyes staring wide into her face.

"You've made the house so pretty for the party," Marybeth said to Vinnie.

"Leanne wanted everything nice."

"Did you see the sign on the door?" asked Leanne. "I made it."

"She's always been good with writing and drawing. She got a certificate in third grade."

"It's a beautiful sign."

"I made it at school. I started going there Monday even though Misty Dawn didn't come home till Wednesday. My class is just for girls who are pregnant or have babies. There's a nursery with a lady in charge, Miss Jackie, and we take turns helping. Tomorrow I'm taking Misty Dawn there."

"Hey, anybody home? It's Uncle Bailey!" He stepped inside. "Oh, hi Mrs. Coggins."

"Hello Bailey, it's good to see you."

"Oh yeah, I'm sorry about yesterday, I was...."

"Never mind, we'll talk about it tomorrow when you come in."

"Yes ma'am. Momma can I help you?" and he fled to the kitchen.

Leanne looked up and met Marybeth's eyes, and quickly looked down again at Misty.

"So it sounds as if you're enjoying your new school."

"Yes, ma'am."

"How many girls in your class?"

"We don't have different classes. There's thirteen girls, but we're all different grade levels. There's only one girl younger than me." Proudly, as if she had accomplished something special. "We're both in eighth grade. By my age I should be in tenth but I stopped going when I ran... when I moved in with Peter, so I have to do eighth grade over again. I don't mind because I never did get the math, but it's boring, almost as boring as real school. Not when we're learning about babies, though. That part isn't so bad."

She pulled the bottle from Misty's mouth – it came out with a pop – and lifted her up to her shoulder, patting her back.

"I'm supposed to burp her half-way through the bottle so she won't get gas," she said. She patted and patted. "Thing is, she never does burp."

"I always used to lay my babies down on their stomachs after I fed them, and the pressure made them burp," said Marybeth.

"Oh no, you're NEVER supposed to put them down on their stomachs. It could kill them. You go in to your baby in the morning and you find it dead."

"There's different rules for raising babies than when mine were coming up," Vinnie said. "Leanne says my ideas are all wrong."

"They're just old-fashioned, Momma, that's all they knew about babies back then."

"Back in the old days, huh?" She laughed. "Well, Leanne's doing great, and I'm proud of her."

Misty was starting to fuss and squirm up on Leanne's shoulder, so she brought her back down and replaced the bottle. The baby sucked vigorously, but then her eyelids began drooping, and her clenching fist loosened. She dozed, startled awake for a couple of sucks, then dozed again, and soon she was fast asleep.

"Oh well, she almost finished it. You want to watch me put her to bed?"

"Happy birthday to you," Bailey bellowed as he came through the kitchen door with a plate of cookies.

Leanne whispered fiercely, "Hush, Bailey, she's sleeping."

"Well, sooo-rry." He put the cookies down on the table. "Just trying to get a little life into the party."

"It's not her birthday anyway, stupid," said Leanne as she carried Misty away behind one of the hanging bedspreads.

"Lucky Dad built this so big, huh?" said Bailey.

"We used to have a mobile home, and my husband built this for a garage, workshop and laundry room. It was going to be nice."

Marybeth wondered what had happened to Leanne's father. She couldn't think of a way to ask, though.

"What did you do with the mobile home?"

"Oh, we don't have it anymore. Would you like some tea?" and she poured a glass without waiting for an answer.

"I bet it stays cool in the summer."

"Yes, and cold in winter. But we do alright. Bailey, save some of those cookies, son, you're not the only one here."

"Sorry Mom. Mrs. Coggins, you want a cookie?"

"No thanks."

Marybeth heard once that there's a silence in any conversation every ten minutes. This silence felt like a room full of doors she didn't dare open. Vinnie nibbled on a cookie, picked at the crumbs on her lap.

"Excuse me a minute, I have to go check on...." and she disappeared into the kitchen. Marybeth heard the water turned on and off. A plate set down, then another. Vinnie's footsteps back and forth, the water again. Some more plates. Vinnie emerged.

"Sorry, I had to take care of something."

Leanne returned to the table.

"You want to see Misty Dawn's room?"

"You just got that child down, so don't go disturbing her."

"I won't disturb her Momma. We'll just look at her stuff."

"Don't you want to open your present?"

It was a big learning center, with dials and bells and cranks that turn.

"Oh wow. They have one of these at school. She'll love it. Come on, I'll put it away and you can see her room."

Behind the bedspread was a different world. A blue rug with big yellow flowers softened the concrete slab. Yellow ducks circled slowly above the sleeping baby. The wall was covered with pictures torn from magazines. Leanne's bed was in the corner, like an afterthought.

"Miss Jackie says if I put up lots of pictures she'll grow up smart. Momma found the rug at a garage sale. She got most of the toys there too."

It was a big carton of toys.

"I know Misty Dawn's too young for them, but babies grow so fast, and Momma got this whole box for ten dollars."

"That's quite a bargain."

"Bailey, how are you doing?" Despite the curtain it was just one room, and though Vinnie spoke softly Marybeth could hear everything.

"Great, Mom."

"How do you like your new place?"

"What new place?"

"I thought you were in your apartment by now?"

"Naw, that didn't work out. I been staying at Ryan's, but his girlfriend bugs me, so I gotta find someplace else."

"How's the job?"

"Alright."

Bailey stuck his head around the bedspread and came in.

"Hey, Lee, it looks pretty cool."

"Shhh, you'll wake the baby."

"Oh man, let's see what's in that box."

"Well, take it out of here so she can sleep."

He hoisted it up and carried it over to the table, dumped all the toys out on the floor.

"Cool."

"Bailey, don't go messing everything up, please."

"It's okay Mom, Leanne'll pick it up, right Leanne?"

"I will not. You be careful with Misty Dawn's things."

Bailey sat on the floor picking over the toys. A brown baby doll with long black hair. A wooden workbench with pegs and a hammer. A device with a tangled network of tubes, and colored levers. Bailey pulled that out and set it on the table.

"Hey neat. Leanne, I'll play you."

He pulled a lever and a ball shot through the tubes into a hole. A fine toy for a six-year-old, if a little advanced for Misty. Bailey and Leanne played enthusiastically, cheering the balls on.

Vinnie and Marybeth sat at the table watching.

"It looks like you did very well at the garage sale."

"I got some blankets too, and a highchair."

Marybeth ate two cookies she didn't want, for lack of conversation.

"Let's sit out on the deck," Vinnie said.

Thank the Lord. They carried their tea out and settled on the wooden benches. Marybeth relaxed, surrounded by flowers, smelling the fresh air.

"That's a beautiful Rose of Sharon. I've never seen one that color."

"My boss gave it to me for my birthday a couple of years ago. The soil's pretty sandy there, but it's done great. With the last two winters so mild it's stayed green right through."

"I have one from my grandmother's yard."

"Oh, you like to garden?"

"Oh yes, I'm out there most evenings and every weekend. It's hard to keep up with it all, especially with the weather so strange. Though I guess I say that every year."

"Do you do it all yourself?"

"Well, when I want a new bed, or a shrub moved or something like that, I have the yard man do it."

"I wish I had a yard man. I try to get Bailey to help out, but he's so... I mean, he doesn't care about gardening."

Vinnie had caught herself before she called him lazy. What *does* he care about, Marybeth wanted to ask.

"Do you grow vegetables?"

"No, just flowers."

Every question was a dead end. But outside, in the bright October air, they didn't need conversation. For a while they sat comfortably, drifting in a garden daze.

"More tea?"

"No thanks. I'd better be going."

They took the cookies and glasses inside. Bailey and Leanne were squabbling.

"Quit, Bailey, you're gonna break it."

"Am not. Look how far he goes."

"Momma, tell Bailey to leave Misty Dawn's toys alone. He's messing them all up."

"Both of you stop now. Put the toys away and come say goodbye to Mrs. Coggins."

She could hear Misty stirring, soft noises of sucking. She was getting in the car when Leanne came out onto the deck holding the baby, half-awake.

"Wave bye-bye now. Thank the lady for the nice present." And she waved Misty's tiny fist. "Bye Mrs. Coggins. See ya."

Chapter Sixteen

Munro was at the dentist, and Marybeth was recovering from the noon rush. Bailey was there, but he took almost as much of her time as the customers. He could ring up a sale, but his mind wandered as he counted out change. It made customers cross. And once he'd insisted that Jason Hargrave had given him a one instead of a ten. They both got hot, and began to get loud, until she went over and apologized to Jason. Afterwards, in the back room, she tried to straighten Bailey out.

"Well, if you don't mind people ripping you off...."

"I've known that boy since before he was born, Bailey. He's not going to steal from me."

"How was I supposed to know that?"

"All you need to know is he's a customer. You don't fight with customers, and you NEVER raise your voice."

"So what am I supposed to do?"

"If you run into something you can't handle, just call me or Munro. We'll take care of it."

"Oh, I coulda handled it. I'm big as he is."

"That's not... look, just call one of us, okay?"

"You're the boss-lady." He moved extra slowly after that.

So he couldn't be on the register, but he wouldn't learn the stock, so he couldn't help customers either. If he was feeling energetic, he'd walk up to someone who was scanning the shelves and ask, "Can I help you?" Then he'd stand there scanning the shelves too, and eventually holler across the store, "Mr. Coggins, where do we keep the staple guns?"

Now the rush was over. The workers from the courthouse and City Hall had come and gone. They bought small items: a screwdriver, screen patches, a few ounces of nails. Raleigh came in. Good thing the rush was over. He liked to talk. While he went on about his family the bell rang and a young man came in. Brand new suit, striped tie, must be a lawyer coming from the courthouse. She looked around for Bailey but saw no sign of him.

Raleigh was looking for an egg timer.

"I wonder if they're all the same. Can you help me check? Here, when I count to three, you turn those over and I'll turn these over."

Raleigh was silent, staring at the falling sand. She saw the lawyer approaching the register and called, "I'll be right with you."

"Look at that. Isn't that something? They're all just a little bit different. I think I'll get the slowest one, give Bethany a little more time with the newspaper. Melissa will probably like it best anyway, with the purple sand."

She heard the bell again and turned to see the door close behind the lawyer.

"Oh, I'm sorry, I kept you here talking and it looks like you lost a customer."

"That's alright, Raleigh, I should have been paying attention. We have a boy working here but he disappears when I'm busy."

"Isn't that always the way? Well, I'd better be going. If I stay out long enough, they may figure out they don't need me, and then where would I be?"

"Now, Raleigh, you know the Commission couldn't get along without you."

He paid cash, they said their goodbyes, and he was gone. The lawyer had left his things on the counter: a drill and a package of CO_2 cartridges. A $52 sale and a customer who wouldn't be back. As she put the items away, she looked for Bailey in every aisle. The door to the back room was closed. She opened it and there he was, asleep in the rocking chair, candy wrappers on the floor, a soda can making a wet ring on Munro's new fishing magazine.

The door opening didn't rouse him. She called his name and he didn't stir. A hurricane wouldn't wake him. She felt sorry for Vinnie, but two weeks of Bailey was all she could stand.

"Bailey!"

That woke him up. He looked blank for a minute, and then stretched.

"Oh, uh, sorry Mrs. Coggins. I guess I must of fallen asleep. Late night you know."

"Well, while you were sleeping we lost a customer. You shouldn't be in here anyway."

"Sorry. I had to eat my lunch someplace, I guess."

"Look Bailey, this isn't working out. I think we have to let you go."

"You mean you're firing me? I screw up one time and you can't even give me a second chance."

"Bailey, I think your heart's not in it. I'm sure you can find something that will interest you more than selling hardware."

"Yeah, I guess you're right. I can't make it anyway on what you pay me. It's barely minimum wage."

It was two dollars more than minimum wage, but she didn't say anything.

"I know some guys starting a band who want me to be their manager. There's good money in that. You want me to stay a couple of weeks till you get somebody?"

"No, I don't think so. We'll get along all right, business is slow anyway. I'll give you a week's pay to tide you over."

"Well, all right, Mrs. Coggins. That's nice of you I guess, to pay me that week."

She sat down at the desk, wrote out the check, and walked to the front of the store with him.

"Say hello to Mr. Coggins for me. He's pretty cool for an old guy. Just kidding. No hard feelings."

It was a relief to have him gone. The air felt fresher. She was a little surprised that Munro couldn't sense the difference when he came in.

"How's your tooth?"

"It's okay. My jaw is kind of tired. She put in a temporary, says the crown will be ready in a week. $1200."

"Ouch."

"I know. Falling apart isn't cheap."

"Honey, I let Bailey go. I didn't wait for you because I already knew what you thought. Besides, I was mad."

"Well, sing hallelujah! It's about time. What did he do? Or not do, I guess more likely."

"He disappeared all through the rush, and even when things slowed down I couldn't find him. Turned out he was in our room taking a nap. It was just too much."

"How'd he take it?"

"Okay, I guess. Says he's going to manage a band."

"I bet."

"I gave him a week's pay, honey. I know he's been here hardly any time, but I hate to send him off with nothing. His mother works so hard, and she's had such a time with him and Leanne."

"Your heart's too big, Maybeth. But that's fine, just don't go adopting the whole sorry family."

"Don't worry, I've had my fill."

Munro went in the back. She stood watching the street for a minute, and then followed him.

"You know, I'd like to go talk to Bailey's mother. I gave him the job because of her. She ought to know what's happened."

"You go on and see that baby again. Doesn't look like there's a lot doing here. I'll work on these invoices and listen for the bell."

"You sure your tooth is okay?"

"Yeah, she's got me so numb I can't feel a thing. Said to take an aspirin after it wears off if it's troubling me."

"Okay, I'll go. But you know there's no hurry on the invoices. I think you should just take it easy this afternoon."

Chapter Seventeen

Leanne was sweeping the deck. The weather was bleak and chilly, and she wore an olive-green raincoat that came to her ankles. She turned as Marybeth pulled into the yard. When she saw who it was, she leaned the broom against the railing and ran down the steps.

"Mrs. Coggins! Hi! You come to see Misty Dawn again? She's wearing that sweater you gave her."

She looked almost pretty. Her cheeks were pink from the cold and exercise, and she was full of energy.

"I'd love to see the baby. Oh, look at the beautiful impatiens."

"Those are mine. They're from the farmers' market. They were just little when I put them in and now look at them."

"Like Misty, I guess."

"Yeah, come in and see her. Oh, wait, Momma's getting ready for work, let me check and see if she's dressed."

"It's really your mother I came to see."

"How come?"

"Oh, I just wanted to talk to her about something."

Leanne's face fell. "I'll get her."

"But of course, I'd love to see the baby."

"I dunno, she's probably sleeping. But you can look at her anyway."

Marybeth leaned on the railing. It was peaceful out here. Across the road was an empty brown field, no houses in sight, just an abandoned wooden shed by the side of what must have been a driveway. Grackles pecked in the dirt.

"You can come in."

Leanne was in the door with the baby in her arms.

"Oh Leanne, isn't she beautiful! She's so cute in those overalls."

Bright red corduroy overalls, and the new white sweater – even for a chilly day it was a lot of clothes, but that big cinder block box trapped all the cold and damp. Two electric heaters warmed the baby's corner. Vinnie was brushing her hair in front of a mirror.

"You want to hold her, Mrs. Coggins?" Leanne asked.

"I'd like that."

The baby had almost doubled in size since the morning Marybeth found her. She was a bulky bundle lying on Marybeth's arm, staring up at her for a long time before she suddenly opened her mouth in a big wet smile. Then she was waving her arms and cooing.

"This must be her lively time."

"Yeah, she still sleeps a lot, but she has this time in the afternoon."

"It's nice, because I can play with her before I go to work," Vinnie said.

"I don't want to keep you. When do you have to leave?"

"About twenty minutes or so. Leanne says you want to talk to me about something?"

"Well, yes, it's about Bailey."

"Leanne, get a cup of tea for Mrs. Coggins. It's so cold in here, we don't want her to freeze."

"You just don't want me to hear about Bailey." But she went into the kitchen cheerfully enough.

"Here, come sit in the rocker."

They went over to the baby's nook. Vinnie sat on the bed and took Misty on her lap. Marybeth picked up a strange cloth doll from the crib.

"Pull the ring on his head." The doll opened up like an accordion, and as it slowly closed, played a lullaby.

"Isn't that nice? It looks like it will play for a few minutes."

"The lady from DFC gave her that. What's the problem with Bailey?"

"Well, I've had to let him go. I'm sorry, but it just wasn't working out."

"He kept missing work, didn't he? I know he missed Saturday." Vinnie's voice was flat.

"Sometimes it's that. But even when he's there, he just can't keep his mind on what he's doing. He doesn't make any effort."

"I know. It was nice of you to give him a chance."

"I wasn't doing any favors; we need the help. But when somebody doesn't work out, they're more trouble than they're worth. We gave him a week's pay so as not to leave him flat."

"No call to do that."

"Oh, I hate to just fire somebody out of the blue."

"He'll just spend it on drugs, you know."

"I wondered about that. Do you think that's why he's so absent-minded?"

"I can't say. Look, I gotta be going. Here's your tea. Why don't you visit with Leanne a bit, play with the baby. Honey, don't get too close to the heater with that child."

"I know Momma, geez."

Vinnie put on a red snow jacket and went out the door.

"She treats me like I'm a kid sometimes," Leanne said. "Should I take your tea over to the table? You can't hold Misty Dawn because it could spill on her, but I'll put her in her carrier."

What can you say to a 15-year-old mother?

"How are you liking school?"

"It's okay."

"How big is your class?"

"I told you before. There's thirteen, only Stephanie's leaving because she got too many points."

"What are points?"

"You get points for everything you do right, like they're bribing you, and then whenever you use bad language or skip an assignment you lose points."

The door crashed open. "Mrs. Coggins, can you give me a ride? Goddamn car won't start."

"Two points," Leanne whispered.

Marybeth followed Vinnie outside.

"I can give you a jump."

"No, it's the starter. I been waiting to fix it till I could pay back my boss for the tires. Now I gotta have it towed."

Vinnie kept yawning as they drove.

"Sorry. I don't get a lot of sleep with a baby in the house."

"Leanne seems to be handling it all well."

"Oh, she is. She's still a kid in lots of ways but she understands about taking care of Misty. I thought she'd be like a kid with a puppy, all excited at first, then they get tired of walking the dog. But Leanne is on top of it with Misty. Some ways it's like before she was a teenager and got ornery. And I think she's doing okay at school. She'll come home and do homework and keep at it as long as Misty's sleeping. She never did well in school before."

"I'm afraid the schools around here don't do very much for a lot of our kids."

"Oh now, Shauna went to school here and she got a scholarship to the University of Indiana."

"What's she doing now?"

"I think she goes from job to job. I don't hear from her much."

When they got to the restaurant, Vinnie asked Marybeth to stay for a cup of tea. "On the house. You didn't get to drink your tea."

It was a comfortable place, with booths along two walls and tables in the middle of the room. She settled in a booth and picked up the menu just to see. Homemade soups, steak and chicken. The special yesterday was beef stew. The prices were low; she and Munro should come here. Vinnie brought the tea.

"Would you like some pie? John makes them here. There's banana cream and chocolate, and a piece of apple left from yesterday."

She knew she shouldn't, but she did love banana cream. She could always skip dinner. When Vinnie brought the pie, a tall man came with her. What hair he had was red.

"John, this is Marybeth Coggins. She gave me a ride here."

"Nice to meet you. That name sounds familiar."

"There are a lot of Coggins around."

"You connected to that hardware store downtown?"

"We own it, my husband and I. My grandfather started it."

"Oh, you're a native. I just came down twelve years ago, got sick of the rat race in Long Island. Things are slower here."

Vinnie broke in. "Well maybe, John, but we'd better get going. The early birds will be here any minute and we don't have the board up yet."

"Vinnie keeps me in line. Well, nice to meet you. You bring your husband here one evening, we'll treat you right."

As they walked toward the kitchen the phone up by the cash register rang. Vinnie answered it and Marybeth heard her say, "Well, you take care of yourself. Drink lots of juice." She hung up and looked at John. "Damn. Susan's sick."

"Oh man, and I gave Nancy the night off."

"I'll just reassign tables. If you take Susan's, Carol and I can cover Nancy's between us."

Leanne

Chapter Eighteen

I don't know how long me and Momma can go on living together. She doesn't get that I'm not her little girl anymore, and she can't tell me how to live. If it wasn't for Misty Dawn, I'd just walk away down the road. Momma wouldn't care.

If she hadn't come home early, or if we aired out the house, it would of been okay, but I didn't want to open the windows because it was cold and Misty Dawn was snuffly. When you light up a joint it smells so sweet and fine, but in a little while you don't notice it. I didn't know the house was stinking.

We'd finished smoking and we was laying on the bed listening to music on Erica's CD player. We were playing *Dream Your Love* over and over. I could listen to Meredith Harmony forever. I never heard the car, but suddenly there was Momma standing in the door. I figured she must be sick or something, and I was going to tuck her into bed and take care of her. But she started yelling at me, didn't care if she woke up Misty Dawn, or that my best friend was listening.

"What's going on here? Smoking dope! You want to make your baby a pothead? What's the matter with you?"

I couldn't believe she was yelling, because I could tell from her eyes she had one of her headaches. Erica got up and said, "Gotta be going, it's late," and she was out the door.

Momma went over to Misty Dawn, who was sleeping and perfectly fine. Like I could of told her if she asked me. Then she flopped down in the rocking chair and covered her eyes.

I asked her, "Did you throw up?" She usually keeps working with her headaches unless she throws up. Just my luck she had to throw up that day.

"I can't talk now." She went over to the bed. "Get this shit off of here." Erica had left her CDs and the player. She started to shove it all on the floor, but I grabbed it and put it on the table. Momma fell asleep right away, so I dragged the rocking chair over by Misty Dawn's crib and watched her sleeping.

See, Momma doesn't understand. Babies are kind of boring. During the week it's fine cause I'm at school I see all my friends. By the time we get home I'm glad just to be with Misty Dawn, and I give her a bath and do homework, and there's good stuff on TV to watch and the day gets filled up. But weekends are a drag.

Sometimes Momma and I go to yard sales or something. But this morning as soon as she had coffee she put on her garden jeans. I knew by the way she was plonked down in the dirt she'd be at it till time for work. Misty Dawn was cranky when she woke up. I gave her Tylenol cause she was hot, and then she fell asleep about 9 and I had nothing to do. We lost our cable because Momma didn't pay the bill, and you can't get anything but two channels. One of them is fuzzy and the other's all gardening shows.

So there was Momma gardening outside and this old guy gardening inside, and Misty Dawn sick and the day stretching ahead of me all empty. I didn't have any thoughts, just feeling gray. I sat at the table for a while, watching the minute hand on the clock. Funny how long a minute is. But you can only do that so long. Like 23 minutes, it turned out.

I went outside but Momma didn't want to talk, and I sure didn't want to garden. It's ok on a sunny day but the weather was nasty. So I went back inside and looked at Misty Dawn for a long time. I was hoping she'd wake up and give me something to do. But she was sleeping hard, snoring a little which was funny because Momma snores too and it's like you could tell Misty Dawn is her grandbaby.

Momma came in for more coffee and said, "Don't go waking her up now." I was just looking at her. Anyway, she's my baby. Usually after a couple hours in the garden Momma's in a good mood, but this morning she got mad every time she looked at me. I was stuck here with a cranky mother and a cranky baby. And before she went back outside she said, "Find something to do, for god sake. Why don't you call up one of your friends and see if they want to do something?"

That sounded okay. I have a phone list for my class. But Tabitha's Mom said she wasn't there. Shameka was spending the whole afternoon at church getting ready for the next day, for some harvest festival or something. I called Brittany and this lady answered the phone and said, "She ain't come home last night. I'm fixing to call DFC and put her on runaway, tell them to take this baby." I said "uh, thanks" and hung up fast. I remembered that Melissa said Brittany was in foster care but didn't want anybody knowing. She sure never told me. I couldn't believe she left her baby with that mean lady.

So I looked at the rest of the list but there was nobody I wanted to call, and then I thought of Erica. She was real surprised when I called; it was over a year since we talked. She said she was meeting some friends at the mall to hang out and I could come. I told her I couldn't go out because of Misty Dawn, and then I realized she didn't even know about the baby.

"Oh man," she said. "You been doing some serious shit." I guess she was right. She said she'd come over after the mall.

When Momma came in from gardening, she was all hot and sweaty even though I swear it was like fifty degrees outside. She was in a better mood, but she sure was dirty. She said she'd take a shower and then make us lunch. I didn't know how soon Erika was coming and I wanted to take a shower too and then do my make-up, so I told her to hurry. But she got so cheered up doing her garden she didn't mind. While she was in the shower I picked out my clothes. I chose this peach sweater with Minnie Mouse in glittery stuff on the front. My boobs are bigger since I had Misty Dawn, so I look good in it. I have peach lipstick that goes with it, not just peach color but peach flavor.

Momma finally got out of the shower. She didn't leave a lot of hot water so I had to be fast. But when I came out she had grilled cheese sandwiches and tomato soup ready on the table, and she knows those are my favorites. I got dressed fast, even if she didn't think so. Anyway, my soup was still warm. We had popsicles for dessert, but I figured I'd wait and have one with Erica. So we were sitting there and Momma said she'd do my nails while we was waiting. Minnie had on a light green skirt so we used green frost. My nails are all bitten but with the nail polish on they looked cool. Momma says when I stop biting them she'll get me fake nails, but I feel like now is when I need them.

Anyway, Erica finally got here. I was feeding Misty Dawn when she came and she was like oh wow. Misty Dawn is drinking a lot now. We moved her up to the six ounce bottles last week. It used to take half an hour to feed her, but now she drinks a whole bottle in fifteen minutes. Some people just prop the bottle up next to the baby but I like holding her, and Miss Jackie says that's good for them. She's the one told me to start giving her some cereal at night so she'd sleep longer, and it worked. Some nights she goes to sleep like 11 and doesn't wake up till 5 or 6!

So anyway, Erica was watching me feed Misty Dawn and going 'oh wow' and 'oh man.' I had her in this bright pink sleeper, and even though she was snuffly she was awful cute, even if it is my baby I'm saying it about. So when I was done feeding her she wanted to play. Erica was all goo goo ga ga at her, and Misty Dawn just laughing and waving her arms around and having a wonderful time. So I guess she's not really sick.

Momma said she had stuff to do before work so she was gonna leave us alone. She changed into her work clothes right in front of Erica. She's kind of fat and has all these veins on her legs, and ugly knees. But she wasn't embarrassed, and Erica didn't mind. I guess I was the only one.

By the time Momma left Misty Dawn was getting sleepy, sucking on her thumb, and her eyes half closed. I told Erica she was real smart to find both her thumbs, but she wasn't that impressed. I don't think she knows much about babies, even though her brother was born when she was about twelve. I remember she hated it when her mom got pregnant, and she didn't want to have anything to do with the baby. She liked Misty Dawn though. We put her down and she was sucking on her thumb and staring at the mirror, and I could tell she'd be asleep in about two minutes.

Then Erica wanted to know about everything. Why I left Peter and what was it like having a baby, did it hurt. I didn't tell her about Peter beating me up. And when I told her about leaving Misty Dawn she said, "Man I could never do that with my own baby,'" and I said she didn't know nothing about it. We almost got into a fight, but then she said "Hey, I brought a present for the baby." And she pulled out this enormous joint. Misty Dawn was sound asleep, so I thought it was OK. Just seeing the joint I got excited, like I couldn't wait to suck in that smoke. I wonder if I'm an addict. I didn't have any weed at all since I left Peter, so I was glad to finally get some.

Erica wanted to know if we should sit on the deck, but sometimes a car will drive by and I figured it would be just our luck. Then she asked if I wanted to open the windows, but like I said, Misty Dawn was starting a cold. She won't keep her blanket on for nothing. So we laid on the bed and smoked about half the joint. I forgot how good it feels. The time went by the way it does when you're high. I felt like I just loved Erica and everybody. I had to go over and stare at Misty Dawn sleeping, and it made me want to cry I was so happy. But stoned and all, I knew I didn't want to wake her up, so I went and laid down again. We played a couple CD's, and we was just listening to Melissa Waters when Momma walked in and the shit hit the fan.

Chapter Nineteen

Bailey's back. Momma's pissed off at me again. And we have to share a bed, me and Momma I mean, not me and Bailey. We moved my bed over by the kitchen and he sleeps there. It's all he does because he's got pneumonia. Momma was tiptoeing and shushing me until she saw Bailey could sleep through anything, even Misty Dawn crying, then she lightened up. Doesn't worry about my sleep, even though I was up and down with Misty Dawn for almost a week.

It was awful. Her snuffle turned into more than a cold. For a few days she had a high fever every afternoon. I couldn't take her to school so Momma kept her, but after a couple of days I was so tired I stayed home. She'd wake up in the morning acting almost normal, like she hadn't been crying all night every hour like a cuckoo clock. I could tell by touching her the fever was gone, and first time it happened I thought she was through being sick. She acted hungry so I tried feeding her, but she couldn't breathe because her nose was stopped up, and she'd scream. The nurse gave us this thing to suck the stuff out of her nose, and that worked okay for a few minutes and then her nose filled up again. It took forever to get through a bottle, and then she'd throw up most of it. We started giving her apple juice, and that worked better. First two days I went off to school, and when I got home she'd be sleeping, feeling pretty warm, but nothing like later in the day, when she was just burning up. The nurse had said if her temperature got over 105 bring her to the hospital right away, cause it could affect her brain, so at first I wanted to take her temperature all the time. That's gross too, sticking it up her butt. Sometimes when you pull it out it's covered with poop. But pretty soon I could tell just by touching her how hot she was. The first night she went from 103 to 105 in less than an hour and I freaked out thinking about what the nurse said, so Momma said she'd stay home from work till Misty Dawn started getting better.

When the fever was so high she mostly slept, but I couldn't. The third night was the worst. Right out of nowhere she woke up screaming and wouldn't stop. You could tell something was hurting but no way to know what. We took her to the emergency room. She screamed all the way in the car. I kept her on my lap because I couldn't stand it, hearing her crying and letting her lay.

It wasn't nothing but an ear infection. They put drops in her ear for the pain, and just like that she stopped crying and fell asleep. They sent us home with other medicine. Momma said it was good thing we got Medicaid.

It was an awful week. Actually it was only five days. I'd been thinking it's hard having a baby; you gotta do for them all the time. But that's nothing like having a sick baby. With Misty Dawn back to normal, it was easy. But man I was tired, and that's how I got Momma so mad at me.

It was the first night Misty Dawn was better. I left her home with Momma again that day just to be sure, and when I came home from school she was laughing and making little happy noises. She took her bottle like she'd never been fed. Momma went off to work and I got her down about 7 and started doing math, but I did five problems and I couldn't keep my eyes open. So I figured the heck with it. I put away my stuff and went to bed. It was so nice hearing Misty Dawn breathing easy. I listened to that tiny little sound maybe ten seconds and I was out, I mean gone. She woke up about 10:30 to be fed, and I know I fed her because the bottle was by the crib the next morning, but I guess I did it in my sleep.

When the phone rang I tripped over the rocker going to answer it. It was Bailey. He was at the emergency room and he needed Momma to come get him. He sounded awful. I could hardly hear his voice but I could hear him breathing, like something scraping on wood. I said she was at work and to call her there and I fell back asleep right there on Momma's bed.

But it turned out Momma had already left work. She got home just a few minutes after Bailey called, and she says she woke me up and I said hi. She asked me how the baby was and I said fine, and went back to my own bed and never said nothing about Bailey. I don't remember any of it. I mean, I remember Bailey calling but I don't remember Momma coming in. But in the morning I was getting Misty Dawn's bottle, all my dreams still half in my head, and suddenly I remembered Bailey called and I looked and saw Momma was home but no sign of Bailey. I didn't know what to do. I figured if he called her at work, she must have told him to take care of it himself, but that didn't seem right. I hated to wake her up because she didn't sleep any more than me the last week but I did it anyway. I said Bailey was real sick and was looking for her, and did he get her at work, and she said no and why didn't I tell her when she got home, and I said I didn't even know when she got home, and she yelled at me and called me a liar, but honest I don't even remember it.

So she got dressed and said she'd go get him and I was wondering how she'd find him because we didn't know where he was living. One of the girls at school said he'd been staying at her uncle's but they kicked him out, and she heard he was staying on the street. But I never told Momma that. It turned out he was still at the emergency room. Momma found him in the waiting room laying on two chairs. The nurse said he had pneumonia and needed taking care of, said he didn't give them any address and he was probably homeless. Momma told that nurse he was her son and he wasn't homeless as long as she had a home herself. And so she brought him home, with a paper bag with his clothes in them, and now here we are, all four of us. Bailey just sleeps most of the time, and at night I get up and give him his medicine. The doctor says it will be a few weeks before he's back to normal. Like Bailey ever was normal.

Chapter Twenty

DFC says I gotta name the father or I can't get TANF welfare. It makes me mad. After my lawyer gave them that paper with all my private stuff, I had to go in and talk to them about it. It was me and Tonya, who's my TANF worker, and this man who's her boss. Miss Bradwell took me there and Momma stayed home with Misty Dawn.

We were in the boss's office. He wrote down all our names, and then Tonya started in to asking about this time when Peter hit me and that time when he kicked me. She sounded like she didn't believe me.

After a couple questions Miss Bradwell was getting antsy, and finally she tells them they have the hospital records from when I had stitches and they don't have to be asking me all that. And the man goes yeah, the question is if Peter's gonna come after me now.

They talked about that awhile, and I told them how he said he'd find me and kill me, and he found me when I was at Judy's. Tonya said, "That was right next door. Did you ever tell him where your momma lives?" and I had to say no. I couldn't figure out how he'd find me either, but I just feel like he can. So the man said he'd think about it and would be in touch with Miss Bradwell by the end of the week.

So Friday afternoon Miss Bradwell called me and said I gotta give them the name or we can have a hearing to have somebody else decide. I'd have to go in and talk about it again and they'd record everything I say. Miss Bradwell wants a hearing. She says the way Peter did me already, and the threats he made, and they got hospital records, that's enough. Even Phyllis thinks I shouldn't tell, but it's not up to her, she's protective supervision, not TANF. Miss Bradwell says it wouldn't get this far except that's how they do it at DFC, they always say no first and then if you push they make a real decision. She says if you lose at the hearing you can go to court, and almost always DFC loses and the person wins. She said to talk to Momma about it.

I hung up the phone and Momma was just standing there. She goes, "What did she want?" I said they want me to tell them about Peter but Miss Bradwell thinks we can change their minds if we have a hearing. But Momma thought Peter ought to support his baby. I guess it makes her mad that he gets away with everything. I think she'd like to see him persecuted for leaving Misty Dawn. She said, "Give him up honey, he's not coming back," like I want him back. It made me mad. I told her Miss Bradwell says it's my decision, and I want a hearing. She asked how it's my decision when I'm still a kid and living under her roof. Said Miss Bradwell should be talking to her. I said she's my lawyer not hers, and she said, "Maybe she's your lawyer but I'm your mother."

Misty Dawn started waking up so I went to fix the bottle. Momma had to go to work and we didn't have to talk anymore. We was both mad and I was glad when she left. I was feeding Misty Dawn, her looking up at me, holding my finger. It's hard to stay mad when you're feeding a baby. Momma's got to understand she can't tell me what to do anymore. I'm a grown-up now with my own kid. I get to decide if they should go after Peter.

If they do, even if he doesn't come over and beat me up, he can visit Misty Dawn and when she's older take her to his house. If a father has to pay child support, he gets to see the baby and be just like a regular father. If that happened, she'd have a stepmother too. And a brother. What if they want to keep Misty Dawn? I bet the judge would let them cause they're married and they live in a nice house. But Peter wouldn't want to do anything like that. He'd move the whole family to Georgia just to get out of child support. Still, it's not right that he can get to be her father when he made me give her away.

I was thinking I wanted a hearing. But then I'd have to go tell all about it again. It's awful telling all these different people about the ugly things he done to me. They look at you like they're bored out of their skull, and they ask questions like they don't believe you, or like they think you're stupid or it's your fault. So when I called Miss Bradwell I still hadn't made up my mind but when she came to the phone I said never mind, let's just tell them his name. And when Momma come home that night she was tired and she didn't ask me about it. I knew it would make her feel better so I told her. She didn't get all told you so on me, just said "Well I think that's a good decision, honey." I hope she's right. I haven't seen any Peter yet, anyway.

Vinnie

Chapter Twenty-One

It was almost Thanksgiving by the time Bailey got back on his feet, but Vinnie didn't have the heart to kick him out. He'd used up all his friends, he didn't have any money, she couldn't afford an apartment for him, and he wasn't really looking for a job.

So there she was, with all of it back on her again, and a baby to boot. Not that Leanne wasn't doing a wonderful job with the baby. She had to give her that. Still, she was a teenager, and she had a mouth on her. Vinnie had been through it before but it didn't last so long; by the time she was fifteen Shauna was good company.

She remembered the things she'd said to her own mother, but her mother used to come right back with a swat in the mouth. That wasn't right, but Vinnie came home tired to Leanne and Bailey fussing, Bailey wanting to watch TV and Leanne trying to sleep. She'd send Bailey to bed, and crawl in herself next to Leanne. And Leanne was a kicker.

Driving home from work she'd pass the on-ramp to the Interstate and think about taking off for California, just disappear, dump the car, change her name, start over. She'd find a place to live near the Huntington Gardens she saw one time on TV, maybe she could get a job there. They had cactuses – she'd never had anything to do with cactuses.

Someday she would travel all over the world looking at gardens. Maybe if she married a rich guy or won the lottery. One was just as likely as the other. She didn't play in either game. She didn't have time to be dating when the kids were little. And the only men she met were married guys who came to the restaurant: insurance men, lawyers, professors from the college.

She was working days. They'd come for lunch and want her for dessert. One of them actually said that to her, pleased with his cleverness. She didn't have any time for them, though she always smiled and stayed friendly, for the tips and for the pride of it. Her job was to make them welcome, make them think she was glad they were there and help them enjoy their meal. Usually she did feel that way. She liked seeing to it that they had a good time, always tried to get them to have some pie. But she wasn't interested in being anybody's dessert. Let these overgrown kids fend for themselves.

She'd been a mother twenty-three years, and now it looked like a bunch more years ahead. She'd be almost sixty by the time that baby was grown.

Vinnie never made Thanksgiving dinner. It was such a big, complicated meal to cook. Before Preston left, they used to go over to Jacksonville for Thanksgiving, to eat with his mother and sisters. Only good thing when he left was she never had to see her mother-in-law again. Suzanne hated her from the day she laid eyes on her, back when she and Preston were in high school. She complained about everything the kids did, and everything they did was Vinnie's fault. Preston didn't stick up for her. He tried a couple of times, but his mother just mowed him down. After he left, Vinnie tried to figure out a way to get the kids over to their Grandma's without being involved. Shauna was twelve then. Vinnie had her call up Preston's sister and ask could they come over and visit. Harriet, bless her, came over and picked up the kids and took them off for a weekend with Grandma and all the aunts. It happened a few times a year for a couple of years. But then Shauna said she didn't want to go, and Bailey and Leanne neither. She said their grandmother spent most of the time talking ugly about Vinnie. So she figured the hell with it.

Harriet called a few times, and Suzanne even called once. Vinnie put Shauna on the line right away and let her deal with it, and after a while there weren't any more calls.

After Preston left, she started taking the kids down to her own parents in Ocala if she had Thanksgiving off. They couldn't do it before, because Preston's mother would fuss. But now both Vinnie's parents were dead, and she wasn't close with the rest of the family. So she always worked Thanksgiving. She'd bring the kids to the restaurant and serve them a big dinner.

She wasn't sure how she'd work it this year though. Misty wasn't old enough to be in a restaurant. When a customer brought in a screaming baby they had to put up with it, but nobody would appreciate her bringing in her own grandbaby. Next year it could be fun, when Misty was old enough to sit up at the table for a little while and mind her manners. But it looked like this year she'd need to do Thanksgiving at home.

Saturday morning she went to Food King early. She looked over the frozen turkeys, but even the small ones were so big. She decided on a turkey roast instead. It would be a lot less trouble and would last two or three days. John would give her a pie.

She was digging through the turkey roasts looking for one with light and dark meat when someone spoke her name. It was Marybeth Coggins, holding a box of hamburger patties. She wanted to know all about the baby, and then Vinnie had to explain how come Bailey was living at home again. When a man walked by and said, "Hey Commissioner, how you doing?", they were standing there chatting like old friends.

"I'm making Thanksgiving at home this year. Usually I take the kids to the restaurant and give them a feast, but I don't think Misty is ready for that."

"Listen, why don't you join us? All the kids are coming, and my grandbaby, he's almost a year and a half, smart as a whip. I don't do it myself because I've never liked cooking. I just order everything here and they deliver on Thursday anytime up till two. If you brought your gang over about 1:30 that would be perfect."

"Oh no. You don't want us butting in on your family."

"I certainly do! It's not butting in, we'd love to have you. Our family – Munro's and mine – we're third cousins you know, though how would you know that, you've never even met him – we always had big Thanksgivings, children at card tables, and a whole separate table for the pies. It feels measly to me, just the five of us – seven now with Ruthie's husband and Scotty, and our Aunt Alice makes eight."

"If you're sure now.... Of course I can't tell about Bailey – sometimes he says he'll show up and then... well, you know about that. We'd love to come, it would be a treat for all of us. But let me bring the pies. I know John will give me some from the restaurant."

"That would be great. Maybe a banana cream?"

It was hard to tell how Leanne would react to anything, but as soon as she heard about Thanksgiving at the Coggins' she started planning their outfits. Bailey promised to be there too. It was a long time since they'd gone anywhere as a family. A long time since she'd been invited into anyone's home, and never someone like a commissioner. They must be rich. What would their house be like? But Mrs. Coggins – she'd have to get used to calling her Marybeth – she was just like regular people, like Vinnie's own family.

It wasn't hard arranging with John about the time off. They weren't very busy on Thanksgiving.

She woke up early Thursday morning. She was making coffee when she heard Misty stirring and a groan from Leanne. She warmed a bottle and went to the crib. Misty was staring in the mirror and murmuring. She smiled when she saw Vinnie. What a nice way to wake up, she thought, and scooped her out of the crib.

"I'll take her, you get some more sleep," she whispered.

"Thanks Momma," and Leanne rolled over. Vinnie changed Misty quickly and dressed her in a clean romper, wrapped her in a blanket.

With one arm full of baby it took two trips to get the coffee, the bottle and the rocker out to the deck. Finally they were set, Misty lying on her lap, sucking furiously on the bottle. Once in a while she leaned over away from Misty, lifted the cup off the floor and took a gulp of the rapidly cooling coffee.

A clear black sky with a slender crescent moon and one last star. Cold, too. When the kids were little, she had loved this peaceful predawn solitude, but working the dinner shift she'd taken to sleeping till 9 or so. Until Leanne came back with Misty, that is. After an hour of listening to tiptoeing and running water, and Misty crying when the bottle wasn't ready fast enough, and finally the door closing behind them, Vinnie was through sleeping. Then she'd get up and sit out on the deck with her coffee, which Leanne left ready for her. In late November it was light at 7:30, and she could watch the mist rolling across the field, ghost-cows drifting through the trees to the water trough.

But the full dark was what she loved best. It was beautiful out here, the sandy road turned white by the bit of moon, and Misty's face somehow with its own light. She had finished her bottle and was ready to play. Vinnie poked at her nose to see her laugh and let her stand in her lap, clinging to her thumbs. But she couldn't keep her wrapped up. It was chilly and the coffee was all gone, so she carried her inside.

Leanne was still sleeping. Vinnie put Misty down in the crib with her activity bag –– it hung on the side, with wheels to spin and plastic chains to jiggle. She hoped maybe she could sleep a little more, and carefully got back into the bed next to Leanne. But Misty was so noisy! She talked to herself in the mirror. She rolled around, batting at things. Leanne was awake too.

"I already fed her."

"I know. Thanks."

"You want to get in the bathroom first?"

"No, you go ahead."

They had the morning to dress, and Leanne took most of it. Vinnie finally woke Bailey at eleven, and to her surprise he got up quickly, showered, shaved and dressed without fussing. By one, they were all ready to go. Bailey carried Misty's things to the car, Leanne strapped her in the car seat, and they set off for the Commissioner's house.

Marybeth

Chapter Twenty-Two

Marybeth woke Thursday feeling the weight of the day. Thanksgiving dinner was always casual, because people didn't want to be fussing in the kitchen; they wanted to visit or watch the game. But she did like to have the house nice.

She spent the morning tidying, dusting, vacuuming. She cut fresh flowers for the table. She had just brought out the step stool and Windex for the smudges on the glass doors when Munro came into the living room.

"Hey Maybeth. It's our day off. Why don't you forget about the windows and come on back to bed for a little while."

He reached around her from behind with his cold hands up inside her t-shirt. She decided you could see the garden okay. Now, if the kids just didn't arrive early.

Munro was in fine form that morning, and she fell asleep afterwards. When she woke up, she looked at the clock and bolted out of bed.

"Oh my gosh, it's almost noon. How did we sleep so long? Honey, get up."

Munro was yawning and stretching as if he had nothing to do all day but lie in bed. No time for a shower, and Munro had left a mark on her neck.

"Now what do I do about this?"

"My brand," he said cheerfully.

"You talk like I'm a cow. Get up, people will be here any minute."

She threw on her best jeans and a clean shirt. No time for the windows, so she put away the stepstool. At least the kitchen looked good. Ruthie hadn't seen it yet, but she couldn't find fault with it. And she looked again with pleasure at the copper pots on the wall.

133

All this fuss and worry about how the house looked. Poor Ruthie could get her in a snit before she even showed her face. This morning's dream emerged from the clutter in her thoughts. Nursing her baby, and suddenly seeing the grime on his neck and arms, his rotting teeth. What could that possibly have to do with Ruthie? The sight of those teeth was so vivid, brown and crumbling like old bone, the baby sucking away at her breast.

Ruthie was still nursing Scotty, and she had an electric breast pump. Marybeth had walked in on her once when she was pumping. She sat on the edge of the bed, her nipple sucked into the clear plastic cylinder with each stroke, and a spray of blue-white milk shooting out. Perhaps it made sense to stock up, but it gave Marybeth the willies. These young women set such impossibly high standards for themselves. She wouldn't want to be raising a baby now for anything. Marybeth had offered to pay for someone to help out occasionally, but Ruthie didn't want any part of it. "Why have children if you're not going to raise them yourself?" she had said. "But it's awfully sweet of you, Daddy."

When the doorbell rang, Marybeth was just taking down the serving dishes. The table was all set with the harvest centerpiece and big cardboard dinner plates.

When she was growing up, Thanksgiving was a huge family feast, a different house each year. The kids at their own table, spilling and bickering, the grown-ups happy to ignore them. No paper plates, no football on TV. After dinner, an endless Monopoly game and a long walk.

Now the family had shrunk to nothing. O.B. had gone to pick up Aunt Alice but the cousins had Thanksgiving with their in-laws. She was lucky that all her children came home. She'd invited Vinnie and her brood to fill things out a little, and because she was all hopped up at the thought of having everyone home. Almost as soon as she left Food King she had her doubts. She didn't know the Ellsworths and what she did know, she wasn't too sure about. How would they fit in? What would Ruthie say? Her family didn't fit together so well but that was family, and they were used to each other.

When the Ellsworths arrived, Munro answered the door and introduced himself.

"Is that your baby? My goodness! Last time I saw her…" He broke off abruptly.

Marybeth came out from the kitchen.

"Hasn't she grown? Leanne, she looks adorable in that yellow dress."

They all looked nice, Vinnie in a silver blouse and black skirt, Bailey with his hair slicked back into a ponytail and his pants ironed. Leanne struck her as a little, well, naked for a girl her size. The hem of her green skirt was closer to her bottom than to her knees, and the orange knit top with spaghetti straps clung to her nipples and showed every roll of flesh. Marybeth couldn't help thinking of a pumpkin. She'd made an effort though, with pearly orange nail polish and wonderful platform shoes, yellow straw with flowers on the front. It all made Marybeth want to go and change. They never dressed up for Thanksgiving, so here she was in jeans, and of course Munro wore his Opakulla University sweatshirt for the game.

Leanne spread Misty's blanket on the floor and set her down with some toys. Misty soon toppled over, but she was happy sucking on her fist and watching all the goings on. Bailey stood at the glass door looking out at the yard.

"I'd love to get a look at your garden," Vinnie said.

"Well, it's not much this time of year."

"You say that all year, honey. Take her out and show her around. I'll look after Leanne and Bailey."

"All right. See if they want anything to drink. There's chips and dips ready in the kitchen."

As she slid the door closed, she looked back and saw Leanne and Bailey side by side on the couch. Leanne sat up straight while Bailey wallowed in the cushions.

When they came back inside, Munro had Misty on his knees, bouncing her gently and talking nonsense. The baby laughed and gurgled. Leanne stood next to them, and wiped the drool off Misty's chin before it could reach her dress.

"Miss Jackie says when they drool all the time it means they're teething. She's early getting her first tooth, but Miss Jackie says I shouldn't worry about it."

"It doesn't look to me like you'd have anything to worry about with a fine fat baby like this." And Munro gave a little squeeze to Misty's leg, which was indeed like a nice firm sausage.

"Brittany says Misty Dawn is too fat, but the nurse says she's just perfect and I'm doing a good job with her. She says once she starts walking she'll lose all that fat."

"Every one of our babies but Ruthie was like this, round and firm and fully packed, isn't that right Maybeth?"

"Yes. Ruthie was like a scrawny little bird from the first day, but the other two were pudges. And they both walked it off."

Bailey had moved over by the TV with the chips to watch the pre-game show. Marybeth filled up the bowl again. The boy from Food King arrived with the dinner, and as she was helping him carry everything into the kitchen, Harlan drove up, followed by O.B. with Aunt Alice. Then Ruthie and Steve arrived.

Steve had a playpen hooked over one shoulder, and a basket of toys in the other hand. At Ruthie's direction, Harlan grabbed the diaper bag. Ruthie came behind them with Scotty, blinking from his nap in the car. When he saw Marybeth at the door, he hid his face in Ruthie's shoulder. Marybeth patted his hand and Ruthie's arm. Munro hugged them both at once.

"Careful Daddy, you'll frighten him."

"That boy's not scared of his grandpa, are you, Scotty?"

He wasn't. He was peeking out at Munro and smiling.

It took a little while for them to maneuver into the living room. Ruthie had Steve set up the playpen by the sliders so Scotty could look outside. She put his talking pig in the playpen, and the basket of toys beside it. She told Munro to take the diapers and diaper bag into the back bedroom.

Leanne was sitting on the couch when they came in, her legs crossed, panties almost showing. Ruthie gave her a cold smile, but she praised Misty lavishly and asked to hold her. Steve was talking to Munro about the team's prospects and ignored Bailey, but Harlan went right over to him and started chatting about the same thing. Marybeth handed Scotty over to Steve and asked Vinnie to help her set out dinner. By the time they got everything on the table, Vinnie was calling Marybeth by her first name.

"My mother had a turkey platter just like this one," Vinnie said.

"This was my mother's. I remember I used to count the children on it and try to match them up with my cousins. Where does your family live?"

"I don't have much family anymore. My parents died a few years back, and the aunts moved away. There's one uncle in Sanford, but we never had all that much to do with him. It's a shame, but I don't know where my cousins have got to."

"It's hard keeping it all going. We have a reunion every other year in April, but that's the only time I see most of them. They all grow up and get married and then there's the other person's family who want them for holidays. I'm just glad all my children still come home."

"We need something for the gravy."

"I broke my gravy pitcher last Christmas. Why don't we put it in this glass bowl? Or should we just leave it in the container?"

"Do you have a ladle?"

"Only a soup ladle – over in that drawer, next to the stove. It won't fit in the container, so we'd better put the gravy in the bowl."

Turkey, dressing, cranberry sauce, gravy, mashed potatoes, sweet potatoes, green beans, macaroni and cheese, rolls. Marybeth had ordered the largest turkey, and triple orders of everything else, but still she worried that there wouldn't be enough.

They were a tight squeeze around the table. Munro moved Scotty's playpen in for Misty so Leanne could keep an eye on her. Scotty's highchair was next to Steve.

"Wow, Mom, it looks terrific!" O.B. said.

"Well now, you know it all came from the store."

"Remember the time at Aunt Ruthie's house when Uncle Sturgis dropped the turkey on the floor?" asked Harlan.

"Stuffing everywhere, man, what a mess."

"O.B., you weren't even three. You can't remember that," Ruthie said.

O.B. looked sheepish. "I guess I've just heard about it so much."

He'd always felt left out, Marybeth thought. Sometimes she thought Ruthie and Harlan deliberately told stories from when it was just the two of them to make O.B. jealous. They were so close, just fifteen months apart, with five years between Harlan and O.B. His name was Patterson, after their great uncle, but Ruthie called him Other Brother and it quickly became O.B. Sometimes she wondered if the other two even remembered his real name.

When they were all seated, Steve said, "Let's bow our heads and say grace."

"Grace!" Bailey burst out, with his donkey laugh.

Marybeth saw Vinnie shift in her seat, and Bailey jump. She must have kicked him.

"Geez Mom, I was only kidding."

Steve glanced at Ruthie with his lips tight, bowed his head, and began his prayer. It was a long one, and the Amens at the end were emphatic.

Marybeth started the platters moving around the table.

"Hey wait, I'm not ready for the gravy yet, I don't have any stuffing. Ruthie, stop hogging the stuffing."

"Don't you want some cranberry sauce?" Marybeth said to Leanne at her side.

"No, thank you. I only like the jelly kind."

"Leanne, all you need to say is no thank you." Vinnie looked at Marybeth. "I try to teach them manners."

"Oh it doesn't matter, we're all family here."

Leanne was glaring at Vinnie. She was so motherly with Misty, and such a child with her mother.

With everyone's plate full, conversation ended for a while. Marybeth was pleased to see plenty of turkey left on the platter, with half the bird still in the kitchen. She relaxed and just watched them all eat, too full of family to eat much herself.

Aunt Alice didn't have much of an appetite either. As soon as she'd eaten a bit and pushed the rest around on her plate, she began to talk.

"They don't let you have seconds at the nursing home except Jello. I told the director it's not right. The state pays good money for me to stay there and if I want a little more chicken or ice cream what's wrong with that? I know what it is to run a kitchen, I told her. I used to be in food service at the University, and you can't get anything by me. I know what goes on. I was in charge of the kitchen at the girls' honor dorm in 1968... no, I'm wrong, I think it was 1964 because the new director came in '65 and I know it was before that. Anyway, I had ordered a whole lot of precut coleslaw. None of the girls liked it, and we had almost ten quarts left over, but I wouldn't let them throw it away. I always told my staff about how my Momma, that was your great-great-aunt, Harlan, you used to call her Dolly but her real name was Dahlia, she was fond of you, said you were the smartest of all Marybeth's children...."

Aunt Alice had always talked that much, it had just gotten a little more wander-y as she aged. Marybeth enjoyed it while they were eating – it blended with the pre-game show coming from the living room. She let her mind float over the sounds, just looking at the faces of her family, thinking nothing much. Harlan getting balder, Ruthie rounder, O.B. at twenty-five losing some of his teenage angles. Munro at the other end of the table, beginning to look pained. She needed to intervene, catch the moment when Aunt Alice paused for breath, even if it was mid-story, because with Aunt Alice it was always mid-story.

"Who's ready for seconds? Bailey, you look like you need some more turkey."

"Yes Ma'am, and some of that stuffing and gravy too." She passed them down and sent all the other dishes around.

"Munro, could you carve some more turkey please? I'm too full to move."

Ruthie hadn't taken seconds, though Marybeth noticed she'd eaten some of everything, including the stuffing and gravy, and the green beans with ham. Last time they were here, for Munro's birthday, Steve had closely monitored what she and Scotty ate, offering a long disquisition on diabetes, heart disease, and cancer, with a side note about revised actuarial tables. He worked for a health insurance company.

Ruthie was expecting again, so you'd think Steve would get fussier about her eating, but he didn't say a thing. Something was different between those two. Ruthie had a little sharp note in her voice when she spoke to him, and he seemed awfully eager to please. She was more like the old Ruthie than when they'd first married. Maybe some of the shine had rubbed off – no surprise after five years.

It was Scotty's first Thanksgiving at the table and he was enjoying it thoroughly. Steve had given him a little bit of everything and made sure he ate his four string beans. Misty had rolled herself into a corner of the playpen, where she lay grabbing and gumming and dropping her toys, but as Munro and O.B. cleared away the plates and Marybeth brought in the pies, she started to fuss. Leanne popped up immediately to get her. She went in the living room to change her diaper while Vinnie warmed the formula in the microwave.

"Why don't you feed her here at the table, so you can have some dessert and keep us company?" said Marybeth.

So Leanne sat back down next to Ruthie.

"Do you find she gets sick a lot?" asked Ruthie.

"No Ma'am, she's only been sick one time, with a virus and an ear infection, but boy was she miserable then."

"I'm surprised. You know they say if you feed them formula they just stay sick, because they don't get the immunities from nursing. Scotty's still nursing and he's only been sick once."

"Same as Misty Dawn."

"Well, yes, but he's a lot older. And I suppose she's in daycare, so she's exposed to all sorts of diseases."

"It's not daycare. My school is just for girls with babies and we have a nursery for the babies. And we all take care of them."

"But she's with all those other babies every day. We didn't take Scotty around other children till he was a year old."

"The nurse at school says it's good for them to be with other babies; it stimulates them."

"Well, I suppose with their mothers so young and all, they're not getting the sort of stimulation they need. Maybe they are better off in group care."

Marybeth was astonished at the attack. What could have gotten into her? She'd never seen Ruthie be ugly with anyone but her.

Misty had almost finished the bottle by this time and she was falling asleep. Leanne asked if she could put her down in a bedroom. Harlan took them back to the guestroom. Marybeth could hear him joking with Leanne as they came back down the hall.

Vinnie's pies were a big hit. Even Steve unbent enough to have a small slice of each, though he advised against any for Scotty. They carried their plates into the living room, where the game was just starting. Aunt Alice sat at the end of the couch and began a story about the visitors who brought pets to the nursing home. But Munro turned the TV up a smidgeon, and she soon faded off, her head back, mouth a little open.

It was a sorry game. Opakulla threw away every opportunity, and the State team caught them all. They were on their third quarterback of the season and the coach still couldn't get it right. Bailey and Munro were both shouters. Steve just sat in a glum slump, with Ruthie looking anxious next to him. Harlan and O.B. groaned through the first half, and then gave up in disgust and started a game of gin, glancing at the TV from time to time when the crowd got loud. Leanne went back to the guest room in the first ten minutes "to see if Misty Dawn's okay," and never emerged.

Vinnie started on the kitchen. Marybeth protested at first, but then gave in, showed her where to put everything, and returned to the game. She was a big Opakulla fan. In that town what else would she be? She didn't understand football all that well, but she liked watching the kids chasing down the field, the long passes, the piling on. She liked the stops and starts of the game, the frantic activity and excitement followed by regrouping, the stomping, grimacing coaches, the hollering fans. O.B. had played football through his junior year of high school. She'd always enjoyed his games. It was more fun in the open air, yelling with the crowd. Still, her own family were pretty good yellers. And it was nice to be together after that huge dinner, all on the same side for once.

When the game finally ended, Opakulla had been crushed 29 to 7, and that was with half the State team recovering from food poisoning. She brought out some leftovers, but nobody was interested. Vinnie went to get Leanne and Misty from the back room. Marybeth had the feeling she had only stayed so Bailey could watch the game. They left, declining the leftovers Marybeth urged on them. Harlan and O.B. were both staying the weekend and went off to shoot pool with friends. They offered to drive Alice home, but Munro said he'd do it. Scotty was down for a nap in Ruthie's old room.

Suddenly she was alone in the living room with Ruthie and Steve. Ruthie was in the recliner, Steve on the couch, and for the first time she worried about what was going on between them. They had always sat snuggled. She might not be crazy about Steve, but it would be terrible if they broke up with a baby on the way. Well, she ought to know better than to worry. She and Munro had their frosty patches, and never thought of splitting. But Ruthie and Steve were both so rigid.

"What ever made you invite those people to Thanksgiving, Mother?" She said it as though they were sharing a joke.

"Well, Vinnie works so hard and wasn't going to be with her family. I guess I felt sorry for her. I knew we'd have plenty, and our family so small this year."

"It was embarrassing. That child with her baby. I can't imagine how her mother let her go out dressed like that. And the boy! I'm just glad Scotty's as young as he is. I don't want him around that kind of people."

"I don't think I know what you mean by 'that kind of people.'"

"Well, if nothing else, a teenage girl and her illegitimate baby. It's like you're saying it's okay to behave that way."

"Now Ruthie, I think we have to be prepared to be charitable to everybody," Steve said. "They're all God's children, and we should forgive them the way Jesus would."

"No. We have to have standards. We can donate to some charity for unwed mothers, but we don't have to be bringing them into our home."

"I don't ask you to invite them to your home, Ruthie. But they were guests in my home, and I'm sorry you couldn't be polite to them."

"I didn't do anything rude. If you want rude, just look at that horrible boy. I was almost ready to go home right then when he made his stupid little joke."

"You were mean to go after Leanne that way. She's doing a good job raising her baby. She couldn't be nursing because they were separated for so long."

"And whose fault was that? Mother, she dumped her in your planter, for heaven's sake. They never should have let her have the baby back after that."

"But see how well Misty is doing. She's just adorable."

"I could see how you felt about the baby; you hardly looked at Scotty. You've got another grandchild coming, you know. I hope you'll find it in you to give her some attention, instead of spending all your time on some teenage girl and her bastard."

Ruthie's eyes filled with tears. Marybeth didn't know what to say. Steve went over and put his arm around Ruthie but she shook it off.

"I think we'd better be getting back," he said. "It's a long drive home, and Ruthie's getting tired. I'll get Scotty's things together, honey. You just sit."

"Oh no, don't you want to wait for your father? He'd be so sorry for you to leave without saying goodbye."

"No, Steve's right. We need to go." Ruthie's voice was calm again, and cold.

But as Steve brought the baby carrier from the bedroom, they heard the car in the driveway. Munro was full of energy after his drive.

"Maybeth, it's a beautiful night. Let's take a walk and I'll tell you all about the time Aunt Alice was promoted to assistant director of food services. It's a nice long story. Hey Ruthie, you're not leaving, are you? I thought maybe we could all play a game or something."

"No Daddy, we have to get home. We'll be back at Christmas, I guess."

"You guess? You will, or I'll come over and get you. Here Steve, give me those things and I'll load up the car. Honey, do you want to pack up some leftovers for them?"

"We don't need any, thanks Daddy."

"You mean we have to eat all that pie by ourselves?"

"You'll manage somehow."

Scotty was dazed and pink-faced from his nap. Ruthie had a long hug for Munro, a quick one for Marybeth. Steve shook hands with

Munro and gave Marybeth a squeeze and a pat. "You'll have to excuse Ruthie – she gets upset pretty easily these days."

When they were gone, Munro got jackets from the hall closet and they set out for a walk. It was a perfect night, with the stars clear, and Christmas lights up already on half the houses. Munro relented and didn't share Aunt Alice's story. She was quiet too, thinking about Ruthie.

Leanne

Chapter Twenty-Three

I've gotta move out of here. I can't live like this. Momma treats me like a baby. She says I can stay till New Years, but no way – that's over a month away. I'll find a place by end of this week, I swear. I called Phyllis twice yesterday, and this morning Miss Melanie at school said she's tried to call her too. But all we get is stupid voicemail. If I hear "Have a blessed day" one more time I'm going to leave a bunch of swear words on her machine. It's her job to help us. She could at least call me.

I can't live on my own because I can't get welfare unless I'm living with my mom or a grown up. But Miss Melanie says even if they didn't have that rule, a landlord won't rent to me because I'm not eighteen and I can't sign a contract. Momma could sign for me but her credit is all screwed up since Bailey's phone bill. Miss Melanie says I could come live with her except for the rules at New Beginnings. I'd have to drop out of the program, and I can't drop out of the program because to get welfare I've gotta be in school. I can't go to any other school with a baby. I wouldn't want to drop out anyway, because then how could I get a job and take care of Misty Dawn?

But it's rules everywhere. Try to move one way and there's a rule, try to move another way and bang, there's another rule. It's like you're in this little box. I can't wait till I'm eighteen but that's more than two years away. I don't know how I can stand it. Miss Melanie says when I'm a grown up it's not all that easy either, because I won't have all these people helping me. But I think she's wrong. I mean, she lives in her own apartment and has a car. She goes to Atlanta for the weekend whenever she wants without asking anybody.

So I've gotta think of somebody I could live with. Shameka and I would get an apartment together but you have to live with a grown up. In Life Skills we had to find an apartment in the ads and make a budget. We found one that takes Section 8 so our rent would only be a third of our TANF checks. It had two bedrooms and two baths. Shameka said she knew where it was and it was pretty nice. It was on the Black side of town. I didn't know how good I'd do living over there, but it was just pretend so I didn't say anything.

Then we went through the furniture ads. Dilman's had the cheapest. I picked a canopy bed and Shameka picked out this modern stuff that had lights in the headboard. We chose a couch, chair and two tables with lamps. You could pay in installments. We added up all the monthly payments, and if we both had part-time jobs we could afford it. Which we're supposed to get after we finish high school. That will be two years even if I go to summer school and take lots of extra credits. So it's like I have to wait till I'm eighteen anyway.

Everything you want to do you gotta wait. I hate it. Old people act like a year is nothing. Momma says time just flies by. I don't know what time she lives in, but my time creeps and crawls. When I'm eighteen Misty Dawn will be two and a half, and I'll still be finishing high school. I don't need all this school stuff anyway. I'm gonna be a graphic designer, where you do stuff on computers.

Mr. Belmont who teaches computer lets me use Photoshop when I finish my Word training. He says I have a flair for it. At OCC they've got a two-year program in graphic design. That's what I want to do, but I don't see why I've gotta study all this English and history, and now they've got a law that you have to take two years of a language. I don't need any of that to do graphic design. I'll never finish high school at this rate.

Everything's set up with rules and wait for this, wait for that. It's so stupid. They act like they know how we're supposed to live. Maybe they've been around longer than us but that doesn't mean they're any smarter. We didn't start any wars or mess up the environment – it was them.

And look at Momma. She's forty-one and nothing but a waitress, living in this crummy garage with a son who's a bum, and Shauna who doesn't want anything to do with her. Momma says maybe she'll come home for Christmas, but Momma will be lucky if she even gets a phone call. And she's got me with her only grandchild and she's driving me away because she's so bossy and says such mean things. I was talking about all these rules and how I have to wait for everything and she goes, "Well, if you'd waited a few years to have a baby you wouldn't be in this mess." Like I don't have any feelings at all. I couldn't believe she'd say something like that, like she wished Misty Dawn hadn't even been born. I would have stomped out of the room but where could I go, the bathroom? This stupid house, if she's so smart how come she isn't living any better than this

Vinnie

Chapter Twenty-Four

Christmas morning started badly, and way too early. The Homestyle Café had been packed on Christmas Eve, and Vinnie had hoped to sleep in till maybe seven or so, now that Misty was sleeping later. Vinnie was dead asleep, between dreams, when the door creaked open and Bailey crept in. He bumped into the tree and reached out to stop its topple, but misjudged. "Motherfucker" he whispered fiercely. For such a tiny tree it made a huge crash, but of course there were all the ornaments. Vinnie turned on the light, Leanne woke up, and Bailey just stood there, staring at the mess, while they stared at him.

"Damn Momma, turn off the light, what's going on?"

"I can't turn off the light, Leanne. Bailey's knocked over the tree."

"I can't wait till I can move out of here. This isn't any kind of a home."

"Could you wait till I have my coffee before you start complaining?"

Misty woke up crying. She never woke up crying. She'd probably responded to their angry voices.

"Hey, everybody. Merry Christmas."

"Oh shut up, Bailey. You woke up Misty Dawn. What time is it? 4:30, Jesus."

Vinnie got up, put on her bathrobe, and went into the kitchen to make coffee.

"You're right, Bailey. Merry Christmas, both of you. Honey, don't just stand there grinning like a fool. Clean up the mess. And see if there's any ornaments left unbroken."

"Sure Mom. I'm sorry I woke everybody up."

"I know. I could hear you trying to be quiet."

Bailey righted the tree and started sweeping.

The lights were slightly askew but only a few of the ornaments had smashed. Most of the mess was pine needles. They had bought the tree two weeks ago, and it was getting a little tired.

Leanne had Misty up and laughing, and she came in the kitchen to fix a bottle. Vinnie could see tears in her eyes.

"Honey, I know it started early, but let's see if we can't have a nice Christmas together, okay?"

"Bailey just ruins everything Momma. I can't live like this."

"Well, I wish I could give you better. It's not easy on me either, you know."

"Yeah, but it's your choice. I didn't ask him to move back in."

"I don't recall you asking my permission to have a baby either. But this is our home, and it's all we have. We need to try to get along."

Thank God the coffee was done. She poured herself a cup. Leanne just glared at her and took Misty, the only cheerful one, back behind the curtain.

"Mom, I'm sorry. I guess I just make trouble for you."

"That's okay, Bailey. Where were you anyway?"

"Oh, just with some friends."

"Well, I know you're grown and I can't tell you what to do. But with all of us in this one room, and the baby here, you should try to get home by eleven or so or find somewhere else for the night. Things are hard here, and it gets too crazy if we can't get our sleep."

"Why do you let her be so ugly to you though?"

"And just how do I stop her from being ugly?"

"You ought to slap her."

"You know I've never believed in hitting you kids. It's just something girls go through, I guess. She's only fifteen, you know."

"I never talked to you like that."

"No, you just kept your mouth shut and did all sorts of things I'd hate to know about." And probably still do, she thought.

"You said she was supposed to be moving out of here."

"She is. But she has to live with a grown up, unless they can't find anyone. Her lawyer has written a letter to DFC, but I hate the idea of Leanne trying to do it all alone. She's so young, and it's not easy going to school and raising a baby without any help. I've been wondering if your Aunt Harriet might take her, though I'd be sorry to have the baby so far away, and it's a lot to ask."

"Well, I just hope she's out of here soon."

Vinnie wished both of them were out of there. Bailey talked as if he was here for good, and she saw no sign he'd ever get a job again.

She pulled out the ingredients for her Christmas muffins – cranberries and pecans added to corn muffin mix. It was her Momma's recipe, and she'd made it herself every Christmas since the kids were little. She heated up milk for cocoa. They'd always had cocoa and muffins while they opened presents. It was the only cooking she did on Christmas day. Christmas dinner was leftovers from the restaurant.

She was past ready to be through with all this. Just to live by herself - the house was fine for one person, and it was all paid for. She let herself dream of how it would be if the kids were gone.

Maybe she'd get a dog to keep her company. She could start saving money at last. She wasn't making a fortune, but tips were okay. She could never figure out where the money went. No rent to pay, but there was always something. You could budget for food and car and electric, but not for all the things that came up when you had kids, and there wasn't enough to budget with anyway.

Sometimes she wondered how it would have been if Preston hadn't left. He was a smart guy; he could have found something else to do. Maybe gone back to school and trained for a different job.

Come to think of it, if she didn't have the kids, maybe she could cut back her hours and get some training. She'd never been good in school, but she'd always kind of wanted to be a nurse. She could get her GED and then do the two-year program at OCC. Susan said the GED wasn't that hard. They coached you, and you could take the test over until you passed.

She was probably ready to go back to school now. She didn't have all the distractions she'd had in high school. Or wouldn't, if the kids would just move out. To come home to her own place, with only the messes she'd made herself, nobody squabbling, nobody whining or criticizing her. How would they ever get through this day? And how would she ever get them out of here?

When the muffins were done, they sat down to open presents. There were more than usual, most of them for Misty: from Miss Bradwell, Miss Knight from DFC, Marybeth, and of course presents from her and Leanne and Bailey. Where would they put all these toys? Vinnie would have preferred a case of diapers. If she thought Leanne wouldn't object, she'd take most of them to the women's shelter. But Leanne would definitely object.

Marybeth had come by the restaurant yesterday bringing presents for everybody. She would have refused them if she could have without being rude. It hadn't occurred to her to buy a gift for Marybeth. She'd enjoyed Thanksgiving, but it's not like they were friends. In fact, it had shown her they couldn't be. They were just too different. Everything was all laid out for Marybeth, with nothing to worry about. Vinnie's whole life was worry. If it weren't for her worries she wouldn't know what to think about. She wasn't jealous exactly – what would be the point of that? – but their lives were too far apart. Vinnie the waitress and Marybeth the County Commissioner. It could almost make her laugh.

She didn't have friends like when she was a kid. Just the girls at work, and John maybe. They all looked out for each other and understood how things are. But Marybeth – she'd never wondered how to pay the doctor, or seen the lights go off in the middle of dinner because the bill wasn't paid. And here was this pile of nicely wrapped presents from her.

Vinnie had given Bailey and Leanne portable CD players with earphones so she wouldn't have to listen to their music, or their squabbling over what to play. The library had CD's.

They liked the CD players, but they were thrilled with the presents from Marybeth. Bailey opened his first. It was a watch with a timer, alarm and calendar. It showed the time all over the world. He pushed all the possible combinations of buttons.

"Oh man, you think it's early here, guess what time it is in Alaska?"

Leanne got a plastic make-up case, like a treasure chest, with twenty little bottles of nail polish matched with twenty little tubes of lipstick, coordinating shades of eyeshadow and liner, a chart to tell you what to wear with what, and five sizes of brushes.

When Vinnie opened her own gift, she was touched. Inside was a plastic pot, with a bare stick thrust in dirt, and a note: "This is a cutting from my favorite rose bush. I grew it from a cutting from my grandmother, and she got it from her own mother's bush. If you've never done roses, call me and I'll give you some advice."

She'd always liked roses but never tried them, because she knew they were a lot of work. She thought they liked the same kind of soil as azaleas, but didn't they need sun? She'd been thinking of a new bed in front where there was plenty of sun. Maybe she could get a couple of rosebushes from Housemart and start a little rose garden. When the kids were gone she'd have more time.

It was a wonderful present, and she wished she'd had the same idea. She could have dug up a bunch of gingers. They cost a fortune to start, but they spread quickly. Well, maybe she could give Marybeth a New Year's present. She could take it down to Coggins Hardware and get her advice on the rose at the same time. Take a batch of muffins too.

After all the shopping and wrapping and care, it only took about twenty minutes to open the presents, leaving a pile of toys and boxes and a heap of crumpled wrapping paper. Leanne dressed Misty in the red velvet dress Miss Knight had given her, and a little elastic headband with a red rosette. She looked very cute and very silly. Leanne put away the other new clothes and arranged all the toys in Misty's crib, but she left the rest of the mess for Vinnie. Then Leanne and Bailey both sat with their earphones on, each rocking to their own beat. As she went by them, picking up the trash, she could hear faint and different rhythms side by side. Well, anything for some peace.

Leanne

Chapter Twenty-Five

Everything's working out perfect. Phyllis talked to Mrs. Coggins, and she says me and Misty Dawn can live with them! I couldn't believe it. We'll each have our own bedroom, and Misty Dawn's is right next to mine. We're moving in next Sunday. Mrs. Coggins called me the day after New Year's and said she'd take me to the mall for new curtains and a bedspread to make it more like my own room.

I haven't been to the mall once since I got back home. All this time with Momma, all I ever did was go to school and come home. Oh, and go to court – that's a lot of fun, I guess. I can't wait to get out of here.

I think Momma was surprised Mrs. Coggins invited me to live with her, but she doesn't say much about it, or about anything. Honestly, her life is so boring, you'd think she'd want to do something besides being a waitress. Look at Mrs. Coggins, she's got her own store, and that big house, and I think she used to be the mayor. They said it on television when they had the story about her finding Misty Dawn. It's funny how things work out. I knew Misty Dawn belonged in that house.

Momma was still home when Mrs. Coggins came to get me. I was hoping she'd take the day off to watch Misty Dawn. But no, she said she can't go rearranging everything so I can buy curtains. I don't know what's bugging her. I'd say she was mad I'm leaving but I know she wants me gone. Man, I'll never treat Misty Dawn that way.

Mrs. Coggins is so different from Momma. She acts like it matters what I think or want. Like at the mall. I had on my black jeans and a yellow sweater and they had a sale on high top sneakers in different colors including yellow. I said those would go nice with my sweater, and she just said, "Why don't we see if they have your size?" and right away we go in the store and try them on and she buys them for me just like that. No talking about how I already have plenty of shoes or we can't afford it or I ought to pay for it out of my own money or anything.

So then we went to Sears. I chose curtains that had blotchy-looking designs in orange and pink, and a pink bedspread to go with them. We got a yellow lamp too. She says I can have my room any way I want as long as I keep it neat. I can even put pictures up. I wanted green towels for the bathroom that's just for me and Misty Dawn, except when people come over they can use the toilet. But she said she had plenty of towels already. She didn't want to buy stuff for Misty Dawn's room either. I wanted to decorate it like a baby's room, but she said it would look enough like a baby's room when we got the crib and playpen and all the toys in there. She said, "We don't want to push Munro too far." I don't know what she meant. Munro is Mr. Coggins, but I don't see what he has to do with it.

When we went by their store to get curtain rings he didn't say much to me, just was asking Mrs. Coggins how long she thought she'd be. She took time off to go shopping with me. Before we left he said, "Now don't get carried away, Marybeth." I think he meant don't spend a lot. Anyway, I guess it will be okay living with him. He was nice to Misty Dawn at Thanksgiving.

After we bought everything, Mrs. Coggins said, "How about some ice cream?" So we went to The Soda Fountain. Mrs. Coggins says they tried to make it like the soda fountains they had when she was a girl, but those soda fountains were in drug stores, and not so fancy. There used to be one across the street from Coggins Hardware. Her father owned the store before she did, and she used to help him. He'd give her money from the cash register for a soda. He'd always say, "Look both ways before you cross." She says she can still hear him saying that every time she crosses the street. But the drug store is empty now. It's been lots of things, last thing was a store that sold underwear and sex toys.

I was embarrassed when Mrs. Coggins said it. I wouldn't think she'd know about that stuff. I know about it because Judy had these dirty magazines and a big pink dildo. She told me her and Creepy Clayton used to use it sometimes. I wasn't too embarrassed by it because we're friends. But you don't want to think of an old lady knowing that stuff. I mean, I guess she has to know about sex, because she had babies, but I don't think people did all that weird stuff when she was young.

Mrs. Coggins finished eating way before me. She just had a piece of pie, but I had a hamburger, fries and a banana split. They give you a little pitcher with extra fudge sauce, and you can choose your ice cream. I got cherry vanilla, caramel chip, and bubble gum. I asked Mrs. Coggins if she wanted a bite but she didn't. She said the pie wasn't as good as Momma's. I told her Momma doesn't make those pies, she's just a waitress there.

After we were done Mrs. Coggins said we should go to her house and get things ready. When we went in it didn't feel like home at all. In my room I kept on holding my purse until she said, "Here, put that down and give me a hand." I guess it will be different after I move in, but I don't feel right there. When I sit down, I don't know how to have my legs, or where to put my hands. I have to think about what to say.

She told me to get some sheets from the linen closet. She has a whole closet with nothing but sheets and towels. It looked like a shelf in a store. None of the sheets go with my bedspread, but she said they won't show when the bed is made. And I should make my bed every morning before I go to school. I didn't like when she said that. I don't mind making my bed, it just makes me wonder, will she make all these rules and act like she's my mother or something?

The room looked cool when we finished. There's a big window, and Mrs. Coggins said we can put some plants in front of it. She asked if I like gardening and said I could help her in the garden. I hate gardening but I didn't want to say no, so I just went uh huh.

I was glad when the clock started ringing and she said she had to get back to the store. The clock rings every fifteen minutes, and then every hour it rings bong bong bong to tell you the time. It's near my room and I'm afraid it will wake me up. I was worried it would keep Misty Dawn up too, but Mrs. Coggins said look how good she slept at the mall, and she slept in her carrier right through us working in the bedroom, and the clock didn't wake her up then. She said babies will sleep through anything.

When we got back to my house the car was there. I told Mrs. Coggins she shouldn't come in because Momma probably had one of her headaches. I opened the door real quiet and carried Misty Dawn over to her crib. Soon as I put her down her face crumpled up and she started crying. Her bottle was in the baby bag so I went to get it. Momma sat up and switched on the light.

"What are you doing?" she asked, her voice all slurry the way it gets when she's sick.

"I'm just getting her bottle, Momma."

She sat there on the bed, blinking and looking around.

"It's gone. Thank you, God."

Sometimes when Momma goes to sleep with a headache it's gone when she wakes up. She went and picked up Misty Dawn to hush her. I said I'd make tea while I was warming the formula, and she said sure. Misty Dawn started crying again soon as Momma put her down. She's getting spoiled.

I made tea for both of us and took some cookies out. I wasn't hungry, but it's what you do when you have tea. I carried it all to the table, and Momma gave me Misty Dawn, and I stuck the bottle in her mouth. All three of us having our tea – Misty Dawn and her Mom and Grandma. It always surprises me when I think of Momma that way. It's easier to think of myself as a Mom than to think of Momma as a grandma.

After one of her headaches, Momma looks beautiful – kind of pink and shiny. She says she feels different then too, like everything around her is clear and new. After a headache she's easy to be with. She asked me what I did with Mrs. Coggins, and I told her about all the stuff we bought.

"It will be nice to have your own room. You'll sleep through Misty's little noises, and she'll probably get more regular about sleeping too."

"Yeah, but I think maybe I'll miss having her sleeping close."

I was looking around and thinking how some ways I'd miss that big old room. I didn't miss it when I was living with Peter. It felt like I was a grown-up then, finished with Momma and Bailey. I was done with being a kid, and that's what Peter said too. He told me I didn't need to be seeing my Momma because we were married and on our own now. Anyway, she could get him in all kinds of trouble if she knew where I was.

I think about it now and I can't believe I let him boss me around like that. I guess that's why it was so easy for him to make me dump Misty Dawn. When I moved in with him, everything I had was his, and all I had was him.

When I move to Mrs. Coggins' house I'll be taking Misty Dawn and all our stuff too. I'll see a lot of Momma, I know, but it won't be the same. When I live here we can ignore each other and just go about our business. It will be different when I come to visit. I wonder if I'll feel like I did at Mrs. Coggins' house, like nothing is mine and I have to be careful where I sit and what I say. When I came home with Misty Dawn it felt like the safest place in the world, and I thought I'd never want to leave it. Now here I am moving again. I've only been back here four months, but it feels like longer.

It might sound silly to miss a place like this, all four of us together with no place to be by yourself except the bathroom, sharing a bed with Momma, who kicks. It's cold, and no matter how bright it is outside, when you come in it's dark like a cave until you turn on the light. But I lived here ever since I was a little kid. I can hardly remember where we lived before except from pictures. It's funny to think Misty Dawn has been here most of her life. I don't count that foster home because she wasn't with me.

I wonder if I'll get used to being at the Coggins'. I'd like to talk to Momma about it all, but when I said about missing sleeping with

Misty Dawn she started fiddling with her cup and then she got up and said, "Here, let me put the baby down," because Misty Dawn had fallen asleep with the nipple still in her mouth. Momma put her in her crib, and then she went into the bathroom, and on the way she said, "Clear away those plates and clean up the kitchen why don't you, you left a big mess in there this morning from breakfast." And our little tea party was over and it was back to normal. Hard to believe I thought I'd miss our house or Momma. I can't wait to be in my pretty new bedroom, with nobody telling me what to do.

Marybeth

Chapter Twenty-Six

Phyllis had said she would do her best to get Leanne there in time for supper. They would probably be there about four. She grumbled at having to do it on a Sunday, when she wasn't on call that weekend, but Marybeth had been adamant. She couldn't take more time away from the store, and Sunday was the busiest day at the restaurant so Vinnie couldn't bring her.

But when Marybeth got back from church, Munro met her at the car.

"That girl and the baby, they're here."

"Oh Mun, oh no. They weren't supposed to be here till four. What did you do with them?"

"I didn't do anything with them, I just moved all her stuff into her room, and all the baby's stuff into the other room. Isn't that what you wanted?"

"But where is she?"

"In her room, I guess. She got here about an hour ago."

"And she's just sitting in her room?"

"Marybeth, she could be doing somersaults for all I know. I asked if she wanted anything, and she didn't, so I left her alone."

It was starting out all wrong. She thought they'd have time together before Leanne arrived. When she left for church, he was sitting glumly on the couch with the newspaper. She kissed him on the head for goodbye and he barely looked up.

When Marybeth first told him what she was thinking of, he'd laughed out loud. Then he saw her face.

"You're serious, aren't you?"

"Of course I am. Munro, she needs someplace to go with that baby, and we have all this room. You wouldn't believe where she's living now. It's a garage and it's got three people living in it, four if you count the baby. Miss Knight says if she can't find her someplace else to live they'll have to take the baby. They only let her stay there because of Vinnie, and now that her brother's moved back in it's just not working out."

"But why us, for heaven's sake? There's lots of people with extra room, honey."

"She can't move in with just anyone. She knows us, Mun."

"I don't want kids in the house again. It's been so nice with just the two of us. You want to give that up for some stranger?"

"But she's not a stranger. We know her, and she doesn't have any place else to go. I couldn't live with myself knowing she'd lost her baby because of me. She dotes on that baby. She's a good mother, honey, and a bright girl, too. We could do so much for her. She knows just what she wants to do; there's a two-year program at OCC in graphic design, and she wants to go there when she finishes high school. She has a gift for drawing."

"Wait a minute. She's in eighth grade, right? And now you're talking about college. Just how long were you planning on?"

"Oh, not all through college. When she's eighteen she can live on her own and still get welfare."

"And now she's what, fifteen?"

"She'll be sixteen in June."

"You can't mean this. You can't be telling me we have a teenager and a baby living with us for the next two years."

"I'm not telling you, I'm asking, but yes, I do mean two years. Mun, you love kids. I thought you'd never get over it when O.B. left and we were on our own."

"Well, I got over it real good. Like I said, we're done with that, Marybeth. Sure, I love our own kids. But I wouldn't want them moving back in with us! And now you're asking me to take in this child, no kin to us, and already in trouble. What do you suppose she'll do while she's living with us? She's no Ruthie you know. We'll be lucky if it's nothing worse than what we went through with Harlan and O.B. She could turn up pregnant again, and then you'll be wanting to take in that baby too. Might as well go whole hog and open a home for unwed mothers."

"Now you're being silly. I told Miss Knight we'll just have to see how it goes. If it doesn't work out, she'll have to find some other place for her to go."

"Sounds like you've already agreed to do it."

"No, I said I'd have to talk with you. But once I mentioned it, she started talking as if it was all settled. She says she has to talk with you too, but it sounds like that's just a formality. In fact, I think she's already talked to Leanne and Vinnie about it. It would be hard to back out now."

"Marybeth, I just don't know what to say. It's like if I sold the house without asking you. Know what I think? You feel bad about Ruthie, and you think this time you can do it right. But there's no do-overs, Marybeth. Now you've got yourself all tangled up in these people's lives. Maybe I should have paid more attention to what was going on. I wasn't crazy about them coming for Thanksgiving, but I didn't say anything, and I think I treated them nice. Now here you've gotten us both sucked into a mess, and I've got no say. I never thought you'd do me this way."

"But it's like I said, it just sort of got away from me before I could talk to you. It feels like it's too late to say no, and I don't know what Leanne will do if she can't come here."

"You really want to do this, don't you? And I really don't, but I guess I have no choice but to go along with it. I don't like it though, Marybeth. I don't like it at all. You did wrong to let it get this far. That's all I have to say."

And it *was* all he had to say. He wouldn't talk about it anymore, though she tried. It had been two weeks of chill between them, as bad as she'd ever known.

Now it had started. Leanne was in the back bedroom. It was too late to back out, too late to talk it over anymore. What had she done?

She went down the hall to Leanne's door, shut tight. She knocked hesitantly, not loudly enough. She tried again. Still no answer. She turned the knob carefully and pushed the door open. She didn't want to wake Leanne if she was asleep.

Leanne was sitting on the bed, reading a teen magazine, wearing earphones and rocking slightly. There were three empty boxes by the closet, where her clothes were already hanging, and an amazing number of make-up tubes and bottles arranged on the dresser tray. Marybeth moved around to the end of the bed where Leanne could see her.

"Hi."

Leanne shoved her earphones up. "Oh, hi."

"I see you've got yourself all settled in."

"Yes, Ma'am." She kept her finger in the magazine.

"Where's Misty?"

"She's sleeping."

"Mind if I peek in on her?"

"No Ma'am." She replaced the earphones.

Misty was much more welcoming. When she saw Marybeth, she startled and then laughed, as if sleeping and waking were a game of peekaboo. Marybeth hung over the crib, and they talked nonsense for a little while till Leanne came in.

"She was just waking up when I came in."

"Yeah, she slept late this morning. I didn't think she'd take a long nap."

Leanne had arranged Misty's things as neatly as her own, though Misty had a lot more than she did. The playpen was full of toys. The carrier and stroller were by the closet.

"Maybe after lunch you'd like to go for a walk? This is a pretty neighborhood, and some of the early azaleas are out."

"I don't like walking."

"Oh. Well, what would you like for lunch? I wasn't expecting you till about suppertime, so I don't have much. Munro and I usually go out for lunch on Sunday after church."

"I don't care. I'm not hungry."

Could she just leave Leanne on her own here? Of course she could, you don't need a babysitter for a fifteen-year-old. But it would be rude to go out when she'd barely been there an hour. She tried to picture the three of them at the Magnolia Inn buffet with the baby. It felt as though Leanne and her paraphernalia were harnessed to her, and she couldn't move around in her own home without this ungainly, awkward clutter dragging along, getting stuck in doors.

"I'll tell you what. I'll make hot dogs and heat up some soup. I'll call you when it's ready."

"I have to heat up her bottle. Can I keep her formula in the refrigerator?"

"Of course. This is your home. Yours and Misty's. Just bring out whatever you have and we'll make room."

Lunch was silent. Leanne's table manners weren't improved by feeding the baby while she ate. With the bottle in her left hand, she grabbed the hotdog in her right and took a big bite, then leaned way forward over the baby for a slurping spoonful of soup. Marybeth wanted to suggest that she feed Misty first and then eat, but she thought maybe it wasn't her place. She tried to start a conversation, but got nothing but yes ma'am, no ma'am. She started telling Munro about the sermon but couldn't even get an uh-huh out of him.

When the kids were teenagers, three conversations at once would fly over the dinner table. She could never understand how they managed to eat so much and still squabble and brag and complain and contradict each other. Sometimes the din overwhelmed her, and she would long to be alone with Munro. It had been wonderful being alone. They could talk or be quiet together, in perfect peace. Now it was silent but not quiet. The peace was gone, everything she did felt awkward, and Munro had closed himself off from her. This was the worst mistake she had ever made, and she was stuck with it. It had to get better, but she didn't know how. Surely they'd all get used to it. But what had she thrown away?

After lunch, Leanne went back to her room with Misty. Marybeth longed to go for a walk, and it would have been fun to take the baby. But she felt she ought to keep Munro company, so she went and sat with him in the living room. Now everyone in the house was a visitor. They were like a bunch of guests sitting around a hotel lobby, or people in an elevator, standing too close and not looking at each other.

Chapter Twenty-Seven

After two weeks they were all more relaxed. Leanne was always up early. She fixed Misty's bottle in the kitchen and fed her in the bedroom. After breakfast she washed her dishes, made her bed and tidied Misty's room before they left for the bus stop at 7:30. She was a model houseguest, but Marybeth missed her solitary mornings.

"She's really no trouble," she said to Munro.

"No, I suppose you're right."

Munro had fallen for the baby. Marybeth came home from church one day to find him lying on the couch making faces at her, while she sat on his stomach and grabbed at his glasses. She reached too far and toppled over. It made them both laugh. Leanne was in the recliner, reading the comics. It was a cozy scene, that made Marybeth feel like an intruder. She changed into jeans and a sweatshirt and went into the kitchen to figure out lunch.

When she agreed to take in Leanne she hadn't thought about cooking. She'd asked her what she liked to eat, but except for frozen waffles, Leanne hadn't given her any suggestions. It would be nice if she'd pitch in. Surely the girl knew how to make a sandwich.

She and Munro had long since divided up the little bit of housework they managed to do. Marlene came in every week to clean. With a third person in the house, Marybeth felt they should divide it up again, but she didn't know how to approach Leanne, who had so much to do already. Maybe she shouldn't expect anything more of her than taking care of the baby and keeping up with school. She hadn't thought it through, hadn't realized it would mean more work for her.

And how much should she meddle in Leanne's affairs? The second day she asked how school had gone, and got nothing from Leanne but "Okay, I guess." So she figured it was up to Leanne and maybe none of her business. But then Miss Knight came by and asked her how Leanne was doing in school, was she taking care of the baby, had she gone for her Depo shot. Marybeth had never heard of Depo.

"Birth control. She has to have them every month."

"But why? She doesn't have a boyfriend."

"It's normal, we always ask for that as part of the case plan for teenagers. The judge won't order it unless they agree, but they always do."

"Did her mother agree?"

"She didn't have to. It's up to the Department, and Leanne of course. But I don't think Mrs. Ellsworth would have any objection."

"It's just strange, DFC prescribing drugs."

"Oh, we don't prescribe. Our doctor does that. But it's important for her not to miss her shot. You should ask her when it's due. I guess I can arrange to take her, but it would be a lot easier if you did it. And we sure don't want her getting pregnant again. Where would you put another baby? Just kidding," she added when she saw Marybeth's face.

"I just don't understand why, if she's not involved with anyone, she should take hormones."

"It's only a matter of time. Once these girls start having sex, they don't stop."

Marybeth didn't like her attitude, and she didn't want to ask Leanne when her shot was due, or whatever she was supposed to be asking. Leanne had just started to relax with her a little.

"I'll let you ask her."

"Okay, no problem. I need to talk with her anyway."

Marybeth fled to the garden.

About half an hour later, Miss Knight came to the back door and called, "I've got to be going now. Everything seems to be fine. You should take Leanne for her shot next Friday at four. Let me know if there's anything you need."

So Marybeth told Leanne she would pick her up after school on Friday to go to the clinic.

When she arrived on Friday, the girls were getting their babies ready to go home. Leanne was talking to another girl, holding Misty on her hip. The baby smiled as Marybeth approached. The girl was a staff member, and she was reviewing Misty's daily report with Leanne. Misty had napped, finished two bottles, eaten a third of a mashed banana, had two bowel movements, and gone for a walk in a stroller. The walk in the stroller was with Leanne, but they wrote it down anyway.

"Are you ready to go?"

"Yeah. Gotta go get my Depo," she said.

"You go, girl," was the other girl's response, which Marybeth didn't know how to interpret. But first Leanne had to carry Misty around to say goodbye to the other babies. She brought her up close to each one for a "kiss", except for the baby with a cold, where she just waved Misty's arm and said Bye Bye.

The clinic was in a small strip mall, next to a vacuum cleaner store. Though the sign out front said *Women's Clinic*, it was actually a clinic for STD's and birth control. A sign said to take a number if they were here for shots, otherwise to sign in. Marybeth counted six young girls holding numbers. Were they all here for birth control? Perhaps for penicillin instead. Several women as old as she were also sitting, without numbers. Three young men had identical scowls. Was it because of the sign? She thought it was better than if it said Venereal Disease Clinic, but maybe they didn't. Two of the men were like a matched set, one black, one white: short hair, jeans, t-shirts and baseball caps. She wouldn't notice them on the street, but she might cross the street to avoid the third. He was big and beefy, with shoulder length blonde hair and an ugly sore on his lip, which he fingered carefully from time to time. His sleeveless black T shirt said, "Size counts." He had a barbed wire tattoo around each wrist, and a blurry one on his bicep that said something she couldn't make out.

After about twenty minutes they called Leanne's number.

"Do you want me to come with you?"

"Naw. But maybe you could hold Misty Dawn."

She took the baby, and snuggled her close, but Misty was in her lively time and wanted to play. To Marybeth's horror, the blonde man came over and sat down next to them. Misty gave him her biggest smile, and he smiled back. His missing tooth didn't bother Misty.

"Girl?" She was wearing a frilly headband.

"Yes."

He reached out a finger, the same finger that had been touching his lip, and gently poked her in the belly.

"You gonna grow up and give some man all kinds of trouble, ain't you."

Misty laughed and he went on poking her, and Marybeth didn't know what to say, or how to stop him. Everyone else in the waiting room was looking over and smiling. She couldn't say anything about his sore. They probably all had sores too. Suddenly she felt uneasy about the chair she was sitting in, about touching anything in the room. Maybe she should wait outside. But just then a name was called over the intercom. With a farewell poke at Misty the man got up and went through the door beyond the counter. The back of his shirt said, "I like a tight fit."

Leanne came out the same door a moment later. She took Misty from Marybeth and they left. Marybeth wished there was a decontamination center somewhere, something like a car wash. Failing that, she suggested they stop for ice cream. It was such a relief to be out of that clinic. She'd let Miss Knight take Leanne next time, and Marybeth could keep Misty. It wasn't any place for a baby.

"Those shots are making me fat."

Marybeth couldn't see any change in Leanne's size, but maybe without the shots she would have lost more weight after the pregnancy. It was more likely a result of the way Leanne ate. Right now she was having a banana split. Yesterday she had asked whether Marybeth ever bought chips or cookies. Marybeth didn't like to buy them because she couldn't stop herself from eating them all. So Leanne went to the store and bought two kinds of chips and a box of cookies. She wanted to keep them in her room, but Marybeth asked her to leave them in the pantry, because of bugs. She promised not to touch them.

Leanne wasn't paying any rent or contributing anything for food. Though the TANF check came to Marybeth, she had told Leanne she could have it, thinking she would save the money. But she kept coming home with new CD's, and on Saturday she went to the mall and bought makeup and sweaters, reporting cheerfully, "Man, I blew my whole check at the mall. I can't wait till the first of the month."

She was only fifteen, of course, and had never been responsible for herself. It was probably unrealistic to expect her to save money. Marybeth decided to keep the check herself, give Leanne an allowance, and put the rest in a savings account for her. That would give her a tidy amount when she turned eighteen.

Leanne

Chapter Twenty-Eight

I don't know what to do. Mrs. Coggins won't give me my money. She says she's putting it in savings, all but $20 a week, and she'll give me the rest when I'm eighteen. Like it's hers to give. That's my money and she has no right. I called Phyllis but she said it's not her part of it, and I gotta call Tonya. So I called Tonya and she said the money goes to Mrs. Coggins because I'm a teenager, like she's my foster mother or something, and she's supposed to spend it for me and the baby. I'm not in no foster care though, and I don't need a foster mother. I've got a perfectly good mother of my own, only I just can't live there.

I told Tonya that if she's supposed to spend the money on me and Misty Dawn I want to know how she's doing it. She doesn't buy anything for Misty Dawn but diapers and baby food, the formula is free from WIC. And the only special food I get is like chips and stuff for snacks, and I buy that myself. We're not costing her anything. She says she's saving it for me, but I don't believe her. I told Tonya to make Mrs. Coggins give her a list of all the money she spends on me and Misty Dawn. But she says that's not the way it works, and it's not that much money anyway, it wouldn't even be enough for rent if Mrs. Coggins was charging rent. She says I don't understand money; the Coggins pay for electricity and water and trash and heat. But it doesn't cost any more to heat a room because we're there. Phyllis says I need to try to get along with Mrs. Coggins because she's doing me a favor letting me stay there. I say it's no favor when she's getting paid to do it.

They go out to dinner every Saturday. I bet it's because they can afford it now that they have my money. And do they invite me? Oh no, I just stay home with Misty Dawn, like always. She said if I want to go out with friends or something, she'll watch the baby. I should just let her know where I was going and when I'd be back. She acts like she's my mother or something and she treats me like a ten-year-old. It's none of her business where I'm going. If I'm old enough to have a baby, I'm old enough for some privacy. Anyway, who would I go out with? My real friends now are at New Beginnings, only none of them have cars, and they've got their babies, and I don't think Mrs. I'm-in-Charge Coggins will watch their babies too.

I can just see us when Misty Dawn's like twelve, still living with Mrs. Coggins, and Misty Dawn's like "Mom can I go to Suzie's house?" and I'm like "Mrs. Coggins can I go to the movies?" I don't think so.

Boy, that's weird thinking of Misty Dawn being twelve. I'll be – add twelve and fifteen – I'll be twenty-seven! I wonder what I'll be doing. No way I'll still be living with bossy Mrs. Coggins, and I won't be all bossy with Misty Dawn either. I'm going to trust her, because that's the way you have to do with kids. You gotta be friends with them so they'll talk to you.

That was the trouble with Momma before I went away with Peter. I'd tell her stuff about some cute guy and she was like, "You're too young to be thinking like that, there's plenty of time for boys, you don't need to be worrying so much about how you look, you should pay more attention to school and less attention to boys..." and blah and blah and blah. She doesn't know anything about what goes on in middle school. She would of killed me if she knew what me and Erica was doing. But maybe if I could of talked to her about that stuff I wouldn't of got fooled by Peter that way.

Only if I hadn't gone off and lived with Peter I wouldn't of had Misty Dawn. Even if I had to get beat up to have her, and even if I am still in eighth grade, I wouldn't want things different. Sometimes I think what if I didn't have her till I was older and done with school. But then it would be somebody else was the father. And then it wouldn't be Misty Dawn, I guess, but a different baby, even if I named her Misty Dawn. Which I would of, because I chose that name when I was eight. Who would my baby be if she wasn't who she is? Like who would I be if Momma married somebody besides Daddy? I wouldn't be me at all, but some other kid would be me. I'd hate that, but how could I hate it if I was never born? I get all confused when I think about this stuff, but I know one thing: maybe it wouldn't matter to Misty Dawn if she was never born, but it sure would matter to me.

Still, sitting home every night with a baby isn't any fun, and I wish I could go out sometimes. If I had a boyfriend I could do stuff. But how can I meet guys just going to school and sitting home at the Coggins'? Their son Harlan is nice but he's too old, and anyway, he's not very cute. There's guys at my school, but we never get to talk to them. Everything's separate there and I only see them in the halls. Anyway, most of them are Black. Not that there's anything wrong with that. I used to be prejudiced, but at New Beginnings practically all my friends are Black, and they're just like me. I mean, their hair is different and they talk different, but that doesn't mean very much. And they have the cutest babies!

But I've never been with a Black boy and they scare me a little. Shameka has a brother who came to school once with her mother to pick her up, and he was acting like some hot shot and flirting with everybody and later she told me he's only thirteen. I would of sworn he was nineteen at least. It looked like he even had a moustache. Anyway, if I did want to date any of the guys at school, like I said, we never get a chance to meet them.

There's a guy I've seen two times at the clinic where I get my Depo shots. He's pretty hot and he's nice to Misty Dawn – he always makes her laugh. Doesn't pay much attention to me though. Also, I don't know why he goes to the clinic, but it sure isn't for Depo shots. He had a sore on his mouth last time I saw him.

So it's Black guys at school and guys with STD's at the clinic. Better to just stay home with Misty Dawn. But sometimes I feel like it will never end. I know when I finish high school I can go to college at OCC, but that's so long. How can I stand it to live with Mrs. Coggins all that time? Some ways it was better at Momma's. She's just as bossy, but

I've known her all my life, and I can say whatever I want. I don't feel that way with Mrs. Coggins, especially when Mr. Coggins is there. I feel like I should be polite when he's around. It doesn't feel like home when you've got to be polite. But I don't think I could stand living with Bailey again. At least here I can close my door.

It's nice having all this room. It's hard to believe we lived in that garage, me and Shauna and Bailey and Momma. How did we ever stand it? When I was little it just felt normal, and we used to have a lot of fun together. Momma was nice then, not mean and tired all the time. And Bailey was okay when we were kids, even if he picked on me some. Now he's just a slob though, laying around all the time. I don't want Misty Dawn growing up around that.

I don't know if Momma would take me back anyway. She's only called me once since I moved out – it's always me calls her, and she's always in a hurry. When I tried telling her about Mrs. Coggins keeping my money, she didn't want to hear it. She says I should appreciate Mrs. Coggins taking me in, not lots of people would do that. When I tell her my problems she says, "You made your bed, Leanne." I hate when people say that, especially my own mother. I need somebody to talk to but she says she's tired of listening to me complain. I don't know. I just wish I knew how to make everything different.

Chapter Twenty-Nine

Peter came; he was drunk. I hate him. Sometimes I wish I was dead. I don't know what would of happened if the Coggins hadn't come home.

Mrs. Coggins called me about five o'clock and said they were eating out and I could heat up leftovers if I wanted, or should they bring me something? I said don't bother, I'd find something to eat. I looked at the leftovers – it was slimy Chinese food. I didn't feel like cooking eggs. I put Misty Dawn to bed and ate some toast but I was still hungry, and I remembered the moose tracks ice cream Mrs. Coggins bought for Mr. Coggins.

I don't get how they are together. They watch TV in separate rooms, and don't hardly talk to each other. She's always doing stuff for him, like bring him a beer, and he just says thank you like she's a waitress or something. I think he's mad at her, and she's trying to get him not to be. At dinner they both talk to me instead of each other. They say dumb stuff, or they ask me questions and that's worse.

Anyway, she bought this ice cream that she said is Mr. Coggins' favorite flavor. I think she means it's just for him. I don't care, they go out to eat with my money and leave me here with nothing so when I'm hungry I'll eat what I want. I got a big bowl of the ice cream, and made some popcorn, and I was watching the Disney Channel. I like it when they're not home because I'm uncomfortable around them, especially her.

I heard the front door open. I didn't think they'd be home from dinner so soon. I didn't want them to catch me in the living room, especially with the ice cream and popcorn, even though she says it's my home and I should feel free to watch TV or do whatever. I picked up the bowls fast and took them to the kitchen. I started towards the hall and oh my God Peter was standing right by the front door! I couldn't believe I forgot to lock it, but Misty Dawn was wet and bawling when we got home and I was in a hurry to change her so I must of forgot.

So there's Peter. Just him and me. Thank God Misty Dawn was in her room. He looked like a bum, like he hadn't shaved in a couple of days. He used to wash his hair every night and use this fancy conditioner. Now it was all stringy and greasy. He came over to me and grabbed my arm.

"Hey Leanne, whatcha doin?"

He stunk of booze and cigarettes and just plain dirt. I don't think I ever saw him drunk like that before.

"Let go of me. What do you want?"

"I want to see my kid."

I had to get him away from the hall cause I was afraid Misty Dawn would wake up. I didn't want him to find her.

"Come in the living room. The Coggins will be home any minute so you can't stay."

"That's too bad. I been thinking about that hot nookie of yours. I been missing it. My wife kicked me out."

I got him in the living room but he wouldn't sit down, just stood there kind of swaying. His eyes was half-closed.

"How'd you find out where I was?"

"You know, that's pretty funny, your brother told me."

"You're kidding. He'd never do that."

"Well he did. I heard him talking downtown at the plaza, bet you didn't know he hangs out there with all the bums. So he was talking about his sister and her baby, how she's living with the people who own the hardware store, and he said the baby's name, so that's how I knew. I figured I'd come check it out, see my baby."

"She's not here, she's at my mom's house tonight."

I thought that was smart, but then he said, "Okay, so we're alone" and he grabbed me again and shoved me on the couch and fell on top of me. He was rubbing hard on my crotch and it hurt. He stunk so bad.

I tried to shove him off, and I was yelling. Then thank God I heard the door open, and this time it was the Coggins. They both come in the living room.

"Whose truck is...? What's going on...? Leanne what are you doing?"

It was both of them talking at once.

"Get him off me!" By this time I was crying.

"Who is this? What's he doing here?"

"It's Peter, he just walked right in, he's trying to rape me."

"Marybeth, call the police."

"Never mind, I'm going." He walked straight past them and out the door. We heard the truck leaving.

"Leanne, are you all right?" That was Mrs. Coggins. She sounded like a mom, and that's when I really started crying. She put her arms around me.

"I'm calling the police," Mr. Coggins said.

"Please no, don't do that. You'll just make him mad and he'll come hurt me."

"But who is that?"

"That's the father, Munro. Maybe she's right, we shouldn't call. He's gone now, and no harm done."

"What if he comes back?"

"Leanne, you have to lock the door."

"I know, I always do, but...."

"Well, you didn't tonight. We probably shouldn't leave you alone here."

"He's not coming back. He was just drunk. His wife kicked him out."

"So you don't want me to call the police?"

"No."

"All right. But Leanne, you have to be more careful."

That was Mrs. Coggins. She'd started out being nice but then she's got to start scolding me, after I almost got raped.

Mr. Coggins said, "Why don't we get us some ice cream."

I didn't tell him I just had a big bowl of it, but he could probably tell when he opened the box. I said just give me a little, and we sat down the two of us at the kitchen table and ate it together. Then I said I was going to take a bath and go to bed.

I filled the tub all the way and laid there a long time. I kept trying not to think about it but it would just pop in my head, the way he smelled, and how it hurt when he grabbed my arm. I looked, but I couldn't see any bruises.

I hadn't been thinking about Peter all that much. They're supposed to go after him for child support but I never heard anything. Everything at the Coggins' house is so nice you feel safe, like nothing bad could happen there. I mean, that's why I picked their house to leave Misty Dawn. But now Peter knows where we are. I told them he wasn't coming back, but how do I know that? I wish I had a gun. I'd shoot him if he came after me again, I really would.

I got myself all dried off, then I put on my nightgown and got into bed. I was so tired but soon as I laid down I could feel him on me again, and it was like the smell was stuck in my nose. I got up and sprayed on some perfume that Momma gave me. Then I went in Misty Dawn's room. There's a night light in there so I could see her. She'd kicked off all her covers, like always. I stood there watching her chest going up and down. I felt so dirty I didn't want to touch her, but seemed like if we were together we'd both be safe. Finally I scooped her up, all floppy, and took her into my room and got in bed and snuggled down.

I can't believe Misty Dawn slept through all the fuss and yelling. I'm sure glad she did. She doesn't have any troubles at all, and I got so many.

Marybeth

Chapter Thirty

Munro had closed himself off from her. It wasn't so bad at the store, where they were busy, and could talk about orders and deliveries. But even there she missed the glances, the smiles, the little pats. She was as lonely as she'd ever been. It was never easy to get him talking, but she could always pry open the shell if she persisted. Now she couldn't get close enough to try. And Leanne was just so *there*. Even when she was in her room, Marybeth felt her hostile presence. She couldn't say anything right to Leanne, especially since she'd stopped turning the check over to her.

Leanne came into the kitchen one night while Marybeth was fixing dinner and demanded to see the savings account. She showed her the bank statement and explained the account fees. Leanne was furious.

"They're ripping me off. It's my money and I want you to give it to me."

"No, actually Leanne, it's not. Tonya has explained it to you. Look, I'll pay the account fees. I just think you should have some money saved up for when you move out on your own."

"Why are you doing this?"

"I'm just trying to help you."

"Who asked you anyway?"

And she flounced off to her room, leaving Marybeth dry-mouthed and trembling. She knew she was doing the right thing. After all, the money was hers, not Leanne's. She'd have over $4000 when she moved out. Two years. How could they possibly go on like this for two years? It was an awful lot of money. Maybe she should give Leanne more for her allowance. Or just let her have it all. Maybe that way she'd learn about managing money before she was on her own.

She felt old and tired and the beans were burning. No, too late, they were already burnt.

Dinner was glum. And the potatoes hadn't dissolved right so there were little pasty lumps. She couldn't even make instant mashed potatoes. Munro left a mound of them on his plate. Leanne chattered to him and acted as if Marybeth weren't there.

Misty in her highchair was the only cheerful one. Munro gave her a little taste of the lemon meringue pie. She closed her eyes tight, screwed up her whole face, and then in an instant her eyes and mouth popped open and she leaned eagerly toward Munro, but Leanne said no.

When Misty realized no more was coming, she bawled, putting her whole heart into it. Marybeth laughed.

"That's mean. You shouldn't laugh at her when she's crying."

"Sorry."

"I'm putting her to bed."

She took a bottle of formula from the refrigerator and heated it briefly in the microwave. Glaring at Marybeth, she carried Misty away.

"Well, I can't say it's easy having them here, but that baby is a pure treat."

But Munro had shut down as soon as Leanne left the room. He silently cleared the table and began emptying the dishwasher.

"You want me to help?"

"No thanks. I'll do it."

Marybeth went into the living room and picked up her Southern Living magazine. It was last month's issue, but she could look at the pictures over and over without getting tired of them. Munro came in, saw her, and started back out again.

"Did you want the TV, honey?"

"No, that's alright. You're reading."

"Oh, it won't bother me. If it does, I can always go back in the bedroom."

"Well, I can watch in the bedroom."

"No, no, you watch here on the big set, where you can be comfortable. I'll probably go to bed soon anyway."

"Thank you."

He turned on the Stanley Cup playoffs. Munro didn't usually watch hockey, but it didn't bother her. It was nice to hear voices with some life in them. What bothered her was sitting on the couch with her magazine, Munro off in the corner in his recliner. The other recliner was hers, but she felt too timid to sit in it. Before Leanne, this was one of their favorite times, sitting side by side watching TV, reaching over to squeeze hands. Sometimes Munro would make popcorn. When one or the other dozed off, they'd both go to bed. Now he never came to bed until she was asleep.

She went on looking at the magazine, but the gardens of Montgomery didn't interest her. Leanne came in with a bag of chips from her stash and sat down next to Munro in Marybeth's recliner. It would be silly to protest. Instead, she yawned loudly. "Well, I think I'll go to bed." Leanne ignored her, Munro glanced up and nodded.

It was almost midnight when Munro came in and undressed by the bathroom light. They had always slept wrapped up together, but now he slipped into bed and kept to the far side, with his back to her. Tonight she couldn't stand it anymore, and she moved over to embrace him from behind.

"I'm tired, Marybeth."

Her feelings were hurt, and she was angry. She lay in that stew for a long time. They'd been sleeping smashed up against each other for over thirty years. If he didn't want to touch her, he should sleep somewhere else. Over two months of sulking. Everything he'd ever done to annoy her came back, followed by spiteful thoughts of how he was aging. How many times had she gone along with him when she didn't want to? Thirty years of vacations at the beach, though she'd told him plenty of times how she'd like to go on a cruise. When he'd wanted to paint the house that ugly gray, she'd argued with him, but he'd dug in his heels. It looked awful, but she got over it before the painters had pulled down their ladders. He insisted they invite Cousin Jared every Thanksgiving, and she agreed, though she could hardly bear to look at him, a silent hulk sucking out energy like a hole in a photograph. Jared, the one they'd always had to include when they were kids, who didn't like to play girls' games or play rough, didn't like to do anything but tag along, breath whistling in his nose. She'd put up with him for years without complaining and always been kind to him, though Munro claimed he didn't come for Thanksgiving anymore because he didn't feel welcome. She could make a list of grievances if she wanted, but she'd never held on to them, or held out on Munro. Sleeping snuggled kept you loving even when things weren't going well.

She sometimes wondered how either one would survive without the other. Thought of old people in nursing homes who were never touched, except by an aide. No wonder they died. Could this be the end of touching for her? Surely he couldn't hold out for the rest of their lives. In the moonlight that came in around the edge of the shade, she could see him curled into himself and away from her. What a mess she had gotten them into.

Chapter Thirty-One

She woke up late the next morning from a dream of shame and loneliness. Munro and Leanne were both gone. She breathed easier with nobody hostile in the house. She had time for a walk or the newspaper, but not both, and against her better judgment chose the paper. It did nothing for her mood. Chaos all over the middle east, promises of democracy, predictions of disaster. She thought it would be the latter, but it was all too complicated for her to follow. The names alone were enough to muddle her. So she didn't read any of the international news but the headlines, and then went straight to the local section. When the phone rang, she had almost finished the comics.

"Mother, this is Ruth."

"Oh, Ruthie. Mun's already left."

"I already talked to Daddy. I'm calling for you."

"Well, that's nice. How's Scotty? How are you feeling?"

"Scotty's fine. I'm fine. Look, I want to come over and talk, and I wondered if we could have lunch tomorrow."

"But I can't just leave the store in the middle of the day."

"Daddy said he could handle it for the afternoon while you and I visit. Scotty can stay with Jessica."

Something terrible must be happening. But Ruthie sounded so calm and in charge, with even a lunch menu arranged, saying she'd bring over corn chowder and homemade bread. Anyway, if something were wrong, the last person Ruthie would call was Marybeth.

Munro pretended to be casual about it, as though she and Ruthie had lunch every week. He wouldn't tell her anything. She fretted, imagining various conversations of recrimination, confession, forgiveness. It grieved her to be in such a tangle about her own daughter. Once, in the most vicious time of Ruthie's adolescence, she had seen a mother and her grown daughter shopping for shoes, joking and laughing like best friends. She wished they could be like that. But here she was all fussed up about a simple lunch.

Ruthie arrived promptly at noon. Marybeth had set up TV trays on the deck. The chowder was delicious, but the bread was tough and too full of seeds for her taste. Ruthie listened patiently as Marybeth expounded on her garden plans.

"I want to put something tall and orange in there behind the day lilies. Maybe Mexican sunflowers. What do you think?"

"That would be very nice. I wish I had your green thumb, Mother. Steve does our landscaping, but he doesn't really have time, and he doesn't love gardening the way you do."

Marybeth had tried to share the garden with Ruthie when she was small, giving her a little sunny bed of her own. But Ruthie had an aversion to worms and bugs and dirt. When visitors asked Marybeth to show them around the garden, Ruthie sat sneering on the deck. Marybeth had once overheard her talking to her best friend.

"Mother spends all her time in the garden. I don't know why Daddy puts up with it. She could pay a service to keep it nice, then maybe she'd have time to learn to cook."

But today Ruthie praised the garden and offered to bring Marybeth a second bowl of soup.

"I know you don't like these whole grain breads, Mother. Should I toast some white for you?"

It was hard to relax and enjoy it. She was waiting to find out why Ruthie was here. As they were drinking tea and eating Ruthie's oatmeal cookies she finally got down to it.

"I'm worried about Daddy, Mother."

"Why? Has he been talking to you?"

"Well, I've been taking training in pastoral counseling. I guess he felt he couldn't talk to you, and he's so unhappy."

"You mean you're giving him marriage counseling?"

"No, no. Reverend Gerber says that wouldn't be appropriate at all, because we're family. But he's called me a couple of times, just to talk."

"Did he ask you to talk to me?"

"No, it was my idea. He wasn't sure I should. But I'm worried about you both."

Neither spoke for a little while. Marybeth didn't plan to discuss her marriage with her daughter, even if she *was* becoming a pastoral counselor.

She was on her third cookie when Ruthie asked, "How is that baby doing?"

"She's just adorable. She's sitting up by herself. She likes to play peekaboo, and babbles all the time. She's very alert, watching everything that goes on."

"That first year is fun. You have a different baby every week."

"I never liked that stage. I was so tired. It was scary having this little creature who couldn't tell me what she needed, and at the same time it was boring. I liked kids better when they started talking. But Misty is awful cute, and maybe because she's not mine, and Leanne takes good care of her, I don't worry too much. I think maybe she's a born mother, not like me."

"So, you're enjoying the baby."

"I guess so. But a baby in the house changes everything. Well, you know that. And a teenager in the house!"

Not that Leanne was anything like Ruthie. Leanne was stormy, sullen or voluble as the moods blew through. Ruthie had been quiet and deadly, emerging from her privacy to deliver a single venomous remark and then slither away.

"I bet it was tough having three teenagers in the house. I think about that sometimes. We're planning to have three, you know. I don't know how good I'll be with teenagers."

"Nobody's good with teenagers."

"You were. You let us say what we thought. I'm not sure I could do that."

"I don't know any way to stop it. The back talk is the least of it. The things the boys would do! I hid the car keys, but they had already made copies. You were different. I don't think you ever did anything wrong. People used to tell me how lucky I was with you. But the mouth on you!"

Ruthie looked away and poured herself another cup of tea.

"What about Leanne? Is she getting into any trouble?"

"Not as far as I know. The baby keeps her busy. And DFC tells me she's doing well in school. She picks up after herself too, though she doesn't pitch in on anything else. I can't even say she's ugly to me, at least not in anything she says. Oh, we've had a couple of arguments. She thinks I'm stealing her money. And I can't ask her anything, she thinks I'm prying. Most of the time she doesn't talk much. I don't even know how to describe it. It's just the way she looks at me."

"It sounds awful."

"Well, she pretty much keeps to herself when it's just us. She'll come out when Munro gets home, and of course we eat dinner together. She talks at dinner, mostly about the people on TV, from those reality shows she watches after she puts Misty down. Munro gets a kick out of the baby. But it's having this hostile presence in the house, even if we hardly see her. It wears me down."

"It's hard on Daddy, too, I guess."

"I suppose he's been talking to you about it."

"Not really very much."

"But you said he called you a couple of times."

"He did. He didn't tell me any big secrets or anything. A lot of what he says is just what you've been saying, about having a baby and a teenager in the house again. I don't think you know, Mother, how much he loves you. He said he was so happy when we all left home and it was just the two of you. It almost hurt my feelings."

Almost, but not quite, thought Marybeth. You like to have Munro confiding in you. But Ruthie didn't seem to be gloating. And Marybeth wanted her to understand what it was like.

"He won't tell me anything now, won't talk to me. I get the silent treatment from both of them. The only time I feel relaxed is when I go out walking in the morning. I don't mind being alone; what I hate is when I'm home and he's home and I'm alone anyway."

"But I don't understand why you let it go on like this."

"What can I do? Leanne doesn't have any place else to go. This way she can keep the baby and eventually take care of things on her own, when she's older."

"But she's not your responsibility."

"I'm surprised to hear you say that. I mean, you're so religious, what about, *am I my brother's keeper*?"

"Everybody quotes that like the answer is yes, but it was just Cain being sarcastic. If you want to go to the Bible, you need to look at where the Lord tells us that a wife should be subject to her husband in all things."

"We have different views on that, Ruthie. Munro and I are partners, neither one of us is boss."

"I know that's how you see it, but that's the whole problem. It's okay to be business partners, but you can't have partners in a marriage. If you want to know, I think you and Daddy would have been a whole lot better off if you had signed the whole store over to him when you got married. Then things would be clearer between you. You have to have someone in charge, and the Bible tells us it's the husband."

How had Ruthie ever turned out like this? She didn't get it from Marybeth. She certainly didn't get it from Munro, who never even went to church.

"You sound like my Aunt Bethany. She tried to convince your grandma not to let me have the store. She had a fit when I went back to work after you were born."

"Well, Mother, she was right. Don't you see how messed up everything is now? Used to be, children were raised by their parents, and people stayed married. Reverend Gerber says all the drugs and crime and poverty are because women have forgotten their true role. Maybe it sounds like a cliche, but we need to go back to the old days."

"How old is Reverend Gerber anyway? Does he have any idea what things were like in what you call the old days? I know how it was: plenty of drinking and beatings and messing around, and those women were trapped."

"Oh, Mother, I didn't come here to talk about history or listen to a lot of feminist stuff from you. I saw how you did, and I've seen some of the girls I was friends with in high school. It's all about selfishness, if you ask me, everybody putting themselves first."

This was more like the old Ruthie.

"So you're saying I'm selfish because I gave a home to Leanne and the baby?"

"It wasn't your home to give, Mother. It was one more of your do-gooder things, save the world but forget about your own family, like when you were on the Commission. I can't believe Daddy let you do that. It took over both your lives and you pretended it was to help the community, but it was all about you wanting to be a big shot."

"You have absolutely no idea about my time on the Commission, or how I got there. That was something Munro and I decided together. We wanted somebody there looking out for local businesses. And Munro thought I'd be better at it – he doesn't have any patience for committees and meetings and such. There were things I liked about it, but Lord knows I wasn't being selfish. Ask your father what it was like for us then. Sometimes I felt like I'd fallen into a river and was heading toward the rapids."

Ruthie's eyes were shut, her head low. She couldn't have fallen asleep. But then she whispered, "Amen," and looked up again.

"Mother, I'm sorry. I've been praying for guidance. I shouldn't have said those ugly things about you. I'm sure you did the best you knew how. Daddy says you both put us children first, and maybe there's a lot I don't know. I only know how it looked to me growing up, and now being married myself. I've learned a lot from Reverend Gerber and the counseling program. The single most important thing is to put

Jesus first in your life, and then your marriage second, before the kids, before either one of you."

"Ruthie, I can't believe you've been talking about me and Munro with your pastor. He doesn't know anything about us, and I'm beginning to think you don't know anything about us either."

"I didn't go in to talk to him about you and Daddy's problems, if that's what you think. But in our counseling classes we all talk about what we've seen in our parents' marriages."

"Oh my God, that's even worse. What about our privacy?"

"It doesn't go outside the class. We all promise to keep everything confidential, like we're already counselors. And lots of the students have much more terrible stuff to talk about than me. Would you believe there's eight of us in the program and only two of us have parents who are still married."

"And you'd like to keep it that way."

"Well of course I would!" Ruthie was genuinely upset. "This didn't go like I planned. I said things I shouldn't. I guess Reverend Gerber was right that you can't do counseling in your own family. But Daddy's so unhappy, and I thought I could help. I wish you'd just think about it."

"Well, thanks for saying you're sorry. You know, nobody looking at a marriage from the outside really knows what it's like. Maybe I'm wrong to say you're on the outside, but when you're little you don't understand, and then when you leave home you don't know what goes on."

"Children understand a lot more than you think. But we don't need to argue about it. I'm praying for you both, Mother."

"Do you want some coffee before you drive home?"

"No, I gave up coffee again when I got pregnant. I wish I could stay off it for good. I'm praying on that too."

After Ruthie left, it didn't take long to tidy the kitchen. She was at the store by 2:30. Munro didn't ask about Ruthie.

"Things are pretty slow. I think I'll take the afternoon. I'll take care of dinner." And he was gone.

It *was* slow. She sat doing the quarterly sales tax in the back room, where she'd hear the bell if somebody came in, but she couldn't focus on work.

How long had it been since she spent that much time alone with Ruthie? Probably not since that day they had tried to plan Ruthie's wedding, and what a disaster that had been! Maybe Ruthie had had a fantasy of a mother just like she'd had a fantasy of a daughter. She had shown up with magazines, catalogs and a wedding planner list, and left the house in tears two hours later.

That was six years ago. She had certainly changed a lot. Unbelievable to hear her apologize. Maybe Marybeth had something to apologize for too. Her friend Patsy used to say she couldn't cry, because if she started, she'd never be able to stop. That's what it would be like if she started apologizing to Ruthie. She never could do right by her. It was like asking a robin to raise a rabbit.

She had met Reverend Gerber and his wife when Scotty was baptized. Mrs. Gerber looked whipped, and Marybeth would bet she was. It made her itch to think of that sanctimonious little man talking about her and Munro. The whole group of them training to be counselors, listening to Ruthie's version of their marriage.

Was it true what Ruthie said, that children know what's going on? Bits and pieces maybe. But she had puzzled over her own parents, tried to imagine what it was like for them. She thought her father surely couldn't be happy with all the complaining and nagging, but they stayed together till he died. Ruthie probably saw Munro the way she saw her own father: a wonderful daddy who deserved better than what he got.

Always ready to doubt herself, she had wondered for a moment if Ruthie was right. Maybe she should have signed the store over to Munro, stayed home and raised kids. But it was only a moment. One thing she knew was how happy she and Mun were together and how he was behind her in whatever she wanted to do. Especially those years on the Commission.

Taking in Leanne though, he wasn't behind her in that. She couldn't blame him. She had told Ruthie they were partners, nobody the boss, and it was true. But partners don't give away the store unless they both agree. No wonder he'd backed off and shut down. He was as miserable as she was, both of them alone after thirty-five years. If he'd been able to talk to her, he never would have talked to Ruthie. Maybe it was good that he had.

Ruthie was changing. It was a mistake to play counsellor with your own mother, but she'd done fine at the beginning until the real Ruthie slipped out. Maybe Marybeth didn't know the real Ruthie. Her friends didn't think of her as Ruthie-with-the-terrible-mother. That was just a teeny part of her.

Marybeth struggled to see some truth she hadn't understood. Ruthie was a whole person, not put on earth to fret her, not a reflection of her own mistakes, nor waiting to become somebody, but already done, as much as any of us can say we are done. Was it possible for Marybeth to know her now? Even to be friends with her? Ruthie had put down the knives for a good part of the morning. But could she accept Ruthie? She'd never have chosen her for a friend – she tried to avoid a certain type of Christian. But she was family.

Now here she was trying to make somebody else family. It wasn't because Leanne was so appealing. She was just so needy, and where else could she go? Chance brought them together and then each little step led to the next. Leanne was hungry so she fed her, needed a ride so she drove her, needed a lawyer so she found one. And now she was responsible for the girl's whole life! Was it a Chinese proverb – if you save a life you're responsible for it from then on? Did that mean in China they just let someone drown for fear of taking on a burden? She hadn't saved a life, but she had meddled.

Would it be wrong to back out? She'd never said how long Leanne could stay. Maybe Ruthie was right. She owed more to Munro than to Leanne. But where would the two of them go? Back to Vinnie probably, and then lose the baby. It was all such a mess and a muddle. She couldn't stand thinking about it anymore.

She started in on the taxes again, but fortunately three customers came in, followed by a little run of business. She could leave the taxes and stop chewing on her troubles.

When she got home, Munro's car was in the driveway, but there were no signs of dinner. Maybe he was taking a nap. She went back to the bedroom to find him, but he wasn't there. As she entered the living room, she saw him. He was sitting on the couch, facing the picture window. The blinds were open, but he wasn't looking out. He sat hunched over, elbows on his knees, head in his hands.

"Munro, what are you doing?"

He didn't move.

"Mun, what is it?"

"It's nothing."

"But you're sitting there like a zombie."

"Look. I'm trying to work things out."

"What things?"

"Marybeth, we can't go on like this. I don't even want to come home after work. Don't you see what you've done?"

It was true. She didn't want to come home either, to the stranger in their house, to Munro's cold distance.

"You talk like it's all my fault. I've done everything I can to make it better. Here we're eating out together every week and I thought that could be so nice, but you hardly open your mouth then except to shove food in it."

She heard the hall door, and the kitchen light came on.

"Leanne, I haven't made dinner yet. Hold on just a minute."

"We need to finish this, Marybeth," Munro said grimly.

She went into the kitchen, where Leanne was strapping Misty into her highchair.

"The store got busy, and time just slipped away from me. Look, Munro and I have some work to do. Why don't you just fix yourself a sandwich or something."

"Sure." It was amazing how much resentment she could pack into one word.

They went into the bedroom. Her mouth was dry. What did he mean by *finish this*? Where was the end? She sat up on the bed against the pillows, but Munro didn't join her. He took the chair in the corner.

He'd started it; he should say something. But Munro was silent, staring at his hands. Marybeth looked at the clock: 6:48. She waited for the eight to become a nine. Wouldn't think about what was coming. She didn't want to begin. But the minute lasted forever, and still Munro didn't speak.

"You want to talk, but you don't say anything."

He looked at her. Took a breath, but then let it out. She waited.

Finally, he said, "I can't live like this. It was tough when Ruthie was young, but this is worse. I don't feel like I have a home anymore."

"What does Ruthie have to do with it? I can't believe you've been talking to her about us, and then getting her over here to counsel me. Anyway, Leanne is nothing like Ruthie."

"No, she's not. But you don't hear me, Marybeth. I want our home back."

"I don't know what you want me to do. You talk like it's up to me to fix it, but you're not even trying."

"You took her in without asking me and now you want me to just swallow it."

"I guess I do. You've been sulking for over three months. You won't talk with me, won't touch me. It's a lot worse for me; at least she's civil to you. The only time she says more than a word to me is when she's arguing. And she acts like I should be waiting on her. When I said I wasn't making dinner she gave me such a look. So don't talk like it's all your problem."

"Wait. Hold on. Let's start over. That's just right – it's not mine and it's not yours, it's ours. And I guess it doesn't matter whose fault it is, we need to figure out what to do."

She felt every tight muscle relax. This was how they usually did, thanks to Munro. He could almost always turn a fight into a problem to solve together, both of them on the same side. Probably the whole mess was her doing, though she still thought it would work better if he'd just stop sulking about it. But he was right. What they needed to do was fix it.

"Do you think there's any way to make this work?"

"I don't. She's from a whole different world, and we don't love her. We got through the tough times with Ruthie because she was ours. But this one...."

"It doesn't help when you keep bringing up Ruthie. That was an awful time, and she never was with you like she was with me. Still is, for that matter."

"Okay, let's stay away from Ruthie, for now at least. But tell me the truth, do you want to keep them here?"

She'd gotten them into it and planned to let Leanne stay until she was eighteen. But maybe she could get her life back. Still, what would Leanne do? Vinnie wouldn't take her back. And even if DFC would allow it, how could she possibly live on her own?

"She's not your responsibility, Marybeth."

"I'm just afraid they'll take away the baby."

"And would that be so terrible? Don't you think Misty needs a grown mother, and a father?"

"Misty's got a mother. I know she's young, but you can see how she loves the baby."

"That's true."

"And she's good with her – responsible, I mean."

"We're getting off track. It's not up to us to decide if Leanne should keep Misty. Maybe she should, maybe she shouldn't, but it's not our problem."

"We need to give her some time."

"Of course. You have to talk with DFC anyway. I'm not saying we kick her out before they have a place for her to go."

"Do you think they'll let her live on her own with the baby?"

"I don't know. I don't know anything about all that. I don't see how she could afford it."

"Well, but there's welfare."

"And how much is that? $267 a month, didn't you say?"

"I don't know, maybe she can get a job. But it's hard, on her own with the baby and school and all."

Now they were both quiet, waiting for it to sink in, the possibility that they could undo what Marybeth had done.

"What is it, Maybeth?"

She had turned her face away from him. The tears were so close. Hearing her pet name again almost brought them on.

"I don't know. It's such a relief. But I feel like I don't deserve to be relieved, like I should have made this all come out right, do better than I did with Ruthie. I don't know how to be a mother. I'm just no good with girls."

"That's ridiculous. You're not her mother. And even her mother can't handle her. From what you've said, it sounds like she has as hard a time as you did with Ruthie."

"You think I failed with Ruthie, don't you?"

She knew he was thinking hard, choosing how to say it.

"I think it's too bad you two still can't get along."

"But what can I do? She just hates me, picks at me."

"Do you like her?"

"Mun, I don't know. She's so self-righteous. You know how I feel about people who think they know the truth. But today it was like there were two Ruthies. She started out nice, like she wanted to be friends, then she got ugly fast. I'm trying to figure out if we can change. She did apologize, and I've never heard her do that before!"

"It's hurtful for both of you, fussing at each other. I think Ruthie is changing. Maybe she just understands you better now that Scotty's becoming such a handful."

"Well, like my dad used to say, with family you've got a whole lifetime to work it out."

"I hope you'll be able to. I'll help any way I can. Now, what do we do about Leanne?"

"I guess I'd better throw in the towel. I'll call DFC tomorrow and see what they say."

Chapter Thirty-Two

Leanne's case worker had quit. The new worker was in training and unavailable. Marybeth left a message for the supervisor. Driving home from the store, she thought about how to tell Leanne. She'd wait until she'd talked to somebody at DFC. She wondered whether she should call Vinnie first but decided against it.

When she got home, Leanne and Misty were on the floor in the living room. The television was on, but they were absorbed in each other. Marybeth stood in the kitchen, watching them. Bright toys lay scattered across the carpet. Leanne threw a red rubber monkey a few feet away, and Misty crawled to get it. She sat up, gripping it in her fist, examined it carefully, and began gnawing on it, rolling her eyes towards Leanne.

"Misty Dawn, what do you think, that's a lollipop?"

The baby dropped the toy, scrambled over to her mother, and began pulling herself up by Leanne's waistband, T-shirt, and breasts. She managed to stand with a final yank on Leanne's hair, and Leanne squealed, "Ow, ow, ow." Misty laughed. Leanne untangled her fist, and she toppled over.

"She'll be walking any day now."

Leanne stood up, looking alarmed.

"I'm sorry, I didn't think you'd be home so early. I'll clean it up." She began shoving the toys into a shopping bag.

"No, stay out here. The living room's a great place to play as long as we watch her, and I vacuumed two days ago, so there's not too much stuff on the carpet. Do you mind if I join you?"

Misty obviously didn't mind. She crawled to Marybeth, grabbed her pants, and pulled herself up.

"I bet she'll be walking soon."

"She is so bright."

"Yeah, and she's got a second tooth coming. She was screaming and screaming last night. Did you hear her?"

"No, our bedroom is too far away. I'm having a glass of tea before I start dinner. Would you like some?"

"No thanks. Could I have a Coke?"

Leanne was being so pleasant, and it was fun watching her with Misty. Maybe it could work out for her to stay here. But as soon as she thought it, she felt the weight descend again.

She'd been feeling light-hearted all day, despite the aggravation of DFC, despite the crowd of people driven into the store by a sudden heavy rain. A young woman in a tan suit quizzed Munro for twenty minutes about different models of rider mowers. Then she thanked him profusely for his help and said, "I'll check the prices at Housemart. They're putting them on sale this weekend, but the salesclerks there don't know much."

Munro made a face at Marybeth, but then squeezed her shoulder and smiled. They were back on the same side, and she wouldn't let that wall between them go up again for anything.

Maybe she should talk to Leanne now. She poured tortilla chips into a bowl, got out the jar of salsa, and put it all on a tray with their drinks.

"Ooh, thanks. I love those. I'll get the playpen so Misty Dawn won't be getting into them."

"Do you mind if I turn off the TV?"

"No, I wasn't really watching."

Leanne rolled the playpen in and settled Misty in it with the toys and a teething biscuit.

How to start? She could ask her about school but that usually made her clam up. They sat eating too many chips for a couple of minutes. Then, surprisingly, Leanne spoke.

"I'm getting an award at school."

"That's wonderful! What's it for?"

"I designed a web page for them, so Mr. Belmont says I'm getting a service award."

"You must have learned a lot about computers. I wouldn't have any idea how to make a web page."

"Oh, it's easy. You just gotta know how to use Illustrator and GoLive, and Mr. Belmont's been showing me that in my free period. But he says it's not just the programs. You gotta have a creative eye. You can go online and see it if you want."

"I'll do that tomorrow at the store, if I have time."

"You ought to get a computer at home, you know."

"That's what Munro says. But I'm afraid I'll get into shopping on the internet and it will get out of control. There's a woman at my church who ran up over $40,000 with eleven different credit cards, and she's talking about filing for bankruptcy. I'd rather just have it at the store, where I don't have so much time to get into trouble."

"I could use it for my homework, though. And if you get Adobe, and you want me to, I could make you a web page for the store."

Oh dear. This was as good a time as any.

"Leanne, I need to talk to you about something."

"What?"

"Well, I've been thinking... I mean, Munro thinks... really, both of us. It's just, having you and the baby here, it's not working out."

"It is too. What's wrong with it? I didn't do anything."

"No, of course not. It's not anything you've done. We just... we're used to being alone. It's a long time since we had a baby in the house."

"But you said you couldn't even hear her. This is the first time I let her play in the living room, I swear. And I won't do it again if you don't want."

"It's nothing about playing in the living room. I told you, that's fine. We love Misty and she's fun to have around."

"Well then how come you say it's not working out? You want us out of here, don't you? Where am I supposed to go?"

"Oh dear, I meant to talk to you after I talked to DFC. Did you know you have a new worker? Phyllis is gone."

"You mean you called them already, and didn't even talk to me?"

"I wanted to know what your options are before I talked to you."

"So, what are they?"

"I don't know, I didn't get to talk to anyone, I had to leave a message."

"You can't just put us out of here, you know. They're paying you for me to stay here. And they won't let you put a baby out on the street."

"You know I wouldn't put her out on the street."

"But you'd put me out, you mean."

"No, of course not. I'm just saying we need to find a different arrangement, a different place for you to live. You'd stay here till there's somewhere else for you to go. Maybe your mother will have some ideas. Maybe you could even move back in there."

"No way I'll live there again. I don't even have my own room there."

"There's a place, I don't remember the name, where girls can live with their babies while they go to school."

"You mean Mary's Place. Kesia stayed there a couple months. It's terrible – they have all these rules and they want to know all about your business. Kesia says they're like spies for DFC, to see if you take care of your baby right, and all they want to do is get your baby for somebody to adopt."

"Well, that certainly wouldn't affect you. You're wonderful with Misty."

"I don't care, I'm not living in a place like that."

"I'm sure something can be worked out. We just need to hear back from DFC."

"I still don't get it. You said I could live here till I finish school. You're getting paid plenty. It's not like I'm taking up a lot of room, I mean, you weren't using those rooms anyway. It doesn't make sense, and it's not fair."

She grabbed Misty out of the playpen and rushed back to her room, slamming the hall door. Marybeth drank the melted ice. It was such a relief to have Leanne in her room, out of sight. She hadn't started crying till just at the end. A baby and no place to go - how would that feel? They said a lot of families with children were homeless now. Anyway, Leanne wasn't going to be homeless. They certainly wouldn't just put her out on the street.

When she heard Munro's car, she went to meet him outside and told him.

"That must have been tough. How did she take it?"

"She was mad. I guess she's scared."

"Poor kid. Why don't I take you out to dinner and give her some time alone."

"I'd love that. I can't imagine us all eating together. It will be tough getting through the next few days."

"Honey, I think it will take more than a few days for DFC to find her a place and get her moved out."

Leanne

Chapter Thirty-Three

I've got my own apartment! There's a bedroom for me and Misty Dawn and a living room, kitchen and bathroom. You can see woods from the bedroom window. That creeps me out because there's homeless guys living in the woods. That guy who murdered two girls, he was homeless. But it's pretty, to see the trees out the window, and Momma says most homeless guys are okay.

I was really surprised the way it all worked out. It turns out Mrs. Coggins isn't as nice as she pretends to be. She went behind my back and called DFC without even telling me. I don't know what she said, but this guy Jonathan came and talked to me. Phyllis doesn't work there anymore. He said they'd give me one last chance. I could try living on my own, and he would help me find an apartment. I could tell he doesn't think I can do it.

After Jonathan came, Mrs. Coggins was trying to be all nicey-nice and saying she'd help me any way she could and it just wasn't working out. I didn't say it but I'm thinking how it would of worked fine if she hadn't tried to run my life. It's not like I was a slob or stealing stuff or anything like that. I think she was jealous because Mr. Coggins likes me. I wasn't doing anything to lead him on but I think he thinks I'm cute. Not that I would ever of done anything with him – he's too old for me.

I didn't know how I'd find an apartment. All I had was this list of addresses. But then Miss Bradwell called and said Misty Dawn has to have a guardian, which I didn't understand. I thought a guardian was when a rich kid's parents die. She said the guardian works for the judge, and it's her job to find out about me, how I'm doing at school and everything, and tell the judge what should happen with Misty Dawn. She's like a snoop for the judge. I said I'm her mother, she doesn't need no guardian. But Miss Bradwell said I don't have any choice.

It made me mad. I expected some bossy old lady like Mrs. Coggins, but this girl Jennifer called and came over and it turned out she's not a lot older than me. She's in college. She asked me how I do this and how I do that, and she said I'm doing a good job with Misty Dawn. She says it's hard to raise a baby when you're in school. She doesn't think she could do it half as good as me. So she said she could help me find an apartment, and a few days later she had all this information. I can get Section 8 and I can rent from anybody who takes the voucher. The best part is I don't have to pay any rent at all!

Next day Jennifer took me to this office. I filled out a gajillion forms, and we went looking for apartments. All the nicest ones were too far from the bus line, Jennifer said. She's probably right. Even the one I found will take two buses to get to school, and that means leaving earlier and getting home later.

So here we are in our very own home. It's just been three days. Mr. Coggins moved my stuff on Sunday in the store truck. It didn't take very long, because all I have is Misty Dawn's things and my clothes. I need furniture and kitchen stuff and everything. Jennifer says St Xavier's Mercy Mission can give me whatever I need.

I got a cell phone, and I called Opakulla Electric to get my electric and water turned on. They want a $125 deposit and they said the electric in that apartment costs about $85 a month. That's in the spring and fall, when you're not using heat and air. I'll keep the air conditioner off as much as I can, but last night it was so hot I had to get up and take a shower.

Good thing I have some money. It turns out Mrs. Coggins was saving my checks for me like she said. She paid for all the baby food and diapers and stuff herself. I guess except for being so bossy she was pretty nice to me. I have $660, so I can pay the deposits and still have a lot left over. Momma brought over sheets and towels and some dishes, and she made up a bag of dish soap and toilet paper and all the things you can't buy with food stamps. She said she'd look out for things for me at garage sales. She wants to take me to Goodwill, too, to get things, but I want to wait and see what Mercy Mission brings.

It's weird being all alone, with just Misty Dawn. I'm not sure I like it – it's a little scary. At night there's noises, creaks and squeals and rattles, and in between it's too quiet. I wish I had a TV. Last night I woke Misty Dawn up to keep me company, but that was dumb because she was all cranky and crying. I wanted her to sleep with me but without a bed it's hard on the floor. Good thing there's carpet.

My building has eight apartments, but I've only seen two neighbors. Right across from me there's a foreign guy. He looks like an Arab except he doesn't wear that thing on his head. He said hi to me, but I didn't say anything. He could be a terrorist. He has a cool car though, a red Mustang. Next to me there's Stacy with a four-year-old and a baby. The first day, I asked if I could use her phone but she was real unfriendly and said it wasn't working. It's too bad because I could use a friend around here.

Misty Dawn is good company when she's awake – she says Momma now when before she would just say dada and it made me mad. I don't think she knows what it means though. Miss Melanie says it will be a little longer before she attaches words to what they mean. But she knows I'm her Momma. When she sees me she gets a big smile, but with everybody else she just stares. Except Mr. Coggins, he made her laugh. And she smiled at the foreign guy too. Maybe she likes men.

Only thing is, I got nothing to do. Even if I miss the first bus out of school I'm home by 5. Then Misty Dawn's ready for her dinner, and after that we play. She has her bath and a story, and she's in bed by 7:30. Homework takes me about an hour, and then I got nothing to do.

I wish I had a TV. You only get two channels without cable but one of them is Fox, and they have most of the cool shows. Living at the Coggins I missed a lot of my shows. So I hope Mercy Mission will come soon and bring a TV.

If I was friends with Stacy I could go over there and watch TV after Misty Dawn's in bed. I know I could hear her because I can hear Stacy through the wall, with both doors closed, yelling at her baby when it cries. It's dumb to yell at a baby. It's not like they can understand you, and it just makes them cry more. At first I thought me and her could babysit for each other sometimes, but I don't think I want her taking care of Misty Dawn. Besides, it wouldn't be fair, because she's got two kids and I've only got one.

Anyway, what do I need a sitter for? I wish I had some friends. Jennifer's cool, and I asked if she wanted to go out some time, but she said she can't because she works for the judge. It seemed like she was looking for a reason to say no. She probably thinks I'm too young, or maybe she thinks she's too good for me, her being in college. But she doesn't act snotty.

Vinnie

Chapter Thirty-Four

Vinnie had taken the day off, but she woke up early anyway and went into the kitchen to make coffee. From the kitchen door she could see the lump that was Bailey, but he didn't move.

Out on the deck it was light enough to see shapes, but no colors yet. The birds were starting, still tentative. The air was cool and damp. She could watch the sun rise, then work in the garden awhile before the heat got too much. The party at Leanne's school wasn't till two.

She didn't miss Leanne, exactly, but she would like to have Misty here with her. Funny how a baby got to you. She could feel her snuggled up on her chest, see her wet smile. A baby was a wonderful way to start the day, even if sometimes it started a little early. It was all those years of babies that had given her the habit of early mornings.

With Leanne in her own place, maybe she'd see more of her and Misty. She had only visited a couple of times over at the Coggins'. She felt like an intruder, shy to take the glass of tea that Leanne poured for her. She felt like somebody would come home and catch them there. But one time she went over when Marybeth was home, and she couldn't have been more welcoming. She had bought cookies and made fresh tea with mint. She said she'd planted some of the mint that Vinnie had given her, and of course it was taking over the bed. She wanted to give Vinnie some to take with her, but Vinnie laughed and said she had her own troubles.

It was nice, sitting on the couch, looking out at the garden, passing around Misty and the cookies. Marybeth showed Vinnie her seed catalogs. She called them her wish books. Even better, she had brochures for garden tours, in Louisiana, Virginia, and even one in

England. She said she could never go, because she and Munro couldn't leave the store. But she liked to think about it.

Vinnie wouldn't be seeing Marybeth anymore, now that Leanne was living on her own. It was a shame the way Leanne talked about her, like she'd been doing Marybeth a favor by living with them. She'd like to talk with Marybeth, let her know that she appreciated it, but she felt she needed an excuse to call her. Then it occurred to her that she could invite her to the end of school party, to see Leanne get her award. It might be a bad idea – Leanne could be rude and embarrass them all. But Marybeth would know that, so she could decide. Vinnie would call her at the store.

It was 7:30. She had time to work in the garden. The side bed was shady and damp, and the mosquitos were in charge in the early morning. But the front bed was drier, and she had plenty to do there to keep her busy. She put on repellent anyway, in case any bugs decided to leave the jungle and go exploring.

Marybeth was delighted to be asked to the school party. "Let me check with the boss and see if I can get the afternoon off." It was a joke, of course. It must be nice to take off whenever you wanted. John let her take off whenever she asked, she just couldn't afford it very often. She could probably even get a couple of weeks to go on a garden tour, if she ever had the money.

She picked up Marybeth at 1:30. She'd never been to the school, but Marybeth knew where it was. As they got out of the car, Vinnie began to get nervous. How would Leanne react when she saw them?

All the students were seated in the auditorium, grouped by program. Eleven girls from New Beginnings were there with their babies. Vinnie and Marybeth agreed that Misty was the cutest one. Leanne looked around the room and to Vinnie's relief, she waved.

It was a good thing that New Beginnings came first in the program. Although the babies were entertaining, it was clear that none of them would last long. There were twenty-three awards for only eleven girls, and it looked like everybody got at least one. Each girl had to walk up to the stage with her baby to get her award, go back to her seat, and then return if they called her name again.

Leanne got awards for attendance, best grade in language arts, math, and art, and a special award for service to the school. Vinnie was very pleased. Leanne had always struggled with math, but apparently she had figured it out. Maybe things would work out okay. She was so young, it scared Vinnie to have her living alone, but maybe it was just what she needed to keep her out of trouble. And maybe with the baby to love she wouldn't get involved with some creep.

When all the girls had received their awards, they went back to the classroom for cookies and punch. It was amazing how much noise eleven girls and their babies could make. Everybody had to sign everybody else's program. Vinnie and Marybeth were the only outsiders there, and they stood by the teacher's desk drinking green punch until Leanne came over to them.

"Hi, Momma. Oh, hi, Mrs. Coggins."

She acted as if she had only just noticed Marybeth. Still, she was perfectly friendly, the little snake. Vinnie was glad she knew her manners. Marybeth congratulated her on all the awards she had won.

"They never had a service award before, they made that up just for me. Did you see my web page yet?"

Marybeth admitted that she hadn't but promised to look at it when she got back to the store. Vinnie had never used the Internet. Maybe she would go to the library to learn how and take a look at what Leanne had done.

"Guess what! Mr. Belmont thinks I can get a job in OCC's graphics department."

"That's great. You wouldn't drop out of school, would you?"

"No, Momma, it's just for the summer. There's a girl on maternity leave and they need someone to take her place. Mr. Belmont says he thinks they can hire me through the S.T.O.P. program, that's summer jobs for kids. So, Monday I have to talk to Tonya and fill out a bunch of papers at the Career Center. It will be cool!"

It was wonderful to see her so excited.

"Let's go to John's and celebrate. Marybeth, do you have time for some pie?"

It was almost four by the time they got to the restaurant. Marybeth had blueberry pie with ice cream, Leanne had chocolate pecan. Vinnie was tired of pie, so she just had coffee. Leanne told them more about the job. She'd earn $9 an hour. Child care would be only eight dollars a week, DFC would pay the rest.

"It's not fair, because the regular job pays $12. I think if you're doing the same work, you should get paid the same. And he says I'm better than the girl who's going on leave."

"I see what you mean, Leanne, but your child care is almost free. I think you're lucky to get it. Maybe you can even save some money."

"Yeah, now I can get some furniture, and a TV. I've been waiting for Mercy Mission to call me, but they don't, and I'm sick of sleeping on the floor."

"Don't forget they'll be taking out taxes."

"Yeah, but I have money saved and I'll still have the TANF, because they don't count S.T.O.P. wages. So I'll have plenty."

Vinnie knew she couldn't push any further. Leanne was getting that sulky look, with her mouth squinched up. Marybeth didn't recognize it. She suggested a trip to Goodwill for furniture.

"I don't want to sleep on somebody else's old mattress. They have good prices at Dilman's, and that's where I'm going after the Career Center."

Misty was rubbing her eyes with her fist, winding up for a major fuss, but after a couple of whimpers, she fell sound asleep in the car. Leanne was quiet, but she perked up a little showing Marybeth the apartment.

"Oh Momma, I almost forgot. New Beginnings is going to Water World tomorrow, it's our end of school party, and we're not bringing the kids. Can you babysit?"

"Honey, I'd love to, but I took today off, and it's awful late to try to switch around the schedule."

"But Momma, I really want to go. I've never been to Water World. They have a new slide and all my friends are going and I haven't got to do anything fun since Misty Dawn was born."

Her face was turning pink, her eyes too. Vinnie would have liked to help her out and have a whole day with the baby.

"If you'd like, Munro and I could take her, if you don't mind her going to the beach with us. We're taking my grandson tomorrow."

Leanne was extremely grateful, and so was Vinnie, though Leanne's sudden warmth to Marybeth and coolness to her pricked a little. But she was glad. Leanne hadn't been just a kid in a long time. She'd made her bed, but it was a hard one. And for fifteen she was pretty responsible, even if she didn't understand money yet. It would be wonderful for her to get a break.

On the way home, she thanked Marybeth.

"We'll be back-up babysitters for Misty whenever we can. Munro just loves her. It's funny, though. All of a sudden we've got two babies in our lives. Ruthie's baby is due in a month. She's all swollen up and it's hard for her to walk. The doctor wants her to go to term if possible because he thinks the baby is small, so he's put her on bed rest, which isn't very realistic with a two-year-old in the house. Her husband does all he can, and the ladies from her church are taking turns. We're taking Scotty for the day to give her and Steve a break."

Leanne

Chapter Thirty-Five

I had Misty Dawn ready when the Coggins came to pick her up. Mrs. Coggins said they probably wouldn't be back till about eight because it's a long drive. It will be Misty Dawn's first time at the beach.

I like thinking of all the things she'll do for the first time, lots of stuff I never did, like the circus and the Sesame Street show. Momma and Daddy never took us to any of those things. I guess if you have three kids you can't afford fun stuff.

It took a while to get Misty Dawn in the car. Mr. Coggins was holding her while I put the car seat in, and suddenly he gets this look on his face. I could smell it too, so I had to take her back in and change her. But finally we got her in her seat with her floppy rabbit. I waved bye bye and she said ba ba. I'm trying to teach her to wave but she doesn't get it yet.

Seeing them drive away felt empty and happy at the same time. It was strange to be alone with nobody to think about but me.

It sure was easy getting dressed without stopping every three minutes to see about Misty Dawn. She doesn't like her playpen, and I don't use it except when I'm in the bathroom or something, because Miss Jackie says they need to explore. She crawls all over the place. I try to keep stuff up out of her way, but she's always getting into something she shouldn't.

The van came about twenty minutes after they left. Miss Melanie honked and I grabbed my stuff. I was the last one to get picked up, so I was glad Shameka saved me a place. We had a separate van from the rest of DuBois, like they don't trust us to be with the New Pathways guys. It's dumb. What do they think we do when we're not in school? Tabitha is going with Justin, who's in New Pathways, and Carla lives with her baby's daddy, even though the school thinks she lives with her mom, but her mom is an addict and doesn't care what she does. I couldn't believe Carla was coming to Water World. Her baby's due in less than four weeks. We let her have the whole back seat.

It was actually cool being just us, because we're all friends. I think we're closer because we're all in the same boat. But we don't have any cliques or anything, there's not enough of us. The Black girls hang out together more, and I guess the white girls do too. But we're still all friends, and like I said, Shameka saved me a seat. The teachers were real quiet, and after a while we forgot about them and talked about whatever we wanted.

I was worried we'd all have to stay together. On my seventh-grade trip we had to stay in groups of six and it was so embarrassing. My group's mom had this orange umbrella and she kept sticking it in the air and yelling "Group Three, Group Three." This time we just had to be at least two together all the time, and if they saw anybody alone she'd have to sit in the bus the rest of the day. I guess they'd let you die of heatstroke.

There's a special entrance for school groups so we didn't have to wait in line. We raced to the changing room and got into our bathing suits. Everybody had a bikini except Carla and Shameka. Carla had a tankini; you could see her lumpy bellybutton under the top. Shameka doesn't wear bikinis because she has stretch marks. But her suit had a V cut down below her waist, with gold mesh over it that you couldn't see the stretch marks through. She looked good. I wish I was thin as her.

When we came out, Justin was waiting for Tabitha and she went off with him. I hardly saw her the rest of the day. Everybody else except Carla wanted to start at the Double Meteor. Her doctor said she shouldn't go down any slides, she could only do the pool. Melissa said she'd go with her because the Double Meteor line was too long, but I think she was just scared. It was nice of her to stay with Carla though. If she didn't, Carla would have to hang out with the teachers.

The line was really long. It took forever to get to the top, but even being on the ladder was neat, because we could see the whole park. It's an awesome place, and me and Shameka decided to do everything at least one time. It was cool looking down at the tops of trees. I saw a bunch of big black birds in one. The sun was hot and I was wishing I'd put on Miss Melanie's suntan lotion, but Shameka was in a hurry, and anyway, I wanted to get a tan. I haven't been outside hardly at all since Misty Dawn was born. I don't have a lot of time for sunbathing.

Shameka was in front of me, and when she got up on the platform I was looking right up at her crotch. When I got up there I was embarrassed because there was three guys behind me and I knew they'd be looking. The Water World guy told Shameka to get on the slide, keep her hands in her lap, and lie down when she sees the tube. She looked back at me and said, "It's cold!" and then she let go and disappeared.

I'd been looking at how far down it was and I'll admit I was scared. I couldn't see how the slide goes because it was this whole tangle of tubes. I sat down and the cold water pounded on my butt. The guy said, "Let go" and gave me a push, and holy shit I go down and around the curve and here comes another curve right after that and then another, and no way to grab on and slow down. I almost went over the edge. I'm waving my arms and screaming and then right in front of me there's this tube and if I hadn't laid down I would of got my head cut off, and then I'm in the dark and all of a sudden I was falling straight down. I've never been so scared in my life. All I was thinking was let me out of here, but then thank God I wasn't falling anymore, just sliding down and almost right away the tube opens up and I'm blinking with the sun in my eyes and I go shooting into the pool.

Shameka was already out of the pool, and she said, "That was the bomb! You about splashed all the water out of that pool."

"Yeah, it was cool, you want to go again?"

"Naw, look at the line."

And she was right, the line wasn't just on the ladder now but stretched around the pool. It looked like thirty people waiting. Old people were in line too, laughing and goofing around, all lumpy in their bathing suits. You'd think they'd be scared of a heart attack. I was glad Shameka didn't want to do it again, and now I wonder if she really thought it was the bomb or was just pretending like me.

We stood in front of the sign trying to figure out what to do next. Joanne came up and said she had something for Shameka in the ladies' room. I thought she meant a joint, and I couldn't believe it because anybody who came in would smell it. Still, it would be cool to be stoned on the rides, so I was glad when Shameka said for me to come too. I think she didn't want to hang just with Joanne because Joanne is a dyke. Kiki thinks Joanne wants to get with Shameka, and Shameka isn't into that.

So we went to the ladies room. Joanne reached into her bag and pulled out a whole bag of miniature Snickers. There's these signs everywhere, "No outside food, drinks, or coolers." They don't even sell candy bars, so I don't think they should say you can't bring them. Joanne gave each of us four little Snickers, said it would keep us going until lunch.

Joanne wanted to go to Deep River next. We passed Greased Lightning and Flume Fall and I wanted to go on them, but I figured we had all day. Deep River had lots of trees and a grassy place. The slide was open all the way down and I was glad because I didn't want to be in the dark again. There are some cool twisty parts, but you don't go too fast. At the end you fall into a real river, and talk about cold, ohmigod you could only go into that water from a slide, because you sure couldn't make yourself wade in.

You can float down the river on a tube. That was cool. Looking down between your legs it's like an aquarium. I saw some fish and a turtle, and lots of this long grass with little silvery bubbles on it waving in the water. I'd like to be stoned and go floating in one of those tubes.

When we were done tubing we went to the snack bar. The school gave us coupons for fries, and Momma gave me $20 because of all my awards so I got a hamburger and a Coke. The others were already there so we pulled another table over and sat with them. Tabitha came in with Justin and we yelled to them to join us but Justin didn't want to and the two of them sat by the window. She kept looking over at us, and he got mad. Then she was just looking down at her food while he talked to her.

Shameka says she's not going to bother with guys until she's out of school and has a job. They're too much trouble and she doesn't have time for them. I think I'd like to have a boyfriend but only a nice one. Tabitha's boyfriend made me think of Peter, which I never want to do. It's more fun just being with girls. When I said that Joanne started laughing and said, "You got that right" and looked at Shameka, but I told her that's not what I meant.

After we ate we went to the ladies' room. The line was out the door and they only had eight toilets. A woman in front saw Carla and let her cut in, but that didn't help the rest of us. Finally Kiki and Melissa gave up, said fuck it they'd pee in the pool, but I think that's gross. So when Miss Melanie comes in I'm the only one still in line and I'm thinking oh shit, because they said a zillion times they'd better not catch us by ourselves. She asked where were the other girls, and I said they went over to the wave pool, and started to explain, but she was nice and said it was okay, she didn't think I'd be getting in any trouble in line at the ladies' room. She asked if I was having fun. She said she wanted to go on the Double Meteor but she was scared and none of the other teachers would go with her. I told her the truth about what I thought of it, and then she was glad she didn't go. I got to pee at last and when I came out she told me to go straight over to the pool. She didn't need to say that after being so friendly, but I was going there anyway so I just said okay.

By the wave pool it's like a beach, with lots of sand and lounge chairs. There's all these signs, like *Please don't move the lounge chairs*, and *Play Area*, where people were digging in the sand and making castles, and one guy was getting buried by a couple of others. I just wanted to lie out. I found the girls, who were all lying together. There weren't any more chairs close by. I said I'd drag one over from the other side, but Brittany said to the two little kids lying next to us, "You don't want those chairs do you?" and they got up and got out of there. It was mean, but we wanted to be together.

The sun felt so good on my back. I listened to the rest of them talking for a little while, they were telling Carla about labor and she was freaking out, but then their voices and little kids yelling and the sound of the waves all ran together, and I wasn't listening anymore.

I woke up hot and sweaty. Everything looked real bright. Carla was asleep in the next lounge chair. I just wanted to get in the water. The pool was huge, but it was pretty crowded. The shallow end was full of little kids. I went out up to my waist where my friends were. The water wasn't near as cold as on the slides or at Deep River, but it felt good, and I ducked under to wash off the sweat. Then I heard this rumbly sound and the water started rushing past my legs. I could see waves getting bigger and bigger. I was getting knocked all around, but after the first big one I got to where I could jump every wave and float on it. Once I got used to it, it was fun.

Then Shameka said she was tired of the wave pool so we rode one last wave into the shallow end. Kesia wanted to go to Salty Sam's Lagoon. It's supposed to be for little kids, but she said there's lots of cool stuff there. So we got Carla and went over to the lagoon. A bunch of kids were trying to cross the water on a big net bridge. It was swinging and swaying. You could make your own waterfall over these fake rocks, or you could make a big fountain by pulling on this handle thing. It was fun, but it got really fun when the New Pathways guys showed up. They got water cannons and started shooting at us and it turned into a war, girls against boys, and all the little kids got out of there fast. The guys were aiming at our bikini tops. One of Kesia's boobs popped out, and she took her time stuffing it back in. Melissa got Justin right in the balls and he was bending over and howling. Three of them came after her and she was yelling it was an accident, and me and Joanne stood next to her and aimed right in their faces so they gave up. It was all fun, nobody was mad or anything, except I bet Justin.

But the lifeguard started blowing her whistle and yelling, and then an older guy came over and said we had to leave the lagoon because it was for little kids. Matthew said there isn't any sign saying just for little kids, and we have a right to be there because we paid our way in to the park just like everyone else, and the old guy said if he wants to he can throw us all out of the whole place, so Matthew said the lagoon sucks anyway and he's going on the Double Meteor again. I didn't think it sucked at all and I would of liked to stay there and play with the fountains some more. They should of let the girls stay because we weren't doing anything wrong, it was all the guys. But it's like the teachers are always saying, we all had to pay for what a couple of them did. I been hearing that one since I was in kindergarten. I think they learn it in teacher college.

We were hungry again so we went over to the snack bar. Some of the guys came with us, and that was okay. Carla gave me her fries coupon and I bought an ice cream too. Anthony was trying to talk to me but he's too fat and dorky for me. I mean, first thing he says is he's sorry they got us kicked out of the lagoon and he was trying to protect me with his gun. Like I need anybody protecting me. Anyway, the New Pathways guys seem so young, maybe because I spent all that time with Peter, maybe just because we all have babies, so we're a lot more grown up than them.

When I finished my ice cream I wanted to try the Flume Fall, but it was already twenty to four and we had to be at the bus at four. I wished we could of stayed till it closed. But Miss Melanie said they couldn't have got any teachers to go if they stayed that late. It kills me. They're not that much older than us, but it's like they're half-dead already. It was nice of them to take us though.

I had twelve dollars left and I went to the gift shop. I wanted to get Misty Dawn a toy dolphin, but it turned out they were $24.95. Everything I wanted was too expensive. Finally I just got her a key ring with a pirate on it. She likes keys. Momma has a whole bunch in a drawer that she doesn't remember what they're for and I think she'll give me some. The key ring was only $5.95 and with the rest I bought a bag of chips to share for the ride home.

We were sort of quiet on the bus. I sat by the window. For a while I was watching the trees and billboards, but pretty soon I was asleep. I never even opened the chips. I got dropped off first. It was almost six o'clock, and Misty Dawn wouldn't be back till about eight. It was such a fun day, and now I didn't have any fun thing ahead to think about. When Misty Dawn came home I'd have to watch her every second and she'd need her dinner and a bath. I mean, I missed her, but I realized I didn't think about her all the time I was at Water World except to buy her a present, I was just thinking about having fun. Before, I was excited about the job at OCC. Now it just feels like another got-to-do sort of thing. I wish I could just have my life normal again.

Chapter Thirty-Six

I'm glad Jennifer didn't let me take that other apartment. I don't know how I'd get us to day care and work if the bus wasn't right at the end of my street. Baby Angels is close to OCC, but it's still a pretty long walk because the graphics department is across campus. My second day we had to wait fifteen minutes for the bus. It was raining and we both got soaked.

It's cool to finally have a job even if it's not what Mr. Belmont told me I'd be doing. I thought I'd be working on designing flyers, but the girl cut down her maternity leave and is working at home, so I'm just a receptionist. There's only four people in graphics and they're part of the Publications Department that already has a receptionist so there's not much for me to do.

I'm supposed to do the copying, but everybody is used to doing their own and they just walk past me to the copier. A couple of times I said I could do it and they were like "Oh no, that's okay, but thanks." I wasn't doing them a favor, it's supposed to be my job.

Mrs. Seacrist, my boss, gave me the Publications Department policies manual to copy. She wrote it. There's forty-three pages of rules for one office! She's got rules for everything, like how they dress, and how they answer the phone, and no food at the computers, but from what I see, nobody follows the rules. She said she's only been there a few months and she still has to get the policies approved.

She doesn't like everybody wearing jeans and t-shirts, but nobody pays any attention, so I'm the only one besides her who has to dress up. I wear a skirt and blouse and sandals. The second day my top showed my boobs, and she said it was pretty but not appropriate. She said it nice though.

Everybody's nice but they're all way older than me. They joke about their kids and husbands. Half the time I don't know what they're talking about, and when I do it's embarrassing. When there's no guys around they talk pretty dirty. There's one who just got married for the second time, and they say terrible things to her.

Everybody is busy and I just sit there by the door. When people come in I'm supposed to say, "Can I help you?" But hardly anyone comes in except people from Publications and they walk right past me and go to the person they want to see, or to raid our supply closet. The graphics division has the cool stuff – all kinds of colored pencils and things. I don't know why they need them because they do everything on computer anyway.

Mrs. Seacrist says she wants me to inventory the supply closet, and also I'm in charge of the bulletin board for Publications. I have to take down everything that's more than a month old and put up new stuff. She keeps telling me how lucky she is because there are all these special projects that she doesn't know how she'd ever get done if it wasn't for me, but I feel like she's making up jobs for me to do.

Mrs. Seacrist says when somebody is absent I can use their computer and take graphics tutorials. I don't have a computer. They couldn't buy a computer for someone who's only there four weeks. That's the bad thing too. You can only work 100 hours every summer in the STOP program, so I'm only working three days a week. I thought I'd have over $2000 by the end of summer and it turns out I'll only have $900. And I already went and bought my furniture with the money Mrs. Coggins saved for me!

I thought it would be cool to have a job. I thought it meant dressing nice, no one telling you what to do and getting paid all that money. But even if I was drawing, and got to use Illustrator, I don't know if I'd want to do it all day. These people spend the whole day working. When do they get to have fun? I never thought about it before. School is different. Even if the work is boring, your friends are there and you get to talk to each other a lot.

Yesterday I heard Crystal complaining. Somebody in Publications gave her a photograph of dancers and said he wanted it turned into a drawing for a brochure, and gave her the words, and she worked on it on the computer and then the guy came back and I heard them talking. He said, "Can you make the letters more, I don't know, more graceful?" And Crystal said, "I'll see what I can do," but when he left she said to Roland, "Yessir, font-fucker," and they both laughed. So when you do that kind of work it's not like just drawing your own things, you have to do somebody else's ideas, and it's not people who know anything about design.

One cool thing happened though. When I finished the supply closet, I still had an hour left till time to go. I asked Mrs. Seacrist if I could use some of the pencils, and she said just to be sure to watch the door and answer the phone. I was doodling, making curvy lines in red and orange with some blue in the middle and it turned into this strange animal that looked like fire and flowers. Roland walked by and said, "Did you draw that?" I was the only one there and pencils were all over the desk so who else could of done it? He asked if he could use it on a poster he was working on. He would scan it in and then change it some. I said that was okay with me, it wasn't nothing but a doodle anyway. It will be cool to see what he does with it.

I don't like Baby Angels. When I pick up Misty Dawn all the babies are in their cribs. Some of them are crying, but Misty Dawn is just sitting there. Funny, it's me at work, Misty Dawn at day care, both of us bored. Miss Marie said they like to have all the babies ready when their mothers pick them up, so they put on their clean outfits at 4, and keep them in their cribs till their mothers come. She says at first some of them cry, but they get used to it, and Misty Dawn is good, she hardly cries at all. But I've never seen her just sitting still, without even a toy. I don't know how they get her like that, and I don't think it's good for her. She needs to be moving around. That's how their brains grow. At New Beginnings you never see the babies in their cribs unless they're sleeping. If they're not crawling around they're being held, and the teachers are showing them shapes and colors, singing them songs, and playing games like patty-cake.

Tomorrow I'm going to Three C's, that's Coordinated Child Care, and change her day care. Then I have to take a form from Mrs. Seacrist to the STOP desk, and they give me something to take to DFC. It's good I only have to work three days, so I have time to take care of this stuff. I'll call and see if Momma can give me a ride in the morning. The buses would take all day.

Chapter Thirty-Seven

Wednesday night I was feeling good. I had my first week of work, and even if it wasn't as cool as I thought it would be, I was getting paid. But bit by bit, everything went wrong, and all the good feelings leaked out of me. Now I feel like I can't move, can't even get up and go to the bathroom. If it wasn't for Misty Dawn, I think I wouldn't ever get out of bed again.

Thursday morning I planned to call Momma for a ride, but my phone wasn't working. I went over to Stacy's to use her phone. She opened the door, leaving the chain on, and I could see she just waked up, her eyes were barely open, her hair was sticking up and she only had on a T-shirt. She yelled *shut up*! to the baby that was crying, then said, "What?"

I asked her real polite if I could use her phone and she said I woke her up, but she let me in and showed me the phone. She put the baby on the couch with a bottle, set her little boy on the floor in front of the TV with a bowl of cereal, sat down next to him and lit a cigarette. She didn't care if the kids saw her private parts.

When I called FirstCell the lady said they turned off my phone because I didn't pay the bill. I never saw a bill but it was in the package of information that came with the phone. It was $32 and she said I could pay it at Speedyway. Then she told me it's $25 more to turn it back on. I didn't have that much.

I bought four packages of diapers on sale last week. I thought maybe Shameka would buy them from me. Or maybe Momma could lend me the money. I needed to call her anyway for a ride. I started dialing and Stacy said "What are you doing? You said you was just going to make one call. I have to get some sleep. I got to be at work at 12." So I had to leave. I can't believe I thought we could be friends.

I figured I'd call Momma from the Speedyway, and she could pick us up there. I put Misty Dawn in her stroller and we started out. She likes riding in her stroller; there's lots to see.

After you get off my street it's almost like a highway, with four lanes and lots of cars. The Speedyway is eight blocks away and they're extra-long ones, and there's no sidewalk.

There were three phones. One didn't have a receiver and the other two were being used by scary-looking guys. One laid his gun down on the little shelf. The other one kept giving me these dirty looks, not dirty like sexy, but mad. He hung up and said, "You wanna use the phone?" I said yes and he said, "Don't be long." I started digging in my purse for the quarters. The guy said "Here," and handed me two quarters. I held on to Misty Dawn's stroller while I was dialing like they might kidnap her. It was silly but I felt better holding on to her.

Momma didn't answer and the machine didn't pick up. As soon as I hung up the phone the guy grabbed it. I waited in the store until I saw they were gone and then I called DFC to tell Tonya I was coming. The machine said my call would be taken in the order it was received. I waited. The voice came back three times to say the same thing and thank me for my patience, but I wasn't patient, I was just stuck. Finally, I got the receptionist, who said "Just a minute," and then she came back and said Tonya wasn't at her desk, did I want to talk to her voice mail. She clicked something and the machine said my call would be taken in the order it was received. I waited some more and got her again. She said, "Sorry, I'll put you through," and she clicked something and then I got a dial tone.

I'd been all morning and I wasn't any closer to getting anything done. Nothing I could do but walk home. I guess I could of took a bus, but I just couldn't face it. It's two buses to DFC and two back, and no guarantee I could get everything done and still have time to get both buses home. So I decided I'd go early Friday morning.

As soon as Misty Dawn fell asleep I laid down for a nap, and we both slept a long time. When she woke up she was pretty red. I started worrying about Tonya seeing her with a sunburn. It wasn't that bad, but at school the girls are always talking about DFC taking your baby away.

I felt better when I woke up Friday. I figured yesterday was just one of those days. Misty Dawn was only a little pink, and she was feeling fine. All I had to do was take my proof of income to DFC, then go to Three C's in the same bunch of buildings, and get them to change my day care. How hard could it be? Now I'm like, how dumb could I be.

We had to wait a long time at DFC because Tonya was with somebody. Misty Dawn was being a pain. She wanted to get down and crawl around, but the floor looked dirty. I bounced her on my knee, but I couldn't make her happy. All she wanted was to get down. The lady sitting next to me had two little kids with her, and she was yelling at them, "Jeremy, you get over here," and "Rita, you're gonna get a whipping" but they didn't pay any attention. Then she'd ignore them a while till she felt like she had to say something again. They weren't being bad, just they didn't have anything to do but mess with the soda machine and pick at each other.

After I waited about an hour, I went up to the receptionist again and asked about Tonya and she paged her. Somebody came out and said she went to a meeting and would be back at one. I asked could I leave the proof of income for her but the receptionist got pissy and said, "You need to talk to her. But suit yourself. It's not my problem." And she turned around and picked up some papers. I said I'd go over to Three C's and then come back but she acted like she didn't hear me.

At Three C's the receptionist was nice but she said in the morning it's just appointments. They see walk-ins in the afternoon. I went back over to DFC.

We were both hot and sweaty. Misty Dawn had wore herself out fussing so I gave her a bottle and she fell asleep. I was hungry too, but dumb me, I didn't bring anything to eat, and I didn't have change for the vending machines. The receptionist said they don't make change.

Tonya got back at 1:30. I gave her the proof of income form and she said to come back to her office. She looked it over and asked me how I like the job. I said I like it. She said that's good and the pay wouldn't change my TANF check because it's part of the STOP program and they don't count that income. I knew that already.

"But you'll need a new child care referral."

"That's okay. I wanted to change her daycare anyway. I was going over there next."

"No, I mean the rules are changing July 1. Now for child care they're going to count the STOP wages, so your co-pay will go up."

"I'm only making like $360 every two weeks, and they take taxes and stuff out of it. How much will I have to pay?"

"I don't have the charts here, but they can tell you over at Three C's."

It bummed me out, not like I was in such a great mood anyway. But nothing I could do about it. She filled out another referral that showed my new income, and I went over to Three C's.

It was a different receptionist from the morning. She said it would probably be about a two-hour wait, but it could be longer, all these people were ahead of me. I'd done okay up to then, but if I missed my second bus I wouldn't have any way to get home. I was trying not to cry and she said real nice that I could leave the new referral there with her, and call the counselor on Monday to find out what I needed to do. I was worried there'd be more forms, but she said I could fax them from my job.

I was so glad to be done with all that until Monday that I got in a good mood walking to the bus stop. Even knowing I had to pay more, I figured I couldn't do nothing about it, so I might as well just forget it and have a nice weekend.

Saturday with Momma felt like a day off from trouble. We went to garage sales and she bought folding gates I can use to keep Misty Dawn from going where she shouldn't. After that she took me to the restaurant for lunch. John and all the waitresses made a big fuss over Misty Dawn.

Sometimes it's hard to remember why I don't want to live with Momma. But Bailey's still there. She says he's not working. She's worried about him because he's still thin from when he had pneumonia, and she's afraid he's using marijuana or something. That's just how she said it and I didn't laugh, but I said I never heard of marijuana ruining your appetite. I didn't want to say too much because I didn't want to remind her of when she caught me and Erica.

That's the thing. When I stay with Momma she gets all bossy, but when we're not living together she treats me like a grown-up and we have fun.

After I got home the truck from Dilman's showed up with my furniture, and the guys put it where I wanted it. I don't have sheets yet, but I spent Sunday putting everything away in the dresser and watching TV. It was real relaxing.

Monday started out feeling like a day off too. It might sound bad, but sometimes I get tired of being with Misty Dawn all the time. Leaving her at Baby Angels and walking to OCC I felt free.

Karen at Three C's didn't call me back until Tuesday. It turned out I had to sign another form and they couldn't fax it. Sometimes I think they're nice when they want to be and when they don't they tell you a rule.

More bad news. I have to pay $30 a week instead of $8 and pay the extra for last week and this week. And I can't switch her from Baby Angels. I told Karen how they just leave the babies sitting in their cribs most of the time, but she said I chose it, and we have to stay there for thirty days because they can't switch everything around all the time just because somebody changes her mind.

Wednesday morning Misty Dawn woke up with a fever of 100. That's not very high, but I knew it would get higher in the afternoon, so I couldn't take her to daycare. I didn't have any medicine for her. I figured we'd walk to the Speedyway, but first I needed to call work and tell them I wasn't coming in. They must of told me fifty times at the STOP program: you always let your employer know. No way I could ask Stacy again, so I decided to ask my other neighbor. Whenever I see him he smiles and says hello. Even if he is a terrorist he won't hurt us I bet, because the terrorists are real careful not to get in trouble while they're waiting to blow things up.

I figured I shouldn't knock on his door too early, so I waited till 8. I said the baby was sick and my phone was broken, could I use his phone to call my job and he said "Of course, of course," and told me to come in and sit down. So I pushed her stroller in and sat in the armchair.

His apartment didn't have much stuff in it, but it was so pretty. He had pictures of a beautiful place, bright blue water and little white houses going down a cliff. There was a pile of pillows on the floor, and a really big TV. Under the window he had lots and lots of plants, all different colors. He was baking something sweet and spicy. It smelled really good.

I called Mrs. Seacrist. She said they'd manage and she hoped Misty Dawn would feel better soon. I said I was going to the store for medicine. When I hung up he said I shouldn't have to walk with the baby sick, he'd give me a ride. I was nervous, but he was being so nice, and I really didn't want to walk. So I said okay. Then he asked if I would like a pastry and coffee first. And he took this cookie sheet out of the oven with little round cakes on it covered with chopped nuts. They looked so good, and I hadn't had anything to eat.

He put one on a plate and brought me a little cup of coffee. The cake was sweet and syrupy. I never ate anything like it. He said his mother used to make it all the time. He's from Greece, and the pictures on the wall are near where he lives. I took a sip of the coffee, and it was the bitterest thing I ever tasted. I must of made a face, He laughed and said next time he'd have milk for me. He gave me another cake to take the bitter taste out.

He was so nice to me, but not like he wanted anything. He asked if he could hold Misty Dawn, and when I said yes he bounced her on his knee, and made her laugh. He has a two-year-old girl and a five-year-old boy at home and he really misses them. He showed me a picture of them and his wife that he keeps in the desk drawer. If he keeps it on top of the desk he has trouble thinking about his work. He's an engineer. He came to Opakulla to get a master's degree, but he couldn't afford to bring his family with him so he hasn't seen them since last summer.

When I finished my cake he said we should go because Misty Dawn was getting really hot. At the store he wanted to buy the medicine as a present for her. Maybe I shouldn't of said yes, but my money was going so fast. The TANF check was just about gone. We were only halfway through June, and I had to pay all that childcare and the phone bill. When we got back home, he said if I ever need any help to be sure and knock on his door. He shook my hand and went inside his apartment, and I went inside mine.

His name is Nick, and I don't think he is a terrorist. I wanted to ask him more questions about his country, but I felt shy. At first I was worried he'd try to put the moves on me, but he just wanted to help me, like I was his sister. Bailey never treats me like that, though. Maybe it was more like he was my uncle or even my dad.

Misty Dawn stayed sick two days. I went to Nick's again to call Momma to ask if she could take me to Three C's, because I sure didn't want to be riding all those buses with a sick baby. Nick gave me another of the cakes, and a cup of coffee that was almost all milk. He said sometime after Misty Dawn is better he would make me a Greek dinner, and maybe my mother could come. I think he's lonely.

When Momma took me to Three C's she bought me some Tylenol to give to Misty Dawn between the Motrin. I could tell she was worried. She said she just didn't see how I could manage everything. I said I'd be okay, even though I'm not so sure sometimes.

Friday Misty Dawn was all better and we rode the bus to the office to get my paycheck. Everybody wanted to hold her, and she was in a real happy mood. After they finished passing her around, and Mrs. Seacrist gave her a cookie – I thought she should of asked me – and gave me my paycheck in an envelope. I opened it on the bus and I couldn't believe it. They took almost a hundred dollars out of it, and all

I had was $273. After I paid for the phone and the three weeks of child care, I'd only have about $100 left, and had to pay another week of child care before I got paid again. Doesn't seem like there's any point working.

Today is my birthday. I always thought sixteen would be really special, like I'd get my license and have a big party. But I don't know when I'll have the money to get my license, and what good would it do me anyway? I can't afford a car.

Chapter Thirty-Eight

Peter came last night. It was awful. Misty Dawn was done with her bath and I was reading her a story. It's my favorite time, when she's all snuggly on my lap, and she smells so sweet. Momma thinks it's silly reading to a baby that little, but this lady at school said it's important to start early if you want them to like reading, and she gave us all these books to keep. So we were reading about butterflies when Peter pounded on the door.

I was scared. I took Misty Dawn to the door with me. I should of put her in her crib, it could of been anybody there. But I guess I feel like she's safest when she's with me. He started banging again, and I yelled who is it, and he said Peter.

I swear I've never been so surprised. It's over three months ago he showed up at the Coggins, and I kind of forgot about him, so much has happened. I just stood there, and he yells "Leanne, I gotta talk to you." I go, "About what?" and he goes, "Come on Leanne, open the door, we gotta talk." And I did. Stupid stupid me. You'd think after he almost raped me I wouldn't of, but it was like if I didn't open the door he'd just stay there banging on it. Or maybe I'm still used to doing what Peter says. I wish I would think before I do stuff. My life would be a whole lot different if I did that!

Anyway, I did open it, and there he was. He wasn't drunk, but he was skinnier, and he just looked sorry. I don't mean sorry I done what I done, I mean sorry like Momma says it, not worth a damn. He came in and sat on the couch like he lived there, and acted like Misty Dawn wasn't even there. It's his baby, he hadn't seen her in almost a year, and he didn't hardly look at her. He said again, "Leanne, we gotta talk."

I said, "Hold on, I'm putting her to bed." When I came back he was still sitting on the couch. Just looking at him gave me the creeps. I can't believe I used to be hot for him. No way I'd sit next to him, so I sat at the table and said,

"What do you want?"

"Aw now Leanne, don't be that way."

"I'm not being any way, just asking what you want."

"I want to talk about this child support thing."

"You mean they finally got hold of you? Happy Father's Day."

Tonya had told me child support would contact him, and I was so worried, but later on I got mad. She kept saying she didn't know what the holdup was. She said she'd talk to the child support worker, but I don't think she did, leastways she didn't have any news for me about it. After a while I figured they weren't bothering with him, and in a way that was alright. He was leaving me alone and they could leave him alone. But I guess they didn't, and now here he was in my apartment.

He said his wife opened the letter from the child support people and got really mad. She kicked him out and she's divorcing him. All that time he was living with me, and me pregnant, and then Misty Dawn born, she never knew about me! She just thought they were separated while they worked things out. They were going to marriage counseling when he was living with me. He is such a big fat liar. I almost felt sorry for her, but not really. I mean, she's been with him all that time, she should of figured him out before now. Anyway, now she knows about Misty Dawn, and she's through with him. Serves him right.

He showed me the letter. It said he had to pay, but if he didn't think it was his baby, they could do a test, and they could go to court.

"How come you had to go and tell them I'm the father?"

"You are the father."

"Maybe I am, but you don't have to go telling them my business."

"Excuse me, it's my business too, and if I wanted welfare I had to tell them your name."

"You're getting welfare?"

He said it like I was dirt.

"What am I supposed to do? I can't get a real job, I'm only sixteen, in case you forgot. I need some way to take care of her. You never even tried to help."

"I sure did, we put her where she would have a good home. That baby would be adopted and we wouldn't have anything to do with it."

"She's not an it. I must of been crazy letting you make me do that. It's the worst thing I've ever done, besides going with you I mean."

"You better not get smart with me Leanne. You're making me angry."

I used to be so scared of him, and I'd do anything not to make him mad. Now I didn't care. I was too mad myself.

"I'll say what I want, you're not the boss of me, Peter."

That's when he grabbed my arm, hauled me up next to him and twisted it behind my back.

"You're gonna tell them somebody else is the father."

That was really dumb, because they have tests that say who the father is, and anyway, who else could I say? He was really hurting my shoulder yanking my arm up behind me, and maybe I should have promised to do like he said. But I just started yelling stupid stuff like I hope you die.

He probably would of started beating on me, except somebody was banging on the door, and then it opened – it's a good thing I forgot to lock it after I let Peter in – and there was Nick walking in yelling.

"Let go of her."

I didn't realize Nick was so big till I saw him next to Peter. He let go of my arm right away.

"Who is this, Leanne?"

"Who are you?"

They said it at the same time.

"I'm her husband."

"No he's NOT!" I yelled it.

"Should I tell him to leave?"

"Yes, get him out of here."

"I think you need to go."

I was crying by that time, partly because my shoulder hurt real bad, and my arm where he'd been squeezing it so tight, and partly I guess because I was so relieved when Nick came.

"You can have her, man, I'm outta here." Like he thought Nick was my boyfriend. He started out the door, but just before he left he looked at me real mean and said, "If something happens to that baby I guess I won't have to pay child support." He slammed the door and was gone. That's when I started really crying.

Nick put me on the couch and was patting my shoulder. When we heard Peter's truck drive away, he got up and said he'd be right back. I was thinking ohmigod, now Peter's going to hurt Misty Dawn. I went in to look at her. She was fine, she slept through all the yelling and banging around. I was wondering how to keep her safe, could I move away where he won't find us, could I get a gun and shoot him before he comes back, all kind of crazy thoughts.

Nick came back in with milk and a cookie, like I was a little kid that all you got to do is give them a lollipop and they'll stop crying. But actually I'd stopped crying by then. Nick sat down on the floor and asked if he could do anything else. He didn't ask, but I told him Peter was Misty Dawn's father, and just a little bit about how I used to live with him and he made me dump Misty Dawn. He said he didn't know I was only sixteen. In his country a girl like me wouldn't be living alone with a baby, I'd live with my family and my father would look out for me. I said I was scared because of what Peter said about Misty Dawn. He said not to worry, I only had to yell or bang on the wall and he'd be right over. Then he left.

I still felt scared about what Peter said. I took a long shower to get his cooties off me. I had a bruise on my arm. It was creepy because it showed his fingers. Then I got Misty Dawn out of her crib and took her into bed with me. She hardly woke up.

Chapter Thirty-Nine

This was the worst day of my whole life ever. When I was little, Momma used to say, "You don't know what trouble is, Leanne." Well, I sure do now.

It was pouring rain when I left work. Misty Dawn was asleep when I got to Baby Angels. Serena was in the rocking chair feeding another baby, and she said wait till I change her. That's their rule, they don't let you touch your baby before they turn her over to you all cleaned up. I think maybe they don't change them the rest of the day, except if they poop. There's a lot of diapers left in the bag when I pick her up.

So I was waiting for Serena to change Misty Dawn, and then she went looking all over for the bottle top that she lost, so we missed the bus and had to wait half an hour for the next one. The rain had almost stopped but boy was it hot. You could see the steam coming off the sidewalk. Then the bus was late, so I knew I was gonna miss my second bus from downtown, and that meant another twenty minutes waiting at the depot, a creepy place.

Time I finally got home, I was thinking thank God there's only two more weeks of work, even though I didn't know what I'd do the rest of the summer. I was tired and hot, and Misty Dawn felt like she weighed a hundred pounds. I opened the door and when I saw inside, I screamed and almost dropped her.

You wouldn't think someone could make a mess that big with so little stuff. First thing I saw was the TV face down on the floor. The couch cushions were thrown every which way, and syrup poured all over them. My drawing things were all tore up, pencils broken and all the pages ripped from the big pad. In the kitchen broken dishes were all over the floor, and glasses smashed in the middle of a big puddle of fruit punch. The bathroom had toothpaste squeezed on the mirror and shampoo dumped on the floor. What really got me, the make-up set that Mrs. Coggins gave me, every single one of the lipsticks was broken, and some of them used to scribble on the door.

I was walking around like it was somebody else's house that I'd never seen before. It was all so weird but at the same time it didn't feel weird, like in a dream where everything that happens is just the way it's supposed to be. I couldn't put Misty Dawn down because of all the broken glass and mess, so I figured I'd put her in her crib.

The bedroom door was closed, and for some reason I thought it would be ok in there. But I opened the door and it was the worst. The dresser was scratched, it looked like with a knife. All our clothes were on the floor. My beautiful new bed looked like buckets of water been poured on it, and the canopy was tore up. And Misty Dawn's mattress was laying on the floor, all slashed open, and on top was this big turd.

That's when I started crying, when I seen that. It was like somebody had done something awful to her, and I knew it was Peter. I was scared just seeing it, like what if she'd been in her crib, it would of been her all slashed up. At the same time I was mad as hell, and my feelings was hurt too for Misty Dawn, like how could anybody hate her like that? And I remembered how he wouldn't even look at her. In a million years I'll never figure out how I could ever of thought I loved him.

Misty Dawn was all wiggling and fussing, she wanted down real bad. Peter hadn't found the stroller so I put her in it and took her outside with the phone and sat on the step. Everything was so clean and nice outside, still hot, but a whole lot better than inside. I knew I had to call the police, only I wished I could get Nick first, but he was in Miami for a couple of days at a meeting.

So I dialed 911 and told the lady somebody had tore up my apartment. It was half an hour or so before the police got there. I went inside for a jar of baby food and fed it to Misty Dawn and gave her a bottle. She really wanted to get down and play but the only place I could put her was on the grass, which is mostly dirt. She was happy like always. She didn't have any idea what was going on. I mean when I was crying she got upset too, and was patting my face, but now that I was quiet she was fine, glad to play in the dirt.

I was just taking a twig out of her hand before she could stick it in her mouth when up comes the police. It was a man and a girl. I took them in the apartment, and they walked around looking at everything. The lady took pictures and put powder different places to get fingerprints. I said I knew who did it, but she said they needed the fingerprints anyway. They asked me all these questions and I gave them Peter's name and address, which good thing I still remembered it.

When they were all done asking questions and taking pictures, the man asked me if I knew somebody who would help me clean up, or maybe somebody I wanted to stay with. He said they would take me and Misty Dawn there if I wanted. I said I only knew the one neighbor and he was out of town, but my mother would help. He said they'd stay there while I called her. All the time they was doing their stuff and asking me questions I was cool, but when Momma got on the phone, I started crying, and the lady cop said, "Let me talk to her." I gave her the phone and she told Momma what happened and said, "Yes ma'am, I think it would be good if you could come over here." She hung up and said they'd wait till she got there. They were real nice, and said how smart Misty Dawn was, and the man said Misty Dawn reminded him of his little girl.

When Momma got there, first thing she said was "Are you alright? Is Misty alright?" She gave me a big hug. She brought cleaning stuff: rubber gloves, spray cleaner, paper towels and a scrub brush. We went inside and Momma looked in all the rooms. She was cursing real soft. She brought dinner from the restaurant, and she said we'd eat first, so we sat out on the step. It was meat loaf, mashed potatoes, string beans, and a big piece of blueberry pie. You'd think I wouldn't be hungry being so upset, but I don't think anything can take away my appetite.

After we finished, we went back inside. Momma said she'd deal with the thing on the crib mattress first. Told me to keep Misty Dawn happy while she cleaned that up. When she came out of the bedroom she set up the TV for Misty Dawn to watch while we took care of everything else. It was amazing that the TV worked just fine. So we put Misty Dawn in front of it in her stroller. Her mattress was ruined so we hauled it outside. I thought the couch was ruined too, but Momma mixed up some cleaner and water, and started me scrubbing it, and I got all the syrup off, except maybe some in the cracks. Misty Dawn was asleep by then, her head hanging over to one side, so I put her on the floor surrounded by pillows so she wouldn't roll away. Momma got all the broken glass and dishes up and mopped the kitchen floor, and then she cleaned the bathroom while I put all of our clothes away back in the closet and drawers. It made me sick to think of Peter touching all our stuff.

It took a couple of hours and when we were done you couldn't tell there'd ever been anything wrong. In fact it was cleaner than before. Momma said my mattress would dry okay. Nothing we could do about the scratches on the dresser, but the drawers were fine. Only thing wrecked was Misty Dawn's mattress and the dishes. Momma said she'd go down to Goodwill in the morning and get a crib mattress and some plates and glasses.

Momma was scared Peter would come back. She wanted us to stay at her house, but I said no. I can't say why, but I just knew he was done with us. He's too chickenshit to do anything that will get him in real trouble. Momma said at least let her take Misty Dawn. But I had this real strong feeling that it's our home and we belong together. Anyway, Misty Dawn was asleep already and I was tired. I didn't want to pack up clothes and stuff and go across town. So Momma said okay, but she let me know she'd worry about me all night and not get any sleep. Which I know was a lie – nothing keeps Momma awake once she lies down. But it was same as saying I love you, and I didn't mind.

So Momma went home. I checked on Misty Dawn and she was sleeping just fine, rolled over on her side. I sat down on the floor because the sofa wasn't dry yet and watched some TV. Then I noticed on top of the refrigerator the pot of beans I made last week. I stuck them up there to cool and forgot them. With everything so clean I thought I'd wash the pot. When a commercial came on I got it down and opened the lid and then I dropped it on the floor and was jumping around all screaming and shaking my hands, like they was crawling all over me. The nastiest thing I ever saw, little white worms, all mixed in with the beans, millions of them. I wished like anything I'd gone home with Momma, or we'd seen the pot when we were cleaning. Now I had to clean it myself. I took it in the bathroom and dumped the beans in the toilet and flushed, and then washed it out from the bathtub faucet till all the worms was gone, but one got on my thumb. Whole time I was screaming and gagging and crying. I took the pot outside and put it on top of the mattress. I wasn't ever going to use it again.

I know it's wrong but I wish I was dead. My life is just one awful thing after another. Nothing will change no matter what I do. I can't give Misty Dawn what she needs. She's in this shitty daycare center and doesn't even have a mattress anymore, has to play in the dirt because there's no grass. She'll be three years old time I get out of high school and even then I can't get a good job. I was even thinking how to kill myself. I'd have to take her to daycare and then do it, maybe I could walk in front of a car. But I'd never have the nerve. I'm a worse chickenshit than Peter even. Only a real loser would of fallen in love with a guy like him. Misty Dawn would be better off if me and him too was both dead.

Chapter Forty

They arrested Peter! I thought he was so smart, but he's really pretty dumb. He left his fingerprints on everything, so now he's in jail. This lady from the victim office said he couldn't make bail so he's in jail till the trial. She'll call me when he gets out. I don't see what that helps – like I could move somewhere else. I can go to the trial if I want and maybe I'll have to if they want me for a witness. I hope not.

I'm glad he's locked up. I was always thinking I saw him in the street or in a store. I like knowing I won't see him. I hope I never see him again.

After he was arrested, I started wondering about his wife. Why didn't she bail him out? Did he beat her up too? What did she know about me and Misty Dawn?

If they didn't have that little boy I think I could forget about her. I'm good at figuring out the buses now, and I decided to go to her house and let Misty Dawn meet her brother. It was a crazy idea, but it turned out good.

It took over an hour to get there. The bus stop was two blocks from their street, and I passed all these pretty little houses. I'd love a house like that. Momma could help me make a garden. Peter's house had no curtains in the window, no toys in the yard, but a lot of boxes and broken furniture piled by the curb. I knocked and waited a long time before she opened the door. She'd cut her hair. It doesn't look as good short but she's still a whole lot prettier than me, even though I put on makeup to meet her.

"I thought you were the movers. What do you want?"

I could see all these boxes behind her.

"Are you moving?"

"Obviously. Did you come to see the house?"

It was dumb, but I said yes. I hadn't planned how to tell her who I am.

"I told the landlord not to send anybody today, the movers come at twelve and we have to catch the bus. But now you're here you might as well see it."

So she let me in, and I walked all over the house. She was on her phone trying to get hold of the movers, but she followed me. It wasn't as nice as it looks from the outside. It was empty except for boxes. The light in the bathroom was just a light bulb with no shade. The living room carpet had a hole.

"Where's your little boy?" I asked her.

"He's next door. How'd you know I have a little boy?"

"The tricycle by the curb, it looked like a boy's."

"No it doesn't. Shit, I know who you are. You're that girl Peter got pregnant. You're not here to see the house. That's his baby, isn't it?"

"Yeah."

I expected her to say how cute Misty Dawn is, I had her dressed in red overalls and a red and white striped t-shirt. But no. She was pretty mad.

"You're even uglier than he said. You've got a lot of nerve coming here. How do you expect us to support you and your baby? Peter hardly makes enough for us."

"It wasn't me, I didn't want anything from him, just wanted to get away from him, but I had to tell them who he was or they wouldn't give me welfare."

"And now you've put him in jail."

"Well, do you know what he did?"

"They say he busted up your apartment."

"He tore up everything, even Misty Dawn's bed. It was horrible what he did."

It always upsets me to remember how it looked when I got home that day, and I wished I didn't, but I started crying.

"Hey, you don't have to cry about it. You're just a kid, aren't you?"

"No I'm not. I'm sixteen."

"Jesus. So when you met him you were like fifteen?"

"Actually, I was thirteen."

"God, what an asshole. Peter said you tricked him, but I should have known. Whenever he opens his mouth a lie comes out. It's probably good he's in jail. If he thinks I'll bail him out he's got another think coming. Hey, you want a coke?"

Her name was Megan. There was only one coke left so we split it. We sat on the couch. She said Misty Dawn was real cute and wanted to hold her. Said I probably did her and Billy a favor sending Peter to jail. All the time he was living with me she thought he was renting a room somewhere while they were in counseling. I told her how it was and what he did to me.

"I can't believe it. He never hit me. I would have left him sooner if he did. I feel like it's sort of my fault because he's my husband."

I said it wasn't her fault, she didn't even know about it. I was starting to like her, even after that mean thing she said. I asked her if Misty Dawn could meet her brother. Her neighbor was keeping him while she finished packing and would drive them to Greyhound. Now she was all interested and wanted to hear about Misty Dawn. She'd been married to Peter since she got pregnant. Before she met him, she was planning to be a model. She left him two times before, but she always went back because of their little boy.

"But this time we're through. He's nothing but a lying asshole. He'll never see us again."

She was moving back with her parents in Ohio, going to go to college to be a kindergarten teacher. I was sorry because I thought we could be friends, and Misty Dawn would know her brother.

The movers didn't get there till almost one. It was just two guys with a big truck. I would of left earlier only I really wanted to see her little boy. She said come over to the neighbor's and have lunch with them and they'd give me a ride to the depot so I'd just have to take one bus.

Megan carried Misty Dawn. She misses having a little baby. Billy was watching TV but he got up and came running to his mom. He's maybe the cutest little boy I ever saw. I could see how he looked a little like Misty Dawn. Megan asked if I'd let him hold her.

"He really likes babies."

She had him sit in the armchair and she put Misty Dawn in his lap. Misty Dawn liked him right away, she was poking at his face. Megan didn't tell him it was his sister though. I took a picture of the two of them with my phone. I'll show it to Misty Dawn when she's older.

The neighbor was nice. She gave us tuna sandwiches and potato chips. Megan told her everything about me, who I am and who Misty Dawn is and about Peter beating me up. I wished she hadn't. It wasn't the neighbor's business. You could tell they're good friends. I felt left out and like they thought I was just a kid.

On the way to the bus I asked Megan for her address in Ohio. Maybe I could come see her some time, so the kids could know each other.

"Well, see, I don't want Peter to know where I am. He never met my parents, all he knows is they live in Ohio."

I said I wouldn't tell, I wasn't ever talking to Peter again. But she said it wasn't safe.

"I know Peter. When he wants to be sweet he can get anything out of you. If he finds out you came to see me, he'll be after you to help him find me."

It hurt my feelings. She said she'd write me, but I bet she never does.

They left us at the depot. She gave me a hug, and Misty Dawn too, and told Billy to give the baby a kiss.

I guess Misty Dawn will never know her brother. But I'm glad I met them. After everything she told me, I see Peter different. I'm not scared of him anymore. Actually I stopped being scared after he tore up my apartment – you'd think I'd be scareder, but it just made me so mad. Like she said, he's an asshole. He shouldn't of taken advantage of me like that, I was just a kid. Now I'm older, I can stand up to him. If they want me in court to testify against him, I'll go. In a way I feel sorry for him. He's gonna lose his kid and I know what that feels like. He had me fooled and he had me scared, but now I know. Peter's nothing but a loser.

Vinnie

Chapter Forty-One

Vinnie was in the kitchen filling the saltshakers. The rush was over. Old Al always sat a long time after dessert, and there were two kids looking like Halloween, all in black with earrings and cheek rings and god-knows-what rings. They only looked scary. She'd overheard them talking and they sounded just like her and Preston at their age.

Peter was the scary one. Leanne thought he was done making trouble, but Vinnie wasn't so sure. She'd never met him, and maybe Leanne knew better, but she didn't like it. Leanne and the baby were alone and Peter knew where they lived.

"Phone for you, Vinnie."

The phone was by the register. A man's voice.

"Mrs. Ellsworth? I have your daughter Leanne here. There's been an accident."

The baby burned, her daughter was very upset, they thought she should be there. They'd called DFC.

Stupid, she didn't ask how bad or how it happened. So all the way to the hospital her thoughts raced, oh God, what next, why did they call DFC, it was too much for Leanne, taking care of a baby 24-7. If Peter had done something she would personally take care of him, she had a gun though nobody knew it. And one thought kept returning, like a prayer, let her be alright, jumping back and forth between Leanne and Misty.

The emergency room was full, and every clerk busy. She tried to talk to one over the shoulder of the old woman sitting in the cubicle, but the clerk said, "You sign in over there, Ma'am," while the old woman, trembling with a palsy, glared at her.

"They called me to come."

"You need to wait your turn."

She stood in front of the rows of chairs. People were mostly old, mostly Black, some half-asleep. Two young girls with crying babies. How in hell would she get to Leanne and Misty? A burly man in green scrubs came through the door and she touched his arm.

"Please, they called me. My daughter's here with her baby."

"Hold on a minute." He went over and handed some papers to a clerk.

"What's your daughter's name?"

"Leanne Ellsworth, and the baby is Misty Dawn Sewell."

"Oh sure. I'm the one who called you. Come on back."

A long hall of curtained cubicles, and Leanne sitting in one, silent and staring. Vinnie spoke her name and she looked up. "Momma, they won't let me in there, don't let them take her away Momma, they can't have Misty Dawn, she needs me with her."

Leanne was too worked up to tell her anything clear. Vinnie leaned over awkwardly to hold her as she cried, till the burly man came back with a chair. She pulled it over next to Leanne and took her hand.

"Tell me what's going on. How bad is she hurt? will she be okay?"

"It's a bad burn. Your daughter says it was on the stove. But it's just her hand and arm, and we've got a burn center here."

"We need to see her. She needs her mother."

"Thing is, Mrs. Ellsworth, she's in a sterile environment and they're doing all sorts of procedures. We asked your daughter to stay in here because we didn't have time to calm her down and get her all scrubbed and gowned. Let me go check on the baby and I'll come back and tell you how she's doing."

"Misty will be all right, she'll be all right, baby." She repeated it as much for herself as for Leanne, though it did seem to get through to her. She relaxed in Vinnie's arms and stopped crying except for a sniffle.

"Tell me what happened. Was it Peter?"

"No, Momma, I told you he's not coming back. It was me, I was holding Misty Dawn and heating up a can of soup. I went to move the pot off the burner, and when I turned and was putting it on the counter Misty Dawn squirmed. I think she was reaching for it. She slipped and her hand went flat down on the burner and it was red hot. Oh Momma, it was awful, I could smell her like meat, there's circles on her hand and arm like she been grilled, they're acting like I did it on purpose. She was just screaming and screaming and she needs me there, they're hurting her."

"Now, honey, from what that man said she's going to be okay, and I think if we get you calmed down we can go be with her."

They sat side by side in the cubicle. It was cold, must have been 60 degrees in there. Another nurse came in with a clipboard. "Oh, you're not Chapman," she said, and was gone before Vinnie could ask her anything. Another twenty minutes. She went out to the nurse's station where a man in scrubs and a woman in a white coat stood talking. She interrupted them.

"Please, we've been waiting and waiting. My daughter's really upset. Can you tell us anything? It's her baby, Misty Sewell."

"What room are you in?"

"Number three."

"Oh, the burn, yeah, that's Patrick's. We'll page him." The clerk paged him. After ten minutes he still hadn't come.

"Must be on break," said the clerk. "Go back to the room and I'll ask him as soon as he gets back."

She found Leanne asleep, covered with goosebumps, her head sagging over. She went out again and snatched two blankets off a housekeeping cart, wrapped them around her. She heard the page twice more, but still Patrick didn't come.

She had been there an hour and a half when a woman pulled back the curtain, came in and introduced herself as Dr. Marshall. She said Misty was in the burn unit, sleeping. It was a second degree burn, third degree in places, but none of the ligaments or tendons were damaged, so she'd have full use of her hand. Except for some scarring she should be fine,

"When can I see her? When can she come home?"

Dr. Marshall didn't look at Leanne. She spoke to Vinnie.

"There's a man here from DFC, he wants to speak with both of you."

As soon as she left, he came in.

"I'm Hampton Ferrell, DFC protective investigation. Which one of you is the mother?"

"Me."

"And who are you?"

"I'm Leanne's mother."

"Does she live with you?"

"No, she has her own apartment."

"Tell me what happened, Leanne."

"I have to see her. They didn't let me see her yet."

"First I need some information, and we'll decide if it's okay for you to see her."

Oh God, they might not even let her see the baby.

Address, age, was she working, who was the father, a thousand questions before he finally got to what had happened that night. Leanne answered them all. When she came to the terrible moment at the stove her voice got high and strained. Vinnie could hardly bear to hear it again. One minute tired and hungry, ready for dinner, the next minute the baby screaming and soup all over the floor, calling the ambulance that took so long to come, and the baby wouldn't stop screaming.

"Has the baby ever been hurt before?"

"Well, she's not a very good walker, so she falls down a lot, and one time this little boy at daycare bit her and left marks. But she never had anything really bad before."

"Well, I think we can wrap this up in a few minutes and we can all go up and have a little visit. I'll take it to the child protection team, and then I can make our recommendation to the judge. There's not a big hurry because they say she'll be in the hospital for a few days."

"You mean we got to go to court?"

Like the doctor, he spoke to Vinnie, avoiding Leanne's eyes. "Whenever we see a suspicious injury like this we investigate, and usually take it to court. Leanne is so young it might be good for DFC to have control of the baby for a while, maybe get her into parenting classes."

"We already been to court. They gave me back Misty Dawn, and I done parenting classes. You ask anybody, ask Jonathan Loring. Everybody says I'm such a good mother."

"Wait a minute. You mean we're already involved in the case?"

Vinnie explained the judge had given Misty back to Leanne, with DFC supervising.

"But Jonathan says in September he's telling the judge they can close my case. It will be a year from when they took her and I'm doing so good with her."

"I thought it was a new case. This is much simpler, since she's in our custody already. Our system is down, so I didn't know anything about it. I'll talk with my supervisor and we'll figure out what to do. We may want to put the baby in emergency shelter for a while, at least till her burn is better, and we get all the information."

"You can't put her in a shelter. She needs to be with me."

Vinnie put her arm around Leanne, trying to keep her calm. She knew Mr. Ferrell was judging them every minute, trying to figure out if they would burn a baby.

"It's not a shelter really, Leanne. It's just a foster home that takes in babies for a short time while we're investigating."

When she heard foster home Leanne's eyes got big, and Vinnie broke in.

"Leanne, why don't we go see how Misty is doing, and maybe you can hold her for a little while. In the morning we'll figure out what to do."

"I'm staying with her."

Vinnie looked at Mr. Ferrell.

"I don't think you can stay, but let's all go up and see the baby. I'll find a nurse to take us up there."

When he was gone, Vinnie said, "Honey, in the morning you can call that lawyer at Legal Aid. I'm sure everything will work out alright. Maybe she won't have to go into a foster home at all."

Leanne seemed defeated.

"Do you think I burned her on purpose?"

"Of course you didn't! And nobody else does either, or they won't when they've talked to all the people who know about you and Misty. But they have to check on things, because you know some mothers do terrible things to their babies, sometimes even kill them."

"I'd never hurt Misty Dawn."

In the burn unit they dressed and scrubbed like surgeons, but the nurse wouldn't let them touch Misty. She was in a bassinet under a plastic tent, with her left arm covered to the shoulder in a huge white bandage, an IV in her other arm, and a tube in her nose. She didn't move or open her eyes. Leanne stood a foot away, as still as Misty, singing the Barney Song over and over as if no one else were in the room, tears rolling down, until the nurse said it was time to go.

She was quiet as they walked down the hall through the maze of corridors, so shut inside herself that Vinnie felt almost shy. Even when Leanne showed up at home after all that time, they were mother and daughter again, Leanne was still her child to scold, to boss around, to comfort. Now she seemed like a stranger, and she was somewhere Vinnie couldn't go.

At the car she said, "Honey, come home with me tonight. Bailey's gone, and you can use his bed. In the morning we'll call that lawyer."

"Okay." But she wasn't listening. She didn't ask about Bailey. At home she didn't want hot chocolate, or a back rub, just went to bed, saying "Goodnight, Momma."

Vinnie turned off the light, sat out on the deck, thought about Misty lying in her plastic tent, her little body stuck up with tubes and tape, sleeping, she hoped. Thought about Shauna, wondered where she was and what she was doing, when she'd hear from her again.

In the morning Leanne was different, almost normal, except she got up early and made coffee for Vinnie. She wanted to go see Misty right away, but Vinnie persuaded her to wait until at least eight.

"Anyway, we need to go see the lawyer."

At ten o'clock they were sitting in front of Amy Bradwell, and Vinnie had to listen to the story again. The horror of it didn't change, but now it was part of Misty. Misty was the baby who got burned, marked as much by the story as by the scars she would have. She'd lived almost a year with nothing bad happening to her, unless you wanted to count those six weeks she was away from Leanne. Now she's like all the rest of us, thought Vinnie. It made her sad.

Miss Bradwell thought Leanne was still living with Vinnie. It took a while, and a lot of questions, to get it clear.

"So you were living with your Mom until about the middle of January, and then you stayed with Mrs. Coggins until the beginning of May."

"I moved on Mother's Day."

"Okay, middle of May. You said the guardian helped you find a place? They're supposed to notify me when they appoint a guardian. What's her name?"

"Jennifer. Her last name is like Simpson, Sampson, I'm not sure."

"Well, I can find out. I'll need to talk to her, and with Mrs. Coggins too. Can you give me her number? Or maybe I have it in the file."

Vinnie spoke up. "You can call her at Coggins Hardware."

"Okay. We want to get this in front of the judge as soon as possible. I want everybody who's seen Leanne with the baby to testify."

"You should call DFC. Jonathan says I'm doing really good."

"I'll call them. But I have to tell you, right now they're being really careful, because of that little boy whose father killed him last Christmas. Even with what your worker has said, I can't promise we'll get Missy back right away."

"It's not Missy, it's Misty Dawn."

"Of course, sorry. Look, I'll be tied up with hearings on Monday. I'll talk to as many people as I can today, and I'd like to be able to reach you. Will you be home this afternoon?"

"I'll be at the hospital."

"Honey, there's nothing you can do there. The nurses are looking out for her, and she'll be asleep most of the time, with all the drugs."

"I don't care. She needs me with her. You don't have to go if you don't want."

"I'll tell you what," Miss Bradwell said. "I think I can reach you at the burn unit. Just in case, why don't you call me about four and I'll tell you what I found out. The hospital is right across the street, so if I need you, I can come over there. I'll want to talk to people in the ER anyway.

"Can they take her away from me, like for good?"

"Everything you've told me, Leanne, I don't think they'll try. It's called terminating parental rights, and it takes a lot for them to do that. Even if they do try, I don't think they can persuade a judge. That's assuming your worker and teachers and everybody says what you think they will."

"Mrs. Coggins doesn't like me."

"Well, we'll see what she has to say."

"Leanne, it didn't work out with you living there, but she says you're a really good mother," Vinnie said. "I don't think she'd say anything against you."

"Actually, Mrs. Ellsworth, I wonder if you could stay for a while. I need to talk with you. You'll be one of the witnesses, and as long as you're here I might as well get your information."

"I don't like it, everybody talking behind my back. It's like you're trying to get them to tell you bad stuff."

"That's not what I'm trying to do at all. If we have to go to court, I want a bunch of people telling the judge how you are with the baby. It sounds like you're doing a great job, and we want him to hear the details."

Leanne said something under her breath.

"Excuse me?"

Now she yelled. "I burned her!"

"Leanne, it was an accident."

"Yeah well, whatever."

"Why don't you go on over to the hospital, Honey, and see how Misty is doing. I'll be over in a little while."

Chapter Forty-Two

Vinnie persuaded Leanne to stay with her till Misty was out of the hospital. It didn't make much difference because she only came home to sleep. Misty stayed in the burn unit for three days, and Leanne sat in the waiting room, going in every hour to sit with her for ten minutes. She insisted the baby could tell when she was there.

"I asked them to come get me when she wakes up, but they don't do it."

Vinnie spoke to a nurse about it, who said she would do what she could, but they were awfully busy.

"She should go home. She's not doing any good here."

Vinnie did convince Leanne to go to work on Monday. "It will look better, honey, if you finish the job. It's only this week and two days next week. And they'll call you if they need you for Misty."

"Will you call Miss Bradwell? I'm not supposed to make personal calls at work. Anyway, I don't want them knowing my business."

Vinnie called in the morning and left a message. She called in the afternoon and left a message. Then she remembered Miss Bradwell had said she had hearings Monday. But she didn't call back on Tuesday either.

"Can't you go see her, Momma?"

"It won't do any good. I'm sure when she's got something to tell us she'll call. She had all those people to talk to."

"If I had a real lawyer instead of Legal Aid, I bet it would be different."

"I know, but we can't afford a lawyer."

On Thursday they both slept in. Leanne had been at the hospital every night till ten, and up for work at 6:30. Vinnie was glad to see her get some sleep, and to catch up on her own. She fixed a big breakfast. It was almost ten when they got to the hospital. Misty was gone.

"She was discharged this morning," the nurse at the desk told them.

Vinnie was furious. "Where is she?"

"I don't know, you'll have to ask DFC."

"Why didn't you call us? My daughter's been here every day looking out for her baby, and now they take her away without a word."

"It's not up to us. The doctor discharged her to DFC."

Leanne was standing not making a sound, her mouth open and tears pouring down. Vinnie took her arm and led her to the elevator. "We're talking to your lawyer."

At Legal Aid they had to wait. Leanne had stopped crying. After about an hour, Miss Bradwell came out and took them back to her office.

"Where do they have Misty Dawn?"

"What do you mean?"

"They took her out of the hospital and didn't tell me."

"Oh my God. I tried calling you this morning. We have a hearing set for Monday. I talked to Hampton Ferrell last night. I can't believe he didn't say anything to me."

"Can you find out where she is? Leanne sat by that baby all weekend and every night after work. It's not right what they've done."

"I'll do what I can. Like I said, we have a hearing Monday and I'm sure we can arrange for a visit."

"A visit? You said they'd let me have her."

"No, I don't think that's what I said, Leanne. I had to talk to DFC and find out their plans, and now we have to see what the judge says. Hampton was concerned about Misty's burn. They have a shelter home where the mother is a pediatric nurse, and they're asking the court to keep the baby with them at least until her burn is better. But he didn't tell me she was being discharged so soon."

"Can't you call and get some information? The nurses wouldn't tell us anything about how Misty is doing," Vinnie said.

"I'm sure she's doing fine or they wouldn't have discharged her. But I'll try calling."

They sat there while she called. She left a message at the office, and on Hampton Ferrell's cell phone. She left a message for the supervisor.

"That's all I can do. I'm afraid it may be Monday before we get anywhere. I planned to talk to you Friday to prepare for the hearing, but as long as you're here, let's do that now. Leanne, I've spoken with almost everyone and they all say the nicest things about you and Misty. Melanie Lillenthal from New Beginnings will testify for you, and Jonathan Loring will be there. I don't know yet what the guardian will recommend. She had nothing but praise for you, but she was worried about Misty's wound. I haven't heard from Mrs. Coggins."

"I know, I left her a message," Vinnie said. "Her husband said she's in Jacksonville. Her daughter's having a baby."

"Well, that's okay. I'll try to reach her, but even without her, we've got a strong case. I've already prepared with you, Mrs. Ellsworth. I'd just like to go over your testimony Leanne, and then we'll be all set for Monday."

She led Leanne through the story again. Vinnie could hardly stand it. It was worse when the questions started: did she usually hold Misty at the stove? Didn't she have a playpen? Did she have any experience treating serious burns? Whose side is she on, anyway, Vinnie thought.

"The other lawyer will ask these questions, and I want you ready for them. Even if he doesn't, they'll be on the judge's mind, and we need to be sure they get answered."

Monday morning Leanne wasn't talking. Vinnie persuaded her to eat some cereal. They got to court at 8:30. All the seats in the waiting area were full. Vinnie went up to the bailiff and asked where their hearing would be held.

"Juvenile, ma'am? They're here in courtroom D, starts at nine."

He told them to wait outside the courtroom until their lawyer arrived.

At nine Miss Bradwell still wasn't there, and Vinnie went up to the man again.

"She's not here yet, can't we go in? I'm afraid they'll be looking for us."

"No worry about that, there's probably lots before you. What's the name?"

He checked his list.

"You're number eleven. But when Amy gets here, she'll get it moved up. The cases with lawyers always go first."

Miss Bradwell came rushing up to them at 9:20.

"Sorry I'm late. You all ready?"

"I guess."

"Leanne, you look great. You doing okay?"

Leanne had dressed carefully, in a navy-blue skirt with a cotton blouse. She didn't look great, Vinnie thought, she looked numb, as if she couldn't see or hear the hubbub around her. She barely answered Miss Bradwell, but followed her into the courtroom, with Vinnie behind.

"I'll let the clerk know we're here."

They found seats in the middle of the third row of pews. Vinnie watched as a young father surrendered his rights to a baby he had never seen. The baby's arm had been broken, and it looked like the mother was going to lose her rights too.

Miss Bradwell came to the end of the pew, leaning over and whispering. "We go after the next case. All our witnesses are here."

An old couple were up next, the woman in a wheelchair. DFC had taken their grandchildren away because their apartment had holes in the floors and faulty wiring. The judge gave the department a month to find them safe housing, and the worker said, "Yes, your Honor." Apparently, the judge had issued an identical order twice before. The old man pushed his wife's wheelchair up the aisle.

"Okay, the next case looks like it could take a while – Miss Bradwell is on it." The bailiff and Mr. Tillman, the lawyer for DFCW, smiled. "Let's take a recess, be back here by 10:30."

The judge went out the back, and everybody else milled around. Marybeth had been sitting in the last row. Now she came up to Vinnie and Leanne.

"How's Misty?"

"I don't know. I haven't seen her since Wednesday. They won't even tell me where she is. I thought she'd be here."

It was more than Leanne had said all morning.

"I'm sure when we're done here they'll get her back to you. It wouldn't make much sense to bring a little baby to court."

Vinnie thought it might be a good idea to bring all those babies to court. She wasn't sure the judge knew they were talking about real babies.

"Leanne's lawyer says they have her in a foster home where the mother is a nurse, and they want to keep her there till the burn is healed."

"Oh, when I talked to her she didn't say anything about that," Marybeth said.

"What did you tell her?" Leanne demanded.

"There's no call to talk to Mrs. Coggins like that, Leanne, she's here to help you."

"I'm going outside," and she walked away.

"I'm sorry, Marybeth, she's really upset. She stayed by the baby every day and then when we got to the hospital Thursday, Misty was gone and nobody would tell us anything."

"That's terrible. Leanne was always so attentive to Misty. I'm sure she could learn to do the dressings."

"Thanks for coming today. Miss Bradwell said your daughter had her baby."

"She did, a week ago today. I've been staying over in Jacksonville to help with their little boy. I just got back Saturday."

"How is she doing?"

"Everybody's fine. She was on bed rest the last five weeks, but the baby came out ok, and what surprised me, she named her after me!

Ruthie and I haven't always gotten along that well. It means a lot to me."

"I bet it does."

She didn't care what Misty's name was if they could just get her back.

People were coming back in. Leanne and Miss Bradwell came in together and went up to the front. Mr. Tillman was there with the foster care worker, Vanessa Washington. Vinnie sat down in the first row with Marybeth. The judge spoke to Leanne.

"You must be Leanne Ellsworth. You're Misty's mother."

"Yes ma'am."

"You're staying with your mother, aren't you? Is she here today?"

Vinnie stood up, and the judge asked her to come up with the rest of them.

"I like to have the whole family here if possible, so you all understand what's going on. Miss Ellsworth, you understand why we're here in court today?"

"Yes ma'am, it's because DFC took Misty Dawn out of the hospital, and they didn't even tell me."

"Well, that's almost right. I need to decide where Misty should stay while her burns are getting better. I know you want her back with you, but I need to do what's best for the baby, and I know that's what you want too."

"She needs to be with me. I'm her momma and she's missing me."

"I'm sure she is, and you're missing her too. If she stays in foster care we'll be sure to let you see her. Now I'm going to ask you some questions so I understand the situation, okay?"

Vinnie couldn't decide whether the judge was being nice, or thought Leanne was stupid. It seemed like she had already decided to leave Misty in foster care with the nurse and was just trying to keep Leanne from blowing up. She went back to the time when Leanne left the baby, and then how she got her back, and her living with Vinnie, and moving in with Marybeth, and then living alone. It took forever.

She asked her about school and friends, and how she got along with Vinnie, and what she planned for her future.

Finally, she got to the accident, and Leanne told it all over again. Vinnie tried thinking of something else, but it didn't work. She had to hear about that damn can of soup, and Misty's little hand slamming down on the burner. Leanne had told it so many times, it was beginning to sound like a made-up story. The judge didn't ask Leanne any questions about it, and Vinnie worried she would think Leanne was hiding something.

"It's terrible how quickly something like that can happen. You need to put her in her playpen or somewhere when you're cooking."

Leanne looked as if she were about to cry. Vinnie knew it was hard, going back and telling about Peter and leaving the baby, and now this. But she answered all the questions and told the judge she knew she could take care of the burn. She'd watched the nurses, and one of them let her help, and Misty didn't scream so loud when she did it.

"I know you love your baby, and she loves you. Now I need to hear from these other people, and then we can decide what's best for Misty. You can just stand up here if you want to and hear what they have to say. All right, Miss Bradwell, let's hear your witnesses."

First was Melanie Lillenthal. Amy began questioning her about New Beginnings, but the judge interrupted.

"Miss Bradwell, I don't need to hear about the school. I'm on the board. Let's just ask her to tell us about Leanne and the baby, then if any of us have other questions we can ask them. I like to run things informally here so we can get at the truth. Do you have any objection to that, Miss Bradwell? Mr. Tillman?"

"No, your Honor."

"Okay, Miss Lillenthal, tell us what you know about Leanne. You're her teacher, right?"

Leanne was one of her best students. She asked for extra help when she needed it and always did her homework. She finished three units of math in one semester, and two units of language and literature.

She borrowed books to read to the baby and brought them back on time. The baby was always properly dressed when she came to school. She ate lunch with the baby, talking to her all the time, not like some of the other girls who hung out in the playground with their boyfriends. Jackie, who ran the nursery, said the baby was right on target developmentally. Mr. Tillman objected to that as hearsay.

"Sustained. But it's all in the guardian's report anyway. Miss Lillenthal, only tell us what you know about Leanne, not what somebody else told you, okay?"

Next was a nurse from the burn unit. She told about Leanne sitting there all day, singing to Misty when she was awake, feeding and holding her once she was out of the sterile bassinet. She told about the dressings. She said she thought the doctors only discharged Misty because they knew she'd be staying with a nurse.

"Objection, your Honor."

"Miss Bradwell, you can't object to your own witness."

So Amy questioned her when the judge was through, established that Leanne had watched the nurses change the dressings and bathe the baby, and one of the other nurses had let her do it herself, and the dressing looked okay.

Marybeth was comfortable talking to the judge. She talked of how Leanne never went anywhere, but stayed home and took care of Misty, though she and her husband would have been glad to babysit. Leanne did everything for Misty herself, feeding and bathing and laundry, and carried her around everywhere. She never heard the baby crying for more than a few minutes. Mr. Tillman asked her about Leanne moving out, and she just said she and her husband needed their privacy; they weren't ready for a teenager and a baby in the house again.

When it was her turn, Vinnie was nervous, though she had nothing to hide. All she had to do was talk to the judge. She told about Leanne taking care of Misty. About the time Misty was so sick and Leanne sat up with her. How Leanne was always telling her childcare ideas she'd got from books or from the people at school. The judge asked her whether Leanne could move back in with her, and she said it would be fine while the baby was getting better, but it might not work in the long run, because it was just one room, and her son stayed there a lot. Miss Bradwell had asked her that. She didn't like the answer but told her to tell the truth.

"Okay, Miss Bradwell, is that all your witnesses?"

"Yes, your Honor."

"Let's hear from DFC and see what they're recommending. Miss Washington?"

Amy protested. "Your Honor, they said Jonathan Loring would be here. He's the case worker who has been supervising Leanne and the baby since they moved into their apartment."

"Is Mr. Loring here, Mr. Tillman?"

"No, your Honor; he's out sick, but Miss Washington has his case notes."

"Well, Miss Bradwell, I can adjourn this hearing until Mr. Loring is available, if you like."

"I need to speak with my client, your Honor."

"Of course."

Miss Bradwell took Leanne over into a corner, and Vinnie followed right behind.

"I'd like to have him here. He told me, just like you did, that he was ready to recommend terminating supervision in September. But it will mean waiting at least another week, maybe more, and you wouldn't have Misty with you."

"I want to do it now. I think the judge likes me. She'll tell them to give me back Misty Dawn."

"Jonathan's testimony would help us a lot. Even if the judge likes you, she could keep her in foster care for quite a while."

"I don't think so, she was really nice."

"Well, it's your decision."

Vinnie wanted to shake her. Wasn't it the lawyer's job to keep Leanne from making a dumb decision? But she didn't have anything to say about it, even if she was the grandmother. Leanne was determined to go ahead. They went back and stood in front of the judge again.

Miss Washington stated DFC's position: Misty should stay in foster care until the doctor said she needed no more treatment. The case notes were just a list of dates that Jonathan had visited Leanne, with nothing about his plan to end supervision. Next was the guardian's report. Jennifer made the same recommendation as DFC. As soon as she heard that, Vinnie knew, but Leanne looked shocked when the judge spoke.

"Well, Leanne, I think it will be better to leave Misty in foster care until she's all well. It's like she's in the hospital, but a much nicer place. And DFC will arrange for you to visit her every week. Have you ever been to the visitation center?"

"I've been there. You only get an hour with your baby. She'll be scared, staying with people she doesn't know. They don't know what she likes and how she eats. She thinks I went away forever. She has to come back home."

She was crying but she managed to say it all clearly.

"Now Miss Ellsworth, we all want to do what's right for Misty, but you haven't always displayed the best judgment, you know. You're a good mother, but I think she'll be safer staying with a nurse who can take care of her burns, and when they're healed, I'm sure DFC will be happy for her to go back to you. Miss Washington, I want you to arrange a visit as soon as you can."

And it was over. Nothing to do but take Leanne home.

Leanne

Chapter Forty-Three

I've visited three times. First time was three days after the hearing. We didn't have to go to DFC. They've got this new place, like a big playroom, only with lots of couches. They say there's lots of people on weekends, but we were there Thursday morning and it was nobody but me, Misty Dawn and Momma, Miss Washington from DFC, and the foster mom. Her name is Jane Kerrington. She's real pretty, with shiny red hair. She's nice too, and she's taking good care of Misty Dawn. I bet if I asked her, she'd let me take her home and not tell DFC. But I'm scared to ask.

Misty Dawn had on those white shoes that keep her ankles up. The doctor said I should get them when she started pulling herself up to stand, but they cost too much. She looked good, except for the air cast. It covers up where she's burned, but it still makes you think about it. I'd like to never think about it again.

Soon as Misty Dawn saw me, she started twisting around to get off Jane's lap. Jane let her go and she started walking to me, but she fell down and crawled the rest of the way. I never saw her walk before. I sat down on the floor and she climbed up on my lap. I didn't want to cry in front of them but I felt all mixed, happy to see her and awful sad.

I sat in a chair and we played bounce. Momma could find out anything I need to know. I didn't want to talk, I just wanted to be with Misty Dawn. I wonder if she'll remember this time. I don't remember anything from when I was a baby but It's hard to believe when she's bigger it will be like it never happened. I wish she could only remember the good stuff, not the burn and being away from me.

I carried her to the corner where the toys are and gave her a xylophone. Momma came over and played Twinkle Twinkle. I thought it was cool, but Misty Dawn just wanted to do it herself. She grabbed the stick and went back to banging.

In a little while she started fussing and sucking on her fist. Jane said, "I think she's hungry," like I don't know that, but I didn't show that it bugged me. Jane gave me juice and cereal and I put her in the highchair. She likes to feed herself. Jane said she gives her little bits of food to eat with her fingers. I said I'm teaching her to use the spoon, and she needs to have vegetables, and Jane promised to get some. Jane told me what a good baby she is, hardly fusses when she changes the dressing. Only I didn't want to think about the burn so I turned around and helped Misty Dawn, not that she needed any help.

I wiped her off when she was finished and took her out of the highchair. I wanted to read her a story, but Miss Washington said, "I think it's time to get Misty home, don't you think, Mrs. Kerrington?" For the littlest minute I thought she meant my home and when I realized she didn't I felt bad, but I didn't say anything. Momma said they'd be watching everything I do with Misty Dawn to decide if it's okay for her to come back to us, and I figured I'd better be polite. So I said, "Just let my Momma hold her for a minute." Momma took her and Misty Dawn put her head down on her shoulder and started sucking her thumb, real cute.

Jane gave me a picture of Misty Dawn. She was wearing a new blue dress and had a fuzzy fox in her lap that hid the cast. She already took Misty Dawn for baby pictures, which I didn't have money for. All I had was pictures Momma took at Easter.

When I asked about visiting again, Miss Washington said she couldn't do a visit every week no matter what the judge said, but Jane could bring her if the visitation center lady supervised. So we had two more visits.

Jane's husband Warren came on the third visit. He's really nice and I could tell he liked Misty Dawn. She was snuggled in his lap when I got there. After we played and I fed her, she fell asleep in my arms, and I went and sat down in one of the chairs. Jane and Warren were asking me all these questions, like what I like to do, where do I live, do I have any brothers and sisters, and all like that. It felt friendly, not snoopy. I told them about drawing, and they said I should try drawing a picture of Misty Dawn. They asked if I like to swim, and I said yeah, and they said after Misty Dawn comes home maybe I can bring her to their pool. They showed me a picture of their pool. It looks like a place in a magazine. There's a deck with plants all around and a big barbecue grill.

Momma wants me to stay with her until Misty Dawn comes home. I want to and don't want to. It's lonely in my apartment, and I miss Misty Dawn a lot. But when I'm back at Momma's I kind of feel like none of this happened, like there's no Peter or Misty Dawn. It's like a couple of years of my life just got erased. When I'm with Momma I feel like a kid, except Momma's nicer to me now and not so bossy. Not that there's anything to boss me about. I mean, there's no school and my job is over so she can't nag me about getting there on time or anything. I feel like she wouldn't anyway, but still, I like being on my own if I just could have my baby back.

On my last day of work they took me out to lunch and gave me a cool present, a pad of good drawing paper and a set of Prismacolors. They're blendable colored pencils real artists use. I was really glad to be done with my job. I think Mrs. Seacrist was just making up stuff for me to do. I hate doing boring work that doesn't even need doing.

Boring is the story of my life. I never thought I'd say this, but I can't wait for school to start. If I went back to Momma's at least I'd have cable. I spend a lot of time just looking out the window at this little tree. All the other trees are big and covered with leaves, and this dinky one is mostly sticks, with a few spotty leaves. I tried drawing it but it was depressing. That's what I do a lot, draw with my new pencils.

I've got the picture Jane gave me in the bedroom. Misty Dawn is looking straight at me, and her smile is so big you can see all four teeth. You'd never know she got burned, or she's poor. I guess when you're a baby, poor doesn't matter, except when you need medicine or shoes. Babies don't worry about what they don't have. It'll be different when she's older, when the other kids have stuff and she doesn't.

At New Beginnings I go at my own pace. If I work hard I bet I could finish in a year and a half and Misty Dawn will only be two and a half. I could have a job making good money for a couple of years before she even gets to kindergarten. Only thing is, I want to go to OCC for graphic design, so I guess we'll be poor a couple more years.

Sometimes I don't think I can do it. Momma has to pay my light bill. I wouldn't ask except if your lights get cut off the housing people take away your apartment. I don't know if I can pay my phone bill either. I thought I was doing good, but then look what happened to Misty Dawn. When I'm sitting on the bed looking at her picture, I try to only think about her, but this other stuff comes in, and worse too, so then I go draw, because when I'm drawing and trying to figure out the lines I don't think about anything else.

Vinnie

Chapter Forty-Four

Vinnie hadn't seen Misty in almost four weeks. The visits were Thursday afternoons, and she couldn't keep shifting her schedule. She hadn't seen much of Leanne either. She had paid Leanne's phone bill and called her every Thursday to hear about the visit. Half the time she woke her up, and other times it was "yeah, no, I dunno" until she gave up and said goodbye. Once Leanne sounded drunk, and she couldn't get any sense out of her. It worried her, but what could she do?

Now Leanne called and said Miss Bradwell wanted to see them both. They had an appointment on Tuesday morning. Leanne didn't know what it was about. Vinnie thought the baby should be home by now. Leanne said she had been bugging Miss Bradwell, so maybe they'd scheduled another hearing.

When they got to Legal Aid, Miss Bradwell asked the receptionist to hold her calls. She offered them tea and seemed to have all the time in the world. Vinnie didn't like the way she usually was, trying to do four things at once, but the change made her nervous. Something was happening.

Miss Bradwell asked how Misty was doing. Leanne was happy to brag on Misty and said the Kerringtons were going to give her a birthday party if she wasn't home yet and invite Leanne, even though Leanne wasn't supposed to know where they lived. Vinnie thought Miss Bradwell would scold Leanne for breaking the rules, but she just wanted to hear more. What did Leanne think of them, how were they with Misty? Vinnie was twitchy. It felt like Miss Bradwell was just trying to get them relaxed before she got to whatever it was. After she poured more tea, she picked up a pen and pulled out a yellow pad.

"I'm afraid things have gotten more complicated. Mr. Tillman told me yesterday DFC intends to file papers to terminate parental rights."

"They can't do that. It was only until Misty Dawn didn't need the dressings anymore. I was supposed to get her back before her birthday. That's in three weeks. You said."

Miss Bradwell said she was surprised too. All the evidence showed what a good job Leanne had done with Misty. Even Jonathan Loring said Leanne was doing fine. But now that the baby was in foster care, she had a different worker. Jonathon wasn't on the case anymore. Miss Bradwell didn't know much about Vanessa Washington; she'd only been at DFC three months. She'd been talking to the guardian, and they both agreed Misty would be better off in a family. It wasn't supposed to work that way at all. But the guardian was new too. It was her first case, and she was very young, still in college.

"You mean Jennifer? I thought she was my friend. She told me I'm such a good mom."

"Have you talked to her recently?"

"No, last time I saw her was before I got my job."

"Well, she's been talking to the child protection team and the nurses, and she wonders if it was really an accident."

Vinnie lost it. "What the hell is wrong with her, is she crazy? How can they have a college kid making these decisions?"

"Please Mrs. Ellsworth, try to keep calm. I'm just as upset as you are, I assure you."

She didn't seem upset, just tired. It must be just one more case for her. But it wasn't any good yelling at her either. It wasn't her fault. Leanne was behaving better than Vinnie. She just sat still, staring at Miss Bradwell.

"Leanne honey, you okay?" Vinnie asked.

"They think I hurt her on purpose." Vinnie could hardly hear her.

"Look, you have to understand. I don't think they'll succeed. But we have to deal with their petition, and I'm afraid with the way things are now it will slow us down a lot getting Misty back with you."

"What things?"

"Well, we've got the new worker, and the guardian's recommendation. Usually, their supervisors would have kept it from getting this far. And Mr. Tillman should know he doesn't have a legal case. But everybody is nervous now since the little boy got killed – remember I told you? DFC and the guardian had both recommended the judge send him back to his father. After something like that happens things change for a while. They take away a lot more kids and it's harder to get them back. The other thing is the judge."

"What about the judge?" Vinnie asked. "She seemed fine."

"She is, but she's back in criminal. The new judge has been in juvenile before, and we know a lot about him. He doesn't think anything is an accident. And I've heard him say some terrible things about teen mothers."

"So Misty Dawn won't be home for her birthday?"

Vinnie couldn't bear it. Leanne didn't understand. They were going to take the baby away for good, and all she could think about was her birthday.

"I think probably not. But maybe we can get you an extra visit and you can take her a cake."

"I told you, Jane says she'll have a party for her."

"Oh yes, Jane Kerrington. Well, that's the other thing. The Kerringtons want to adopt Misty. Nobody's supposed to be talking about adoption at this stage, but Mr. Tillman has always been straight with me and he told me what's going on. You see it happen. The foster care worker is impressed when she's got a baby in a good home, because so many of them aren't good, and she's not that involved with the mother, so naturally she wants the baby to stay where she is. And like I said, Vanessa Washington is new. She doesn't know how many of these adoptions go wrong."

"Aren't there any rules?" asked Vinnie.

"Yeah, I've gotta follow all these rules for visiting and TANF and everything, and they get to do whatever they want. It's not fair."

"No Leanne, it's not." Miss Bradwell sounded discouraged, all her energy gone.

"They can't adopt her unless Leanne agrees, right?"

"No, of course not, not until, I mean not unless, they get her rights terminated. What I'm saying is, I think they are trying for termination because they have a good home for her."

"She has a good home already. I'm her Mom and she needs to be with me. Everybody knows that. They can't love her the way I do. She'd feel it. She'd miss me. She'll get all messed up."

"Whoa now, Leanne, you're talking like it's decided. I brought you in here to tell you what's happening, and to figure out together what we should do."

And she started explaining their choices. The first question was whether Leanne wanted to oppose termination. Miss Bradwell assumed she did, but she had to understand that they could lose. They would probably win, only it might be a few months before they got Misty back.

"When you say there's a chance we'd lose, what kind of a chance, like what are the odds?" Vinnie asked.

"I can't give you a number. The law is definitely in our favor. But like I said, things are screwy now. I'd say there's maybe a ten percent chance they would win a termination."

"But if we don't fight it, it's a hundred percent, right? So I don't see any reason why we'd just lie down for it."

"Well, it's complicated to think about, because of the Kerringtons. Leanne, are you paying attention now? It's all up to you." Leanne wasn't looking at either of them, but down at her hands, picking at the skin on her thumbnail.

"I'm listening," she whispered.

If they lost the termination fight, the Kerringtons would adopt and Leanne might never see Misty again. If they didn't want to risk that, even though she didn't think it was a very big risk, they were in a strong position to negotiate an open adoption, where they could visit with Misty sometimes, and know her as she was growing up.

"You mean I could take Misty Dawn to my house? Could I have her on her birthday?"

"That would all be something to work out. We'd meet with them and their lawyer. We wouldn't agree unless we had what you wanted. If we can't get what you want, we'd oppose termination."

"What I want is Misty Dawn home where she belongs."

"Well then, we should oppose termination, do our very best, and hope we win. And I think we will."

"And if we don't, Leanne might never see her baby again."

"That's true. It's a hard decision. That's why I wanted to talk to both of you. I'd like you to go home and think about it for a few days. I don't have to file an answer until August 18, so you have some time."

Leanne

Chapter Forty-Five

Jane is such a phony. The day after we talked to Miss Bradwell I had a visit. I didn't think Jane would be there, but her and her husband both came. They acted like nothing was different, all smiley, talking about how cute Misty Dawn is and what she's doing. They never said nothing about adoption. I guess they didn't know Miss Bradwell had told me.

Jane wanted to talk about the birthday party. I pretended I was all excited, and in a way I was. A year ago she was so teeny and I was scared holding her, afraid she'd break. Now she's walking and almost talking, and she feeds herself. Jane says she won't take the bottle anymore, she uses a sippy cup.

We spent the whole visit talking about what Misty Dawn was doing, and about her party. Jane says she's sure DFC will let us do it at their house instead of the visitation center. I bet Miss Washington will do whatever the Kerringtons say, not like if it was me asking. Jane said she'll get a cake, and me and Vinnie and whoever else I want can come. I'm mad at Momma though, and I said she'd probably be working.

The night after we talked to Miss Bradwell, Momma and I had a big fight. I was crying in the car because I was scared they'd take Misty Dawn away, even if Miss Bradwell said she thought we would win. I keep going in circles. Misty Dawn's gotta be with me so I can't let them adopt her, but if I let them adopt her I can still see her, and if I don't let them I might have her back with me or I might never see her again.

I don't know how to figure out something like that. Momma said I didn't have to decide it right this minute, and we should take our time and talk it over. She said I should come home with her for lunch and stay the night. I shouldn't be alone with something that hard.

I didn't want to argue, also I was hungry. Mostly though, I just wanted Momma to tell me what to do. But she wouldn't. In fact, she didn't want to talk about it very much. She said I needed to think about what it would be like if I kept Misty Dawn, and if I lost her. How it would be if they adopted her but I could still visit and see her. How I would feel for each of those things, and how it would be for Misty Dawn too. She said I should think about all this stuff. I asked her what she wanted me to do, and she wouldn't say. She said that shouldn't be part of my decision. But what made me mad came later.

We had grilled cheese for lunch, that's what she always makes when I'm feeling bad. After lunch we sat on the deck, even though it was hot. She brought out lemonade with mint – it's real sweet and I like it a lot. I said it would kill me to give up Misty Dawn. Momma said no, when your heart breaks it doesn't kill you, you just wish it would. I figured she was thinking about when she gave away her baby, and maybe when Daddy left too, except I remember that, and it didn't seem like her heart was broke at all. But I was just a kid. Maybe I didn't know.

I asked her if she was sorry she gave away her baby and she didn't answer for a long time. Then she said, "What good would it do to be sorry?" I asked her if she ever thinks about him, and she said not so much as she used to. I wonder what she thinks about. Is it about him as a baby, or what he'd be like now? She doesn't know what he looks like or what he's doing. He could be dead and she wouldn't know it. That's what it would be like with me and Misty Dawn if we went to court and lost.

We sat out on the deck for a long time. We didn't talk a lot. I was getting sleepy in the sun, and then it was time for Momma to go to work. I turned on the TV and watched cartoons and the shopping channel. It kept me from thinking about any of it. But I fell asleep in front of the TV and didn't wake up until almost 8:30. And when I woke up, I knew what we should do. I couldn't believe nobody had thought of it. I'd ask the judge to give Misty Dawn to Momma. It would be like she was still with me. We could share her. I could work and go to college and it wouldn't be so hard.

I had this idea all by myself. When I did what Momma said, and practiced how it would feel, it felt good thinking of Misty Dawn with her. Besides feeling okay when I thought about it, it would be the best for Misty Dawn. She'd be with family, she wouldn't be leaving me, and Momma is good with her and loves her.

Momma came home about 11:30 with a whole bunch of fried chicken and half a chocolate pie. I said, "Momma I've got it all figured out," but she said we'd talk at dinner. While she took a shower I heated up a can of corn and set the table. I made it look all nice. She came out in her bathrobe with her hair in a towel and sat down and took a piece of chicken. But when I told her my idea, she just said, "No," mean and loud.

When I was thinking how it would be, I never even thought about her saying no. It's her own grandbaby, and she's always saying she loves her so much. I guess not, if she's willing to let her leave the family. I tried to get her to explain, but she just kept saying, "That's your baby for you to raise." So now I find out she thinks I should tell Miss Bradwell I want to fight. Easy for her. She probably doesn't care if she never sees her again. I knew what she was thinking: you made your bed, you lie in it. After she gave away her own baby and told me it hurt so much, now she doesn't care if they take Misty Dawn away from me.

It hurt my feelings bad. She's my mother. She could fix everything so we wouldn't lose Misty Dawn, and she doesn't even care. I just wanted to get away from her and be by myself, but all I could do was go out on the deck and wait for her to go to bed.

I sat out there a long time. It wasn't as hot as in the daytime. I kept looking at the stars. I always thought I'd be showing them to Misty Dawn when she gets older. I could remember Daddy showing me the consolations, and I never could see any pictures up there until one day I could. I saw the hunter, and after that I could always see it. Thinking of showing Misty Dawn the stars, I really missed her then. I could almost feel her on my lap up against my stomach. What if I never got to do that again? But how would it be, just visiting her once a week? Would they let me have her at night?

Before the burn I would of told anybody that Misty Dawn was fine and she belongs with her Mom. It's just now I'm starting to wonder. The birthday party, that makes me wonder too.

The Kerringtons don't live anywhere near a bus stop, so Dr. Kerrington picked me up. He acted real nice and asked how I was doing and when does school start and all that. Their lawyer must of told them Miss Bradwell talked to me, but they still pretend they don't know. I can pretend too, and I acted all friendly. I said his car was cool; it's a Jaguar convertible. We talked a little about his car, and a lot about Misty Dawn. We drove through the south side of town and went through this fancy gate. You wouldn't have any idea all those houses were back there. The road was twisty with big trees everywhere, and I could see a lake behind the houses. At their house there was birthday balloons tied to the mailbox.

The house is amazing. The whole back is glass. You can look out and see the swimming pool, with chairs all around it, and then past that, through the trees, you see the lake.

We went inside and straight to the playroom. It has all the toys on low shelves, and a big TV with a whole bunch of DVD's, every kid movie you ever heard of. There's armchairs for grownups. Emily is five. She's real cute, with long brown hair. Misty Dawn was sitting on the floor with her, playing roll the ball. When she saw me she got that big smile and started walking to me without holding on. I picked her up and gave her lots of kisses, and then she was wiggling because she wanted to get down and play.

Jane said she'd show me Misty Dawn's room, and we went upstairs. Her room is all decorated with Winnie the Pooh. Above the crib there's a big picture of him with a balloon, and by the changing table there's a shelf with a little plastic Pooh and Tigger and all the rest where the baby can see them.

Jane said it was time for the party, so we went back downstairs. Emily and Misty Dawn were in the playroom on the couch, and Emily was reading The Color Kittens to Misty Dawn. That was my favorite book when I was little. I couldn't believe Emily got all the words right, but Jane said she has it mostly memorized.

When they finished the story, Jane said we should go in the kitchen and start the party. Emily carried Misty Dawn and I was afraid she'd drop her, but she did fine, and it seemed like Misty Dawn was used to it. In the kitchen the table was all set up. There was a pink tablecloth and plastic Happy Birthday plates, and balloons tied to the chairs. Lunch was sandwiches made with cookie cutters, cream cheese and jelly for the kids and tuna salad for the grownups, including me.

It was fun to be in a real house instead of the visitation center. Emily wasn't bratty like you'd think she'd be with all those toys. She sat next to Misty Dawn and helped her. I cut up a star and a heart, and Misty Dawn finished most of it and a whole sippy cup of milk. I finished her sandwich; I liked it better than the tuna fish. Then Jane brought out the cake and lit the candles. It had a big orange sun coming up over a blue lake with pink clouds, Jane said because of her name. Dr. Kerrington said, "But it's not misty, the sky is all clear." They were joking with each other, and all of a sudden I felt lonely and just wished I could take Misty Dawn and go home.

Then Jane said Misty should blow out the candles. They'd been practicing blowing the whole week. I put the cake in front of her but she just kept pushing out her lips like a fish and no air came. Jane said I should blow it out for her, but Emily said, "She has to make a wish." Jane said she was too young to make a wish, so we should all make one, and not tell what it is. I knew what they were all wishing. But I couldn't figure out mine. I wanted her back, only everything was nice at the Kerringtons' house, and everything was crummy at my house. And

Peter could come to hurt her there, but he's too chickenshit to mess with the Kerringtons. But even with my crummy house and Peter, I'm her Mom and she should be with me. So then I just wished I knew my wish, and I blew out the candle. It made me sad not to have a wish.

Jane gave a little piece of cake to Misty Dawn. She mushed it in her hand, and then sucked it off her fist real good. I only took a couple bites of mine. I liked it but I was feeling bad. Jane gave me a towel to clean up Misty Dawn, and I held her on my lap for the presents.

First I opened Momma's present. It was a party dress with a pink top and fluffy white skirt, and pink patent leather shoes. Dr. Kerrington said, "When's she going to wear that?" but Jane said, "Hush, Warren, I think it's adorable." Emily's present was a DVD of Teletubbies. Jane and Dr. Kerrington gave her a big brown teddy bear. Jane told me the eyes and nose were made of thread so she couldn't choke on them. It bothered me a lot. She thinks I don't know anything about babies, because look how I let Misty Dawn get burned. And then she said, "Now it's time for your present from your mother, Misty Dawn, and that's the best of all." I just wanted to go somewhere and hide, because I bought her a teddy bear too, with yarn eyes and nose, only mine was about as big as one of the legs on the one they gave her. But I had to open it there in front of them. Jane said how cute it was, and she could sleep with it in her crib, but everybody knew it wasn't as good. Then Jane said they had a present for me, because Misty Dawn's birthday was a big day for me too. And it was the same picture they gave me on the first visit, only it was big, and they put it in a silver frame with flowers on it.

That was the last present, and Misty Dawn was falling asleep. So Jane said, "Why don't you put her down for her nap, and then Warren will take you home." I went upstairs and put her down in her crib and covered her with the blanket. I looked all around the room again and thought about how when she wakes up she sees all the Poohs and Tiggers and Eeyores. I don't know why, but I took Kanga and Roo off the shelf and put them in my pocket. Then I went downstairs and Dr. Kerrington took me home.

At home I went and laid down on the bed. I was fiddling with Kanga and Roo, and I kept feeling sad that I didn't have a wish. Miss Bradwell says I've got choices, and Momma says to think about them all, but one of them I don't even have to think about, because I know that's what I want. So I just have to think about the two, never seeing her or seeing her sometimes, and that's not a hard choice either. I guess where I get confused is, if I do one thing I get the best or the worst, and if I do the other thing I get the middle – that's giving her away but getting to see her. I don't know how to figure out something like that.

I can't believe Jennifer thinks I burned my baby on purpose. She saw how I was with her. The girls at school say I'm spoiling her with all the cuddling and laughing when she's bad. I know people do terrible things to babies, but nobody could think I would do that. Still, it was my fault. Everybody knows you don't hold a baby near a stove, and usually I never did. I always stuck her in her playpen when I was cooking. But she was fussing and I was just pouring out the soup. Now she'll have scars because I wasn't careful. I should be the one with the scars.

That's not the only bad thing I did either, even if it's the worst. One time when we were both sick, I didn't change her all day and she got a bad diaper rash. It took a week to get it cleaned up. I didn't take her to the doctor because I was scared they'd yell at me. And one night she wouldn't go to sleep in her crib and I finally gave up and took her into my bed even though everybody says you shouldn't. In the middle of the night I went to the bathroom and left her there sleeping, and she rolled over and got stuck between the mattress and the headboard, and she could of died if I hadn't come out right then. And there was a time she wouldn't stop crying no matter what I did, and finally I put her in her crib and sat out on the doorstep and let her cry and cry. If people knew those things they would of taken her away a long time ago.

I couldn't stop thinking about all that stuff. And I was thinking about how it was for Misty Dawn with the Kerringtons. Emily was like a big sister for her, and you could tell Jane and Warren were really good parents, because Emily was so kind, and she had good manners too. She was really smart. She was only five but she was already reading. It seems like Misty Dawn could have a really good life with them. I remember how it was for me when I was little and the other kids had all this stuff I couldn't have, and we lived in that stupid garage. Maybe if I really love her I should let them adopt her and give her that good life. She'd have a whole family, and never have to struggle. She'd have it easy, and have what I never had. And I bet Jane would let me see her lots.

Vinnie

Chapter Forty-Six

Miss Bradwell said they should both come to the meeting, so Vinnie drove Leanne to the lawyer's office. She couldn't tell if Leanne was still upset with her. She sat looking out the side window. Vinnie was pretty sure she was crying. No wonder, giving up her baby. Where did she get the courage to do it? Or was it courage? Maybe she should have fought. How could Vinnie understand it when she could never make sense of what she'd done herself?

She hadn't heard from Leanne the whole week after Misty's birthday, and when she went by the apartment Leanne wouldn't answer the door. The last time she knocked and knocked until a neighbor told her to go away, people were trying to sleep.

Finally, after a week, Leanne called and told her, and said they had to meet Thursday with the Kerringtons and their lawyer. The lawyer's office was in a new office park, with trees and rolling lawn, and a pond with irises around it. The flower beds weren't touched by the heat and storms, not like Vinnie's.

They got there right on time. Miss Bradwell was just getting out of her yellow Volkswagen when Vinnie pulled into a parking space. Leanne didn't say a word, not even hello. She had been so quiet in the car, and she stayed quiet as they walked from the glare of the afternoon sun into the cool lobby, with its dark reflective glass that made it feel like three in the afternoon on no real day of the year.

Miss Bradwell reminded them again: the Kerringtons could make promises about visits but the law couldn't make them keep the promises.

"You don't have to keep telling me that. I made up my mind."

Vinnie understood because Leanne was just like her. Deciding was miserable, but having things settled was a relief, no matter if it tore your heart to pieces.

The receptionist ushered them into the conference room where Dr. and Mrs. Kerrington and their lawyer, Mr. Benefield, were already sitting on one side of the long table. Mrs. Kerrington said, "Hi Leanne," but Leanne just mumbled something. Mr. Benefield was an old man in a gray suit, his manner formal but warm.

"You must be Leanne Ellsworth. I'm Jay Benefield, it's nice to meet you. That's right, just take that seat, and Mrs. Ellsworth, why don't you sit right here next to your daughter. Miss Bradwell, I don't believe we've ever met."

They shook hands. Vinnie wished Miss Bradwell looked more like a lawyer and wore a suit, instead of that drooping skirt and cotton jacket. It probably didn't matter, but it felt shabby. Leanne looked better than she did.

"Well, Miss Bradwell, what do you propose?"

She laid it out for him, what Leanne had agreed to. A monthly visit, a visit at Christmas and on Misty's birthday, a phone call every week when Misty was old enough. This was less than Leanne wanted, and a lot more than she could probably get, Miss Bradwell had told her. Sure enough, Mr. Benefield said they couldn't agree to that. The phone calls would be disruptive and confuse the child. The standard arrangement was an annual letter and photograph to the birth mother, but the Kerringtons had agreed to birthday and Christmas visits too.

Miss Bradwell said the standard arrangement didn't apply, because Leanne had already had the baby a year – it wasn't like with a newborn. If they couldn't reach a satisfactory agreement, they were prepared to withhold consent and contest the termination. The state didn't have grounds for termination.

Mr. Benefield said juvenile court was unpredictable, and with all the disruptions at DFC there seemed to be a lot of terminations that weren't, strictly speaking, legally justified.

Suddenly Leanne spoke up. "It doesn't matter. Whatever they want."

Mr. Benefield barely smiled. Miss Bradwell said she would like to speak with Leanne privately, but Leanne said, "You don't have to explain any more stuff to me. He's right, it will just mix up Misty Dawn."

Miss Bradwell looked at Vinnie. "Maybe you and Leanne would like to talk?"

"She can't tell me what to do. I'm not a kid, and it's up to me, not her. She gave away her own baby, and she wouldn't even take Misty Dawn."

Vinnie wanted to slap her, but even more she wanted to put her arms around her. She couldn't do either one, of course, so she just sat there. The Kerringtons kept their eyes on Mr. Benefield, and he spoke only to Miss Bradwell. It was as if Leanne and Vinnie were just embarrassing intruders in this room with the polished table and the view of the pond through the dark glass.

"It sounds as if your client has made up her mind, Miss Bradwell."

They talked a little more, about getting DFC to transfer the case to a private agency that could turn the adoption around quickly, asking the judge to waive the waiting period since the baby was already in the home. On and on, none of it about Leanne or Misty. She would be gone, her first grandbaby, nothing but a picture every year, maybe a visit if Leanne would let her come too. She could stop all this legal stuff, just say, "I'll raise her, I'm her grandmother, she belongs with family." But she'd made up her mind too, and this time, it hadn't been that hard, not like when she was a teenager. She'd already raised three, and maybe not done so good with any of them. She was tired; she couldn't start over with another one, another eighteen years. It's not like they'd never see Misty. It would be different if she was going to some terrible place, but the Kerringtons were nice people, and they sure wouldn't have to struggle like Leanne, or like she would, for that matter. Still, if it were up to her, Leanne would have fought for Misty.

Mr. Benefield said he'd draw up the agreement, and his secretary would send it to Miss Bradwell. He turned to the Kerringtons.

"I believe we may be able to finalize the adoption by the end of September, if the judge will waive the waiting period."

"Can we go now?" Leanne said. Vinnie could tell she was about to cry.

"Yes, we're done. I'll call you when I have the papers." Amy opened the door and followed them into the reception area. A tall young man was sitting near the receptionist. Leanne stopped so suddenly Vinnie bumped into her.

"What are you doing here?"

"I'm signing the papers, just like you."

"Momma, it's him," Leanne said, her whisper so fierce she could have been yelling.

"I thought you were in jail," Leanne said to Peter.

"I got out last week, no thanks to you."

"They were supposed to tell me. You'd better not come near us again. I got a gun and so does my Momma."

That was ridiculous. Vinnie did have a gun, but Leanne was too young, and she hoped she hadn't gotten hold of one.

"Don't worry about that. I don't want anything to do with you or your brat. When I sign that consent, I'm free. You won't see any more of me."

Amy and the receptionist both looked nervous. The receptionist stood up and said to Peter, "I'll see if Mr. Benefield is ready for you."

"I don't get it, why does he have to consent?"

"They need the father's consent for the adoption," Amy said.

"He never paid any child support, he never even changed her diaper. How come he gets to say?"

"That's the law, Leanne. Both parents have to consent, unless the court terminates parental rights."

"Well I'm not like Peter. I'm not giving away my baby just like that. He's not any kind of father, but I'm a good mother, and if he's signing papers, I won't do it. Let them go ahead and try to terminate me."

"Oh my god," Amy said under her breath. Vinnie heard it, but Leanne was yelling at Peter.

"You'll never see Misty Dawn again, or Billy either. I saw Megan. She's taking Billy where you'll never find him. You aren't even a man, you're just a big bully. Even my brother thinks you're a loser. I'm not scared of you anymore, I'm twice as smart as you and I'm going to college and make a good life for my baby."

The receptionist stood between Leanne and Peter and took his arm. "Mr. Benefield is waiting, come into the conference room please."

Amy herded Vinnie and Leanne out of the reception area. "Well, Leanne, I think you've surprised everyone."

"So now what happens?" Vinnie asked.

"DFC will have to file a petition to terminate Leanne's rights, and we'll contest it. I'll call you as soon as I get the papers."

"When do I get to see Misty Dawn?"

"I'm not sure, I have to talk to DFC."

"She needs to be back with me," Leanne muttered, but she followed Vinnie out to the car. Vinnie sat a moment before she started the engine.

"I'm proud of you, Leanne."

"Cause I stood up to Peter?"

"No, I'm glad you're not afraid of him anymore, but yelling at him like that? That was dumb. But I'm proud you're fighting for Misty Dawn. You're a good mother, and I don't care what stupid stuff is going on at DFC and with that judge – I think you'll win and get your baby back. And if you lose, you know what? I don't know how, but we'll appeal it."

"I'm sorry I said those things about you in front of all those people, Momma."

"That's okay, honey. You're in a world of hurt."

They were halfway home when Vinnie said, "We need to celebrate. If you were older, I'd say let's have a drink, but we'll go out for dinner, somewhere besides John's."

In the last hour her heart had tumbled from past to future and back again. Lose the baby, keep the baby, now what? She'd take them to the Lakeside Grill. Leanne could look for gators and enjoy the sunset. And Vinnie could have a drink.

Leanne

Chapter Forty-Seven

I think I'm the luckiest girl in the world. The biggest thing is I got Misty Dawn back. Miss Bradwell says that lawyer from DFC was just trying to scare me so I'd let them do the adoption. When I changed my mind they dropped the whole thing, and two weeks later she came back home.

She was away from me almost three months, but it feels like she never was gone. Sometimes I get tired, being with her all the time, but when I think how it could of been I'm ashamed. I just feel bad I missed so much when she was with the Kerringtons. She doesn't take a bottle anymore. She runs and climbs, and I have to watch out she doesn't get hurt.

Jane Kerrington called me up and wants to be friends, like she didn't try to steal my baby. She wants me to come over and let Emily play with Misty Dawn. In a million years I wouldn't go back to their house. They'd probably figure out some way to trick me, and anyway, there's bad memories there. It was terrible trying to make up my mind, and I can't believe I decided to let Misty Dawn go. That's another reason I don't want to let Misty Dawn know the Kerrington's, because I don't want her ever to think her mother didn't want her. I don't trust them. They'd probably end up telling her and then maybe she'd feel bad, seeing what she missed out on.

But me and Misty Dawn, we won't always be poor. I'm working at Coggins twenty hours a week! That makes me too rich to get welfare, but I got more money than I did before and I still have the rent voucher and food stamps. I don't have Medicaid anymore, but Misty Dawn does. I just have to hope I don't get sick.

I don't have to pay childcare. I bring Misty Dawn to the store with me after school – we put her in a play pen in their little room, and leave the door open, and if she needs anything, there's always one of us can help her. Best thing, I still get to go to New Beginnings. That's not just for girls on welfare, but any girls who have babies. I went really fast and I've almost finished tenth grade, and when I do I can take a couple of design courses at OCC that will count toward graduation and get me started on college. I could get my associate degree by the time I'm eighteen, Miss Melanie says. She says she never saw a girl work so hard. She thinks after I'm done at OCC I can probably go to Opakulla University. In a million years I never thought I'd go to college. Momma is so proud of me.

We're different now. It's like Momma's my best friend. She hurt me so bad when she wouldn't adopt Misty Dawn, but it turns out she really hoped I'd fight to keep her. I guess I understand, she raised three kids by herself, and starting over with a baby – that's a lot. You got to be thinking of them the whole time, and you care about them more than yourself. Even with all the hard stuff, I love Misty Dawn deeper than anything.

Momma says watching her grow is like watching flowers bloom. I remember when Peter made me give her up, how I tried to picture her older, and couldn't see past that teeny face with the greasy looking hair. Her hair is light brown and wavy now, with that sweet baby smell.

When I ran away with Peter, I thought I was so grown. But I was just a kid, and it was easy for him to get me to do whatever he wanted. It's like he had me in a little tiny box, and he could take me out and play with me or beat me up.

What if I hadn't of changed my mind, and the Kerringtons adopted her? I wouldn't even know her and she wouldn't know me. In a way, Peter's what saved us. Seeing him at the lawyer's office made everything so clear. Usually I make up my mind and that's it, but I guess I hadn't really decided, and when I saw him I knew. No way would I do like him. So Peter, he's through with my baby, and I think he's lost his little boy too. He's not smart enough to find out where they are and move up to Ohio to be with his kid.

I used to think Peter was smarter than me, but like I said, he's just a loser. I'm almost sorry for him, even if I hate him. He's lost his kid, and that's the worst thing that can happen. Momma feels like she's lost Shauna, but you never know. Maybe she'll come back some day. Mrs. Coggins said she used to be real separate from her daughter Ruthie, but then when Ruthie grew up more, and had her second baby, they started being friends. I guess it takes some people a long time to grow up all the way.

Even Bailey is changing some. He got a job in the music store. He's worked there two months and Momma says he hasn't missed a day of work. He loves it, and he's learning guitar. He's even paying rent to her! I never thought I'd see that.

Even if I'm only sixteen, I been through so much I feel like I'm grown. I know what I want and I know how to get there. Me and Misty Dawn, we're always gonna be together.

Acknowledgements

I want to thank: My friends and family of course - faithful and enthusiastic supporters

Joan Leggitt, publisher of Twisted Road, and the editor of my dreams. She is ALWAYS right.

All the book groups who have invited me into their homes or Zoomed with me, because they wanted to sit around and talk about my first book. I hope they'll invite me back to discuss this one!

Walter Cummins, Stephanie Dickinson, Sue O'Neill, Susan Haigh, Tony Gomes, Talia Carner, Marie Aronsohn, Xu Xi, Larry Zuckerman, excellent writers who invited me into their long-standing critique group, Two Bridges, and have taught me invaluable lessons about doing this work we all love.

About the Author

Elizabeth McCulloch was born in Buenos Aires, Argentina, and lived in New England, the Midwest, Canada and the South before putting down roots and finding her home in Gainesville, Florida almost forty-five years ago. Previously a lawyer, then a teacher, she has had children of various stripes: one born, two foster, one step, and the granddaughter she raised with her husband. She has been writing fiction for thirty-five years. Her first novel, *Dreaming the Marsh,* is an environmental fable involving a giant sinkhole, prehistoric creatures, and a fair amount of magic and romance. Find more about Elizabeth on her webpage: elizabethmccullochauthor.com.